PAMELA NORSWORTHY

WAR BONDS

A NOVEL OF WORLD WAR II

Black Rose Writing | Texas

The author grants the final approval for this literary material.

First printing

This is a work of fiction. Names, characters, businesses, places, events, and incidents are either the products of the author's imagination or used in a fictitious manner. Any resemblance to actual persons, living or dead, or actual events is purely coincidental.

ISBN: 978-1-68513-371-9
LIBRARY OF CONGRESS CONTROL NUMBER: 2023948139
PUBLISHED BY BLACK ROSE WRITING
www.blackrosewriting.com

Printed in the United States of America
Suggested Retail Price (SRP) $22.95

War Bonds is printed in Garamond Premier Pro

*As a planet-friendly publisher, Black Rose Writing does its best to eliminate unnecessary waste to reduce paper usage and energy costs, while never compromising the reading experience. As a result, the final word count vs. page count may not meet common expectations.

To Uncle Jase Norsworthy, for sending the cherished gift of six pages, single-spaced, all caps feedback at the perfect time;

And to my father, Col. Floyd Harris Mason (Ret.)
B-17 pilot and wing commander of the Bloody 100th,
Thorpe-Abbotts Airfield,
POW, hero, dad.

I miss you both.

WAR BONDS

PROLOGUE

Paris, 1954

The pianist entered from the wing to polite applause, offered a crisp nod of her head, and took her seat at the piano bench. She inhaled, shoulders lifting, releasing, a recalcitrant strand of hair escaping from her bun as she leaned in to play. She seemed familiar to him somehow, the lissome curve of her neck, the confident fluidity of her hands and fingers, the graceful way her body moved forward and back with the music. The melancholy nocturne brought him immediately back to the dangerous, hopelessly conflicted time when his life and soul were at risk. His stomach clenched; his shoulder radiated a deferred pain. No, he reminded himself. The threat is past.

It was an impetuous decision, coming to Paris for a few days, but he'd been anxious to see his son, newly hired as an aeronautical engineer at Avions Marcel Dassault. They had not met since the boy's wedding and the father greatly wished to get to know his daughter-in-law a bit better.

The son had secured four tickets at Salle Gaveau for a program of piano music by Polish composers, performed by promising students from the Conservatoire de Paris. Many were Jewish musicians whom the faculty of the Conservatoire trained free of tuition. Gestures like this were still common across the continent, those who survived the war seeking to elevate the fortunes of those who had suffered so acutely and, perhaps, assuage their guilt for allowing the brutality to advance as far as it had. After a hurried bite in a nearby café, the group walked through the brightly lit streets to the concert hall, settling in just as the program began.

And now. This girl. This oddly familiar young woman. He looked down at his program for the name of the pianist: Ilsa Stroński, age 19, Poland. Could this be? Could it be the same family? After the concert, he would seek her out, to ask.

CHAPTER ONE

To be prepared for war is one of the most effective means of preserving peace.
–George Washington

England—as war arrives

Colin gazed through the schoolhouse window, transfixed by the excavation of the hills, feeling a tremble in his bones as the earth gave way. He wished he were outside, charging up the growing mounds of earth where he could proclaim himself king of the hill in front of Hugo and the other boys, former strangers into whose lives he'd been suddenly thrust. In his mind's eye, he raced ahead as the others flailed, their frantic missteps causing them to slip and roll helplessly to the bottom, the fragrant, newly overturned earth smearing their shorts and sweaters and knee socks as they tumbled. Colin, on the other hand, would be the sure-footed one, conquering the hill and earning the admiration of the men working to flatten the land, who might then let him join their labors. He could assist them, he thought, by rolling stones out of the way so their machines could push through the squelchy, soggy meadow.

Colin and his classmates had grown accustomed to the relentless rumble from the earthmovers, their eerie, oddly mechanical sound punctuated now and again by a screech as metal scraped ancient rock buried beneath. The children couldn't know this intrusion on the quiet, pastoral hills of East Anglia was a prelude to the aggressive machines that would soon swarm and darken the impossibly blue English skies. Interspersed between the sleepy villages and the farms stood centuries-old estates, newly requisitioned for the flying men moving in. The lords of these manors did not object. But they did wince when swaths of pine trees that once anchored the countryside were felled. Whole conifer forests that had endured for generations, vanquished by the earthmovers, the trees giving their lives to the war effort as all of England knew it must do.

Colin had fallen in love with the tailored wildness of the landscape that surrounded his new home—so unlike London's crowded streets and noisy lorries. And to think of how bereft he had felt that afternoon a year ago, when he returned from school to find his mother stuffing his clothes into his small valise, apprising him they were headed straightaway to the train station.

"But Mummy," he'd cried, "I don't want to live in the country! You said if something happened, I would go to Leeds with the grands."

"Yes, well, Grandmother loves you very much, but there are no children around that huge estate, are there? Not a one." She would not meet his eye; her voice was high and clipped, not at all how she usually sounded. "Grandmother's afraid you'll be lonely and we don't want that, do we?"

"But, Mum, aren't the talks still going on? You said the prime minister would sort things out with the Germans. There can't be war if they're still talking, right Mum? So, I don't need to go just yet. I can stay here with you." Colin folded his arms and gave a nod, hoping his argument convinced her.

"The time for talking has ended, Colin. The Germans have attacked Poland. They've gone and done it. The war's begun. I'll be working extra at the hospital and with your father gone, you'd practically be fending for yourself, my sweet boy, and I can't have you doing that." She knelt, holding him by his shoulders and locking her eyes on his, her "I mean business" look on her face. "So, we will finish packing your things, then you'll be taking the train along with lots of other children for a holiday in the country. That's it. It's decided."

Taking a train—alone! That put a new light on it. The prospect of such an adventure intrigued him. But with his usually even-keeled mother rattled, her eyes watery and red, Colin kept this to himself. Instead, he'd thrust out his lower lip and set his face in a way he hoped would assure her he'd miss her, that he was sad to go, but he would do his duty.

Colin's sixty-mile trip from Kings Cross had taken hours longer than expected because of all the children collected along the way and the many other trains crowding the tracks on a similar mission. The elaborate and detailed plan to remove children from England's cities had been developed over many months, just one element of war preparations that had run quietly in the background throughout the prime minister's futile peace negotiations with the German chancellor. Once England declared war, the children's evacuation was immediate. At each stop on Colin's journey, volunteers with too-bright smiles boarded, bearing trays of cheese sandwiches and non-specific compliments.

"Such sturdy children," one exclaimed.

"Brave indeed, all of you!" said another.

"And you're headed to lovely families—truly lovely—where all this will be sorted out and you'll be safe and make loads of new friends! You'll see."

Their stilted pronouncements did little to soothe the sniffles and bewilderment of the youngest refugees, those traveling without a shepherding sibling or older family friend, who felt the exodus not as a grand adventure but a jarring dislocation. The eyes of the volunteers glittered as they swept over the assemblage in the train car. "Child refugees," Colin heard one breathe to another, shaking her head. "*English* refugee children," another clarified. "With gas masks and ration books. Peace in our time, my arse. God save us all."

Colin's stomach heaved.

After the third stop and the third variation of the grand adventure, morale-building pep talk from a third round of volunteers, the children from London lost interest in both the message and the limited menu, one stage-whispering that "a shortbread biscuit would hit the spot right about now, but do you 'spose we'll see a tray of those? Not hardly." That round of sandwich-bearing volunteers slinked away with full trays to await the next train, their own spirits sagging.

The train resumed its journey and with the coach more crowded, many children grew more chatty—whether from nerves or uncertainty, or from the opposite, that they'd begun to relax a bit. In the company of strangers, they had identities to invent. Who might they be, out from under mother's constant tutelage on proper deportment, or daddy's impervious rules? They tried out stories and spun tales for their seat mates of their lives in the city, where neighborhood chums were headed, and who among their families remained in London.

The littler ones boasted about how fast they could run, the high trees they had successfully climbed, their mastery of complex puzzles and chapter books. The older boys—barely in their teens and protected from conscription for the next number of years—were all bluster and bravado, describing with certainty how the Wehrmacht would be stopped in France because of this older brother or that uncle who was brave and fierce and could single-handedly push 'em back to the Rhine. In the manner gifted only to boys their age, they punctuated their stories with the sounds of machine gun fire, then bombs dropping slowly, inexorably, from great heights, a foretelling of the massive explosions the Allies would cause behind German lines. Their inspired table reading of the prosecution of the war left the littlest riders mesmerized, wide-eyed, impressed. For Colin, it filled in details of the current reality that his parents had kept out of his hearing. Once an architect, his father was a soldier now, training somewhere secret. He wasn't supposed to say where, he whispered to his travel companions. In truth, he didn't even know.

As the older boys continued their competitive storytelling, tales growing taller and the telling more animated, a dark shadow of worry settled into Colin's awareness, carving out a neat, defined space. Try as he might to push it out of his mind, the worry migrated to the center of his thoughts, expanding as the train's steady progress bore him farther away from all he knew. And so it stayed, rarely receding—an axis, so to speak—around which Colin's every thought turned.

The train slowed, reaching its destination at last. A quiet rolled through the car. The youngest children, who'd begun the day anticipating the excitement of a train journey without their parents' fussy supervision, grew quiet as if suddenly realizing the train ride was not the point, an immured adventure that would conclude with their return to the familiar. A sense of displacement settled over their faces and in their chests, and even the most rambunctious grew pensive, straining to see out the windows to get a look at their new home.

They could see the village, yes, but also endless acres of meadow beyond that, where cows and sheep grazed under the watchful eye of a quick-moving sheltie, who circled and barked to ensure her charges didn't nibble too far afield. Horse carts ambled over rutted, muddy roads that wound through acre upon acre of farmland, past half-timbered homes constructed of white-washed stone, ancient wooden barns, and lean-to sheds that had seen better days. This was not London or even Birmingham or Manchester: this place was remote and rural and quiet. The train hadn't just taken them north: it had taken them back in time. They saw no city workers bustling to their office buildings or shoppers musing over the wares of street vendors. No rhythmic whoosh as the Tube approached a corner stop. Just a quiet, green and golden landscape they would soon learn smelled mightily of livestock and earth and rain. Elsworth.

Their minders—schoolteachers and nurses, mostly, who had chaperoned the trip—directed them to exit the train and line up along the wall of Elsworth Station.

"Quickly now, here we go then!" one enthused, with an overly spirited clap.

So much cheer, Colin thought, knowing that when the grown-ups overdo it like this, it means they are worried about something they aren't willing to talk about. He straightened the name tag pinned to his coat and gathered his things—the valise containing his clothes, ration book, identity card, a photo of his parents, and a jar of plum marmalade—and the gas mask that fit his thin face so poorly. He strode purposefully off the train car, winding around children who had slowed to consider if perhaps they just sat back down in the carriage they would magically return to their parents.

Already arrayed, facing the station wall, dozens of families gathered in clusters awaiting the evacuees' arrival. Families missing men, or if there were men, they were grandfathers or lame on one side or nearly blind. It was mostly women and their children who began quickly appraising the goods—the children they'd agreed to shelter for who knew how long. They assessed what they could, scanning the tired faces to see whether a child seemed happy or withdrawn, anxious or easygoing. They considered the quality of the children's jackets, their hats, their shoes, how recently they'd had their hair cut, their ages, and which chores they'd be suited for.

A man with a bullhorn welcomed the children to Elsworth. Reverend Haywood Dowd, the parish vicar. Kind and clear eyes peeked out under wildly bushy eyebrows that hung like awnings on his rumpled face. Providing a measure of symmetry was the elaborate mutton chop beard he'd worn for forty-five years, an emblem of another era, an earlier war. His meticulous attention to it, the daily trimming and sculpting and tweezing, his vain and loving devotion to it proved reassuring to his parishioners, proof that this tireless worker for Christ was in fact fallible and human, one who could understand their own vanities and doubts, their petty grievances and larger heartbreaks. But those eyebrows, clucked some in his flock. How is it Mrs. Dowd doesn't tell him the brows could use some tending, too?

"A delight, truly, that you're here, children," he bellowed.

More cheerfulness, Colin worried, can't be a good sign.

"These families you see before you are ready to welcome you into their homes for however long that may be. This isn't London, is it?" he tittered, eyes wide with the outsized understatement. "Not a bit. But we quite know you'll like it here, children. We do. And to you, Elsworth families, the entirety of the British Empire is indebted to you for the generosity you are showing these dear children."

After a quick prayer beseeching God to be in and among them all, he announced it was time to begin.

A woman stepped forward immediately, her face determined, her eyes narrowing as she called out, "I'll take that one." She pointed to one of the oldest boys, a sturdy redheaded 13-year-old named Wilbert, who blushed furiously as he realized she meant him. His eyes darted in the vicar's direction. The older man nodded vigorously and began a series of complex, fairly incomprehensible gestures—lifting, pointing, sweeping—which Wilbert interpreted to mean that he should now gather his things and depart with his new family. One family after another echoed the cry, "I'll take that one," and moved in to claim their choice. The chaperones trailed behind, making notes of who went where, securing names and addresses and a telephone number if there was one. Slowly the line of children thinned, many walking off with exaggerated slowness, woodenly, casting glances over their shoulders at their former train-mates—friends they'd made only hours before but who seemed so much more familiar than these villagers who were taking them off to who knew where.

A woman with a boy about Colin's size approached. "We're the Hughes," she said quietly, placing a hand under Colin's elbow and drawing him towards her. "I'm Ivy and this is Hugo. He's nine years old. You'll be staying with us."

She was small and blonde and moved with slow and gentle purpose in response to Colin's shy reluctance. Her eyes crinkled at the corners as she smiled. In that moment, Colin surrendered to the reality of his current situation. He nodded, a lump building in his throat, tears gathering in his eyes, because while this pretty lady seemed friendly and nice, she was still a stranger and so unlike his own mother.

"Pleased to meet you," he managed, extending his hand as his father had taught him to do. "Thank you kindly, ma'am. I've some marmalade for you from me mum."

"Marvelous. We'll have it for breakfast then, won't we? And your name, young man?"

"It's Colin Clarke, ma'am. I'm ten," he choked out, humiliated that his voice betrayed his sudden sadness and rush of homesickness.

Hugo eyed him with obvious disappointment, shoulders slumping, arms crossed, nose wrinkled like he smelled bad fish. "We've a weeper, Mum," he sighed. "Let's switch 'im."

"Hugo Milton Hughes! Is that a way to welcome a newcomer? One who's had a long journey? Who doesn't know you or me from Adam's house cat?" Ivy glared, leaning in and over her young son, blue eyes intense and fixed. "I've a mind to leave you right here, then. Let you find a new family for yourself. Is that what you'd like?" She turned to Colin. "Sincere apologies, Colin, for Hugo's lack of hospitality. He is working on cultivating a kinder temperament. It's clear there is still work to do." This she said with clenched teeth, eyebrows raised unnaturally high. Clearly, this conversation was well-worn territory between them. "Seems we'll be needing to talk to the vicar again, Hugo."

Hugo stared at the ground, red to the ears.

Colin forgot his own sadness, enthralled for the moment by this small but fierce woman who dared drop the cheerful façade the rest of the grown-ups had taken pains all day, at every stop, to maintain.

Nearby, twin girls—hardly five years old—clutched one another, sobbing, unwilling to acknowledge the insistent urgings of two different women, each prepared to house only one child.

"There, there. It's a small village," offered one woman, all business and ready to end the whimpering. "You'll see one another at school and at church. It's time now, my girl. You'll see your sis soon enough. Here. Let me take your things."

Their sobs grew louder and more hysterical as they pleaded for their mum—their real mum—and for their home, for Marty, the family pup they loved and missed, even as the aspiring adoptive mothers worked to pry them apart.

"We're off to a good start then, aren't we?" one of the women sighed as the vicar approached.

"Problem, ladies?" he asked over escalating howls.

"They're not budging," said the first woman. "I can take one child, but not both. I'm sorry. We've a newborn at home. That's the best we can do."

"Can you shelter them at the vicarage, perhaps?" asked the second. "Just for the foreseeable. Surely, we'll be sending them back to their homes in no time. You and Mrs. Dowd can play grandparents for now."

The vicar paused, face still and serious, as he considered the request. His parishioners bore hardship better when they believed the vicar had it worse than anybody. But two little girls? His own children were grown, he was 68 and doing his utmost to convey calm and surety to congregants who had already sent husbands and brothers and sons off to war. Truth be told, he was weary. He was worried. There were so many reasons for him not to take this on. Little tiny girls! Two of them!

"We had planned to take an older girl," the vicar stuttered, "so, well, perhaps..." He paused, mouth working as he tried to get his words out.

"Well, wouldn't you know, the words of St. Paul seem to have foisted themselves upon me in this very moment, ladies—'I can do all things through Christ which strengtheneth me.' Isn't that just the way things work? For the fact I've preached those words countless times, it seems, now, I must trust them. Let me find Dorothy and discuss this. Grant me just a moment."

But the prospect of being taken off by this bearded, vest-wearing man with the booming voice, with the huge eyebrows and gray sprays of wiry hair springing from his ears, prompted fresh howls, cries so full of distress that Hugo was drawn out of his recent shame, transfixed on a situation far more dramatic.

"Mummy," he said. "Those little ones. They're trying to send them to different houses. Can we go see, please?"

The tenuous and newly formed family of Colin, Hugo, and Ivy made its way toward the wailing twins, their own disappointments momentarily forgotten. Ivy smiled at the two women.

"Afternoon, Muriel, Rowena. Quite a day, yes?"

The twins quieted at Ivy's greeting, the melody in her voice drawing their interest. Ivy knelt to speak with them.

"Hello, girls. Welcome to Elsworth. I'm Ivy Hughes and this is Hugo. He's nine. And this is our new friend, Colin, who is ten and was on the train with you. Do you have names then? What are you called, each of you?"

A staring contest ensued. Ivy waited. The girls, gripping one another's tiny hand to stave off any separation, exchanged a glance, one telegraphing to the other to proceed.

"Margaret," one of them whispered. "She's Patricia, but mummy calls her Patsy. We are four and half and we have a dog called Marty, but we couldn't bring 'im."

"You share a name with Princess Margaret—now what about that! And Patsy—such a modern name, isn't it? Please to meet you." Ivy stood, then called for the vicar to return to the little group. "I can take them—both of them," she said. "They'll settle in better if they have one another."

"But Ivy, can you manage?" asked the vicar. "With William gone? Perhaps we can place the boy with someone else."

"No," insisted Hugo, his attitude fully reformed. "He's comin' with us. Two and two. Two a them and two a us. Boys and girls."

"Well, what about that?" said the vicar, allowing himself a small smile of relief.

"The Lord giveth, and the Lord taketh away, eh, Vicar Dowd?" laughed one of the women, prompting him to speak a quick prayer of thanksgiving for Ivy's generosity.

"That's that, then," smiled Ivy, after the vicar's amen. "Girls, you're coming with us and you're coming together. Alright? No need for tears. It's all right. We've a kitten who's needed some younger friends to play with while Hugo's at school."

CHAPTER TWO

The day of individual happiness has passed.
–Adolf Hitler

France—as the Occupation begins

Lieutenant Gordon Clarke knelt, back erect, fingers laced behind his head, and stared at the Unteroffizier who trained his machine gun on the remnants of the Allied force in France. The German lifted his chin, jaw muscles grinding, his finger tapping astride the trigger. The circles under his eyes betrayed a deadening fatigue that Gordon understood all too well, one that would surely seep into the very bones of every soldier arrayed across the Continent over the coming days, if this war couldn't be settled soon.

The soldiers garrisoned in Calais felt both terror and relief: the dive bombers and Panzers had turned toward Dunkirk and while blasts still resounded down the French coast, they were no longer tearing through stone and flesh in this ancient citadel, in what had become the soldiers' last refuge. Gordon was proud of his battalion's stand but they'd never had a chance, overrun by an enemy well-armed and well-trained, whose might and speed introduced them to a war unlike anything their fathers had known; the weapons the Allies brandished seemed like those of children compared to the German arsenal. With their gas masks and entrenching tools, the English high command had prepared them for the last war, not this one.

Gordon resolved not to dwell on what might await them in enemy hands. He and the others needed to focus only on surviving this day, then the next. Water. Food. Sleep, perhaps. The men he commanded were barely twenty years old, after all, conscripted into a war that had been vague and ill-formed in their imaginations; they had expected an ennobling adventure that ended in victory. They believed this most especially because their side had won the last time. And now they knelt, subdued and still, watching the tongue of a German soldier play over his chapped lips as if he were looking for just the right target to shoot.

The German advance, Gordon feared, would continue until Paris itself fell. Europe would be fundamentally reshaped, but perhaps that would mean their captivity would be brief. They'd be released once some sort of quid pro quo could be struck—Germany getting something to add to the Sudetenland or whatever it was they felt they were entitled to—and then Hitler's bloody plan to reverse the terms of the Treaty of Versailles would reach its denouement. Poland and Austria had been annexed into the German empire and perhaps there was some argument for this. A few refinements to several more boundaries, then, Gordon hoped, order would return to the continent. He and his men could return home. He could live in peace with Beryl and Colin.

The German commanding officer approached, bellowing specific orders to his staff assistant, who nodded officiously and directed the Allied soldiers to stand. They were moving out.

The officer smiled, surveyed the enemy fighters, and then gave a sharp nod. He turned to his assistant. "Prepare them to march. Some water beforehand. But that's all." He turned back to face the men of the tattered battalion.

"Vas du das Krieg est uber," he announced, his glee hardly contained.

For you, the war is over.

As they stood, a British private maneuvered closer to Gordon.

"Sir, where are we going? Can you ask them to keep us here? Can the colonel just tell them we could bunk here and wait?"

Gordon turned to the soldier, a teenager, really, his face covered in soot, blood crusted under his ear.

"It's not up to us, Fletcher. Keep your head down and follow directions. Don't give them a reason to shoot."

And with that, a line of Allied soldiers departed from the citadel they'd failed to defend, to begin the journey eastward, across France and deep into the Reich.

.   .   .

For miles, they marched, French, Belgian, and Dutch among the captives, each looking for a familiar face, or at least a familiar uniform to march alongside. They re-sorted themselves as they went, hoping their captors didn't catch on, inching closer to men who spoke their own language and might have an idea of how to get out of this mess.

Over days, two dozen of Gordon's troops managed to maneuver closer to him, a makeshift platoon prepared to follow his lead. They spoke in low tones, caps drawn low over their brows, their quiet alarm intensifying with every step that took them farther from home and freedom. Their route traversed northern France, through acres of wheat belonging to astonished farmers whose rural isolation had to this point kept news of France's late misfortune from them. German machine guns and rifles, whether slung over a shoulder or casually aimed in their direction—at their children, their livestock—quickly convinced the farmers to cooperate with German requests to feed the captives.

But who had the stores to feed the thousands of POWs who just kept coming over the rise, their boots flattening seedling crops that had just gained purchase in their fields? Farm women prepared soups and stews using everything at hand and in their storehouses—onions, potatoes and other root vegetables, greens from dandelions that had just begun to appear in the grazing pasture. But there was never enough.

The German officers overseeing the massive prisoner relocation fared better. Should a host not offer a menu that was suitably hearty—they had many more miles to travel after all and were on duty every minute of the day—one of the many sharpshooters in the ranks simply drew his weapon and fired. One German officer raved about the outstanding blanquette de veau he'd enjoyed outside Lille, thanks to a straggler calf, the last in a cluster of cattle heading out to graze. The farmer who owned him was incensed and demanded compensation: his son, he said, had bottle-fed the calf through many difficult months to ensure she thrived and brought a good price at market. The officer responded that indeed the farmer had received his recompense: had he not heard the satisfied belches of the German officers at the table?

At night, Gordon and his fellow prisoners dropped where they stood, their bodies and boot prints ensuring these fields would not yield healthy crops this growing season or next. They fashioned pillows from stalks and dried grasses, grateful when a cooling breeze crossed their filthy faces, for the gift of sleeping under a clear sky. A few sought out what shelter they could in barns and shacks along the route, but most preferred the safety of the larger group. No sense drawing unneeded attention.

After Lille, they continued through Belgium, cutting south of Brussels. They arrived at a sugar beet farm belonging to an old man and his frightened wife, who days earlier had learned their land had been appropriated as a staging area for POWs headed east and German units headed to France. A spring-fed stream ran through the property and the Germans directed small groups of prisoners to make their way to the stream bank should they wish to bathe or rinse some of their belongings. June was giving way to July: they'd been on the move for more than a month and the men were hungry, smelly, and, in many cases, ill-tempered with worry. But here, at least, they had a moment to rest.

Gordon removed his jacket first, then his boots, socks, pants, underclothes and laid them aside the stream. Wading naked into the water, still startling cold for early summer, he dropped gingerly on the stones at the stream bottom, letting his arms go limp in the water, watching the filth float away from his skin as the stream did its work. He exhaled, feeling he'd been holding his breath since the fight was lost at Calais. The water, so clear and purposeful as it moved downstream, the sun highlighting the eddies as they swirled and jumped around rocks in their path, proved restorative. He lay back in the stream and let it cover his head, rubbing his face and neck to remove the grime, pretending for a moment that he was outside London, swimming in the lake with Beryl at her family's home.

"Genug jetzt!" shouted a guard, signaling for the men in the stream to finish so others could undertake their ablutions. Gordon knee-walked to the bank, a familiar hand extending to pull him from the water.

"Here we go, sir," said Private Fletcher, cutting his eyes toward the German guard.

"I appreciate it, Fletcher," said Gordon.

"Hughes is off, sir," the soldier breathed, continuing his move past Gordon into the stream.

Gordon didn't directly respond. But as he sat to dry himself and began to dress, his eyes met the soldier's and he gave a wink of acknowledgement. Hughes had fled, then, sometime around their crossing into Belgium. It was what many hoped to do, now that it was clear the hostilities would not be resolved quickly. Many men had slipped away, soundlessly, taking advantage of a guard more asleep than awake, or one who stepped a few feet off the road, forced to attend to the urgent demand of bowels that had not responded well to the inconsistent diet and physical rigors of the march. The Belgians and the French had the advantage: those able to drift out of the lines could melt into a familiar countryside. They knew where to head for safety to quickly secure the jackets and caps that instantly transformed them from soldiers to villagers. For the British and the Dutch, it was more perilous. Their unfamiliarity with the terrain and the language meant they had to proceed more slowly, relying on strangers who might or might not turn them in. Gordon knew of three Brits no longer in the ranks and two had not fared so well: one had tried to stay back in Lille, shot dead in a hayloft where he'd attempted to hide when it was time to move out. The surprised shriek of the farmer's daughter had given him away and the Germans, instead of pulling him up and forcing him back in the line, simply drilled him with a bullet in case others got the same idea. A second had miscalculated his opportunity to escape, believing his guard distracted by the arrival of two SS officers, eager for an update on the progress of the prisoner relocation. The young Heer guard seemed especially eager to impress the SS men, perhaps hoping to be promoted into their ranks. As he offered a thorough report on their progress since Calais, his eye caught the British soldier inching toward an outcropping of tall shrubs and trees. When the

Brit was about ten feet away from the forest that could hide him, the guard lifted his machine gun.

"Entschuldigung, meine Herren,"—Excuse me, sirs—he said with a curt nod, before firing a quick burst that cut down the soldier. He then resumed his recitation of the successful relocation of the POWs, brushing aside the extravagant praise of the visiting officers while at the same time crediting himself with contributing in key ways to its unqualified success.

Whenever a burst of bullets echoed through the hills, Gordon knew a man had not timed his escape well.

And now Hughes. Gordon said a quick prayer as he dressed, pulling his still-filthy clothes over damp skin, hoping Hughes was sitting at a farm table somewhere, enjoying a proper meal, and plotting his route back home to England.

In late July, the contingent decamped to the main train station in Brussels, where some of those wounded in the battle for France had recovered enough to join them. No passenger rail for them, however; they were loaded into train cars meant for livestock, sixty men to a car with a bucket for pee and excrement. So, thought Gordon. There is something worse than endless marching. There's this.

CHAPTER THREE

Friendship is born at that moment when one person says to another:
What! You too? I thought I was the only one.
–C. S. Lewis

Elsworth, England

Their business concluded at Elsworth Station, Ivy and her charges began the short walk home. Patsy clutched Margaret's hand and Margaret clutched Ivy's, Hugo playing tour guide as the boys sauntered behind. The Hughes' two-story brick home sat on Boxworth Road, Elsworth's main street, Hugo explained, a few steps from the greengrocer, the tiny post office, and Vicar Dowd's Holy Trinity Church. Cattycorner from the church, Hugo pointed out a white plaster building that sat at the head of a vast spread of open farmland. "The schoolhouse," he said. "Mrs. Helms is headmistress. She's alright. Could be worse."

The group entered the house, the girls forgetting their present misery and charging ahead once they spotted the promised kitten.

"She's called Marigold—gold stripes, see?" explained Hugo, as the twins moved to encircle the sleepy and slow-moving kitten, dropping to the floor in a coordinated twin-ballet, placing the startled kitty between them, their knees blocking her escape.

Hugo helped Colin tote his bag up the polished wooden steps to his room, where a pallet had been fashioned on the floor next to Hugo's narrow bed, a chamber pot visible underneath. A washbasin sat on an old oak dresser next to a photo of a soldier whose slight build and sandy hair looked a lot like Hugo.

"Your things can go here," Hugo offered, pulling out a dresser drawer. "I've moved me own things over to make some room."

"That your father?" Colin asked, pointing to the photo.

"Tis," responded Hugo, eyes slow to meet Colin's before he turned to take in the cherished photograph. "He used to be the butcher here. Now he's with the BEF. Shipped out last week."

"My dad is in the service, too. It's partly why I've had to come here. Mum's a hospital nurse. Wouldn't leave me by myself even though I could have managed fine. But she's worried the Jerrys are coming for us, so she sent me out of London. Just until my dad gets back."

"I bet they've met," declared Hugo, invigorated by the idea of his father serving the Empire alongside someone familiar. Well, not familiar, exactly, but the father of a friend. A new friend.

"Maybe," offered Colin. "We can write them and find out. So, Hugo, is the loo up here?"

"The privy's out back," Hugo replied. "You have a loo back home? Inside your house?"

"Yes. We do," said Colin, pausing a moment to think about the additional considerations inherent when the privy is out of doors and not in.

"The school has a loo," said Hugo, with a measure of pride. "Inside. Mostly because of the boys who used to go outside to piss who wandered off. One lad made a regular habit of it. His father was a plumber. So, he built us an inside pot. We're not so different from London, I'd say."

"Not at all," mumbled Colin.

Ivy climbed the stairs, laden with quilts and a pair of eiderdowns. "I'll be putting the wee ones in my room for now," she called, her use of the term "wee" sending the boys into a fit of laughter, any lingering awkwardness arising from their initial meeting now safely dissipated. Unsure of what prompted their snickers, Ivy was nevertheless pleased at their conspiring and the considerable energy Hugo seemed to be expending to welcome Colin and perhaps regain his mother's trust. She continued, "I expect the girls will want to keep a close eye on us—and that cat—until they get their bearings."

Indeed, their endless fascination with the kitten, so silky and portable and so unlike Marty the dog who had been less cooperative with their games, helped mightily as Margaret and Patsy navigated the jolting transition to their new home. They were from Manchester, where their father oversaw the massive operation at the Avro aircraft factory. Tasked with producing as many Lancaster aircraft as possible, he was deferred from military service to essentially live at the plant and keep the lines moving. The factory was a prime target for German bombs aiming to cripple British aviation capacity, so he had dispatched his wife, infant son, and Marty the dog to extended family in Cardiff and the twins to Elsworth. It was the safest decision for them all, but being sent off from their mum and dad was not something little girls could easily understand. At night, they cuddled together face to face on a thin mattress heaped with a mound of old quilts, the soft eiderdown drawn under their chins, Marigold between them, tears dotting their smooth, round cheeks. To Marigold they whispered their deepest worries in their first months in Elsworth, confessing how much they missed mummy and daddy, which foods Ivy placed before them they didn't really like, the pungent smells of the countryside that were unfamiliar and strange. Marigold listened intently except for the times she fell asleep.

Ivy welcomed the chaos and demands the city children introduced to her household. The daily work of squeezing everyone successfully through dressing and bathing and meals and school lessons, the clamor of the boys racing down the steps each day and the quiet plotting as the girls worked to corner Marigold so they could put a bonnet on her head and place her in the old pram. A blessing, this, she thought to herself, a distraction for Hugo and for her, with Wills off somewhere learning how to preserve the Empire.

Before his conscription, Wills was Elsworth's butcher, sharing space with the greengrocer, a two-block walk from their house. They had come to Elsworth for the job, thinking that once he had some experience, they'd move someplace more interesting. That was ten years ago now. Wills had taken to the people and the work, learning their proclivities and exactly those cuts of meat each customer preferred. In the early days, some villagers accused him of selling low-quality meat that turned tough upon cooking, prompting Wills to do a bit of investigation around their cooking techniques. He ushered several chronic complainers into Ivy's kitchen of a Saturday for simple cooking lessons he told her were necessary to prevent innocent rump roasts and tenderloins from becoming shoe leather—and to ensure he stayed in business. Indeed, under his gentle tutelage, his customers' skills improved. The cooking lessons eventually turned into weekly dinners; attendees brought vegetables and breads and desserts to complement Will's roast, which was always the admired centerpiece. To show their gratitude, the customers—now friends, really—showered the Hughes with fresh vegetables in season, eggs from their chicken coops, and biscuits and cakes every December to wish them a happy Christmas. Kind and dear—all of them—they had stood in the gap when Ivy, her own mother long dead, struggled to find her footing as a new mum. Dorothy Dowd, the vicar's wife, arranged a little caravan of people who came to the house for several months to manage the laundry, get supper started, dust and clean a wee bit, and most importantly, take the baby for a stroll in the pram so Ivy could fall into the deep, restorative sleep her body required after a difficult pregnancy and protracted labor. When her stillborn daughter was born two years later, they swept in again to console Ivy and Wills in their heartbreak and assure them that life would go on. The villagers' interest in Hugo remained avid as he grew, indulging him with small gifts and treats while steering him toward proper manners when he, as little boys are innately compelled, grew unruly. There were no Saturday cooking lessons now, with Wills gone, but there was plenty of activity with four children in the house. Ivy believed Elsworth had taught her to be open-hearted and grateful in a way she might not have been had they lived elsewhere. All those years of accumulated kindnesses fortified her now, as she navigated these days without the love and company of her husband.

As fall turned to winter, the newly constituted and expanded, somewhat improvised Hughes family found a workable, shared rhythm. Vicar Dowd appeared at the door one afternoon, having walked over from Holy Trinity with a refurbished bicycle that at one time belonged to his grandson. The parish board did not entirely approve of the time he devoted to getting this and other cast-off bicycles in working order; the vicar knew displaced children needed more than the prayers of strangers to help them settle in, so he ignored the board and pressed on with the blessed ministry of bicycles. Margaret and Patsy were on the list to get theirs once they fulfilled the prerequisite of growing just a bit taller so their feet could reach the pedals.

On their bicycles, Hugo and Colin explored the village, bumping across the cobbled streets and pedaling through the countryside that was transforming before their eyes into runways and tarmac. On Saturday mornings, Ivy packed them a pair of hard-boiled eggs, a bit of fruit, and some cheese so they could ride out beyond the schoolhouse and sit under the trees and watch. Their bellies full, the boys would lie back in the meadow, the sun warming their bones, and discuss England's plight and that of their own families. Their fathers would return soon, they decided, since things over in France seemed stalemated. Soon, the armies would want to go home. And when Colin returned home after that, the boys vowed they'd become pen-pals because they'd discovered there was nothing like having a close friend your own age—"We're more like brothers, really" Hugo said more than once—with whom to chew things over. These meadow mornings were Colin's favorite times—free of adults, apart from the raucous rush of the city in which he'd been raised—and he was sad when the weather turned too cold to linger outside.

Colin, Ivy observed, tended to grow pensive at the close of the day, the shadow of worry for his mum and dad ever present. So, she spoke frequently of Colin's mother, inquiring as to her habits and routines to replicate what she could, reminding Colin to post a letter or card to her because surely Mrs. Clarke awaited the postman every day to bring news of him. As the calendar turned to 1940, Margaret and Patsy matriculated into school, having turned five and needing something beyond cat-chasing and games with one another to occupy them. They were a bit young, but they were smart and schoolmistress Helms abridged the longstanding rules to allow them and other evacuees their age to enroll in the January term. It was but one of the formerly hard and fast rules amended in Elsworth because circumstances demanded it. Ivy found the girls' anxiety lessened when they spent the day in the company of other children.

By spring, talk of the children returning to the cities gave way to whispers of imminent invasion. The German advance had not been stopped by the uncles and fathers and big brothers of the British Expeditionary Force, despite the confident pronouncements of the children on the train six months earlier. France was imperiled, and the English were scrambling, feverishly building airfields for the fighting men of the Royal Air Force who were, even now, taking to the skies over the French coast in a futile effort to stanch Germany's advance. Perhaps with the new prime minister, England's fortunes would improve.

As Colin's father was marched toward a POW camp inside the Reich, the War Office notified Ivy that Second Lieutenant William Hughes was missing. Despite repeated inquiries, the War Office had failed to locate his body and could not confirm his presence in a POW camp. They knew only that he had not been evacuated at Dunkirk but was believed to have survived the fall of Calais.

Haywood Dowd volunteered for the Home Guard and once he received his uniform in late summer, he wore it almost exclusively, even under his clerical robes every Sunday. It was the least he could do, he explained from the pulpit, what with two grandsons in the war—one in the RAF and the other serving in an artillery unit. His parishioners quietly remarked to one another that he was preaching as well as he ever had, less stale and stuffy and more inspired than in previous years, one even making such a comment— obliquely—to Mrs. Dowd. But it wasn't that her husband had suddenly developed new powers of oration, she knew. It wasn't longer nights spent in his study, more carefully crafting messages for each Sunday's worship. It was simply that now, when he urged the congregation to pray; when he read aloud the Psalms of David that lamented unjust conflict waged by cruel aggressors that, in the end, God would set to right; when he preached of painful sacrifice and ultimate trust in God, they heard and believed because this was the truth, the hope, to which they now staked their lives.

CHAPTER FOUR

But if we fail, then the whole world, including the United States,
including all that we have known and cared for,
will sink into the abyss of a new Dark Age made more sinister...
Let us therefore brace ourselves to our duties, and so bear ourselves that,
if the British Empire and its Commonwealth last for a thousand years,
men will still say, "This was their finest hour."
–Winston Churchill

London—as the Blitz begins

Beryl moved through the quiet flat, gathering the things necessary for her workday—her gloves, her pocketbook, the apple and crackers that would suffice for a meal—crossing and recrossing the worn floorboards, unconsciously delaying her departure. She stood under the dim light in the hallway, placing her nurse's cap just so over her dark curly hair, wondering when the purplish circles had become so pronounced beneath her eyes. The cat rubbed at her calves, his aloofness having evaporated soon after Gordon, then Colin had left. It was hard to remain remote when there were so few people around to notice it. Even cats of great reserve sought human contact now and again.

It had been a year since Beryl had sent her son out of the city, the right decision not only for Colin's safety, but because she now spent nearly all her waking hours at Grove Park Hospital, working from the early evening until the sun rose. The volume of patients was intensifying—alarmingly. For months, the Germans had directed their firepower at the ports and airfields: now bombs fell day and night across London. The government warned invasion was imminent, but what does one do with that kind of information? Short of catching a boat to America—across seas humming with U-boats and laden with mines—what were the options? One simply continued to do one's duty, going to work each day, offering service to others, protecting what one could—both human life and, to a lesser extent, one's belongings.

At first, Beryl had tended to the terrible, shredding wounds of evacuated soldiers of the British Expeditionary Force, but now civilians filled the wards. Women whose homes betrayed them, collapsing into ruin around them, heavy wooden beams issuing lethal blows. Children who should have been sent to the countryside a year ago, buried under mounds of brick that moments before formed the sturdy wall of a schoolhouse that had stood for three hundred years. The pain of watching Colin pull away on that train, pain that had hollowed her out and left her bereft and breathless had been erased and replaced with something else entirely: whenever she thought of him, miles away in Elsworth under another family's roof, out of her influence and care, she was overcome with a gratitude that quieted her twirling thoughts and affirmed that her decision to live apart from her beloved little boy was righteous and generous. "Children are safer in the country," posters on public walls in every English city read. "Leave them there." She had expected her parents to take him, given the space and resources of their estate. In fact, they had room for perhaps six or eight children, but at the eleventh hour, her mother had rejected Beryl's request, saying at her age, she couldn't possibly keep up with a little boy, war or no war.

Beryl had managed to travel to see Colin four times now, finding herself both glad and alarmed at how easily he had assimilated to village life, so much simpler and slower-paced. He would have academic ground to make up, surely, when he returned to London. If he returned to London. As Beryl followed this curlicue of thought, the best educational path to ensure Colin an expansive future, a shroud of shame settled over her. "God, forgive me," she breathed, knowing that on this night, like the others, she would surely encounter mothers whose only hope would be that their children would live.

With her colleagues at the hospital, her neighbors on the street, the news agent she chatted with on the odd afternoon as she picked up the latest newspaper, she shared the unspoken commitment to survive the next twenty-four hours with her chin up. Just this day. To get through the immediate challenge, solve the next urgent problem, obediently follow the newest directives of Prime Minister Churchill's government. No musing or second-guessing. No public positing of theories on how long the battering might continue. Was it cowardice or courage? Was it wise to project ahead, to decipher telltale signs or read between the lines, to consider if the battle was already lost? No. All of England had collectively decided, apparently, to trust, to pray, to summon the resolve to follow through with one's obligations and duties, despite the possibility that the next wooden beam careening from the ceiling might have your name on it. That was the shared sense of things—at least the sense that people would acknowledge to one another. We're in this together—doubters not wanted. But in her own head, alone in her flat or out back in the garden under the Anderson shelter Gordon had fixed before he reported for duty—her thoughts spun and collided. She wondered if her cloistered life was the only way to live amidst the terror. Because that's what the constant bombing created—abject terror as one street corner after another was hit, scarring her beloved city and the psyches of its residents. If the end of the world was at hand—or at least, the end of a free world—Beryl wondered if she'd regret spending these days like this. Despite dutiful, solemn examples around her—the Prime Minister first and foremost—she heard rumor there were some in London approaching the crisis differently. Like those in the Bible who believed Jesus' return was right around the corner, so they stopped being earnest and dutiful. They'd had parties. Sex and drunkenness and all that. And there was talk that the very same thing was happening at some of London's finest hotels. Was that wrong? Or was she wrong, with her spartan life, working to the point of exhaustion, living alone, and missing those she loved? It seemed all pleasure was gone for now, squeezed from daily living, as husbands left wives to take up arms, families fractured through loss and relocation. As she flattened herself out under the garden shelter, bombs whistling through the air and dropping dangerously close by, Beryl ruminated.

Their life together had been sweet, hers and Gordon's, even when it grew complicated, Beryl bending toward modernity in ways Gordon had not anticipated. He had studied architecture, his drafting table now her preferred place to sit and sip her tea. They had met when she was nineteen at a summer party at the country estate of her parents' friends. He'd arrived late (on purpose, she always believed, impossible to miss), so they had not been properly introduced. Once she saw him, she was transfixed and tracked him like prey. He was a head taller than most men there, his face lean and sculpted under a blonde head of hair. His alert blue eyes betrayed uncertainty as to whether he wished to engage fully with this particular party and its assorted female guests. Beryl intercepted him at the punch bowl where they commiserated over the fact no invigorating spirits had yet been added. "Perhaps we should do so," she'd offered, eyes twinkling, earning Gordon's immediate interest and admiration. Much to the dismay of the other girls at the party, they had departed together and had not been apart since.

Over her parents' objections, they'd married young, Colin arriving less than a year later and quickly enchanting his grandparents, erasing any notion that Gordon and Beryl had not formed the most perfect family in the most brilliant way. A family trust ensured Beryl could afford help, but after those first sleepless, colicky months, Beryl released the nanny, much preferring to manage her baby on her own. When Gordon completed his studies, they moved from her family's estate to London where Gordon's parents lived, a decision Beryl's mother protested vigorously given that Beryl's older sister still lived at home. But Beryl wanted to enter nursing school, not because she intended to become a nurse but because science had always interested her and she found women with educations mildly subversive and most intriguing. To her surprise, her curiosity intensified with each class and clinical instruction. She discovered broad fields of inquiry opening to her that formerly she had not known existed. The miraculous beauty of the human organism became her fascination, its intricate chemistry and the ongoing mystery of its persistent functioning and ability to heal itself. It amused her to think of how small her world had been before, the notion that one might pursue education not to enhance one's mind and capabilities, but to reposition oneself in society, in the eyes of others. It saddened her, actually, because she was quite sure most women still saw it exactly that way, most assuredly her own mother.

The time she devoted to earning her degree had produced some tension in her marriage, Gordon not quite understanding her quest and sometimes finding the demands of her schedule inconvenient. He was not a temperamental artist, as some of his colleagues tended to be, but he did work in great sweeps, ideas and solutions coming to him in a giant, profuse draft. He objected to anything that interfered with him giving himself over to this force, uninterrupted, hour upon hour, believing that if he missed the creative moment that offered a brilliant path forward, he was not guaranteed that it would return in just the same way. Beryl found this notion a bit silly, as if the muse of architectural creativity stamped her foot and left the room if one weren't paying sufficient attention. Gordon loved his new son, but sometimes found himself at a loss when the baby screeched and yammered when Gordon attempted to work. More than once in those early years, he had looked at Beryl, beseeching her to quiet him; more than once, she had suggested he scoop up the baby and take him out for a stroll so she could complete preparations for an upcoming clinical. Colin's paternal grandparents were of no help, in part because Gordon's father suffered frail health but more significantly, because they came from an older, more formal world that left them innately uncomfortable with the unpredictability of young children.

"But, Beryl, I have a deadline," Gordon pleaded one morning, when Colin was just beginning to toddle around the flat, happily yanking newspapers and ashtrays and cups of tea off table tops, his parents ill-prepared for his sudden mobility. "My client must see these drawings very soon and I cannot concentrate with Colin bashing about."

"My darling," she responded, hands on hips, approaching him at his table. "Shall I say it another time? I have deadlines as well that I complete in and around caring for the baby. You have an office to flee to during the week—hours of blissful quiet that I seldom enjoy. When you are home, you can hardly expect me to manufacture the quiet of a library."

"Why, though, are you devoting this much of your time and energy to this? Do you truly plan to work as a nurse one day? I can't see it—and I do not mean that unkindly, Beryl, because I know you are capable. But now that we've a child..."

She looked at Gordon and heaved an indulgent sigh. Her beautiful, imaginative, mildly self-involved husband.

"Whether or not I eventually work out in the world, I love every bit of this learning—the depth of it and all it requires of me. It assures me that I measure up to you. I don't want to become my mother—sociable and complaisant, yes, that's the good part, but a lady of leisure who can't even hold a conversation over dinner about what's happening in Europe. You have work that stretches and challenges you; this challenges me and I hope keeps you from growing weary of me."

"Now that's an impossibility, love," he said, placing his hands on either side of her familiar, cherished face—the deep green eyes, the swirl of dark hair. From the start, he had liked how she stood up for herself, how funny she could be and quite naughty, too, spiking the punchbowl at parties, marrying him despite family misgivings, letting the nanny go. And now here she was doing it again. He deserved exactly this. "You've got me. Forever. Yes, I do love your smart brain. It attracts me, gets me juices going, all that sensuous grey matter swirling around in there, winking at me. And I love what's right beneath it," he said, placing a kiss on each eyelid, then her freckled nose, then her full, smiling lips.

Gordon became more comfortable as the years passed and Colin grew conversant, thoughtfully reflective, and curious about how the world around him functioned—how it all fit together. Now it was the father, when they gathered at night for dinner, who rambled on and on about the marvels of this child—about their conversation just that afternoon that revealed insight advanced for a child his age, supported by an expansive vocabulary Gordon suspected was quite, quite unusual.

"Yes, love, Colin's a real boy now!" Beryl had chided, and they'd laughed at this change of roles, Gordon utterly besotted as Beryl had been when Colin was tiny, both now enthralled with this little family they formed.

Gordon's work had been well received, and he progressed through the firm, taking on projects that challenged and satisfied his considered talent. But then this. He was conscripted soon after war was declared and deployed with the British Expeditionary Force to France, quickly promoted to lieutenant thanks in part to an education that included a working knowledge of German. But his service was short-lived; his battalion was surrounded by German troops at Calais. He was declared missing, the War Office at first only able to tell her he'd not been among those evacuated out of Dunkirk. And then, months later, a letter arrived from the Red Cross, affirming his registration at a POW camp in Germany. She'd received one other letter since, a note in Gordon's own hand.

I think of you in the garden in the warm evenings and know you'll be glad of my comfort when you do so. We are busy within and without, with industrious schedules meant to secure our ongoing health and wellbeing in this novel acreage of the German Reich.

It sounded translated from some ancient language. No concern expressed for Colin, no inquiries about her work, their friends, her parents. Nothing specifically about Gordon himself. But in these few words, the stilted syntax, she recognized he was advising her to stay in the Anderson shelter—it would comfort him, he was saying, to think of her protecting herself this way. The next tortured sentence could mean various things— that the prisoners travelled outside their camp to jobs somewhere, or that they were working on something significant within the confines of the camp. By "health," Beryl feared he meant that doing precisely as the schedule dictated was his best hedge against being shot dead. It was clear he was housed in newly acquired territories outside the former boundaries of Germany.

The Germans work relentlessly with keen commitment and without fatigue in the rolling hills and the beautifully constructed industrial factories, overseeing the trains that bring new residents to homes of necessary work.

"Homes of necessary work?" How had that slipped past the German censors? Work camps, he must mean. But what other point was he trying to make? What else had he hidden in his apparent compliment of the German work ethic? Reading and re-reading, she concluded he was saying the Nazis were primed and prepared for this war and would not give up easily. He was in the countryside but aware of churning factories nearby. They were building new structures across the conquered countries, probably. Trains transporting "new residents"—did he mean more POWs? French troops, probably, captured in the fall of Paris. Most disheartening of all, he did not sign his notes with any profession of love, which is what she needed from him most of all. He closed with a simple "Yours, Gordon." She worried he was suffering—either psychologically or physically or both and this odd prose was a way to convey this to her, that he was alive, but not well.

Running late now, she returned the marmalade to the larder, gathered her things, saluted her cat, and headed out the door. As she pulled her key from the lock, the air raid siren sounded. Should she head back through the flat to the garden? No, she decided. Better to walk to the Tube station and wait there until the all-clear.

CHAPTER FIVE

Comparison is the thief of joy.
–Theodore Roosevelt

Inside the Reich

When Gordon recalled their naïve, shared hope at the moment of defeat at Calais, hope for a quick repatriation and resolution to the European conflict, he felt both foolish and ashamed: foolish for misjudging Germany's vast ambitions so completely and somewhat embarrassed that his country—wholly triumphant in The Great War—had been so ill-prepared to take on this one, facts both dependent and related. England and America, too, had done their best to ignore Hitler's bellicosity and the dwindling freedom within his borders, as if not discussing it diminished the threat. Gordon was privately ashamed of himself too—and he was not alone in this—for not acquitting himself better in France or at least escaping after capture. Again and again, the Calais survivors replayed with one another the pivotal sequence that led to their internment two and half years ago: how the Nazis had pushed them to the coast, bombed them mercilessly, and cut them off. Which British military genius had made the call that allowed their lethal isolation? The saving grace for the captives was learning much later that their capitulation, the delay it had caused in the progress of the Panzers, had led to the evacuation at Dunkirk that saved countless Allied lives.

Gordon and those who survived the trip from France were housed first at a camp at Sandbostel, where daily they were tantalized by the sounds of townspeople outside the gates, greeting one another as they went about their business, the happy shouts of children pedaling bicycles to school, living ordinary lives, as if there weren't prisoners of war housed in the barracks plainly visible through the barbed wire. And perhaps that explained why Gordon and his fellow prisoners were transported after a year to a more remote outpost. They were now encamped in Sagan, once a Polish town but now firmly in German control, residents of Stalag-Luft III.

If an Allied POW, a guest of the Reich, didn't die of malnourishment accelerated by dysentery that suddenly, spasmodically emptied his bowels, depleting him of the minerals needed to keep a heart beating—or if he did not contract TB or typhus—the next mortal threat was the overwhelming boredom that could cause a man to lose his mind and try to make a break for freedom. It had happened twice in Sagan that Gordon had witnessed, the failed escapees mown down by machine gun fire from the guard tower when they tried to get up and over the small section of fence that could not electrocute them. There was a deadening sameness to these days; standing in formation at *Appell* morning, noon, and night as each name was called and camp rules reiterated; daily rations of barley water the Germans had the nerve to call soup and the hard, black, rocks they called bread; the unremitting stench that overspread the camp thanks to latrines that spilled their contents with every hard rain. Was combat worse than this suspended animation? Gordon wondered. At least in battle, he'd been on the move, headed somewhere, even if it was headlong into enemy fire.

The most sanguine and respected among the prisoners were those who did not constantly yearn for the world outside the barbed wire even as they expended considerable mental energy devising ways to rejoin it. It was their sworn duty as soldiers to try to escape. Gordon coped by organizing his day in much the same way he had before the war, as a span of time in which he had assignments to accomplish, appointments to keep. His ability to compartmentalize, to identify then accomplish small objectives, kept him from despairing at the big picture—endless captivity and no control over his life. Gordon rose before dawn and stood for roll call, his only goal to cooperate and get on to breakfast. He ate his rations without acknowledging the foul taste and the lack of calories and nutrients that had caused his body to soften and shrink. With fellow prisoners, he peeled potatoes, swept the barracks, and cleaned latrines as ordered. He took his exercise around the perimeter of the camp, although his jog had become a walk, and now that walk was slowing. Once in a while, he joined in the soccer games in the main yard, a useful interval for exchanging information unnoticed but still perilous, given the rocky, uneven yard that challenged even the best athletes. A deep gash in a shin or a broken ankle could bring fatal complications.

Only briefly, before he fell asleep at night, did Gordon permit himself to contemplate his family. He read and re-read the handful of letters he'd received via the Red Cross, then pictured Beryl's smiling green eyes, mirrored in their son's, both of their noses surely covered with a spate of freckles by this time of year, both with dark curls atop their heads, Beryl's more unruly and untamed—an ongoing frustration to her—and Colin's clipped shorter as a young boy's should be. Young boy. He was 13 now. Three years since they had said their goodbyes. Gordon closed his eyes and prayed, begging God to protect them from harm and beseeching the Almighty to end this war before his son had to join the fight.

Then, with effort, he pivoted from these dangerous thoughts, away from the black whirlpool of loss and loneliness, the Charybdis that could pull him under. It would not serve him to grow despondent here. It would lead to death. So, in the stinking darkness, his prayers concluded and snores filling the barracks, he applied his concentration instead to all he had observed that day—new and recurring patterns in the movement of the guards throughout the camp, in the operation of the electrified fence, in the times of day when the gate swung wide. He drew conclusions and made mental notes of those things he would share with his superiors.

The prisoners were mostly segregated by nationality and rank and spent the bulk of their hours in the company of the two dozen men housed in their barracks. The regular Heer officers showed begrudging respect for the senior Allied prisoners; they communicated news and revised policies through the top British flag officer, Lieutenant Colonel Herbert Leonard, observing their enemy's military chain of command. When a POW was to be punished for a perceived infraction—late for *Appell*, failure to properly clean latrine spillage from a walkway, or simple intransigence—their commanding officer was notified before the offender served his sentence, usually a span of days in a locked cell on even more limited rations. But while the regular military observed the broad outlines of the Hague Conventions, the Waffen-SS, Gordon observed, were uniformed thugs; wild-eyed, fervent believers who lived to demonstrate their singular dedication to the Party even if that meant ignoring universal military protocol and policy. The Waffen-SS came regularly to review camp operations and invariably found grievous issues they insisted be addressed immediately. Whether they expressed their displeasure to the camp commandant was unclear. Their preferred moment to notify the captives was at the final *Appell*, of the day, when the POWs were the most tired, the most irritated, when their fuses were shortest and they tended toward despair. Properly baited, any one of them could have a fatal overreaction as an SS-Standartenführer stood in front of them, toe to toe, barking incomprehensible orders in their percussive German, spittle landing on the prisoner's cheek or in his eye. More than one POW had moved to strike his interlocutor, earning jail time or worse, depending on the mood of the visiting officer. Gordon took satisfaction knowing the SS's lack of soldierly discipline and impulsive decisions would quickly thin their ranks and cost additional German lives. At least he hoped so. It heartened him to think of the lot of them continuing on in this war, officers promoted not because of their astute minds but party purity. As they preened in their ribbon-covered uniforms, the lightning bolt emblems on their hats and lapels signifying their vaunted positions, Gordon prayed each one would make spectacularly stupid decisions that would accelerate their undoing.

On one late-spring day, the prisoners were ordered to gather in the wide yard at the back of the camp, an occurrence that often coincided with the arrival of new POWs. A Nazi garden party, the long-timers had taken to calling it. The first time they were invited to such a soiree, the men had been reticent to leave their bunks, concerned they were furnishing their captors an efficient opportunity to machine-gun them all at once. No, the camp commandant assured, it's simply to allow for some housekeeping. The gathering meant the guards could make a thorough search of the POW quarters—all at once, no *Kriegie* interference. The camp guards were older, many slow-moving, too old to fight at the front but eager to be part of the war. Some limped noticeably or suffered other infirmities, but their hearts were true; they served the Fatherland with serious purpose. That is, except for the Poles conscripted into this service. Having survived the Blitzkrieg, now adapting to the occupation, Gordon observed the Poles' loyalties shifted as opportunities presented themselves. They obeyed the Germans to keep their families safe. But in exchange for cigarettes and chocolate—which they consumed away from the camp so the Germans did not see—they furnished certain essentials for the prisoners' wellbeing. There was the bucket in which the prisoners cooked their *Kriegie* hooch, fermenting raisins that arrived in the Australians' Red Cross packages to make a horrible-looking cocktail with a gratifying alcoholic kick. The Poles had smuggled the two-gallon bucket in for them, hiding it underneath the barracks' floorboards. But that was just the beginning. For the right price, they secured thread and buttons and bits of fabric to help transform military uniforms into civilian clothes, blank paper of just the right sheen and weight that forgers could transform into documents for escapees, and odds and ends like coiled wire for the current project: constructing a radio receiver. The newest POWs would likely have something to contribute; fliers were trained, as they bailed from their aircraft, to grab a tiny piece of something useful and shove it up a nasal passage or elsewhere, so deep that it would remain undiscovered even in a strip-search. When the German guards planned a camp-wide sweep, the Poles, from all appearances, supported the search in helpful and efficient ways: in actuality, they stayed ahead of their German colleagues, removing contraband before the guards arrived, and relocating it to barracks that had already been searched.

For the prisoners, the garden party was a spirit-lifting reunion that let them remember themselves, let them recall and reclaim their identities as husbands and fathers and brothers—as men. Hope was renewed and contained within each healthy, unfamiliar face—most of them airmen shot down over Germany or France, a few captured in the African hostilities—not yet dead-eyed and thinned out, men still vigorous and relieved to be among the living, flesh and blood proof that the Allies were still fighting this war. Americans were now filtering into the camps, young bomber pilots and gunners forced to unceremoniously exit their burning aircraft under withering German fire, leaving compatriots dead in blood-spattered turrets.

The long-timers—ranking officers first—encircled the new arrivals to absorb the latest news of the war. The Americans, they learned, were taking over RAF bases in East Anglia, but their early bombing runs had been near-disasters with unsustainable losses of aircraft and men. But at least America was in the fight now. That would surely turn the tide, Gordon and the others believed, or slow the Germans, anyway. What was Churchill's plan, now that the Americans were in it? They sought news about their former air bases and questioned the new arrivals if they knew how this town or that village was getting on in the war. After the initial, consequential questions, they inevitably probed for that dearest bit of information—whether the new captive might know someone they knew. If, on the off-chance, they held a person in common, an authentic link to the world before the war.

"York?" a young British Second Lieutenant called out. "Anyone from York?" and moments later three soldiers were at his elbow, comparing addresses, favorite pubs, running through names of girlfriends—current and past—along with those of brothers and sisters, relatives and friends. A close listen revealed they had no friends in common but it didn't matter: standing in front of another man who knew your hometown—the very lanes you'd walked, the park where you'd played cricket, the church where you were confirmed, the pub where you'd sung and spilled ale with your mates— affirmed for the prisoners that the places they ached for were solid and real and still existed in full color with their familiar smells and beloved quirks and the cherished memories attached to them. It affirmed the rightness of fighting this war, if only because those moments in those places bore repeating.

Despite serious effort, Gordon had not found anyone who knew members of his family or Beryl's. He'd learned through the new arrivals of the terrific bombing London had sustained and that there had been a respite as Hitler opened the Russian front. He met an officer who had worked at Grove Park Hospital who confirmed it remained untouched by bombs. Two other prisoners, both new to the camp, thought that perhaps they'd shopped at Densmore's market—maybe—and while the details they offered didn't seem to fit with Gordon's remembrances of his neighborhood market, just hearing another human being say "Densmore's" transported him right inside the shop that smelled of fresh flowers and tobacco and the faint scent of a piece of fish or two that would best be popped into a stew immediately. Many officers in the camp were Londoners, one a lawyer in civilian life who had prepared contracts for Gordon's architecture firm, though not for any of Gordon's projects. He had listened patiently as Gordon spoke at length about the uninspired environment in which they found themselves, all right-angles and utilitarian function, poorly situated for the prevailing weather patterns and constructed without a thought given to the movement of the sun. Better positioning could have introduced more sunlight in the barracks and in the mess, keeping the whole of it brighter and dryer and perhaps more tolerable. More thoughtful design, Gordon explained, could have obviated any number of issues but clearly, the Germans were applying their efficient and disciplined design brilliance elsewhere. The patient, erstwhile lawyer nodded in agreement.

Standing in the guard tower, camp commandant Oberst Reinhard Schröder observed the gathering, mutely wishing his English were more serviceable so he could better understand the words the prisoners exchanged, if only to get a better sense of when the Allies might be willing to quit the fight. A Heer Colonel, not SS, Schröder proudly served in his teens in the previous world war, having been loyal to his country years longer than he'd been loyal to the Nazi party. In fact, he harbored deep worries over what Germany would be like when hostilities ended. The Fatherland would be victorious, he believed, but what caliber of leader would Hitler be in peacetime? The Führer seemed born for crisis and conflict—often creating it unnecessarily, Schröder believed. The commandant supported the German thrust into France and the Low Countries, but when he'd offered pointed insights in a staff officer meeting, questions about the overall strategic approach in the prosecution of the war, he was chastised for impertinence. That, plus his failure to seek a transfer into the Waffen-SS and an assortment of small missteps, had cost him a field command. These days, he kept his war analyses to himself. He had a prison camp to run, and he determined to do so in ways that would eventually earn him notice and favor when peace arrived.

CHAPTER SIX

The United Kingdom has become
"one vast aircraft carrier anchored off the north-west coast of Europe."
–The Journal *The Aeroplane*

England—as the Americans arrive

There were days the wind whipped the rain sideways, little knives nicking human skin. Bundling up against the cold air was one thing, but a cold rain was a different challenge entirely. It found its way inside sleeves and up over the tops of boots and down jacket collars where it diffused silently, expansively, overcoming any residual warmth it encountered. The haste with which Kimbolton Airfield had been constructed abetted the rain's objectives over the airmen's efforts to stay dry. It pooled on the runways and taxiways and flowed briskly into the stone walkways between the buildings. It ran in streams underneath the corners of the Nissen huts and puddled, pulling socks and cigarette butts and the detritus of the day into a chilly whirlpool bath. Jack Henry Philip's blood ran thin to start with: growing up on the Florida panhandle had not prepared him well for this island in the North Sea. And it was only October. Late October, 1942, but still.

The route that had brought him here was a circuitous one, now that the skies over the Atlantic were as perilous as the seas beneath. The pioneer squadrons of the 379th Bombardment Group flew their B-17's to England via the southern route, flying from Florida to Borinquen Field, Puerto Rico, then hopscotching several islands en route to Parnamirim Air Base in Natal, Brazil for a night's layover before the grueling six-hour leg that came next. From Natal, the fliers crossed to Africa, stopping first in Sengal, then up through Algiers for what turned out to be a memorable few nights in Casablanca. Despite promises made to girls back home, some of the men were intent on enjoying as many of life's pleasures as they could, in case they had more days behind them than ahead.

From Africa, they crossed northward into England, heading for Kimbolton. Built for the Royal Air Force Bomber Command, the field was now designated USAAF Station 117 to serve American heavy bombers. The shining waters off the coast looked both familiar and strange to Jack's eyes when he'd first piloted his bomber low and slow up the length of England. Rocks and crags in front of dense pine forests, instead of the miles of sugar sand shoreline he'd grown up with along the Gulf. But the dots of small boats, the gleam of the sun on water, the gulls wheeling and cawing, diving into the deep for a snack—all this reminded him of home.

The day President Roosevelt declared war, Jack was home from college, two classes short of completing his engineering degree at The University of Florida. He and his fraternity brothers had anticipated returning after Christmas for a final, glorious, beer-drenched semester in Gainesville. Instead, Jack was abruptly and unceremoniously graduated from the University making him eligible for the draft, because he needed those last two courses in fluid mechanics far less than the country needed him in the service. He enlisted, seeking a position in the Army Air Forces. After barely ten months of training, first at Harding Army Air Base in Louisiana and later close to home at MacDill Field, his squadron got orders to England. After assembling briefly for final training and instructions at Fort Dix in New Jersey, they executed the complicated flight plan to England. In just days, they would begin bombing runs across the Channel. For now, it was daily training in the cockpit—touch and go's to continue to get the feel of the aircraft—intel briefings, weather briefings, technical briefings, and updates on the dismal situations in the Pacific and North Africa. That and sloshing through the base to the mess hall, the officers' club, or out to the hardstands to inspect their aircraft and catch up with the mechanics taking refuge in the tents meant to keep them and their tools out of the rain.

As Jack stood smoking and talking with his ground crew one misty afternoon, he noticed two young boys outside the fence, leaning on their bicycles, watching the Americans work.

"Can we help you, young men?" Jack called.

The boys exchanged a glance and dissolved into laughter.

"And what's so funny about that?" Jack asked.

"Nothing, sir. Nothing. Sorry," said the taller one. "We just wanted to hear you talk. Seeming as you're a Yank."

Jack excused himself from his conversation with the two mechanics, pulled his jacket collar up around his ears, and strode toward the boys in the drizzle. The smaller boy hopped on his bike, prepared for a quick getaway, but the other one stood bravely, shoulders back, as Jack grew closer.

Hugo and Colin had developed a somewhat proprietary posture toward Kimbolton, first watching the construction workers from their schoolhouse window, then venturing over on their bicycles countless times to monitor progress. When the first of the American bombers began arriving, the boys made daily pilgrimages to watch the waves of lumbering, impossibly loud B-17s descend. They came on Saturdays to watch training flights, astonished these enormous beasts could even lift off the ground. Surely, the giant bombs they carried would bloody well demolish the Germans. How could a little Messerschmitt or Junker fighter possibly knock these out of the sky? The Americans, too, were a source of endless fascination—so brash and loose-limbed but at the same time, intense and serious-minded. These were different creatures from the boys' more buttoned-up fathers. They seemed to follow an entirely distinct set of grown-up rules, drawing attention to themselves in ways the boys had been taught not to do. They hooted and called to one another when they came into Elsworth, walking three abreast so other shoppers had to navigate around them. They laughed loudly and unselfconsciously, drawing disapproving looks from those who found such behavior roguish, intrusive. They loved their planes and fussed over them endlessly. They gave them names and painted girly pictures on the nose— something Hugo and Colin found brilliant and bold. Village neighbors did not necessarily agree.

"And what more would you young fellas like me to say?" Jack asked. "Any particular words y'all achin' to hear? Want me to sing a few bars of 'I've Got a Gal in Kalamazoo?'"

More laughter erupted from the boys at the way he said "Kalamazoo" and his slip-slidy way of talking. One word rolling into the next. Saying "y'all" and calling them young fellas. Fellas! That was new.

Hugo and Colin exchanged a look, both working with great effort to compose themselves. Colin got a hold of himself first. He offered a small bow. "Thank you, sir. That's quite good. No need to sing. Truly. Are you a pilot, sir? Can you fly that aeroplane?"

"Are you a spy, son, asking all these questions?"

"No—no sir," Colin stammered, horrified. Hugo prepared again to make a run for it until they recognized the smile behind the American's eyes.

"Listen, I can't stop you from seeing what goes on here from your side of the fence. Heck, we've just moved in and taken over your farmland, haven't we? But I can't talk about any of it because you never know if the Jerrys are listening."

The boys exchanged a wide-eyed look. "I knew it," Hugo mouthed silently, prompting a grave nod from Colin.

"And y'all best not talk about it either, boys. You know that. I'm sure you're seeing a lot here in your little village now that all us Yanks have moved in. Bet things have really changed."

"I'm from London," volunteered Colin, "not Elsworth. Got moved here before the Jerrys started bombing. Three years ago. I live with Hugo and his mum."

"I'm from Elsworth," Hugo offered. "We watched them build this airfield, but we thought it was for the RAF. Nobody told us the Yanks were moving in."

"Well, we are. And not just here. But now look at me, saying too much. So, okay, you're Hugo. And what's your name, son?"

And so began the first of many, many visits between the friendly and frequently shivering American pilot from Florida and two young boys who were rapidly becoming young men, aching for dads whom they worried they would not see again. These Americans, short and tall, stout and lanky, some olive-skinned with exotic last names, others so red-cheeked and ruddy they could be mistaken for Brits—their very presence brought hope. The reinforcements had arrived—like in American Westerns when the cavalry rode up over the hill just in the nick of time. The popular song the BBC played on a loop proclaimed, "The Yanks are coming:" and so they had.

After that first conversation, in which they thanked their new Yank friend profusely for his time and promised to return the next day, the boys practically vibrated with excitement. Racing home through the rain, pedaling hard through the village to the point they thought their lungs might burst from their chests, they cut through the garden of Holy Trinity, rounded the corner to the house on Boxworth Road, and tore through the front door.

"Mum!" Hugo called as they charged into the house. "Mum! We've met an American soldier! A pilot. Over at Kimbolton Airfield."

"What's this?" asked Ivy, emerging from the small kitchen in her apron, wooden spoon in hand. The rich smell of onion and herbs wafted from the soup pot simmering on the hob. Vegetable soup tonight for supper. "You got one to chat, finally, did ya?"

"We didn't stay at the front gate this time," said Colin. "We followed the fence 'round back and this American bloke was out on the runway talking to his mates. The aeroplane mechanics. He saw us and just walked over and asked us if he could help us."

"He asked if we were spies for the Germans!" cried Hugo.

"Spies!" said Ivy, looking them up and down. "Well, are you?"

The boys' laughter spilled through the house. Hugo clutched Colin's arm, doubling over at the very idea. Ivy's hand came unbidden to her chest and she breathed, gratefully, deeply, for this rare and precious moment. Here are the Hugo and Colin the war has taken away. Happy, mischief-making schoolboys these circumstances rarely allowed them to be.

"What if we are?" responded Colin finally, wiping a tear from the corner of his eye. "Maybe I'm a Jerry spy who's been planted here—not from London at all but from Berlin and I'm listening and watching and radioing back secret messages that are decoded by other spies..."

"Are you now? And what have you disclosed so far?"

Colin tapped his lips with his forefinger and thought a moment. "That we need paratroops on a rescue mission for Marigold to save her from Margaret and Patsy. That no matter how loudly the vicar preaches, there's always a parishioner or two asleep in the back of the church. That the Jerrys may as well give up because Brits are far braver and with the Yanks in the fight, the Germans will be pushed back and drowned in the Ruhr!"

Ivy smiled. Oh, this boy. This boy who felt like her own, at turns serious and silly, who had become just the companion her Hugo had needed—that she needed for him—after Wills had disappeared. There was grace contained in Colin's mischievous sense of humor, so precious in these serious, sullen, worrisome days.

"Mum," Hugo followed up thoughtfully, finger pointed in the air. "He must be a double agent then, if he's talking the Jerrys into quitting."

"Oh, if they would quit, my boy. Right this minute. But since you've figured all that out, Hugo, it must mean you're a spy as well. How did this happen that I've got two young and handsome spies right in my midst? I should have known, what with all the secretive trips you've made to the airfield to gather intelligence there. What kind of wanker am I to have not even noticed before now?"

More laughter drew the twins into the sitting room.

"What is it, Ivy-mum? What's so funny?" Margaret demanded, hands on hips, as Patsy nodded at her side, the cat—a kitten no more—hanging in limp resignation over her narrow shoulder.

"The boys were chatting with Americans today, girls, some of those soldiers who fly those very loud aeroplanes we see now."

"Can we meet one, too?" asked Patsy.

"Yes! I want to meet Americans!" cried Margaret.

"Perhaps we can, girls. Maybe we can have them for dinner here. Wouldn't that be something? But they are busy, busy—they have important missions to do, so we'll have to see," said Ivy, much to the chagrin of the boys, who wanted nothing whatsoever to do with sharing their American with little girls.

CHAPTER SEVEN

The great deceivers of the world begin by deceiving themselves.
They have to, or they wouldn't be so good at it.
—Molière

Sagan, German Reich

Reinhard Schröder was rather enjoying his wartime post, billeted for the past three years, with his wife, Annalise, in a manor house requisitioned soon after Poland was pacified. The home had belonged to a Jewish family, now relocated elsewhere, and contained rooms of carefully curated furniture, much of it burnished cherry and mahogany, devotedly cared for and in pristine condition. Drapes of dark, richly textured fabric hung at the windows, sumptuous brocades that were repeated on some of the upholstered furniture in the sitting room. Left behind were silver and brass menorahs that Schröder had melted into candelabras for the formal dining table. There were closets full of linens, some of them antique with intricate hand-sewn lace borders, all of them clean and pressed and fresh-smelling; the butler's pantry held dozens of place settings of English bone china and finely cut crystal—hundreds of stems for wine, champagne, brandy. The music room at the back of the house opened to the gardens and featured a Steinway grand piano, which, once tuned, offered a resonant and glorious timbre. A guest house stood adjacent, where Annalise's family and other important guests stayed when they came to visit. While Annalise had protested their move from Berlin—home to her parents and sister and second only to Paris in her mind as the nexus of European culture—she had come around once she took in the amenities their large, new home offered.

Given the location of their post and the uncertainties of the time, they'd sent their two children to boarding school in Geneva and while Annalise professed to missing them intensely, she rather liked having her days more or less to herself, rising later in the morning and lingering over her coffee, not having to remind them to finish their lessons or contend with music teachers who carped that her children must practice more faithfully. After ten years of motherhood, her time was once again her own. Daily, Annalise played the Steinway, working through a lyrical Strauss waltz, the technical demands of a Bach counterpoint, sight-reading her way through the Chopin sheet music she found in the piano bench. Afternoons found her in the vast garden, snipping gladiola and iris stems to bring inside, paring back branches on the rhododendron, and enjoying the corn-cockle and larkspur that grew wild in the warmer months at the entrance to the woods at the back of the property. She passed many contented hours with the botanical encyclopedia in her lap, dreaming of new cultivars she could introduce.

From the music room, French doors opened to a red-bricked terrace holding a large weathered wooden dining table, surrounded by oversized planters bursting with red geraniums that would soon bow their round heads in surrender as cooler weather settled in. It was the ideal setting for Sunday lunch when the children came for summer holidays, for relaxing with a good book, and for entertaining—most especially Reinhard's superiors when they came each quarter to inspect the camp and review his performance. And now Annalise had plans to enhance its loveliness. She envisioned a wooden arbor with crossed beams to create some shade on the *Terrasse* and still allow the sun to peek through. She would train vines to run up the sides and eventually over the top for a sweet-smelling drape. It might take several years to reach its full impact, but if the posts were artistically carved, the structure would enhance the home and the garden immediately. She sketched it out for Reinhard and presented it to him one evening after supper.

"And this is?" he asked, eyebrows arched and skeptical.

"It is an idea to make our home more welcoming, Reinhard. The *Terrasse* needs to be finished."

"It is finished," Reinhard replied. "The foundation is solid, the furniture suits it, and your flowers are thriving."

"But imagine, darling, if we built some wooden posts on either side of the bricks, here and there, and created a beautiful arbor." She pointed out details in her sketch. "And see, it would go up this side with a lintel across and the second post here. Just picture it, Reinhard, covered with trellis roses or jessamine or even ivy. It would be enchanting—heavenly. I can't imagine why it wasn't included in the original design, or at the very least, constructed soon after the house was occupied." She sat back in her chair, blue eyes bright and hopeful.

"And who is there to accomplish this, Annalise?" he asked reasonably. "Every capable German workman is serving the Fatherland now—as he should. There is no carpenter I can call and I most certainly cannot devote a moment's time to this. It is critical for me—for us—that I oversee operations at the camp with the utmost competence. It will reflect well on me—on us—when the war is over and the Führer selects the men he wants beside him to lead Germany in peacetime."

Annalise reached across the dining table for Reinhard's hand.

"I was thinking about just this problem," she smiled. "Can you—would it be improper—to use some of the prisoners in the camp? You've placed some on work details outside the camp, so could we not have a work detail here? Reinhard, think about it. It's not entirely fair. Had we stayed in Berlin, we would have had a larger staff than just a housekeeper and cook. And I often need some help with the heavier work."

"Annalise," Reinhard replied sharply, "we are very near a war zone. We are extremely fortunate the war has not separated us. I had expected to serve at the front—I could be in Leningrad, you know. So, I hardly think this posting has shortchanged either of us—or that German resources should be spent this way... redecorating."

They had slipped from discussion to argument and Annalise, aware of the pivot, slowly, sadly withdrew her hand. She averted her eyes from Reinhard's gaze and stared out at the garden. He, in turn, watched her. The light blue eyes focused in the middle distance. The long, elegant fingers steepled together at her narrow waist as she formulated the words she would use to continue making her case. Her sinuous legs, crossed, the muscles of her calves lean and taut. After twelve years of marriage, she remained utterly compelling to him. Ten years his junior, she retained a young, lithe frame, her smooth, fair complexion framed by silken blonde hair she often wore loose. He frequently considered her attributes in comparison to the wives of his peers—only to himself, of course. The other wives had their value, certainly, but were more matronly in their appearance with hips that had begun to broaden, hair tinged here and there with silver, chins with flesh growing a bit loose and soft. It gave him distinct pleasure to enumerate all this. Annalise looked barely beyond her teens, a deep source of pride for her husband, as if he had foreseen how her beauty would endure or had somehow fostered it.

"I am only seeking," she said finally, eyes still fixed on the distant woods, "to keep myself occupied while my children live in another country, away from my affection and influence. My own children! I did not choose this, Reinhard. I came at your request—in loyalty to you—to serve your needs. I only wish to ensure this place feels like a true home, one that warmly welcomes your superiors so that they evaluate you more highly, so that you can reach the professional standing to which you aspire. I am only seeking," she repeated, "to keep myself busy and cheerful so I can survive living in this... this dreadful, backward, place. This... Polish nightmare."

He knew she was prone to melodramatics, but this was the first time she'd expressed her dissatisfaction so directly. It would not do to have a visibly unhappy wife in a competitive, highly monitored political climate. He would let her twist and sulk a little bit before he rescued her because this was the bargain they had struck within their marriage—moments of high passion, stepping right to the line of abject hopelessness, then staying there for a moment to feel fully the angst and sorrow and disappointment. Then one of them would relent, would rush to soothe and obviate the other's distress, begging forgiveness, forswearing enduring love and loyalty. As for building the garden arbor, a request he could easily grant, he would be the one to move them to climax, denouement, and resolution. At the right moment, of course. Reinhard had his own bit of dramatics to perform, more restrained and measured, to ensure he remained as compelling an individual to his wife as she to him.

"And for me, Annalise—how do you imagine I like running a camp for failed Allied soldiers, having to answer to the impulsive children of the Waffen-SS? When I expected to command a Panzer division of twenty-thousand trained soldiers? Do you think this is the war I asked for?" He slapped the table with his open hand, gratified when she startled at the sound. Then he bluffed. "Let me clarify for you, Annalise, that while the current situation is not what either of us anticipated, it is hardly nightmarish. Should you wish to return to Berlin, where I gather you would live more happily with your parents, that is surely an option you may take."

A tear slipped down Annalise's cheek, her last card to play to convince him of her loneliness, her disappointment, her need.

"You would have me leave you, Reinhard?" she asked weakly, pain clouding her eyes.

And within a few moments, as she expected, he stood and pulled her to him, lifting the strands of her hair from her forehead and kissing her there. She wrapped her arms around his middle and buried her head in his neck.

"My dearest," he whispered.

"You have your command, Reinhard, your career, such as it is," she said through tears. "I am here alone in this... this near wilderness, managing a barely competent Polish housekeeper and a Polish cook I would have fired long ago had they worked for us in Berlin. And without my son and daughter to pour my life into as I had always wanted and planned. We used to play music together, do you remember? We took them to the best museums and concerts and ballets. We led a full life—one of culture and refinement. And now I live this partial life, away from all I've known, while you progress, with your ambitious plans to serve the Fatherland in a prominent way, a decisive way, once this war is over. Well. What of me? Is it so selfish on my part to wish to ply my creative energies into something beautiful that helps us impress the very people who may one day recommend you for an important role in the Reich?"

"Dear Annalise. Lovely Annalise. It pains me that you do not know how much I value all you've done to make our home a happy one. The flowers you spread throughout this house and garden that greet me each morning. The sumptuous menus you devise, even if the cook struggles to master them. Your patient indulgence with the household staff. Your habit of welcoming me with a perfect pour of wine at the end of each day. And your affection, dear one. Your constant demonstrations of love. You have made this a happy home, Annalise. I am a fortunate man. Forgive me for not expressing more clearly my gratitude."

She sensed the tide had fully turned her way and lifted her head, allowing their eyes to meet.

"I shall see to your request tomorrow."

With that, she laid her hand flat on her chest and sighed, satisfied at both her performance as the well-meaning, suffering wife and at Reinhard's heroic turn as protector, provider, deliverer. Reinhard clasped her hand in his, then reached his other hand towards his wine glass. Then he guided her up the stairs to their suite of rooms so they could celebrate a proper reconciliation.

.   .   .

Annalise was correct: POW work details set out daily from the camp and although her husband didn't tell her this, they were rather easy to requisition. Some details harvested fields, others helped build or reinforce bridges, still others worked in factories that the Nazis claimed did not support the war effort but of course, any labor the POWs handled freed able-bodied Germans to build armaments or transport supplies to the troops. Reinhard's search for a carpenter led him to Gordon Clarke, who claimed to know not just building architecture but project design and construction.

While the last thing Gordon wanted was to make life more pleasing for a damnable Nazi officer and his wife, the opportunity to get out of the camp at regular intervals—to do something productive with his hands with tools and diagrams and simple math, and to get a feel for the countryside in which he found himself—felt like an answer to prayer. After consultation with Lieutenant Colonel Leonard, he consented to the work. As Leonard advised, he would not rush. This building project would receive the time and concentration needed to ensure its utmost value could be leveraged.

Within the week, Commandant Schröder, his driver, a guard, and Gordon assembled at the camp gate to travel the few miles to the commandant's house. The duty guard reviewed Gordon's gate pass granting him exit from the camp, then nodded toward the waiting Mercedes-Benz staff car, its small Nazi flags adorning either side of the hood, a misleading signal that these four men were setting off on a mission of import to the Reich. Gordon climbed into the back of the staff car, breathing in the smell of the soft calf's leather and noting the spotlessness of the interior. Had he been closely observed, one might have noted the rhythmic movement of Gordon's mud-covered heel as he worked to transfer the dirt from his boot to the carpet under his feet. A small act of resistance. Having decided to spend a portion of his lunch hour on this errand, Schröder sat beside him, *Schirmmütze* cap in his lap, revealing him to be younger than Gordon had imagined, mid-40's, salt and pepper hair, his face more pleasant and his jaw softer when his teeth were unclenched. He seemed completely preoccupied with the task at hand, as if Gordon had not been under armed guard in the camp minutes before and was simply a hired man contracted to do some work. The commandant explained what he expected of Gordon, both in terms of the quality of construction of the arbor and respectful deportment toward his wife. The guard amplified the commandant's orders, translating some of the remarks. Gordon nodded as they rode past the small, quaint homes and businesses of Sagan, noting landmarks where certain roads intersected and the dense pine forests that circumscribed the town.

"Jawohl. Sicherlich. Was auch immer deine Frau wünscht." Yes, sir. Certainly, sir. Whatever your wife wishes. His barely accented German surprised the other three men.

"Lieutenant Clarke, you are full of wonders. First, you claim architectural talent and now, you speak to me in German," responded Schröder, thrown by this development, mentally reviewing what he might have said in the POW's presence that he would not have wanted him to understand.

"Jawohl," Gordon responded, explaining he'd developed a working knowledge of German at university when he'd studied some of the great German theologians.

"Well, with Herr Hitler, we've little use for them now," Schröder quipped. "Our Führer has assumed the role of head theologian at this point—determining for himself who are the true chosen ones of God, along with those who are most clearly not."

Schröder asked how much time Gordon needed to complete the project. Gordon responded he would first review the wife's initial sketch, survey the property, measure, and from there, turn to design and acquisition of supplies. He would have a more accurate timetable after today, an answer that satisfied his new boss.

They arrived at a lovely old manor house that had clearly belonged, at some point in its history, to an owner of means, a far larger estate than any Gordon had seen en route. The driver pulled the vehicle around the back of the house, jumping out to open the door for the commandant, then standing at attention at the driver's side door. Gordon and the guard opened their doors themselves and walked the few paces up the pebbled drive to the garden gate, the guard at the rear, sidearm in hand. Schröder used a key to unlatch a tall wooden gate and they stepped through, pausing to take in the tableau. It was glorious, verdant, the very antithesis of the world Gordon had inhabited since his capture. Deep red flowers overspread a Rose of Sharon hedge, with foxglove and yarrow interspersed—the last blooms of summer, erect and vibrant and untroubled that the growing season was near its close. Profuse red geraniums sprang from pots and window boxes. Linden and birch trees overhung part of the sideyard offering shade, their leaves just beginning to lose their deep green. Gordon's mind went first to the person who, year upon year, had created this soothing oasis—the hours of work and planning it represented—who'd then been forced to abandon it. He thought next of his own garden in London, tiny in comparison, where he and Beryl nurtured pots of herbs to use in the kitchen and cultivated one bed of roses and another of Scottish wildflowers. He could see it in full, midsummer color. He remained there a moment before pulling himself back to the more extravagant and somewhat unanticipated present.

Amplifying the abundant visual beauty, a melody floated through the open doors at the back of the house. A piano etude. Schumann? Strauss? Gordon guessed as his mind followed and absorbed the exquisite sound. The men waited, each holding his breath, straining to hear every note as the piece reached its melancholy peak then concluded in the plaintive diminuendo. Then quiet. The men exhaled. Gordon almost applauded, astonished that there still existed a select few in the world safely insulated from the violence raging across the continents, a select few with the means and capacity to cultivate and appreciate artistic beauty, its ethereal poignancy.

A young woman emerged from the doors at the terrace—a daughter, Gordon thought at first, before realizing with a start that no, this must be the commandant's wife. Gordon heard the jangle of her bracelets, the staccato strike of her high-heeled shoes as she crossed the red bricks, feminine sounds that, like the beauty of the garden, the rise and fall of the music, seemed wildly incongruous to the recent experiences of his life. She was fair in the favored German way, translucent skin, light blonde hair restrained into a chignon at the back of her neck, pearls dotting her earlobes. Her bearing was formal and authoritative. She wore a plain beige chambray skirt, narrow and snug on her hips, that almost looked army-issue. It was topped most incongruously by a cream-colored satin blouse, unbuttoned at her long neck, the very low V inviting the gaze of three of the men who stood before her. Her husband seemed not to notice.

"Annalise, this is the *Kriegsgefangener,* Lieutenant Clarke, here to construct your arbor. Clarke, my wife, Frau Schröder."

Her eyes locked on Gordon's, her face unreadable but not unkind. He could smell her. Unlike her bland-colored wardrobe, her scent was complex and exotic—ambergris, if he had to guess. He thought at once of the faint rosewater perfume Beryl preferred, how she dotted it at her temples and behind her ears, how he inhaled it when he buried his face in her neck, in her hair.

"Lieutenant Clarke," the woman acknowledged. "Thank you for agreeing to work for us. Perhaps it will be more enjoyable than the typical activities in which you engage. I understand you are trained. I have the sketch for you. I am no artist so it is very rough, but I can explain how I want this built. Please come this way to the table for us to begin."

Her English was accented, but far better than her husband's. He followed her to the table where a silver tray held a gleaming tea service, along with orange slices, tea cakes, strudels, and a saucer of marmalade. Gordon salivated at the sight and smell of them.

"Annalise," her husband called. "I trust you have what you need to begin your collaboration. I must return to camp but Friedrich, of course, will stay here to supervise."

To guard me, Gordon translated, although he saw the sidearm was now holstered.

"Yes, darling, of course." She waved a distracted hand in his general direction. "Until this evening, then," and she returned her attention to the table where her sketch lay. Staring now at her back, her husband gave a curt, superfluous nod, called out that the driver would return in four hours' time to retrieve the lieutenant, then turned back through the gate to his car. When she heard the engine start, she addressed Gordon.

"Please, have what you'd like," she said, pointing toward the tray. "But first, I must ask you to use the washroom. Friedrich, please escort the Lieutenant to the lavatory."

They entered through the kitchen, where Friedrich greeted two women in the middle of preparing the day's meals and polishing many place settings of silverware. They eyed Gordon with surprise and extended no welcome. Friedrich directed Gordon on to the servants' washroom where he availed himself of the first flush toilet he'd seen in three years then soaped and washed his hands and his arms and his face with clear, clean, unscented water—quite unlike the poorly filtered taps in the camp.

Gordon emerged, nodded to the women who seemed approving of his efforts, and followed the guard back outside. Frau Schröder stood at the table studying her sketch, one arm supporting her weight as she leaned over the drawing, the other at her hip, causing the lapel of her blouse to fall open, allowing a glimpse of the fine lace of her undergarments, the rise of her breast.

"My, you're a tall Englishman, aren't you?" she observed. Their eyes met and as she straightened, Gordon moved his eyes down, just a few inches, to the middle of her chest, the dip of the V. If she wished him to notice her, he would. If she was laying a trap, he preferred to find out sooner instead of later.

A smile played at the woman's lips. "I can see that we are both eager to begin," she said.

CHAPTER EIGHT

In wartime, truth is so precious
that she should always be attended by a bodyguard of lies.
–Winston Churchill

London, 1942

In the pre-dawn, the hospital halls were blissfully quiet—just a soft brush of movement as orderlies returned gurneys to inventory and nurses made scheduled checks through the wards. Beryl tamped out her cigarette, then secured her unruly and overlong fringe with a pair of bobby pins. With a slow exhale, she reached across the receiving desk, her tired mind fit only for the most basic of tasks: stacking the patients' folders alphabetically so the day shift workers could begin with some semblance of order. The wards of Grove Park Hospital remained at capacity, beds full of civilians mangled in months of bombing, but the pace of new admits and the numbers of family members circling the halls in worry had eased now that Germany had turned its attention to its enemy on its eastern flank. London was still standing, barely, residents gaining courage with every onslaught withstood: the Nazis had not swum across the Channel and climbed upon their shores yet. The soaring Coventry Cathedral might be hollowed out, but her walls stood, proud and defiant.

Beryl's workdays were busy, steady now, a change from the frenetic breathlessness that had characterized the prior year, the careening from ambulance bay to bedside to operating room, summoned by doctors in need of immediate help. She could now pause for a meal and a smoke mid-shift and visit the loo when she needed to. She had a moment to place dutiful telephone calls to ensure her in-laws were safe. But her hyper-vigilance did not recede. Within her, adrenaline coursed uninterrupted, every nerve ending poised to respond to the next threat. These many months of compressed, intense worry about Gordon, about Colin, about Britain's very survival, had altered her internal chemistry and physical appearance—her brow perpetually creased, braced for the next round of bad news. Although she worked to hide it, she lived in a state of irritation over small things that didn't used to annoy her. When she lay down to sleep, her mind would not quiet. It fought to stay aware, on guard. She carried through her work at the hospital bone-weary and at times a little muddle-headed, her need for genuine rest and restoration acute. But she soldiered on—chin up and brave, calm and reliable—the performance exacting a cost she did not acknowledge. Now was hardly the time for such considerations.

Carrying on day after day—maintaining one's sanity, really—required a case of intermittent amnesia. One did well not to formulate a list of the accumulating losses because the list was too long, too devastating. Like other Londoners, Beryl had learned to simply step around the piles of debris en route to Grove Park, forbidding her mind from dwelling on what this pile of rock and brick had been hours before when it sheltered living, breathing human beings. She tried not to tally the number of the hospital colleagues, neighbors, friends of hers and Gordon's who had been so dreadfully unlucky in the barrage. Because luck was all it was, really. There was no outsmarting the bombs that fell. The people who'd been lost, Beryl chose to remember discretely as singular accidents detached from the overall death counts. Glenda, the lead nurse who had done the most to bring Beryl along and sharpen her clinical skills—the one who gave all the young nurses confidence they could handle the constant need, had only wished to get home to sleep off a long, demanding string of days on the ward.

"Be off with you, then!" Beryl had smiled. "All's well here. The day workers are arriving, so why not go while you can?" And with a cheerful wave, Glenda slipped out of work a few minutes early on the last morning of her life. Walking her usual path home, she was caught beneath a compromised wall that suddenly gave way, raining bricks on her, peppering her head and body, fatally compressing her spinal cord as she tried to crawl to safety. The nurses on the floor who had loved her like a sister received the news with tight nods and clenched jaws. There was no place for full-scale weeping and sorrow because acknowledging the depth of the loss, surrendering to the grief, would render them unable to take care of those who could still be saved.

Diagonally across from the Clarke's row house, a line of hodgepodge buildings stood, their architecture indicating that each had been constructed in disparate decades under wildly different budget considerations. There were several shops, with tidy family flats above, mostly wooden structures with stone footings. These shops comprised the neighborhood hub, along with the tavern one block over, their worn and familiar presence an extension of the homes that surrounded them, comforting especially to the lonesome many who had sent children to the country and husbands to war. At Densmore's market, Beryl secured what foodstuffs she could, trading ideas with other shoppers on how to best use the limited supply of canned goods and scrawny produce. Cecil Densmore and wife Kate owned the small enterprise, the challenge of providing for their three children impossibly complicated by the bombings and blockades that interrupted supply lines and forced even broader rationing. Whatever their own worries, the Densmores remained generous and practical: they somehow managed to keep an inventory of cigarettes tucked underneath the front counter (a password and secret handshake practically required for purchase) and could locate supplies of extra milk for babies whose mothers feared they were not growing properly. Kate would privately prevail on her customers to forgo a bit of this for a ration of that. The back end of the bargain might take months to complete, but the Densmore word was true. Just apprise Kate of your need—sugar, to bake a birthday cake, or extra tea for relatives coming in to the city—and she set to work, devising a strategy that could involve any number of trades to make the thing happen.

On Saturday mornings, Beryl moved with greater purpose as she made her way home from the hospital. She stopped home first to offer the cat a bit of milk before heading across the street to Densmore's—the cat usually coming too but trailing her at a distance. And there in the market, a group gathered—shoppers, neighbors, friends of friends—eager to share. Precious snippets from a soldier's postcard. An extra egg a hen had miraculously produced. Greens coaxed from the backyard garden. Cigarettes unearthed from a seldom-used bureau, a tad stale but still satisfying. Kate offered cups of tea while the Densmore children improvised war games with sticks for rifles and pine cones for hand grenades. The cat was the lone Nazi in this war tableau, eliciting shrieks from the children as he appeared suddenly from under the shelving or around a corner. On occasion, Beryl had brought small squares of chocolate to give the children, bounty mailed to her from an RAF officer she had treated at Grove Park—a survivor of Dunkirk. Afterwards, he had been sent to America for a particular type of flight training. He then spent a good portion of his paycheck expressing his gratitude to the hospital staff back home with gifts of chocolate, tea, and what became, in transit, very smelly cheeses. Bennie, the youngest Densmore child, had never tasted such a thing as chocolate. That first time, shyly accepting the proffered piece, the boy popped the morsel in his mouth and closed his eyes in bliss. He sank to the floor of the market, nappied bottom dropping between his chubby knees in utter surrender to this singular taste. From then on, the Densmores— children and adults—called Beryl "Chocolate Lady," recalling her generous gift and perhaps to encourage her to direct future such benevolences their way.

The woman who ran a hair salon next to the market made a point to pop in to Densmore's on Saturday mornings so she could catch up on how neighborhood men were faring in the war. A red-haired Scot, Jesse was the widow of a German bookkeeper, forced to leave Bavaria just as the war began in Poland when accusations surfaced that her veins carried Jewish blood. Her appearance seemed to belie that notion with her clear blue eyes and ivory skin, a furious rosacea occupying her cheeks. She and her late husband had no children and rather than return to live near family in Scotland— relatives who vehemently disapproved of her liaison with a German—she set up shop in London and worked quickly to assimilate in her new hometown. She had been pleased to leave Germany, she said, because the government had grown so radical, not at all the place she had settled with her dear husband twenty years earlier. His heart would have broken had he survived to witness Germany's subjugation of France. Somehow, the doors of Jesse's salon remained open, despite a tiny clientele. Women employed in the war industries had limited free time to indulge in an afternoon at a beauty shop. They'd sooner snip off their own fringe and tie their hair in a bandana. Jesse remained optimistic that after the war, her business would blossom. She only needed to hold on until then, although how she could accomplish that remained in question. Typically, Beryl stopped in after her overnight shift at the hospital—the first customer of the day—when she needed a shampoo or trim. Ensconced in the salon chair, she chatted mindlessly with Jesse, taking in the smell of the rosewater (her favorite) and lavender that permeated the place, a respite from the acrid air outside and the sharp antiseptic smell of the hospital. The experience was something akin to time travel; Beryl was 22 again, carefree and newly married to a brilliant architect with the world at their feet. In these rare few hours, her shoulders relaxed, her heart slowed, her scrunched forehead smoothed.

Adjacent to Jesse's salon stood a three-story office building. Ornate but artless wooden carvings hung over the main door, an attempt to lend age and stateliness to the structure and confer a sense of experience and wisdom to the insurance vendors who rotated through the premises. In times of war, insurance is a tricky business. And on the far end of this row of buildings was a lending library where Beryl and Colin had once spent happy, quiet hours first perusing the lovely picture books, then as Colin grew as a reader, favorite chapter books like *The Railway Children,* with its devious spies and glamorously wealthy Russians—and more recently, pouring over maps to track Hitler's moves across Europe.

And then came the morning when Beryl had rounded the corner as she returned from work to see pages and pages torn from the spines of these books; pages wafting and swirling in the air, dislodged from their once-secure and orderly shelves, their tales and truths now spinning and intermingled and confused atop the collapsed stone that was once the library. Jesse's salon stood untouched, as did the office building, windows dusty but astonishingly intact. Beryl's home across the lane was safe, as were the adjacent homes of her neighbors. But the Densmore's market was gone, sheared off and mown down, splintered wooden planks now burying what had once been a vital place to find courage in community. Out front, two of the Densmore children sat atop a wooden crate, dirty and dazed, the girl staring blankly. When the air raid siren had sounded hours before, their parents rushed to corral the children into their garden shelter. But Bennie, unreasonable and disoriented in the way of abjectly exhausted toddlers, wrenched his hand free of his father's and ran back inside and up the steps to retrieve his frayed favorite blanket. Cecil and Kate had charged after him in panic, unable to see him in the dark, the actions of all three perfectly timed to intersect with the arrival of a German bomb that obliterated them all. Their surviving children sat mutely, fingers interlaced, as a Home Guard volunteer knelt before them, gently inquiring about relatives who might be able to take them in.

Jesse emerged inconsolable from her shop, tears streaming, hands tying and untying the strings of her work apron, unsure whether to stay or go home, saying again and again that this one was too close, that she'd just thought that it would befall others—not her, not here.

"Jesse, love, it wasn't you. Really, it wasn't. The salon is standing. Your life is intact," reasoned Beryl, a flicker of impatience in her tone. She pointed toward the children. "It's those two who've lost everything. Their parents, their baby brother, and their home. You and I are right as rain, no thanks to the Germans. Remember that."

"Aye," Jesse nodded. "We are. We are. It's just that my whole life is in that shop and had I lost it..."

.   .   .

Beryl never saw the children again. They were taken off to relatives in Cornwall—safer for them anyway—another of the many losses that she worked hard not to tally. But losing this little family and the community that had coalesced around their Saturday conversations produced a silent heartache in Beryl about which she could not speak, fearing it would surely untether the frayed cords with which she held herself together. She still visited Jesse's, but their conversations were more sober now, especially since Jesse remained jittery and anxious for months after the bombing.

Glancing at her watch, Beryl resolved to stop by Jesse's after her shift to get her fringe snipped off and out of her eyes. She stubbed out her cigarette, tidied the files, closed out with the ward clerk, and departed for the salon.

. . .

Jesse Jordan had found the weekly gatherings at the market essential to interpreting what was happening—or the British understanding, anyway, of what was happening. She listened solemnly, nodding as the women and the few older men still in the neighborhood shared cherished lines of the letters they received that pointed to how their son or brother or husband was faring. Taken together, their dispatches comprised for Jesse a vibrant and full picture of the war—the raging, seesaw battles in North Africa, the vast expansion of the RAF, now training fliers at countless bases across England, Beryl's husband in a wretched camp for prisoners somewhere in Germany. And of course, they dissected the increasing privation—the limited food, the scarcity of dry goods—relaying the latest news from cousins or in-laws or friends elsewhere in Britain and comparing it to their own daily challenges. What Jesse would not give for new hair clippers with a better hinge. Hers left her hand aching with the maneuvering she had to do to make a straight and even cut. But factories in England needed every scrap of metal for ammunition, not scissors. Jesse faithfully sharpened her blades as best she could, knowing her small base of customers were generous in these times, forgiving minor irritations like imperfect haircuts that simply could not be helped.

One soldier son of the neighborhood, Jesse learned, worked with the RDF—something to do with radio waves that detected incoming planes—and more than once, his mum outlined in detail what the series of detection towers along the coast could accomplish. After the third or fourth explication, Jesse finally grasped that this invention could actually spot German planes headed across the Channel so Hurricanes and Spitfires could knock them down before they dropped their lethal payloads over land. News of this development was not something found in daily papers. Propaganda posters crossly asserted that "Careless talk cost lives," but the market conversations were hardly careless or ill-considered: they were weekly succor for families mad with worry over the present danger they and their soldier faced, a brief moment that allowed them to drop the public façade that all was well and puzzle through the facts they knew about the Allied effort. In this gentle company, they could shed a tear of sorrow or proudly share news of a promotion or medal earned. No danger, because it would not extend beyond their little circle.

And indeed, the talk ceased entirely after Densmore's was lost. The group did not reform elsewhere, in part because each had work to do to figure out how to fill this new hole, where they could now turn for the support that Densmore's had provided. They walked new paths home from work to take them past new shops, making for longer days peopled with less-familiar faces. But in truth, there was no effort made to find a new gathering place because doing so would only call to mind the many Saturdays they'd gathered, with the Densmore children scurrying through the aisles, the cat in their sites, Kate making hush-hush deals in service to her neediest customers, Cecil presiding proudly over all of it—his vital contribution to keeping wartime spirits lifted.

. . .

The bell on the door jingled as Beryl made her way inside the salon. Jesse stood at the front desk, rifling through her paper receipts, calculating, perhaps, how long she could afford to keep the shop doors open.

"Hello, love," Beryl called.

Jesse lifted her head, eyes meeting Beryl's but not seeing her. Then she recovered herself, masking her worry and greeting her customer.

"Beryl. Hello. Sorry. Just wrapped up in the ledger. Thoughts elsewhere. But I'm happy you're here. I miss seeing you. Judging by the look of ya, you're in genuine need! That fringe is astonishing. Looks like they've got a mind of their own!"

Beryl laughed. "They are the bane, Jesse, of my every waking hour. Flopping in my eyes and not minding the bobby pins. But I know you can solve what's become a rather serious condition."

"Aye, I can," responded Jesse, guiding Beryl to the back for her shampoo.

With a deep inhale, Beryl sat back in the washing chair, head tilted over the sink basin, taking in the languorous scent of the potions lined up on the shelf behind. If this war continued, Jesse would soon run out of these magical elixirs. Her well-provisioned shop would close. Surprising it had lasted this long.

"Any new word from your husband?" Jesse inquired as she combed out the wet strands.

"Yes, in fact, I've received another letter. He's well—as well as you'd expect."

"Two years now, right?"

"Longer, actually. You know, Jesse, I don't even count the days anymore. Don't find it helpful. We don't truly know if we've lived another day closer to defeat or a day closer to the way things used to be. My boy—all the way up in Elsworth. I thank God every night—I do—that he is safe there, away from this bloody bombing. But we can't get these years back, can we? None of us can, I suppose."

"And Lieutenant Clarke?" Jesse pressed. "What news did his letter offer?"

"Truly, not much, Jesse. The censors black out any hard information. He's received three postcards from me through the Red Cross, even though I write every week. He's aware of the damage in London."

"And how would he learn of that, do you think?"

Beryl paused. It was a question she'd considered again and again. Did the Nazis terrify their British captives with news of the destruction in England? Did they hint at it? She suspected the camps were more porous than the captors might have liked.

"I'm not sure what they hear officially from the camp officers, but when new POWs arrive in the camp, they bring news. In his letters to me, Gordon continues to talk about our garden and his hopes for me to spend long hours there in the evening—wants me in our Anderson shelter, is what he's saying. He raves over his occasional package from the Red Cross. He also talked about a work detail he's assigned to—architectural work of all things, constructing some sort of wooden arbor over the garden in a nearby house.

A simple project, really, too simple for his talents but it beats hard labor, I'd say. Isn't that rich? The Nazis beautifying their surroundings as they bomb humanity all to hell."

Jesse listened, nodding kindly, sympathetically, making notes in her head of all Beryl had shared.

CHAPTER NINE

Jews are being transported in conditions of appalling horror and brutality....
In Poland, ...the principal Nazi slaughterhouse, the ghettos established by the
German invaders are being systematically emptied of all Jews... None of those
taken away are ever heard of again. The able-bodied are slowly worked to
death in labor camps. The infirm are left to die of exposure and starvation or
are deliberately massacred in mass executions. The number of victims of these
bloody cruelties is reckoned in many hundreds of thousands of entirely
innocent men, women, and children.
–Joint Declaration by members of the United Nations
December 17, 1942

East Anglia, England, 1943

They had christened their B-17 "The Florida Gator" in homage to their
pilot and instead of the more common rendering of a pin-up girl, they'd
painted toothy jaws on the nose and a cartoon of a Nazi soldier, drawers
down around his knees, with this helpful subtitle: "Taking a Bite Out of
Hitler's Ass." And indeed, Hitler's ass was more visibly exposed now with
the Allies taking Tobruk from Rommel's Afrika Korps and the Red Army's
valiant stand at Stalingrad. But the Nazis now occupied the entirety of
France and ongoing intelligence pointed to mass evictions of those they
deemed undesirable from the Loire and southern France. Trains bearing
refugees continued to thunder across the Reich, newsman Edward R.
Murrow declaring over the BBC radio broadcast the fliers tuned into each
day that the purpose of these camps was not concentration, but
extermination.

In their early days at Kimbolton, Jack and the nine other men of the Gator had flown sorties only as far as France, to pound a steel center in Lille, the railroad marshaling yards farther north, and to stir the waters of the U-boat pens at Brest and Lorient. Across and back, a handful of hours in the air with the sparkling if frigid waters of the Channel below, convenient for bailing out if needed. But it was clear, now, they would soon trade those milk runs for higher-risk missions and higher-risk targets in Germany thanks to improved fighter aircraft that could better shield the bombers from German fire. Not shield, really, but at least these little friends, as they came to call them, afforded the lumbering Fortresses the time and space to drop their payloads over targets and gave them a fighting chance to return to base. The P-51 Mustangs—re-engineered with more capable Rolls Royce engines— and P-47 Thunderbolts could theoretically accompany the B-17s all the way to Berlin, hang out while the bombardier spotted the target in his bomb site and did the deed, then escort the crews home. And while advancements in the capability of the fighter escort aircraft degraded the German counteroffensive, it did not disable it. The cost to the Allies—in men and materiel—was still horribly, painfully high.

When Jack sat down to breakfast, he knew some of the men he broke bread with would not be present at dinner. Perhaps he would be the unlucky guy decapitated by anti-aircraft fire or, if fortune prevailed, fall to earth and find himself a POW. Beginning ten, eleven hours after a mission commenced, the crewmen who had prepped the planes—seeing to the engines and loading the bombs and ensuring the flight and electrical systems were running perfectly—made their way to the top of the control tower, searching the skies for returning B-17s, counting them as they came in. Every one that failed to return to its hardstand at Kimbolton meant ten men lost. Ten telegrams to wives or more often parents that explained with deep regret that their airman was killed or missing in action. The 379th Bombardment Group had lost a squadron and a half already—18 aircraft and 180 men who flew bravely into the fight against tyranny because their country needed them to. Farm boys and accountants, engineers and postmen, graduates of midwestern high schools and the Ivy League, who were asked to save the world and agreed to do it. Men whom Jack had come to know and respect during their months of training and men whose loss he tried not to think about too often lest he grow distracted and share their fate.

The Brits did what they could to help the fliers avoid despair, given the unrelenting, high-wire tension of their work. Scores of British girls in their teens and twenties staffed the Aero Club—a string of Nissen huts on the base where the men could blow off a little steam. Busses ran several nights a week collecting fliers from other bases looking to have a little fun with the guys at Kimbolton. There were card games—bridge but more often, poker—a piano to pound, libraries of books and magazines, and a favorite option, listening to the radio, both the BBC and the German propaganda they could pick up from a signal out of Luxembourg. But what most of the American soldiers wanted to do was dance because that meant they could get their hands on willing young women eager to do almost anything to support Americans who were crucial to winning the war. Often there were lively bands doing their best renditions of "Moonlight Serenade" and "I'll be Seeing You;" other times, the tinny phonograph offered recorded versions, the little speaker unable to replicate the bass as it sounded live, so deep that it vibrated through the very bones of the dancers, feeding their yearning and sense of dark romance. And while some of these liaisons became instantly sexual, producing a useful and distracting counterpoint passion to the high drama of the skies, others did not. Often, these girls and boys—close in age and both suffering the same piercing wartime disruption—simply became friends. He told her all about the girl back home; she told him about her soldier in Tunisia or somewhere in the Pacific or worse, interned by the Axis. Many of the girls invited the airmen and their crews to their homes for a meal and to meet parents and grandparents, little brothers and sisters, the family pet. A meal circumscribed by rationing, but rich in the soul-sustaining nourishment that unfolds when keeping company with kind people in a warm home, comfortably seated on an ancient sofa with doilies draped just so across the padded arms, the smell of tea laced with cinnamon wafting in the air.

For Jack, it was his meals with Ivy and the constellation of children that comprised her household that relieved the tension, that restored him and allowed him to close his eyes and sleep at night. He and his co-pilot Buck Myers had a standing invitation to dine with the Hughes on Saturdays and when they weren't flying or in pre- or post-mission briefings, they headed over to Boxworth Road. The men repaid Ivy in military-issue cigarettes and chocolate, along with tea bags and sugar packets lifted from the Aero Club. Buck was a Chicagoan, a graduate of Northwestern who took a degree in journalism and worked at the Tribune before Pearl Harbor. His fastidious fact-gathering contributed to his success in the cockpit and, more widely, the success of each mission he flew. There was not a detail that escaped his notice, from the readings on his gauges to how the aircraft responded to changing demands and variables, to the evolving defense strategies of the Germans. The mission debriefs were always longer when Myers was involved, but Jack, and indeed every man in the group, appreciated his precision. Luck, they knew, favors the well-prepared.

Given the hundreds of questions Hugo and Colin posed to the fliers at these dinners, Jack joked the boys could probably fly a B-17 themselves at this point. Colin worked to understand the physics of flight—of lift and drag and pressure while Hugo was all numbers: how many squadrons in a group? How many groups in a wing?—his brain quickly extrapolating how many aircraft the United States Army Air Forces, Eighth Air Force Command must be massing on their missions across the Channel—and how many thousands might be spread across the English countryside. With their fathers gone, Jack slipped into their lives as a surrogate, called upon to answer questions of military strategy, wartime economies, along with the basics of geometry and what made girls the way they were. One evening, with Ivy overseeing the twins' bath in advance of church the next day, the conversation turned to when Jack and Buck thought the boys' fathers might return. Jack replied that Colin's dad would be freed from his POW camp at the war's end when the Allies won.

"But when do ya think that'll be, Jack? This year? Another year?" Fourteen now, his lengthening frame and deepening voice presaged that adulthood was not so long away. Colin made his inquiry as if returning his father to England were somehow within Jack's power to effect. Looking into eyes shrouded with concern, Jack wished he could lie to make this boy happy for just this moment, to assure him the war's near finished—that soon, soon, his father would be restored to the family. But no. He owed him better than that.

"The good guys have got to get a foothold in Europe, son," Jack began. "The bombing we're doing is for sure demoralizing the Nazis and slowing 'em down—but we're a long way from them quitting. So, the generals are figuring out the best way to get troops into France and then on into Germany. And that's gonna take a while. Maybe a few more years."

Colin nodded, calculating. How old would he be when his father returned? Sixteen? Eighteen? Would he attend university someday, or would England need him to follow his dad into the British Army? The first of the evacuees with whom Colin had arrived in 1939 were now approaching their eighteenth birthdays. Wilbert, the red-headed boy who'd arrived on his very train, had received a letter from his mother that the conscription board was already looking for his registration papers.

"But you're certain we can smash the Germans?" inquired Hugo. "I mean, if we didn't win—I believe we will, for certain, but say we didn't. Would they let Colin's dad go if they won? Or can they keep them because they came out on top?"

"Prisoners of war are repatriated when the conflict ends. Both by the losers and the winners."

The boys considered this, then Hugo heaved a sigh and looked Jack square in the eye. "And what about my dad?" he asked. "What do you think his chances are?"

Buck and Jack exchanged a long glance. Responding to Hugo's question proved much tougher duty. In the unsteadying years since Hugo's father was declared missing in action, Colin's presence had helped give Hugo something solid to lean on when his worry over his father got the best of him. Hugo aspired to be like the slightly older boy, mature and grounded, and was past the sudden crying rants—tantrums, really—that had characterized the previous year.

"Hugo," Jack began, believing there was little chance that now, after three years, his father still lived. "We'll just have to wait and see. I'm not losing hope. Don't you either, okay? We don't know nothin' about nothin' 'til we know somethin', right?"

And despite his fear, the hollow feeling in his gut that stayed with him most of the time, Hugo smiled and slowly shook his head. "How is it you Yanks never, EVER learned how to speak properly?"

"Hey, buddy," laughed Jack, "when we win this thing, and we ship out for home, you're gonna miss hearing us talk. Know what I mean?"

Hugo did. He knew Jack spoke the truth.

The door knocker sounded, and Colin leapt to his feet. His mum. She was to have joined them for dinner and finally meet Jack and Buck, but had not arrived in time. This happened frequently, passenger train schedules subjugated to the army's claim on the rails.

Colin opened the door and there she stood, slightly disheveled from a long day of waiting and postponed plans, but beaming at the sight of her beloved boy, healthy and safe.

"Mum! What was it? A broken-down train?" he asked, reaching his arms to hug her, both of them noticing that he had crossed a threshold: he was taller than she and had lost the last traces of the round, boyish face with which he had departed London three years ago. He pulled her head into his shoulder, the grownup, proprietary gesture surprising them both.

"My sweet one," she said, her face a mixture of pride tinged with sorrow. "You have eclipsed me! I'm now a squat old lady with you growing this tall in just a few months. You're a man. You don't even need your old mother."

Colin laughed with genuine delight. "Yes, mother, you are so bloody old. Ancient! Time to move you into a home for the aged, where they can feed you your meals all mushed up. Let's hope your pension covers it."

"Actually, there are days I would be more than happy to eat mush if I had someone to prepare it for me," she replied.

"Looks to me like you haven't been eating all that much," he said, stepping back and apprising her. "That skirt is practically dropping off you."

"Never you mind. It's just the work, Colin. Terribly busy. But I'm fine and have plenty to eat and I do not wish you to give it another thought because I want to hear all about everything here."

Hugo and the men stood quietly in the sitting room and watched, warmed by Colin's obvious joy and not wishing to intrude on it. These two were so obviously related, appearing more like siblings than mother and son. Their green eyes shone, hers more tired and drawn than her son's, but happy still.

"Mrs. Clarke!" Hugo called finally, stepping up and extending his hand before she pulled him into an embrace.

"My other son," she smiled. "You've gotten taller too! Taking good care of each other, I see."

"We are, ma'am. And here are our Americans—the ones we've told you about."

She turned to greet Jack and Buck, surprised when her heart caught at the sight of them. These were the young men whose exploits Colin detailed in his letters to her, their bravery and kindness and patience. They appeared so much like the hundreds of airmen who had practically taken over London since the Americans had joined the war. But this pair was standing in for two missing fathers, providing a sense of normalcy, sturdiness, to the boys' interrupted lives. Not to mention a bit of excitement.

"Our Americans!" Beryl echoed, surprised by the tremble in her voice. "I am honored to meet you both, Officers, and so grateful to you for all you've done for Hugo and Colin—and for me."

Jack spoke first. "You've got it backwards, ma'am. It's the boys who have kept us on our toes since we've been here. They remind us what we're fighting for. You've got a pretty smart kid there."

Buck agreed, extending his hand and joking that he stayed up nights studying his flight manuals to stay ahead of the boys' questions.

"And who might this be, coming to my cottage at all hours?" Ivy called as she descended the steps, Margaret and Patsy skirting around her.

"Mrs. Clarke!" squealed Margaret. "What have you brought us?"

"Margaret!" Ivy intervened. "We've discussed this. You do not go asking adults for gifts like that. It is entirely improper, even when you know the adult quite well. Remember? Try again."

"Hello, Mrs. Clarke," Margaret began in a monotone. "So lovely to see you."

"I hope you had a safe journey," continued Patsy.

"I did, girls. Thank you both awfully for asking."

"Dear Beryl. Hello. Delays again?"

"Ivy, I do apologize for being so tardy." She smiled and reached to hug Colin's foster mum. "The train left Kings Cross, moved a few miles, then just sat on the sidings. I considered just turning around and heading home since I've missed the meal and all."

"Indeed. That would be hospitable. We shall dispatch you back to London with an empty stomach and hope for the best. Sorry. You're out of luck." She winked at the boys. "Come, let's warm a bite or two for Colin's mum."

In fact, Beryl had brought a gift for the twins: *The Quest of the Missing Map*, the newest Nancy Drew mystery which they received with enthusiastic appreciation before charging up the stairs where they could read aloud to one another, chapter by chapter. The men joined Beryl at the table as she ate her meal, pouring her a bit of the Kentucky bourbon they'd brought from the base exchange, chuckling as her eyes grew wide and surprised at the first sinus-clearing taste. Halfway through her soup, she asked if Jack would pour a wee bit more. Then a spot more after that. With his mother seated next to him on the long bench, Colin appeared content, settled, watching his mother tell her stories as if he were committing each nuance to memory for later, when he needed to summon a bit of her. As she finished her meal, Beryl relaxed against her boy and he reached his arm around her, snugging her in to his side.

They talked of the radical changes that had seized the world, British and American women working long hours in factories and businesses because there weren't enough men to hire. Buck volunteered that his grandmother in Chicago watched a collection of toddlers every weekday while their mothers worked and found she rather liked helping the war effort in her own particular way. They discussed the pinch of rationing and how the tight supplies of food in the shops freed up cash the Brits could contribute to the War Savings Campaign while the Americans purchased war bonds to fund the fighting. They talked of London, Beryl describing how the stone walls and tower of Christ Church Greyfriars stood, the roof collapsed into the nave—brought down more than two years ago on a particularly vicious night of the Blitz. Now, in 1943, Londoners had chosen not to lament the loss, but to see it as a magnificent symbol of their own steadfastness in the fight.

"It's Gordon, you know, who's made me this way—makes me see all this," Beryl said. "I take scores of mental notes about what he might observe with all this glorious architecture taking this beating—like the Wren churches—and I imagine the meaning he would ascribe to it."

"And dad will appreciate it when he returns," said Colin. "He'll have a lot to catch up on."

"Let's hope for all our sakes," added Ivy, "that these two Yanks here and all their brethren make that happen soon."

Jack leaned slowly across the table, one hand clasping Ivy's, the other reaching for Hugo's.

"We're on it," he promised. "Number one goal. For all of you."

"I'd say the Florida Gator's doing her part," said Buck. "Our sturdy little girl has got a bite. The Luftwaffe's only chipped off a little of her paint at this point—nothing serious—and probably because they took issue with our little message to Hitler. Those Nazis are so thin-skinned." At this they all laughed, Beryl feebly attempting to convince them she didn't entirely approve of their crass cartoon, but no one bought her motherly indignation.

The fliers detailed for Beryl how the war had come calling for them, pulling them out of comfortable lives they believed were headed in a safe and predictable direction. But Pearl Harbor put a quick end to the idea the United States could sit out this war and since then, every ounce of American energy had turned to equipping the arsenal of democracy.

"You weren't already trained as a pilot?" Beryl asked.

"Hardly, Mrs. Clarke," interjected Hugo, a grin on his face. "He was an ale-swilling university boy. Probably good for nothing."

"Hugo—that was our secret, man. And here I thought I'd be able to fool everyone into thinking I know what I'm doing flying the Gator. Yes, I'll confess that is probably an accurate description of my previous focus in life, although I gotta say that feels like a million years ago. I earned my degree in mechanical engineering, Mrs. Clarke. The University of Florida, class of '41."

The men offered broad accounts of their missions to date—describing the unearthly feeling of piloting their B-17 into the air, watching as one bomber after the next climbed into the sky to the initial rendezvous point. How they waited, circling over the glistening waters of the Channel as hundreds of bombers arrived from bases across East Anglia, the mass of them then forming up in staggered rows to minimize the prop wash—the wake turbulence—thankful every time they were not consigned to Purple Heart Corner, the plane in the lowest right-hand corner of the formation and therefore the most vulnerable. They described the concussive jolt of the German anti-aircraft fire that began as they crossed over France and how it built into a continuous, truculent fervor over Germany itself. Colin added the details he'd learned and found fascinating: that each man on the crew had an electric warming suit he plugged in when the bomber reached 17,000 feet altitude to keep ice off their oxygen masks and prevent frostbite. That the Florida Gator had dozens of pock marks from flak—some the size of soccer balls—and she still flew steady and true. That the Americans were making progress, he believed, destroying targets that would fatally compromise the Nazis' ability to wage war.

"Exactly that, Colin. Just so," said his mother, proud of this perceptiveness but still missing, a bit, the little boy he'd once been.

The hour grew late. As Buck and Jack cleared the dishes and Ivy and Hugo busied themselves with washing and drying, Colin whispered what had become a frequent pitch: that he pack his things and head back to London with his mother.

"I would not have a moment's peace if I were to do that, Colin. Your dad is trusting me to keep you safe."

"I miss you, mum. Mrs. Hughes is the absolute tops—she really is. And Hugo—we will be friends for life. I don't want to sound ungrateful. But I worry about you a bit. And I miss us being a family."

"Let me say this again, love." Beryl looked him steadily in the eye, her hands in his. "You've no need to worry about me. I'm well. We're both exactly where we ought to be. We're still a family, my sweet, wherever we are. And here we have an extended family. Not at all what we planned, is it? But it's a gift to us both. Let's remind one another of that when we get blue, alright?"

Hearing just a bit of what Beryl had been saying, Ivy sidled up and reached an arm around her.

"Any word of Wills?" asked Beryl quietly so Hugo would not hear. Ivy gave an almost imperceptible shake of her head, then leaned into Beryl's embrace. "I'm still praying, you know," Beryl said. "Every day."

"I'm counting on it," Ivy whispered.

The kitchen tidied, Ivy suggested Beryl stay overnight rather than attempt to get a seat on the midnight coach. She could squeeze onto the loveseat in the sitting room and leave after church in the morning. Beryl had stayed over on more than one occasion and as appealing as that sounded, Jack had another suggestion: he could requisition the jeep or perhaps even a staff car and return her to London tonight, provided his CO approved. Beryl attempted to demure, protesting this was way too much to ask, too much of an inconvenience, but she was ultimately unsuccessful.

"You didn't directly decline, Mrs. Clarke, so I'll take that as an affirmative," Jack smiled. "Let's swing by the base and get the ok and we'll head south."

"Well. Yes. Certainly. I would appreciate it so, Lieutenant. The only time—I promise—it's just that the train may take half the night and if it truly would not interfere with your responsibilities. I would be grateful. So grateful."

"One, condition, ma'am. You call me Jack."

"Right. Yes, Jack. And I'm Beryl."

And with another round of hugs and handshakes all around, they were off.

. . .

They dropped Buck at the base and, after obtaining permission, Jack swapped the jeep for a staff car that would afford more comfort across the sixty miles to London. Beryl curled into her seat, relaxed and warmed by the bourbon, repeatedly expressing her thanks, to which Jack replied that he now understood just where Colin's fine manners had been cultivated. He listened as she talked about her work at Grove Park, the heart-rending cases she handled one after the next, then blocked out so she could attend to the next patient in front of her.

"Sounds wearing," said her driver.

"Tis," she responded.

They mused over the expected acceleration of the war now that the U.S. Army Air Forces were better trained, better equipped, and more strategically astute about what needed to be done, Beryl impressing Jack with her wide knowledge of aircraft and their capabilities, the geographical considerations, and her own analysis of when she believed the Allies might invade Fortress Europe.

"And here, I thought you were a nurse—not a military tactician," observed Jack, struck by both her reasoned insight and the easy, relaxed way she expressed herself.

"We're all living this stuff, Jack, every detail, because we want so much to see signs of progress. And on top of that, I've got to study long and hard to stay ahead of my son with all he knows."

They talked of Gordon—what she knew of his situation at this point and how Colin seemed to be handling it. She praised Ivy, her surprising strength and her loving generosity towards Colin, but even so, Beryl missed him desperately and knew that her influence as his mother had been diluted, interrupted, readjusted in ways out of her control. Necessary, yes. She knew that. But it grieved her. Much to Jack's surprise, the tears came.

"My apologies, Lieutenant. Jack. You didn't know this long trip could get even worse, I'm sure, with me feeling sorry for myself like this." Beryl pulled a handkerchief from her sleeve. "It's just been a long day. And I'm not used to topping it off with drink."

"I can't imagine how rough this is for you. With your husband locked up—and being apart from your boy. I have to tell you; I miss Colin on the days I don't see him. He and Hugo brighten every single one of these foggy, freezing cold, pea soup days. And Colin is so curious and bright—very good at math, you know. He stays right with me through very complicated expositions on the physics of flight. He's interested in every bit of it. Just remind yourself: you've been the best kind of mother because you've been selfless and committed to keeping him safe and out of danger until this thing is wrapped up. And it will be wrapped up. Not right away, but eventually. And then you'll get your family back."

His kindness did not have its desired effect, eliciting instead a fresh a torrent of tears. Beryl attempted a smile as they fell and readied herself to respond.

"You are as dear as Colin says you are. He's told me so much about you and the crew through his letters. Your base and your plane and these long chats you have with him at Ivy's and at Kimbolton. I am so, so very grateful to you." She blew her nose, then shook her head, trying to clear it. "Do you know, Jack, this is most I've allowed myself to dwell on this in four years— the most I've said to another human being about how dreadfully difficult life has been? One of the very few times I've allowed myself to just feel the pain of it, the despair, because I bloody well have to keep it out of my head or I'll be useless at the hospital and likely kill a patient in the process. I'd be of no use if I didn't push this from my mind every single, god-awful day and simply go to work, do my job, come home, feed the cat. Chin up and all that. I cannot count the number of my friends killed in the Blitz. I'm not saying people I heard of or people I was acquainted with. Friends—dear friends who were a regular part of my life and deserved to live. Deserved it probably more than I. If I actually counted how many are gone now, I would lose heart. And I can't do that, can I? We can't. We mustn't. Gordon and Colin do not deserve for me to grow faint-hearted. But inside... sometimes, it wrecks me."

He reached over and took her hand and she didn't resist, removing it briefly to shift gears, then reaching for hers again. She laid their clasped hands in her lap, then brought his to her face, pressing it into the tears that flowed for Glenda who had trained her, for Bennie Densmore and his sweet family. For the innocent children they could not save at Grove Park, punished for the sins of power-mad adults. Then it poured out, all the competing emotions she'd kept to herself over these many months, the oppressive loneliness, if soldiering on, playing pretend and ignoring the loss and the horror, was the best way to endure it. If enduring was enough. Or if living in this shuttered way would close off essential parts of her that would remain inaccessible for the rest of her days, whether those days included her family reunited or more heartbreaking loss.

When they arrived at her flat, she began to apologize for falling apart, attributing it to how familiar he seemed to her, their connection to Colin, his Yankee informality that seemed to invite her to let down her guard. And of course, the bourbon.

"All your fault," she said. "Ply the lady with liquor and look what you get."

He offered her a cigarette, then lit one himself, drawing on it slowly, thoughtfully, reaching again for her hand. "I've learned you have to release the floodgates sometimes, Beryl," he said, exhaling and looking out the window of the staff car at the quiet, dark city. "Gotta relieve the pressure and just feel, you know? Feel it as much as it hurts to do it. Doesn't make you weak or less courageous. You let it out and then you have room to handle more. You've had way more than your share too, with all you go through at the hospital every day. That'd be enough to keep me hidin' in a closet. So please don't be so hard on yourself. No one expects you to be perfect."

He turned to her, suddenly aware of how close they sat, the feel of her hand in his, the wisps of her breath. He believed he'd never seen a more beautiful, sorrowful, honest face. A face that didn't deserve the grief it bore, that she worked relentlessly to hide to preserve a veneer of normalcy for her son. And, because Jack didn't know what else to do, had no other tricks in his bag to soothe this woman whose tender courage had impressed him so, he leaned over and kissed her, her tear-drenched and eager response surprising him utterly.

CHAPTER TEN

Illusion is the first of all pleasures.
–Voltaire

Sagan, German Reich, 1943

There was some urgency to complete the arbor before winter set in and the ground froze. But securing the concrete in which to set the series of balusters that were now part of Gordon's design proved an obstacle: they would have to wait until they could get some leftover supply shipped in from one of the Nazis' many construction projects ongoing throughout Poland. Reinhard said there were massive endeavors underway across the Reich commanding large stores of cement, brick, and wood. It frustrated Annalise entirely that the vaunted Reich was not well enough organized to send the very limited and minor items she needed. When Reinhard finally had some say, after the war, his competent leadership could surely improve government efficiency. What she could not confirm but nevertheless suspected was that her straight-arrow husband failed to leverage the under-the-table network that could have secured the supplies in a week's time.

In the interim, Gordon drew up working plans and introduced some detail to the structure. He drafted and revised, requested more drawing paper and pencils, and revised some more, acting the part of the exacting artist driven by his talent to be thorough and careful. Gordon added elaborate corbels, proposed a more delicately carved lintel, always soliciting the Frau's impressions and thoughts, taking her input and promising to incorporate it into the next revision. He recommended they use cedar for not one, but three columns on either side—drawing an objection from Frau

Schröder who worried the red hue would clash with the red brick *Terrasse*. Gordon promised that with time, the columns would weather and lose the orange overtones in favor of a rich ochre. Alternatively, they could paint or stain the pillars which provoked many long discussions of paint and stain shades and how they wore over time. Their debates over this and every best choice to be made for the project moved easily from German to English and back. When they had trouble conveying nuance and specificity, each would try another language to make a point. Sometimes French worked.

On his workdays at the manor house, the cook, Clara, brought him a thick soup or stew and warm buttered bread at midday. He would break from his work and sit on the terrace, savoring the peppery flavor of the chicken or beef broth, the sweet scent of the butter—so pungent after years of unflavored potatoes and watery soups. He smuggled anything he could back to the barracks, Annalise observing this without comment from the earliest days. As time went on, the assortment of fruits and breads at breakfast doubled in size, a small burlap sack appearing on the table that soon became Gordon's tote bag. Clara began bringing four, five thick slices of bread with his midday meal.

"Is the lady of the house aware of this abundance you're sharing with me?" Gordon asked her the first time she appeared with an entire warm, crusty loaf.

"She is aware of most things," Clara responded enigmatically, looking around furtively to ensure Friedrich was not nearby. "What news do you have of the war?"

"Same as you, I would imagine," Gordon responded guardedly.

"This, I doubt. We only hear what the Germans wish us to hear."

"And you think there is another side to the story?"

"My dear Lieutenant, I know there is. We know there is, even though the only radio reports we are permitted to hear are those here in this house, the German propaganda."

"And yet you work for the commandant and his wife."

"Helene—she is the housekeeper—and I worked for many years in this home for Dr. and Mrs. Stroński. He delivered our babies, restored our children after infections and accidents. We worked for them even after the

Nazis invaded because they were good and fair people who treated us with respect. They begged us to leave their employ for our own safety, so we made it appear that we no longer worked here. I moved out and took my things to my sister's home, and we returned sporadically to cook and keep the house. The day the doctor and his wife were taken from this house—a terrifying scene I shall never forget—they lied to the Gestapo taking them into custody, screaming that Helene and I stopped working for them long ago. Mrs. Stroński said we,"—here her voice grew pinched and her face strained—"we spat on them when we quit because they were Jews. They accused us of arriving on the premises that day only to ensure the house would be properly cared for until the new German occupants arrived. They yelled that we were vipers, snakes. But that is not what they believed. None of this was true."

"Do you know what happened to them?" Gordon asked.

"Sobibór," she said. "Because of their false testimony, we were protected, assigned to stay and run this house, the Germans believing that here were two Poles who held proper loyalties. We have been paid fairly well and live under less scrutiny than some of our neighbors because of what the Strońskis led the Germans to believe." She paused and her eyes swept over the terrace, the garden, the guest house, the large main house. "I feel guilty for this every day, that my burden in this war is not heavier."

"And is there something you wish from me?"

"The truth," she said simply, looking around again, then pulling from her deep apron pocket portions of a radio transistor. "Dr. Stroński left this for us, but it is far too dangerous for us to use. We would be killed if they found it. So please, take it. Use what you can of it. There are more pieces, but this is all I can give you now."

Gordon's heart thumped as he scrambled to hide the components, first under his shirt, then in the burlap bag meant to transport his leftovers. Clara hurried off, hoping her presence had not been missed in the kitchen. Her actions placed her at substantial risk and that inclined Gordon to trust her, at least for now.

When the driver questioned what Gordon was carrying as he left the house that afternoon, Annalise had sharply replied that the sack carried drawings she wished the prisoner to study before he returned the next time—a statement clearly false, given the lumps plainly visible in the sack and the lingering aroma from the bread it exuded.

"Further, there is no need for you to concern yourself over things I, myself, am overseeing. Friedrich is also here, as you know, and my husband would not appreciate your overstepping. Verstehen Sie?"

The driver nodded, pulling himself up straight, clicking his boot heels together. He had no choice at this point but to believe her—the commandant's wife—and be quiet. He could decide later whether to pursue the truth some other way.

Gordon observed Frau Schröder to be more forthright out of her husband's presence. She knew her mind, challenging Gordon to arrive at design solutions that satisfied her down to the smallest details—no different from his clients back in London. Occasionally, she would suggest something outlandish—"I'd like a stone pediment seven meters wide at the top wherein you can carve figures representing the leaders of the Reich"—laughing coyly at Gordon's confused reaction before he caught her joke. She joked often, her posture relaxed unless Friedrich or the staff were about. On the odd mornings when the commandant was slow to depart for the camp or when he worked at home, she seemed a different person. She became more puerile, magnifying trivial things. She followed her husband out to the staff car, pressing him on which would more perfectly complement the *Zwiebelkuchen* they would share that evening—a sweet white wine or dry— like it was an issue of great consequence, nodding with rapt attention to his wise response. Even her voice changed, its pitch slightly higher, the inflection more child-like, an apparent stratagem to ensure the commandant believed himself firmly in charge of her.

The driver took Friedrich and Gordon to the house two or three times a week, depending on the Frau's schedule and whether there were any pressing issues to decide about the project. Concurrently, Clara continued to funnel vital resources his way, streamlining the procedure by baking wire and other small pieces of the radio inside the bread, hoping they survived the oven heat.

Gordon wondered at what point his foot-dragging on the arbor work would become too obvious for the Frau to ignore. But for this, she was partly to blame, sitting down at her piano, the doors to the *Terrasse* open to Gordon as he sat sketching at the table—playing waltzes and scherzos and nocturnes that she knew arrested his attention entirely. She told him she had studied briefly at the Conservatoire de Paris before her marriage but was not among the most gifted students and, at eighteen, could not summon the drive to become one. She was home on holiday in Berlin when she met her husband. The proposal of marriage from an officer whose fortunes appeared on the rise provided a timely exit from school that mollified her parents. The children had arrived quickly thereafter and as she had occupied herself with their raising, Reinhard charted his course in the emerging Reich, learning, unfortunately, that his blunt and straightforward analyses of the geopolitical landscape were not always welcome.

When the staff car returned to camp late or amid a hard rain, the duty guard would simply wave it through, failing to ask for the return of the gate pass, unwittingly providing additional canvasses on which the camp's captive forgers could practice their craft. The men in Gordon's barracks, especially those attached to real work details, teased him about babysitting a Nazi while they were exhausting themselves harvesting potatoes, tilling fields, shoveling trucks out of the mud. Several lamented not having chosen to attend architecture school themselves. Gordon's commanding officer warned him to keep his eyes open and not assume he was safe outside the camp. The Gestapo shot first and asked questions later, most certainly if they came upon an apparent escaped POW in a private home. The SS wasn't much better, often spicing up sudden executions with a bit of torture beforehand. Lieutenant Colonel Leonard had made these concerns known to the commandant who had assured him the armed guard posted at the house would intervene and handle any questions regarding Gordon, should those separate agencies come across the unusual arrangement. While Leonard was pleased with this unexpected source of radio components, he urged Gordon to remain cautious with Clara because, if discovered, the Germans could pressure her in ways both irresistible and lethal.

The weather turned for good by late October and Gordon's lunch breaks became less pleasant, but still far superior to any day spent wholly in the camp. With the colder weather, Friedrich had taken to staying in the kitchen with Clara and Helene. Gordon found them to be talented actresses, attentive to Friedrich's needs, responsive to his jokes in ways that relaxed him and lowered his guard. He kept the Lugar holstered nearly all the time now, except when visitors came to the house and he wished to convey his tireless vigilance guarding the POW. Then, he would stand off from the terrace, pacing with the gun in his hand. At intervals he would stop, plant his feet wide, extend his arms and point the gun at Gordon as he worked. Once the premises were clear of visitors, Friedrich would return to the kitchen and resume his visits with the staff, sipping coffee, enjoying a smoke. For Friedrich, wartime service had much to recommend it.

As sleet fell one November afternoon, Gordon sat hunched under the canopy of linden trees, breaking off pieces of bread from a loaf he had tucked into the neck of his uniform shirt—a feeble attempt to keep it dry. The loaf felt too light to contain any contraband: he would take the bulk of it back to camp this afternoon. While the POWs exchanged most commodities through a complex bartering system, Lieutenant Colonel Leonard had adjudged that Gordon's contributions of food—because of their provenance—would be reserved for men in the worst shape, those fighting off infections for whom some additional calories and nutrients could be life-saving. As he felt the icy splinters hit his face and slide down his neck, his hands turning red from the cold, it seemed impossible to imagine that there were people right now, in this moment, in some parts of the world who lived under no threat, with loved ones in warm homes, enjoying laughter and cups of hot tea. He wondered if they even recognized and appreciated their good fortune. Pray God, Colin and Beryl were among them. While Colin was not in the company of own family, his father hoped he was well-fed and safe, with people who loved him and cared for him in Gordon's stead.

"Lieutenant!" Frau Schröder called from the *Terrasse*, scarf on her head, umbrella raised. "Lieutenant, please come here! Bring your things."

Gordon quickly made his way to the French doors at the back of the house.

"This weather is unbearable. I have told Clara to make a place for you in the kitchen." She pointed toward the back door that led to the kitchen. "But first," she paused, looking apologetic. "I can no longer tolerate your smell. You reek of sweat and...frankly ... excrement."

And whose fault is that? Gordon wanted to ask. The entire camp smelled this way and would only worsen with the frozen rain now falling. He was a bit surprised her husband didn't smell this way.

"My apologies, Frau Schröder, but there is not much I can do to fix that. Thank you for the invitation, but I am happy to stay out here to finish my meal. It is delicious and again, I am truly grateful to you for everything. I will return to work in just a few minutes. My apologies for subjecting you to my... my unpleasant situation."

"I'm more than aware, Lieutenant, that you cannot fix it, but I can. Please use the bath in the guest house. I have called Reinhard and apprised him of my concerns, and he understands it is necessary for our continued work together. Clara will launder your uniform and return it to you when it's dry. In the meantime, you will find old garments of my husband's in the guest house that you may wear. Friedrich will show you where to go." And with that, she turned and entered the doors to the music room, leaving him shivering and astonished.

.   .   .

Gordon ran the water hot—the hottest he could get it. The bathroom filled luxuriantly with steam, bringing to mind the soupy mists of his home, of London and life with Beryl, which seemed ever more remote, a fantasy world to which he longed to return. He closed his eyes and saw the old claw-footed bathtub in their flat, roomy enough for the three of them, baby Colin slippery as a seal, chest to chest with Gordon, Beryl soaping them both with slow, massaging circles, the water fragranced with drops of lavender oil.

And what to make of this intimate gift Annalise had proffered? Kindness only? Or did he truly smell so foul she could no longer tolerate it? With no way to know, he resolved that his safest course was to continue observing the defined formality of their working relationship, to assume no deepening connection.

Gordon emptied and refilled the bathtub a second time so he could rinse with reasonably clean water. Skin warm and reddened by the hot water and abrasive soap, he climbed out of the tub, dried himself quickly, and dressed in the breeches and tunic he found on the dresser. The sensation of clean clothes on clean skin, no grainy dirt chafing at the bend of his knee or elbow, no silt dropping on his shoulders as he finger-combed his wet hair, made him feel civilized in a vaguely familiar way—the way of life before the war.

He crossed the yard from the guest house and made his way in the kitchen door where she waited at the servant's table, armed with her file of recent notes about the arbor. Clara and Helene were not present; Friedrich paced in the hallway that led from the kitchen to the front of the house. Annalise looked up and read Gordon's grin as he entered the room.

"Ah, then that was acceptable to you, I see," she smiled, happy. "You did not take my request as an insult. You look refreshed. A new man."

"I am, most certainly, Frau Schröder. Thank you."

"And this will inspire enormous design creativity," she needled.

"I can't promise that," said Gordon, "but at the very least, I won't disgust you."

"Oh, now, you do not disgust me. Not in the least." She ran her eyes over his frame. "Reinhard's old clothes look well on you. Very acceptable. They would not fit over his middle these days. It's... broadened just a bit over the years and at that, I'm being kind." She paused, as if waiting for him to agree with her.

"Friedrich," Annalise called. "Your ceaseless pacing annoys me. Is there not something better you can do with your time? Please join Clara and Helene in the dining room. I am fine here. We have work to do and I do not wish to be distracted."

"Jawol, mein Frau," he responded, turning on his heel.

"The commandant seems to be in top shape for a man his age," said Gordon, picking up the thread of their conversation, approaching the table. "Very vigorous and energetic, it seems to me."

"He commands your prison camp, not a front-line unit. He has a desk job, Lieutenant, anathema to a career army officer. He is not yet old, perhaps ten years older than you, and his superiors found him wanting."

"These things are hard to figure, ma'am," Gordon offered. "I would not pretend to understand how officers are evaluated for promotion in the Wehrmacht." He hoped asserting his lack of context would persuade her to move their conversation to safer territory. It did not.

"They are capricious, you must know, and they insist on loyalty. Devotion bordering on mindless subservience. That was Reinhard's obstacle, but between us, I can't say I would have preferred he act differently. He is his own man, which is a dangerous position in the current climate, so he keeps his views to himself. But thankfully, he is also a man confident enough in his powers to allow me a certain latitude. To have you here to beautify my home and even," here she stood and reached out to smooth the collar of his tunic, "to dress you up to look just like a German ready to enjoy an evening in Berlin's most raucous Biergarten. I only wish it were possible to do exactly that, but it seems that opportunity will not be afforded us."

Then she placed both hands on his chest and looked up at him, tilting her head, pursing her lips. "Yes," she repeated, "an entirely new man."

It was the first time she had touched him and the coy, playful expression on her face did little to mask a surge of heat within her. "Out of that dirty uniform, you hardly seem like the enemy."

. . .

Over the course of a few weeks, it became their habit that Gordon would bathe most mornings after he arrived, Friedrich stationed at the door, Reinhard essentially apologizing to Gordon for insisting that he abide this request, what he termed his wife's unreasonable petulance. Clara washed and hung his threadbare uniform in front of the kitchen fireplace to ensure it was clean and dry before he had to return to camp, slipping items in the pockets that she thought could be useful to the POWs like socks and string, pencils and pens, even a map of Sagan. Gordon and Frau Schröder now met at the servant's table in the kitchen to discuss the progress of the arbor—the wood inlays he considered incorporating which would take additional time—but more and more often, she turned their talks to other things. Of her parents in Berlin, where she wished she had stayed, and of her children in school in Geneva. More typically, she explained, officers with an eye toward advancement sent their children to Nazi schools, where they could be more completely immersed in the culture and mission of the Reich. Indoctrinated, he wanted to interject, but did not. Annalise had not wanted a political education only: she wanted her son and daughter to receive a classical education as she had, replete with music and foreign language instruction and access to the broader European culture. Finer things, she believed, that would matter again when the war concluded.

"Reinhard was not happy with my decision, but in marriage, one must give and take. And I have done most of the giving, as women do, as he has plotted his career and future. He is a decent man but not the—how shall I say this?—the romantic hero I once thought him to be when I was younger. I had expected his promotions would open the world to me but now I find myself alone here in this house in the middle of nowhere with all my friends back in Berlin enjoying their glittering lives. And you, Lieutenant? What of your life in England?"

And about this, he lied, spinning a story as he spoke, of an intense but failed love affair made all the more disappointing because he wished to father children and now, most likely would not.

"Children. They are wonderful, of course, but a demand. A mixed blessing. Don't misunderstand: I love my darlings totally and I miss them. But once children arrive in a marriage, their needs tend to come first and one's self comes second. My capacity to collaborate with you on this project, for example, would be far more limited were they here." She meant privacy, he knew. With children about, she could not linger over tea with an English prisoner, could not reach to brush off a stubborn speck of lint only she spotted on his tunic, or stand so close as he worked that he felt her breath.

At the end of their conversations, Gordon poised to leave, the staff car idling outside with the driver at the wheel, Annalise developed a habit of introducing a new topic or posing an urgent question about architecture or art or his creative process that she insisted he fully explain in this moment.

It happened so often that Friedrich knew not to intrude to hurry Gordon along, but to wait outside the door until Annalise dispatched Gordon from the kitchen. She would make her inquiry, invite Gordon to re-seat himself, then elbow on the table, chin in her hand, she would listen to him, looking for a split-second too long in his eyes as he spoke, so intimate and unblinking a gesture that Gordon felt his pulse quicken. He returned her penetrating gaze, silently beseeching her to understand fully what she was doing here, the danger inherent in what she proposed.

CHAPTER ELEVEN

There is a destiny that makes us brothers,
No one goes his way alone;
All that we send into the lives of others,
Comes back into our own.
–Edwin Markham

East Anglia, 1943-44

After four years together, Hugo and Colin were more brothers than friends. Rarely was one seen without the other, pedaling around Elsworth on their various missions and adventures. Hugo-and-Colin, people said, as if it were one word. When Ivy prevailed on one to bring in some wood for the fire, they both did it. When she needed something from the greengrocer, they both went, summoning the proprietor if they could not find the exact item Ivy requested. When the twins turned eight, the boys planned a series of lessons to teach them to ride the bicycles the vicar had brought, believing that simultaneous instruction might foster healthy competition. And indeed, Margaret's desire to assert (she was nine minutes older than Patsy, after all) dovetailed nicely with Patsy's wish to not, for once, be second, so both girls picked up the whole exercise rather quickly.

In one respect, however, the boys differed greatly from blood siblings; each knew the other's weaknesses and fears and chose not to exploit them. Hugo relied on Colin's intuitive understanding of mathematics and the physical sciences to help explain some of his trickier school lessons, noting to Ivy that Colin explained it more clearly than Mrs. Helms. Colin deferred to Hugo when it came to processes and organization of their non-school time—cricket first with the mates in the schoolyard, then a trip over to Kimbolton, but home in time for chores before dinner. "Gotta make sure he doesn't spend every minute of the day just thinking his great thoughts," Hugo explained when what he really meant was that Colin didn't get the blues as often when Hugo kept him on the move. Hugo was a little smaller and more compact, giving him an agility and athletic quickness that inspired admiration instead of jealousy in Colin. Having lost their fathers, they looked to one another for affirmation, each granting it capaciously. Having absorbed consequential losses already in their lives, they had learned, as most in Elsworth had as well, that pettiness and little envies wasted time and energy. It was one of the great gifts of the war.

The boys had arrived at a shared worldview, often shaping their ideas in those hazy minutes just before sleep. As they lay whispering in the dark, their brains let go of conventional lines of reason and became freer to untangle complexities in creative, unbounded ways. When the war ended, they resolved to take a flat in London together and perhaps attend university. After they made their fortunes (they outlined no timetable for this but assumed it would be immediate), they would return to Elsworth and open a bicycle shop that would also offer flying lessons once Colin had his aviator's license. They would purchase Kimbolton for their private airfield once the Americans no longer used it. "When it's over" was the recurring preamble to so many of their plans and it seemed, based on the broadcasts from the BBC and the latest reports in the newspaper, that finally, hopefully, things might be heading in that direction. The Germans had lost Stalingrad and Tunisia but were doing their utmost to hold on to Italy. The Allies were island-hopping across the Pacific, wrestling the determined Japanese for territory, inch by inch in costly, bloody battles that left the tropical sand black with blood. Jack's long-ago joke about the boys being spies notwithstanding, they were astonished to learn there actually were real Nazi spies in England—gobsmacked in Colin's words—one spy arrested in London as he attempted to jump a freighter to Algiers. But what Hugo and Colin found most electrifying were the rumors of resistance in Paris, brave people who operated under cover of darkness to disrupt and sabotage. Their secret, independent machinations meant that the War Office might not know everything about everything and everyone everywhere. In this, Hugo and Colin placed a measure of hope.

The next Sunday at Holy Trinity, the boys were stunned to see the successful outcome of one such undercover effort when Vicar Dowd's grandson—a flier in the RAF—returned from the dead. His grandmother at his side, he sat serenely in the second pew, in uniform and looking well, despite having been shot down six months earlier and declared missing by the War Office. On this particular Sunday, the vicar abandoned the Anglican lectionary and chose for his scripture the eleventh chapter of John, the story of how Lazarus was raised from the dead.

"Hear the word of the Lord to Martha as she discovers her beloved brother is restored to her," he intoned. "'Said I not unto thee, that, if thou wouldest believe, thou shouldest see the glory of God?' Good people, I cannot explain why Lazarus was returned to his family—was it his extraordinary faith or the faith of those who loved him? Nor can I fully understand why our own Oliver is back among us while others in this congregation whom we love have been irretrievably lost despite fervent prayer. It is a question for which we will not have an adequate answer until we see the Lord face to face." His eyes misted as he turned to look directly at his grandson. "It is enough for us now to rejoice that one of our beloved is returned to us. God desires us to continue to believe as the sisters believed and trust in God's providence to face what lies ahead. It is incumbent on us all to lift prayers in praise and thanksgiving for His magnificent gift, and ask that He might, in his benevolence, extend it to others whom we love and hold in prayer."

After the final hymn and the benediction, Flight Sergeant Oliver Dowd stood in the narthex with his grandparents to receive the handshakes and well wishes of the parishioners who had prayed to God for just such an outcome. But instead of asking to hear the story of the loss of his aircraft and how he'd gone from missing to standing there, alive and breathing, congregants inquired about his plans, where he would deploy next. Despite his fever to know how Oliver got here, Hugo did not want to breach the protocol that the congregation seemed to innately understand, so he simply shook Oliver's hand and welcomed him home. He'd ask Jack later if he had an explanation for this.

After school the next day, Hugo and Colin climbed on their bicycles and pedaled over to Kimbolton, waving hello to the private in the guard shack who called out as they zipped by that Lieutenant Philip was in a briefing and would the boys please wait outside his quarters? These were perfunctory orders only. Hugo and Colin were fixtures on the base now, younger soldiers ruffling their hair and teasing them like they did their kid brothers, older officers, parents themselves, inquiring about progress in school and the sports they played and followed. When the men had passes to London, they would invariably hunt around for treats to bring back to the boys and the twins—a comic book, strings of licorice, a deck of cards—the normalcy of offering these small kindnesses counterweight to the high drama that characterized each bombing run they undertook.

The boys parked their bicycles and instead of waiting at Jack's Nissen hut, they ambled over to the mess hall looking for Buck or other members of the Gator crew. Clearly, they were all otherwise occupied. A staff sergeant approached, gave them a friendly smile, flipped a pack of gum their way, then headed toward a waiting jeep that would take him out to a B-17 waiting at its hardstand.

The base was humming with activity—busier than the boys remembered it ever being, confirmed by the now-daily thunder that resounded over Elsworth as the bombers rose in the air. The Florida Gator had fresh pockmarks in her every time the boys saw her, wounds the ground crews patched up to keep her airworthy, laughing at the damn Jerrys who were too slow on the uptake to shoot the Gator down. Soon, some of the flight crews on the base would complete the required twenty-five missions, making them eligible to rotate back to the States. Hugo and Colin pushed the idea of Jack's departure from their minds: it was a terrible thing to even imagine.

The doors to the briefing room swung open and out into the daylight emerged dozens of squinting pilots and crew, many of them running through the details they'd just heard, stopping short when they saw the boys.

"Fellas," called Jack to the boys. "Y'all up to no good again?" He nodded to the men he was with to urge them to go on as he took some time with the boys. He stood in his fleece-lined leather flight jacket, the collar pulled high on his neck, hands plunged deep in his pockets, working to shake the chill.

"Here only to keep you in line, mate," responded Colin with a grin. "Blast, Jack! It's all of eight degrees and still you shiver as if we're in the midst of an ice storm. This is about as good as it gets in February around here. We're enjoying it, hey Hugo? Not even wearing our long underwear!"

"That's about forty-five degrees where I come from, so to me it feels like the dead of winter. So, what's up?"

"We've got some questions for you," said Hugo.

"No! Questions? For me? Well, that's new," he joked. "We can sit in the mess and talk. I'll get y'all some Cokes from the O-Club—I could use something a bit harder right about now—and meet you over there. Then we'll get down to business."

·   ·   ·

Settled in the corner of the mess hall, the boys described the events of the previous day. Hearing of the sudden appearance of Flight Sergeant Dowd at Holy Trinity, Jack smiled, lifted his beer in salute, and gave a little hoot. "Good for the ole' vicar and his family. Glad to hear it."

"So, how did he make it home?" Hugo pressed. "Who smuggled him out of France?"

"Probably a whole slew of folks," responded Jack, who then filled out the broad details of what the boys had already begun to piece together, that a chain of resisters had likely found the good sergeant and hidden him for some period of time. Then someone had guided him southward through France, handing him off, one partisan to the next, along the treacherous route through the Pyrenees, then probably into Spain. British intelligence would have received him there and arranged for transport home. "But I'm guessing here, fellas. That's probably close to what happened and now I need you both to forget every bit of it because talking about it makes the way home that much harder for the next guy. I'm serious. That's why nobody was talking about it yesterday. Promise me you two won't blab to anybody about it—not at school or anywhere and if you hear talk about it, shut it down."

"These guides—they're not soldiers?" asked Hugo.

"Not usually. Maybe some are, but they're all kinds of people who can blend in and stay out of sight so they don't get caught. It is dangerous business, boys. No trial by jury if they're caught, you know what I mean? They got more courage and guts than most people do, I'll tell you that."

"Wish they'd found my dad," he murmured.

"And hidden him and got him out," finished Collin.

"I do too, fellas," responded Jack. "Boy, do I." Jack looked at Colin, the green eyes serious, earnest, so like his mother. Beryl. He wondered where he stood with her after he'd overstepped that night. Jack planned to make things right as soon as he had the chance. He felt some urgency to do so.

They sat a few more minutes before a throng of about fifty men—hyped up and hollering, having survived their bombing run—descended on the mess for an early dinner. The boys finished their Cokes and made their way outside, thanking Jack as they customarily did, a ritual that had evolved from formal handshakes and stiff head nods to Jack cuffing their hair and pulling them in close for an embrace. "It's what we Southern Yankees do, boys," he'd explained. "Can't help it."

Hugo and Colin hopped on their bicycles for the trek home, riding slowly, side by side, considering what they'd learned. Jack had provided startling answers to their questions and filled out their understanding of things they had suspected, but there were many things they still didn't know about the fight in France, details they would remain unaware of for months to come. Namely, that after worship the day before, after the handshakes had concluded and the long line of congregants dispersed, Oliver Dowd had made his way over to Ivy, asking his grandmother to take Margaret and Patsy to the garden so he could have a moment with their foster mother. And as the two of them stood in the chancel, sunlight gleaming in distinct rays through the prisms of the ancient stained glass, Oliver had pressed something small and sacred into Ivy's hand that brought an immediate rush of tears, prompting Flight Sergeant Dowd to reach out with haste to hold her to ensure she remained upright.

CHAPTER TWELVE

That which we are, we are –
One equal temper of heroic hearts,
Made weak by time and fate, but strong in will
To strive, to see, to find, and not to yield.
–Alfred Lord Tennyson

Occupied France

It wasn't that William Hughes was particularly courageous. Neither was he foolhardy. He had simply availed himself of an awkward and ultimately deadly set of circumstances that set in motion his fortuitous escape.

When the prisoners taken at Calais and their German overseers passed outside Lille, more than one POW took refuge in the farmer's hayloft—several hoping for a chance to flee, all grateful for a soft place to rest. The farmer's daughter, who, at eighteen years old, had never been five miles from her family home, found the sudden occupation of the farm enthralling. The noisy arrival of the Germans with their modern trucks and staff cars and the thousands of captives impressed and appalled her. The POWs were grimy. But the Germans. Some of them were beautiful, especially the ones in charge of directing this transfer of prisoners. They seemed taller than average men, sharp, and so sure of themselves in a manner she found attractive. Powerfully so. She felt some shame for this, but it did not quench her interest. It was partly their uniforms, decorated with ornate emblems and ribbons, the significance of which she knew nothing. Most had good teeth and a lot of them, straight noses. Their hands were not calloused and rough like the boys she knew. When, as she served them supper, one of them began conversing with her in French, he earned her delighted response. Her parents were horrified, their eyes flashing a warning she pretended not to notice. That night, they reprimanded her, reminding her that these barbarians had taken over France, killed her countrymen. She must maintain her distance.

After her parents fell asleep that night, she slipped soundlessly from their shared room, pausing to quiet the dog as she began to stir, making her way to the hayloft to meet her German. She had resolved she was ready to give herself over to whatever he asked—it would be her first time—believing it could offer a path that could take her away from the tedious and never-ending work of the farm and toward a more interesting life. Their encounter was not what she expected—his body out of the uniform did not have the same allure—but the whole thing was bearable and didn't last overly long. They slept and at dawn, as the first rooster crowed, she leapt from the hay to head to the cow pen so her parents would think she had risen early to see to her chores. As she did so, she tripped over a muddy boot—that of a hidden POW who had lain quietly beneath the hay at one side of the large loft throughout their sexual congress. This is when she emitted her mortified scream, prompting the German to shoot the man not because he was attempting to escape, but because he could give witness to the violation of this naïve French girl. The shattering sound of the gunfire brought the girl's parents and a contingent of Nazi officers to the barn, where the German—now dressed except for his boots—calmly announced he'd found a man attempting to flee and had executed him accordingly.

Buried under the hay, next to the dead POW, William Hughes held his breath, relieved when the girl's family arrived because at least there would be witnesses to give testimony to his death. But the cacophony of accusations, realizations, recriminations covered him. The parents pulled the girl roughly from the loft, her mother slapping her face, hissing through clenched teeth that she was an embarrassment, simple-minded, and selfish. The German strode from the barn, head high but face enflamed, earning quiet plaudits from his peers for both his conquest of the pretty girl and preventing an escape. When the assemblage moved out that afternoon, the girl stood and watched them, face anguished and tear-streaked as she began a reckoning of all she had lost.

William stayed hidden the remainder of the day and through the night, showing himself when the farmer entered the barn and climbed to the loft to remove the body of the dead POW the next day.

"Oh, mon Dieu," the farmer breathed as William pushed through the straw and slowly sat up. He had lain in the blood of the other man for a day and a half, his uniform soaked through on one side and across the back, the metallic scent attracting insects and rodents that twirled hungrily about him.

"Je pensais que tu étais mort," he said. I thought you were dead.

"Je vais bien," William responded. "This poor bloke saved me." And knowing enough French and English between them to communicate what they needed to do, the men maneuvered the dead soldier—a Belgian fighting for France—down the loft ladder and placed him onto a wagon. They would bury him in the woods after sunset.

The farmer brought William into the house, where his wife, daughter, and young son stared in fear and disbelief. Their dog barked furiously, incensed at this stranger appearing in the kitchen.

"Albert!" his wife shrieked, leaping to her feet, the kitchen knife dropping from her hand and clattering to the floor. "Sucre! Soyez silencieux! Gilles, por favor, le chien." The boy pulled Sucre the dog to his side and demanded her silence.

"All's well," the father assured them. "Sit. All of you. This is Guillaume, William. He is British. He is not wounded. The blood belongs to the one the Nazis shot. We must clean him up and hide him."

A hushed but spirited exchange ensued, in which the women vigorously challenged the wisdom of helping an Englishman when the Germans had so plainly demonstrated the punishment for those who did not respect their rules. After the events of the past two days, the daughter's appetite for drama had been sated, and she wished for nothing more than to return to the safety and sameness of her life before the contingent of captors and captives had arrived. The boy, a lanky fourteen-year-old, looked intently at William, eyes wide and staring at the blood-soaked uniform.

"Vous êtes resté silencieux ? Tout le temps?" You stayed quiet? The whole time? the boy finally said.

"Silent? Yes. I did. Oui," William responded.

The boy put his face in his hands and shook his head as his father pled William's case.

"Did I fight at Verdun—see with my own eyes, good men cut down next to me—to give in to the Germans now?" Albert asked reasonably, looking from face to face. "How God has blessed me with each of you. With a farm that year after year rewards us for our hard work, producing well and providing for our needs. I have coveted this tranquil life and I wish it still. But we cannot ignore what has happened. The Germans have brought the war to our doorstep. One of them took advantage of my own child. We will not cower. We will do our part. All of us. Ginette, heat some water so he can bathe. Prepare him some food. Gilles, show him to the bathtub. Sylvi, fetch some of your brother's clothes for him to wear."

·   ·   ·

William slept fitfully that night and the next and the next, naked between soft, sweet-smelling sheets, well hidden in the farmhouse attic, no vermin nipping at him for the first time since Calais. In his dreams, he heard gunshots. He felt the warm ooze of the other man's blood, moving silently, relentlessly toward him, except this time it overwhelmed him, moving over his face and covering his mouth, cutting off his air. He heard the German soldier say, "You are next," in English clear and distinct, which startled him awake, his heart pounding, moments passing before he realized he'd been spared. That he lived astonished him. What recompense could he even begin to offer this farmer who insisted on protecting him at such great cost?

Albert directed Wills to stay in the house during the day so he could retreat quickly to the attic should a neighbor stop by. The signing of the Treaty at Compiègne and the establishment of the government at Vichy after Paris fell introduced distrust and suspicion among formerly friendly neighbors. As the occupiers began to post directives in the villages of Northern France, requiring residents to turn over weapons, radios, and other contraband, everyone wanted to know what everyone else intended to do—abide the new rules or ignore them? Were the Germans likely to take action if they did not comply? The imposition of rationing caused a second fury, with families turning to neighbors ostensibly to barter the items they lacked, but more often to share indignation over these new limits. They had grown this wheat and now it was being seized and shipped to Germany? Their anger swelled, but what could they do, really? Despite their earlier promises, vows, declarations of loyalty to France, Albert knew people didn't truly know how they would behave until the time came. Some French soldiers had fought to the death or to the moment of capture in the opening days of the war while others simply laid down their arms, removed their uniforms, hid, and attempted to return home. Civilians would be no different. Some would show selfless courage that endangered their lives. Others would bow to their fear and protect themselves and those they loved, keeping their heads down as best they could, trying only to stay out of the Nazis' way. Still others—those for whom Albert reserved his deepest contempt—would trade on any information they collected to improve their own lot. And now with this Treaty, it appeared there were plenty of those willing to collaborate and do the Germans' bidding. Albert said he would need some time to discern who among those he knew might be willing to help them and who would happily turn in an English soldier to earn special consideration from the Gestapo.

They had burned Wills' uniform and since Gilles' pants proved too narrow for him, Ginette loosened them by inserting some fabric at the waist culled from old grain sacks. With this, his transformation into a French peasant was accomplished. Through the summer months, members of the family drilled him to improve his French, doctoring it with a bit of Dutch that might help him pass as Belgian were he discovered, chiding him when, in frustration, he would blurt out a phrase in English. His anxiety dissipated in the kitchen when he cooked alongside Ginette, the two of them trading techniques, Wills' repertoire expanding thanks to the herb garden out back of the kitchen and the wild greens culled from their fields. Sucre the dog learned a thing or two that summer, too, Gilles patiently training her to alert the family when a visitor approached, to stay completely quiet when ordered, and to bare her teeth on command.

Living as they did on acres of open land, two kilometers from the next farm, the mechanics of returning Wills to England would entail resources they had not yet accumulated and help from others not yet identified. Every day required a resolute courage that was tested with each bit of news visitors brought to their door: a villager shot when her neighbor heard the faint static of her radio one still evening and dutifully reported this to the occupying authorities. Another, executed for his vociferous objection to the removal of his Jewish wife from their home. She and their children had then been placed on a train heading east. A third, shot by a firing squad and the body hanged in the village square for hiding a downed British pilot, his activity accidentally exposed by a onetime friend who had spotted the parachute and was overheard whispering the story in the village café.

And yet, here was Wills—safe for now—a hearty bowl of garbure before him, dressed in clean clothes that were not stiff with muck, the family around him risking their very lives for him while those with whom he'd been captured were headed to a certain hell. He thought of Ivy, who was surely suffering with worry in Elsworth—what had she been told? Fletcher, whom he'd marched next to and commiserated with over those many weeks, knew he had not been in the contingent that departed Lille. Did he assume Wills was the soldier shot dead in the loft? He hoped that word would get to Ivy that he had been seen after Calais, healthy and well. And while he desperately wished to return home to Ivy and Hugo, his months on this farm had placed a new mission before him, one he could not in good conscience avoid, one he would undertake as soon as the pieces fell in place.

CHAPTER THIRTEEN

Whose bread I eat, his song I sing.
–German proverb

Inside the Reich, 1944

One morning, Gordon awoke with an unfamiliar pain in his gut. Like his fellow POWs, he suffered a variety of ailments that never really resolved—scabs that failed to heal, odd rashes that came and went, and bowel irregularities—always that. Underlying all of it, persistent fatigue. But this was something new, a cement block parked in his stomach. He felt it when he moved, so he worked to position himself to make the feeling recede. It remained ever-present and rock hard. And the heat—when had it become so very hot this late into September? But was it September? He drifted back to sleep, looking to retreat from the pain that seized his middle.

"Let's go, mate. Up and at 'em." It was Fletcher. What was he doing? Gordon wondered. Why so loud?

Then there were two of them—Fletcher and McGruder at his side, in his ear, yelling that Gordon needed to get up and out to the yard for *Appell*.

"Sleeping in, are we, sir? There's none a that here," said one.

"It's late, Lieutenant Clarke," pleaded the other. "Come on now, or we'll get in trouble too."

Gordon attempted to rise from his bunk, surprised to find the world had become gauzy, vague, its edges blurred and indistinct. There was something glimmering, twinkling at the edge of his vision. It was rather pleasant. He wanted to go there, to enter this indeterminate world that had emerged as he had slept. As he moved upright, he was hit first with lightheadedness, then a weakness that brought him to his knees. He was half-walked, half-carried to the yard, where his bunk mates held him upright at *Appell*, inviting wry looks from others who assumed he'd overindulged on *Kriegie* hooch. Lieutenant Colonel Leonard demanded Gordon be seen by the camp physician when next he came. That would be several days off, as the doctor only visited once a week.

By the time Dr. Hildebrand did his examination, the typhus had fully set in. A vivid rash crossed Gordon's chest and torso and was making its way down his limbs. He had not eaten in three days, able only to tolerate the smallest sips of water. He was admitted to the medical building not because there was belief he could be saved, but to minimize the contagion. As he lay in the ward, marginally cleaner than his barracks, on an actual mattress, nurses noting his vital signs and his obvious decline, offering him sips of water (although he perceived none of this), he dreamt.

He dreamt of Colin when he was small, when they used to visit the park and the library. There was no film of misty rain; it was hot, arid, as they walked walking through sun-flecked gardens and city blocks. There was his boy, forever seeking detailed answers to questions about the world around him—like why did the cabbie pushing a pedal on the floor of the taxi make the thing go? What was the connection? And what was right above them at this moment as they rode the Tube? And how did the Tube-builders know how strong to make the tunnels so they didn't cave in? How many pounds did the walls hold up? And flying. He was fascinated by flying and the apparent impossibility of it all, prevailing on Gordon to read him all he could find on the Wright Brothers and how they'd figured it all out, then wanting to discuss it with his dad, step by incremental step. He would be an engineer, Gordon thought—or perhaps an aeroplane designer. A technological career, so unlike his own artistic appetites. Who would have imagined? And Beryl. Beryl who had pushed him to know his son—to handle him when he was tiny and squalling and to converse with him when his words came—when the habit was to order children about and make them mind, or let the women handle the child-rearing entirely. He could see them now—walking—he didn't know exactly where they were headed, but it struck him that it looked more like what he remembered of his current locale than England, Beryl in a sundress and sweater, dark hair framing her face. He was surprised; she looked the same as he remembered her in 1939. Not the first gray hair. But with Colin, he could not formulate a picture. He saw his boy from the back, a bit taller, broader, walking away from him. Gordon wanted to call out but he could not locate his voice, activate the series of muscles and tendons needed to accomplish this. He had the urgent need to say goodbye, but more importantly, to thank this child for all he had taught him. For forcing him to be a little less selfish. More careful with his time so he could reserve all he could for his family. More honest with himself. More fair. This is what children teach you, thought Gordon, because it's easier to change your awful stubborn habits when you realize that to not do so will disappoint this little person to whom you are the moon and the stars and the firmament. And so you must be. Had he been that to his boy? He wished he could ask him, but Colin seemed not to be listening to him. He just kept walking farther off, so instead Gordon said a prayer to God to thank Him for His beneficent gift.

Would Beryl survive this—becoming a widow so young? He knew she would for their son. She would find a way to return joy to Colin's life. She would fight to give him everything he needed to heal from this terrible loss, even finding a new father, perhaps. He could trust her to do that. She was capable and resourceful. She would hate being described like this—sturdy and dependable, like a car or a motorbike. He could not let her think that was all he loved about her, so he began making a list, his roaring fever convincing him he could communicate this directly to her, reassure her of the limitless things he loved about her. First: her brain. She was smarter than most of the men in his firm had been, practically seeing around corners as she discerned complex patterns whether in her chemistry class or as she observed Hitler's rise. She could have been a doctor, had she wanted. But she had wanted Gordon and Colin too. Her body, the perfect way his arm fit across her shoulders when they walked, hers looped around his waist. Her narrow waist, the flat stomach over the curve of her hips, he could see even now. He had a sudden remembrance of their arms and legs intertwined, of the easy way they fit together and how making love silently after the baby came introduced an intimate, compressed vigor to their bed. He saw her face, the beautiful green eyes revealing both passion and contentment, an eagerness for what awaited them. He felt her encouragement, her absolute belief in him. But then she withdrew, giving him a smile and a quick, apologetic wave before turning to join her son. His wife and child were walking into their future without him, he realized, and this is what they had to do. He understood and wished he could release them from feeling sad about it. As they moved farther away, another figure approached, emerging from a lush garden in full flower. He detected the scent. He knew this scent. The commandant's wife. She was speaking loudly angrily, insisting on her way. She was in charge. In his mind's eye, he saw her wearing a uniform—a man's uniform like her husband's but one that fit her beautifully, impressively, tight across her breasts, unbuttoned to mid-chest, but only Gordon could see. It was for him. Gordon was seized with guilt: he wanted to apologize to her for his inability to finish the arbor over her *Terrasse*— such a shame, really because he had wasted so much time dragging everything out so he could surveil the commandant's residence and report back and reap the many benefits from working there for as long as possible. But now he felt remorse for all that because he had not been honest; he could have finished within two weeks. And now she didn't have her arbor. It would not be ready for her party. This must be why she is so angry. He attempted to speak to her and then he recalled that there was a good reason he could not tell her the truth. He did not know what this was.

And then someone turned off the furnace. At last, Gordon thought. It had been blasting nonstop since he had arrived here. Where was here, exactly? No matter. He was glad the proprietor had finally turned it off. His parched lips stuck to his gums but thankfully, someone was pouring water over them. The wetness found its way past his lips, slid down his neck and puddled at his head. He attempted to swallow, giving a little cough as he did, feeling like his throat contained muscles that had not been worked in some time. After one sip, two sips, three sips, he fell back, exhausted from the depleting sadness of his dream and from the overwhelming dehydration the nurses were attempting to address. But something had changed. He felt a movement of air, which brought a little chill. Perhaps the innkeeper would bring him a quilt now to warm him up. When did he arrive here at this inn?

He wanted to summon someone to ask, but where was his voice? He could not locate the parts of himself that could make him speak aloud. A nap then. I will solve this after a rest, he thought. He slept, the aroma of ambergris still in the air.

CHAPTER FOURTEEN

He is most powerful who has power over himself.
–Seneca the Younger

London, early 1944

His kiss proved a torment to her, evidence of the very flawed and false person Beryl had long suspected she might be. What kind of wife and mother does this, whirled the dialog in her head—your husband a prisoner, your country under siege? She'd always seen herself—and this was vitally important to her—as a woman of sound judgement, of demonstrated loyalty and certitude, qualities that signaled maturity and selflessness, that helped her cope as the war had subtracted, one by one, the people and things she loved. She looked for this in others, but the strain of the war had hardened her, contracting the leeway that she had once instinctively, happily, given those around her. Her first impulse now was to judge, as she did with one young nurse who laid out of work pleading a sudden onset of sniffles—best not to bring the infection to the ward—who'd been spotted heading out on a date after her shift, a date that clearly spilled into the next morning. Beryl did not pass judgements directly, publicly, as she had watched her mother do, and never called the young woman to account. Instead, she railed silently inside her head and withdrew from those she believed were not living up to her expectations. She had grown harsh, the smug corollary to each judgement being that she, Beryl, would never do things so base, so improper. Now that she felt she had, she reserved the harshest judgement for herself.

Her embarrassment and anger had built in the days since Jack had driven her home, costing her sleep and erasing her appetite. Her heart ached because she had kissed the American hungrily, greedily, and had he not kept a few feet's distance as he took her to the door and bid her goodnight, she might have pulled him across the threshold for much more than a kiss. What was he—eight years younger than she? She played and replayed what had happened on an endless loop as she walked to the hospital and tended to patients in the ward, and most of all, during her off hours, when she lay alone and ashamed. She remembered each detail of the trip home to London, his reaching for her hand and her using it to dry her tears. "Bloody awful," she breathed to herself, "why on earth?" her muttering prompting Dr. Lowell, the attending on her shift, to inquire if she was speaking to him.

"No... sorry. I'm just working through a bit of a problem," she replied, pulling herself back to the current moment, eyes fixed on the clipboard in front of her.

"Nurse Clarke, if I haven't said it, let me say it now," he began and here she waited for the doctor to blast her for her distraction and carelessness. "I don't know how we'd have managed so well without you. You're one of the few who never complains and I know we ask a lot of you. It has not gone unnoticed. You've been heroic, really. And if you're a bit tired by this point, believe me, we understand. We're all bloody knackered."

Having never seen a breach in her professional demeanor, Dr. Lowell's eyes grew wide in surprise to see tears glimmering in Beryl's eyes, to hear the break in her usually strong and confident voice.

"And you, doctor," she responded, gratefully, embarrassing him just a little, "are a prince to say so out loud."

·   ·   ·

The unrelenting demands of her work, the privation of the war, the absence of Gordon and Colin, the loss of the Densmores—meant there were no voices in Beryl's life that regularly encouraged her, reminded her that she was only human. That she was still worthy. Living alone for years now, she received precious little feedback from other human beings—the kind of thoughtful input that refutes errant conclusions and redirects unhelpful trains of thought.

As Beryl got some distance and stopped agonizing over her physical contact with Jack, she was able to consider the value inherent in his words and the echo of them she heard from Dr. Lowell. How both their assertions had been so unexpected and felt undeserved, but had enveloped her like a blessing and opened a portal to tears she had needed to cry months and years earlier, tears that began to wash away the notion that she was either one thing or its opposite. If they were right about her, then she was not beyond redemption. She recalled the outlook she possessed before the war had demanded so much of her, when she was less reactive with herself and others, when her instincts inclined her more often to give the benefit of the doubt. Living apart from Gordon and Colin, she'd had no one close enough to her to remind her of this, to evince tenderness in favor of judgement. Jack had pushed between the scaffolds she'd erected to keep her life intact and people at arm's length and suggested she forgive herself for not managing the impossible perfectly. He confirmed that what she was doing was brutally hard, and in saying so, kindled gratitude, relief, and a tiny ray of hope within her that she might survive this, however it turned out, that she might someday be able to relinquish the judge's seat and return to a beneficence with herself and others. She did not have to stay the closed-off woman that recent circumstances demanded. As she took small steps in this direction, the roiling in her stomach calmed and sleep came more easily.

Three weeks after their encounter, Jack turned up at the reception desk on her ward at Grove Park. She saw him before he saw her, striking and substantial in his olive drab service uniform, the khaki tie slightly askew, his fingers working his garrison cap. Her hand rose first to smooth her hair, then to her own uniform, to straighten her skirt as she moved down the hall toward him.

"Jack—hello! Is Colin alright?"

"He's great, Beryl. Just fine. Sends his love. Wants you to know biology is not getting the best of him."

She smiled. She would stand here all day to hear tidbits like this.

"Says he has you to thank for that—and his dad for his math skills. So, Beryl, could we meet later maybe?" Jack asked. "After you get off?"

"Well, I'm mid-shift—can't exactly get away this moment but as you've come all the way to London... You're on a pass, I'm assuming?"

"I am. Another five missions checked off, so they send us away on three-day passes. Our schedule is gonna be pretty full coming up real soon, so a lot of us are taking the time we can. I apologize for not telephoning first." He dropped his voice and looked at her steadily. "I didn't want to give you the chance to say you wouldn't meet me."

"Of course I would meet you," she responded, hearing the intimacy in his voice. "Jack, I'm fine. Really. We're fine. I'm glad you've come. We've got some air clearing to do, I know that, but all's well. Truly. You started me thinking, and that's what I've been doing. Not saying it's been easy. So, I work until six tomorrow morning and take my meal break around midnight. Not exactly good for arranging dinner with friends."

"Tomorrow's fine, really. I'm booked at the Dorchester—have some briefings with some muckety-mucks in from—never mind about that, I guess. Listen, tomorrow is fine. Do you want to meet for breakfast at the hotel? Or should I head over to your place?"

She considered the safest course. "I'll come by there when I'm out of work. I'll have to run by my flat to feed the cat first so it may be seven, seven-thirty. Shall we meet in the café?"

"Yes. Great. Perfect. Thank you, Beryl. Appreciate it. I'll see you in the morning."

"Right, Jack. Tomorrow then."

. . .

He waited, consuming cup after cup of ersatz coffee—the hotel often ran low and substituted a foul chicory—before switching to tea an hour later. The waiter circled attentively at first, before discreetly concluding no further service would be needed as this was not, after all, a party of two. She changed her mind, Jack realized, and would not meet him. He did not fault her. He had clumsily, dishonorably, stolen a kiss from a married woman, betraying her, and her husband, their son whom they all loved, and himself. He had come to apologize—to promise never to overstep like that again. But privately, he wished it could be different for them, that there was a way forward that did not involve deceiving people who loved and trusted them.

At nine, Jack rose and paid his tab, walking out of the hotel unsure of his destination. The truth of it was, when he pictured his time in London, he had pictured it with her. He passed shops just now opening their doors and thought about what he might bring back to the boys and the twins, wincing because this complication with Beryl robbed a bit of joy from the enterprise. He thought about what lay before him. They were on the cusp of a major air offensive in the war, one that could prove pivotal, the specifics complicated and closely guarded. If he was soon to fly his last mission—if something were to go wrong—he would like to depart with a clear conscience, her forgiving him for crossing a boundary. Jack meandered eastward, winding through Covent Garden, then turning north toward Kings Cross. Along the way, he noted the hundreds of American airmen that outnumbered the natives, each of them soaking in the veneer of normalcy that was London, working hard to not think ahead to what awaited them upon their return to quarters. After an hour of wandering, it was clear his feet were taking him towards her, a magnet pulling him inexorably in her direction. So be it, he thought. Maybe he would just walk past her flat as a way to say goodbye.

Across from her place, he could see a new business going in, reconstruction of some sort of retail business that had stood on the corner at some point before. They were also rebuilding a library, from the looks of it, evidence of the resilience of the British that had surprised the Germans and heartened Churchill.

As Jack stood across the lane facing Beryl's house, he saw her front door standing wide open, a cat holding sentry on the stoop. He jaywalked madly across the street and ran up her steps, standing in the open door and calling her name. He heard her before he saw her—her wracking sobs, the keening of one who has lost all hope. As his eyes adjusted to the dim light inside the front hallway, he saw her in a heap, as if she had fallen, legs splayed out beneath her, a piece of paper in her lap. She appeared at first not to recognize him until he came to her and repeated her name. She answered by handing him the paper she held. It was from the War Office, informing her of notification received from the International Red Cross, that First Lieutenant Gordon S. Clarke had succumbed to typhus whilst a prisoner of war in the custody of the German government. She would be notified at a later date as to the disposition of his body. His effects had not yet been released, but once the Office had received them, the death would be confirmed. At this, Jack summoned the cat inside, closed the door, then knelt before her, pulling her into his arms in vain attempts to soothe her, believing that in some way, his wish to be with her had caused this.

. . .

He stayed with her, helping her onto her bed, telephoning the hospital with the news of Gordon and to say she would be out for several days, preparing cups of tea and broth that she had no interest in. By late afternoon, grief and shock exhausting and disorienting her, she fell asleep, her lovely face red and anguished, knees drawn into her belly like a small child. Jack telephoned the base and was granted an extra day's leave—beseeching his commanding officer to please, please keep word of Colin's dad to himself because of how it would magnify the heartbreak were the boy to learn the news haphazardly. He ambled through their flat, looking at the many framed photographs—of Gordon and Beryl's wedding, of a younger Beryl at nursing school graduation, of newborn Colin in the arms of his clearly proud father, of a school-age Colin who more obviously resembled the boy Jack knew and loved. He studied the picture of Gordon—Colin was growing tall like his dad—and he wept over the ruination, the waste, the irreplaceable loss. He returned to the bedroom, pulling a worn quilt over Beryl's restless frame, removing his shoes and his uniform shirt, then dropping into the armchair next to the bed. He shook his head in disbelief and anger. The damn Germans. They'd probably left Gordon alone in his bunk to die a miserable death. What a lucky man, until that moment, Gordon had been. Father to a great kid like Colin. Married to a strong, beautiful, utterly devoted woman who was so unlike the girls Jack knew in college. She was older, of course, a mother who had experienced the breadth of life, vastly different from the sorority girls he'd dated, many who cultivated an interest in him but seemed unconcerned with much beyond the Florida state line. This war had broadened Jack's understanding of the world and he would not return easily to the provincial life he'd led before. Jack closed his eyes and soon he dozed, awaking at intervals to hear the cat mewling, sadly, insistently.

At midnight, she awoke, her eyes swollen and dull, surprised to see Jack in the chair and willing only to sip a bit of water at his insistence. She asked him to feed the cat, because she'd not done so all day.

"I got sidetracked," she explained.

When she'd arrived home that morning, the post had awaited her. Once she saw the return address on the envelope, she'd wanted to rip it up or stuff it back in the box, to refuse delivery. Instead, she'd walked into her house, opened the letter, and judging from the blue bruises emerging on her knees, collapsed. She spoke calmly, her voice low and robotic, as if she recounted events that did not directly involve her, that did not utterly devastate her life. Jack listened and nodded, moving onto the bed with her and holding her hand. As the night wore into morning, she stopped talking and inched her body into his, gripping the arm he placed protectively around her as she prepared for another convulsive round of tears. They agreed Colin did not need to know right away—that Beryl would tell him herself on the next visit she made to Elsworth. Or maybe they would do it together.

Jack awoke at mid-morning, taking a second to remember where he was, the sad reason he was here. He heard water running in the bath, so he went to the kitchen to splash some water over his face and put the kettle on for tea. He found bread in the cupboard and sausage in the larder, heating the meat on the stove and drawing the interest of the cat who gave Jack a long look, trying to figure out what this stranger was doing here. The cat followed him as he carried the tray of food and drink back to the bedroom.

Beryl lay against her pillows in a bright, floral robe, her wet hair fanned out from her face, eyes aimed at the ceiling but seeing nothing. "I telephoned the Clarkes—Gordon's parents," she whispered. "They already knew. Their letter came two days ago, and they didn't think to talk to me." She ran her hands through her wet curls. "His father is mad with grief. His mother was so quiet. She could not speak."

Jack crossed soundlessly before her, placing the tray at her bedside. She moved over, inviting him in beside her. "Are you able to stay here a bit longer?" she asked, "Until I get my footing and figure out what I'm to do next."

"Yes. Planning on it. I've got forty-eight hours before I need to be back. Can you eat something? It might help."

"I'm not hungry, if that's what you're asking. But if you say I need to eat, I'll do it." He offered her the cup of tea first, which she held between her palms for warmth, her eyes looking at him but her thoughts elsewhere.

"Do I get his body back?" she asked. "Or does this bloody war take even that from me?"

"I don't know, Beryl. I'll find out. Sometimes there are issues when there's a contagious disease."

"I want the memorial service in Elsworth. I want that old vicar to do it— the one who gave Colin his bicycle. There are people there who know and love my son and will help him through this."

"That sounds like the right thing to do."

"But I need to tell Colin. And Jack, I'm not sure I have the words to do that yet."

"I know, Beryl. I know. We can wait a bit." This typified their conversation throughout the day, she looping back to things already decided, he soothing her, affirming all she said.

She decided suddenly that she wanted out of the bedroom, to tackle the idea of sitting upright and facing the world instead of seeing it from a recline, so they moved to the living room, Jack toting the tray, ever-hopeful that she would take some nourishment. She asked him what he was missing and whether he could be in trouble for staying with her this long. He told her he'd spoken to his C.O. and that the schedule had room for him to be here now, because next week, all hands were required on deck. It would be significant.

"Significant?" she questioned. "In what way?"

"We're gearing up, Beryl. Gotta take the Luftwaffe out of the equation if we're gonna bring in an invasion force. And that's happening next week.

We're throwing everything we got at 'em. You'll see. But it's hush hush, of course so..."

She nodded, then sipped her tea finally, heaving a great sigh and attempting several bites of the sausage before setting it aside in favor of some nibbles at the toast Jack had slathered with her plum marmalade. At that moment, there was a light rap on the door and they heard Jesse on the stoop, worry in her voice.

"Beryl? Beryl, are you alright in there? It's Jesse."

Beryl tied her robe about her a little tighter and nodded to Jack, who rose and opened the door. Jesse registered surprise at seeing an American serviceman in his T-shirt standing behind the door.

"Hello, ma'am. I'm Jack. A friend of Beryl's."

"I'm Jesse, her neighbor, well, her hairdresser really, but I haven't seen even a sign of her in a few days and I was getting a little worried about her, so I thought perhaps..."

Beryl interrupted the monologue. "I'm here, Jesse. You needn't worry. We've just... had some bad news. Jack has been here helping."

"News! What is it, Beryl? Colin? Gordon?"

Again, Beryl nodded at Jack, steeling herself to hear him speak the words out loud.

"Gordon, ma'am. Beryl's been notified that he suffered an infection in the camp. It was fatal."

"Oh, my word," she exclaimed, hand over her mouth, easing her way over to Beryl and crouching in front of her chair. "My poor darling. What can I do? How can I help? I'm so terribly sorry."

Beryl reached out a hand, her smile wan and sad.

"I know. I know you are. Thank you, Jesse. I'm managing. In shock still, I suppose. Jack will be leaving—when Jack? What day do you go?"

"I've got until the day after tomorrow," he responded, "so maybe you'd be able to check on her after that."

"Aye, I will," affirmed Jesse, "and how fortunate she's had you here to assist her." Jack heard the slightest question in her voice, as if challenging them to explain their evident intimacy.

"Jack has befriended Colin, Jesse, in Elsworth. He is stationed at Kimbolton. He was in London when I received this news and I'm very grateful he was able to do this, to be here. Because next week will be big, right Jack? The Americans are going to throw everything they've got at the Germans. I believe that's how you said it."

In her fatigue and grief, Beryl was unaware she had made this disclosure. Jack winced, a rebuke of his own irresponsibility, sharing too much and putting her in this position.

Jesse's attention pivoted away from her friend upon hearing this bit of news. "Oh, yes? And what is your part to play in this?"

"Beryl, I believe you misheard me. It's been a long couple of days and she's been sleeping on and off, Jesse. I'm not sure what she thinks she heard me say. But yes, my pass expires in forty-eight hours and I'll be returning to base. Routine duty."

At this Beryl froze, recognizing her mistake, turning her attention to the cold cup of tea in her hands. Jesse looked at Jack just a beat too long, trying to determine what exactly was going on, her face revealing the calculations underway in her brain.

"Routine duty. Well, good for you, then," she said finally, but her abrupt shift, from sympathetic concern for her newly widowed friend to intense and specific interest in Jack's upcoming duty, had been obvious to them both.

"Alright, Beryl, my dearest. I shall take my leave. Lovely to meet you, Jack, despite these dreadful circumstances. Good luck. Beryl, I shall return in two days' time to see how you're faring. But if you need anything— ANYTHING—before then, please ring. I'm right across the street." With that, Jesse made her way out the door, clearly preoccupied by what she'd learned in her few minutes inside Beryl's flat.

·   ·   ·

Later, after enjoying her lovely, if spare, afternoon tea, Jesse pulled out her writing paper to memorialize the day's news. She had nothing startling this time—nothing like the early information on the RDF towers she'd sent, along with the rough sketches that approximated their locations. She'd been proud of those. It had been an enormous risk, but it had miraculously gotten through and explained why the British had been so good at intercepting German planes during the Blitz, forcing the Luftwaffe to reconsider its strategy. Her other gem was learning through the parent of soldier in North Africa of the numbers of battalions the Americans planned to send to reinforce the lines. Not that it had mattered in the end, really.

In previous missives, she passed along Beryl's hunch that incoming prisoners to Gordon's POW camp were the primary source of information on the situation in London and the thrust of the Allies' current strategy. She imagined her information reassured camp officers that their prisoners hadn't somehow gotten access to BBC broadcasts. Jesse shared that Lieutenant Clarke worked in a private home outside the camp, believing the German censors would now know to keep a close eye on the letters the Clarkes exchanged. She hoped her latest letter cum report would forewarn the Luftwaffe that the American fliers were ramping up for something big, but she was probably too late. All of it she wrote using a code that camouflaged locations and reinforced her identity as a none-too-bright hairdresser with a meager clientele in London, a pen-pal commiserating to American friends about nothing much at all. She sealed it up, addressed it to the post office box in Iowa and mailed it off. Returning home, she watched to ensure she wasn't followed. She expected her latest contribution would earn high praise from her handlers.

Fortunately, for the Allied effort, she was mistaken.

CHAPTER FIFTEEN

The paradox of courage is that a man must be
a little careless of his life even in order to keep it.
−G. K. Chesterton

France, 1943-44

Four months before he was welcomed in the sanctuary of Holy Trinity
Church in Elsworth, Flight Sergeant Oliver Dowd fell out of the sky over
France on a moonless night, his fifteen-minute descent profoundly peaceful
after the chaotic moments that proceeded it. The flight engineer of the Avro
Lancaster, he was seated next to the pilot when flak had risen suddenly in
the night sky to tear through the side of the Lanc, a piece of metal cannon
fire embedding itself neatly into both the essential controls of the cockpit
and the pilot's neck, fatally opening his carotid artery. As the plane began an
uncontrolled descent, the wireless operator, an Australian, calmly ordered
the remaining five crew members to bail. With a cheerio and a God's speed,
he leapt into the night followed quickly by the others. Just three of them
made it to safety, landing in an open meadow close to the Belgian border:
the wireless operator, the bomb aimer, and Oliver. The gunners, the
navigator, and, of course, the pilot, were never seen again.

With France now wholly occupied by the Nazis, the men believed there
were fewer resisters with the means to get them to safety. Each flier was
equipped with an escape kit: a French passport with a fake identity, a
compass, a bar of soap, a razor, fishhooks and line, a morphine injection,
sulfanilamide tablets, Benzedrine tablets, gum, chocolate, matches, French
Francs and German marks, a page of phrases in Dutch, French, and German,

and a map of the European continent printed on a scrap of silk. These were, however, of limited use in the disorienting dark.

As the final survivor floated to earth, the two who proceeded him sprinted in his direction, madly balling up the parachutes that had saved their lives but would now give them away. They flattened themselves into the earth, waiting for the Lanc to reach her end. Within moments, they felt a menacing rumble vibrate beneath them as the plane plowed into the ground several miles away, the bombs they had hoped to drop on a German oil refinery at Regensberg detonating instead into a French wheat field. The Germans would come looking for them immediately. They lay on their bellies, heads together, devising their next move—a run to a stand of trees in the distance where they could hide. Before they could act, a wagon approached, creaking over the rutted road that bordered the meadow, a farmer out to investigate. He slowly surveyed his property for anything untoward, the horses ambling along and drawing closer, their snorts audible to men who wished they could will their bodies to sink wholly into the ground. The wagon drew to a stop. The man jumped down and darted suddenly in their direction. As he neared, each flier prepared his response: one held a razor, a second rose on his haunches to run, and Oliver, dutiful grandson of a cleric, prayed that God would send an angel. As the man approached in the darkness, he began to whistle. After a false start, the noble melody asserted itself. The *Marseillaise*. Still whistling, he crept over to the three fliers and motioned them into the back of the wagon, helping collect their chutes, then turning his rig around towards a farmhouse hardly visible in the distance. At some point, his tune transitioned into *God Save the King*.

He pulled the wagon into a barn and carefully closed the doors behind him. As he ushered the men out of the wagon, they realized their nimble, slightly built rescuer was a young woman, her hair tumbling to her shoulders as she removed her cap, eyes shining at their surprise. She directed them first to don civilian clothes from an assortment hidden between stacks of horse blankets in the mule's stall. She then brought them into the kitchen and presented her mother, who had prepared them tea along with baguettes and cups of soup. The lights remained low; just a few flickering candles on the table, away from the windows. As the men ate, the young woman nodded a goodnight and turned to leave the kitchen. Before she departed, her mother reached for her daughter's face, cupping her chin. Then she pursed her lips in a kiss in appreciation for her daughter's good work. After the meal, the woman brought them into the living area and lifted a section of floorboards. The men climbed down into the crawl space and were soon fast asleep, cocooned atop and beneath soft cotton quilts.

. . .

They awoke surprisingly refreshed, relieved to have survived the night, knowing the next part of their journey would be fraught with peril. Over a breakfast of eggs and hash, they met the farmer and his teenaged son, Gilles. Albert's English had vastly improved: two years of rescuing British and American pilots demanded it. While the English typically had a working knowledge of French, the Americans rarely did.

"We are just south of Lille," he explained, pointing out their location on their RAF maps. "We can arrange transit for you, but it has become more challenging. Until a few months ago, the Gauleiter for this region had trusted his ring of French informants to track the movement of their neighbors and to report unusual patterns. It was this group he would send out to hunt for Allied fliers when a plane went down. Would it shock you to learn the French 'helpers' proved unreliable? They would look and look and look but their luck was poor. So now, the Nazis send their own searchers and they leave no stone unturned. They cover a wide radius from the point of the crash and return to places they've already checked, hoping to catch a resister off-guard. We must stay ready. You will need to remain here for a number of weeks—perhaps longer. It will be safer when the weather turns colder. The Germans are not as fastidious in their searches when there is snow on the ground. But we will get you home."

"And what of the informants who were so terrible at informing? Are they part of this effort?" asked Oliver.

"Oh, no, no." replied Albert. "There were seven men—the mayor of the village among them. Executed by firing squad in the yard of the Catholic church."

"And yet, you are willing to do this?" asked Ryan, the bomb aimer.

"We are. Because you are willing to give your lives to restore our liberty. It is a fair exchange, no? The only difference is that you wear a uniform to signify your allegiance while we," and here he gestured to his family, "we have our allegiance engraved on our hearts."

.   .   .

That afternoon, a clanking diesel engine announced the approach of a Nazi staff car. An officer on the Gauleiter's staff stepped out, scanning the farmhouse windows, hand placed on his sidearm as he neared the front door. A junior officer trailed several paces behind. The driver remained with the car. At the familiar and foreboding sound of the engine, each member of the family moved into position. Albert and Gilles slipped silently out through the kitchen door, Gilles rubbing dirt on his tunic and the knees of his pants so it would appear he'd been hard at work all day. Albert picked up his pitchfork and positioned himself near the entrance to the barn. Ginette busied herself in the kitchen, pouring stock into her iron skillet and stirring it with a wooden spoon, placing bins of root vegetables at her side to complete the scene. Sylvi directed the dog to lie down on a specific section of the floor, then waited silently behind the door for the German's knock. Still, when his knuckles rapped on the wood, she jumped. She exhaled and exchanged a smile with her mother.

"Oui, monsieur?" she said brightly, opening the door wide to make clear she had nothing to hide.

"Good afternoon, mademoiselle," he said, sweeping into the house, eyes casting about the room. "Are you alone here?"

"She is not," said Ginette, moving into the room from the kitchen. "I am her mother. My husband and son are working in our fields. May we help you, monsieur?"

"I'm looking for information, madame, after the crash last evening of a British aircraft. We found evidence of four bodies, both in the aircraft and, not far from here, one hanging in a pine tree very close to your property. A British soldier with poor aim, apparently." He smiled at his joke. "So, there are three men unaccounted for. It is these we are looking for. We need to know what you might have seen." He moved into the center of the room, eyes continuing to scan, looking for anything out of order.

"I heard it last night!" Sylvi volunteered, one hand on her chest, the other reaching for the Offizier's arm. "It was just horribly loud and frightening. I stayed in my bed and pressed my pillow to my ears, afraid it might have been the Allies bombing us. Do you think they are, Herr Offizier?"

"Never that, mademoiselle. Not here. You are safe from the Allies. Madame, what can you tell me?"

"I must be honest, sir. These plane crashes frighten me so, that I simply stay in my bed, hoping the locks on the door will hold should an invader come to rob or rape us. Am I to understand that you wish us to involve ourselves when a plane crashes like this? We would have no weapons with which to bring any prisoners into your custody. And I would be so frightened if they intended to harm my Sylvi. I could speak with my husband, who has some farming tools we could put—"

He cut her off with an impatient wave, clarifying that he did not expect her family to take direct action, only to report anything important they had witnessed.

"Your husband, then. Where is he?"

The younger officer stayed in the house, Sylvi distracting him with questions about his work, laughing flirtatiously at his one-word responses as if he were a brilliant and witty conversationalist. Ginette walked the other man through the kitchen and out the back door to the barn, where Albert posed with his pitchfork in the hay. The Officer repeated the questions he'd asked the women, Ginette then repeating them to her ostensibly hard-of-hearing husband. Albert shook his head and pointed to his ear, saying he had not heard the crash, but he appreciated the forewarning that enemy soldiers might be in the area. The Offizier appraised him through narrowed eyes. A critical part of his success involved differentiating between harmless old men and those intent on sabotaging the Nazi war effort. In this case, he saw nothing to raise his suspicions, but this farm would remain under surveillance.

He took a quick turn through the barn, Gilles accompanying him and chattering alongside him. He informed the Offizier that he was nearing eighteen now and wondered: did that make him eligible to serve in the Wehrmacht? His facile babbling had become the quickest way to get undesirables out of their home and, indeed, after a quick perusal of the barn, the Offizier headed back to the house. They passed through the kitchen and as he walked through the living area, his gaze rested on their mongrel dog, lazing happily in the sun that fell through the window at the very spot she lay. When the man reached to give the dog a pat, she lunged, teeth bared, a furious bark followed by a low, persistent growl. The Offizier jumped in surprise.

"Non, non, Sucre! Bad dog!" Ginette exclaimed. "Gilles, you must get this animal under control before she bites someone. My apologies, Herr Offizier. She is still a pup and unpredictable with strangers."

"Yes. I see that," he responded, ruffled and annoyed. "Good day to you then." Both visitors walked quickly out the door.

Sucre listened intently to the sound of the diesel engine as it pulled away. Once she could no longer hear it—and this was minutes longer for her sensitive ears than those of her human family—she moved away from her spot on the floor to allow the floorboards to be lifted and the fliers to emerge from the dank crawl space. Gilles presented the dog with a hambone for her excellent performance.

"Good girl, Sucre. Magnifique," he said as he rubbed her ears, her fur purposely left matted because it made her look more fierce.

·   ·   ·

The Gauleiter's man returned three times that week, his suspicions never yielding the fruit he'd hoped. Had he approached in a quieter vehicle, he might have had better luck. Oliver and the two crewmen hid there six weeks, moving from hayloft to attic to crawl space to mule stall, helping muck out the barn and contributing in whatever ways they safely could to express their appreciation. On an early November morning, Albert exchanged their fake French passports for forged German-issue papers and announced they would depart the next day. Their peasant tunics exchanged for business suits, Albert buried them in the back of the hay wagon before an unfamiliar man appeared and jumped into the driver's seat. He took them south to a shack just outside Paris, where a bookish man appeared, put fedoras on their heads, handed Oliver a briefcase, and gave the others small valises.

"I am an accountant. You are my assistants. We are visiting clients in Orleans who may have to liquidate their holdings. We will travel by train from the Bréguet-Sabin station and all of you will fall asleep the minute you are seated. Nothing—and I mean nothing—shall wake you."

They climbed aboard a horse-drawn fiacre for the trip to the station, their guide reminding them to appear familiar with, not astounded by, their surroundings. What they saw was Paris subdued, bent under the weight of occupation, although the smiling German soldiers who filled the sidewalk cafés seemed not to have noticed. There were but a handful of cars on the streets, most of them belonging to the German military command since gas was unobtainable. Bicycle-taxis pedaled past them as well as an occasional bus. But the quiet of the city was unnerving. Parisians, known the world over for their cosmopolitan confidence, moved listlessly through the streets, their very postures conveying their contempt for the occupiers. As the fliers crossed the station to board their train, they assumed the same defeated torpor as the Parisians around them.

When they arrived at the Orleans station, their accountant exited the train at one door as he directed them to another, where a new guide fell in step with them as they walked, deftly guiding them out a seldom-used exit and into a waiting truck. He took them to a dilapidated barn where they abandoned their business suits for farmer's clothing. The next morning, he was gone and a young girl appeared to begin the trip southwest toward Bordeaux. They began on foot, the men wondering how she was able to discern the path through dense woods, across streams, up rocky hillocks. After three days, she left them with some bread in the chill darkness of a pine forest, walking off without a word. Hours later, a rickety cart pulled by two skinny horses arrived, the driver giving a nod to indicate the men were to ride in the back with his supplies and tools. Amid a light snowfall, this guide transported them to Bordeaux, depositing them at the banks of the

Garonne. He left several blankets to fight off the cold, instructing them not to light a fire. They were to bury the blankets under the pine needles when they departed. With the hooks and wire from their escape kits, they fished the river, catching several carp that they consumed cold and raw.

Two days later, just as the fliers were beginning to think they'd been forgotten, two young men arrived with food and warm coats. The group hiked for a day and a half into the foothills of the Pyrenees, arriving suddenly at a well-camouflaged mountain cabin. The door opened. A fire blazed in the hearth—permitted irregularly when they had a good fix on the movement of German patrols. They smelled a warm stew on the stove. But to Oliver, far more significant than any of these amenities, was the person standing at the stove stirring the stew. William Hughes, grandfather's butcher from Elsworth. He moved to speak just as Wills put down his wooden spoon and turned to greet the newest fliers he would escort into Spain. Wills' eyes registered mild alarm at seeing vicar Dowd's grandson, indicating this was no time for reunions. Wills introduced himself to the three fliers as Carlos, shaking hands with each, locking eyes with Oliver long enough for the Flight Sergeant to realize he must not speak.

After the meal, when the men had bedded down, snores resounding through the cabin, Wills inched his way to where Oliver lay, placed his hand over his mouth, and shook him gently awake. Oliver started, then recognized Will's face inches from his own, tears streaming from his eyes. "The less we say," Wills whispered, "the safer we are."

Wills handed his wedding ring to Oliver, who clenched it tightly and nodded. Soundlessly, the men embraced.

·   ·   ·

After a brutally cold hike through the Pyrenees, their escape route improvised and extended because of a suddenly closed border crossing, they arrived at a hilltop monastery. There, two Benedictine monks, one with a pistol in his cassock, brought them the final twenty miles into San Sebastián, where they found the Spanish police assiduously disinterested in them. The bribes had been paid. A British embassy attaché—in actuality, an agent with the British foreign intelligence service MI6—picked them up in an embassy car which drove them first to Madrid, then eventually to Gibraltar. There, the men, along with a dozen other escapees, climbed aboard a Dakota military transport plane that took a roundabout route back to England. And after two weeks of debriefings, followed by a week of leave during which Oliver slept a solid sixteen hours a night, he made the trip to Elsworth to see his grandparents and to hold his whispered conversation in the Holy Trinity chancel with an overjoyed Ivy.

CHAPTER SIXTEEN

War is both the product of an earlier corruption
and a producer of new corruptions.
–Lewis Mumford

Sagan, early 1944

The notion of Gordon dying when his presence offered the one pleasurable thing in Annalise's life was flatly unacceptable to her. So she resolved to make him well, even if, in doing so, she put herself at risk. It was a week after he missed his appointed day at the house before she realized he was gravely ill and several days beyond that before Reinhard reported the diagnosis of typhus as they shared breakfast.

"Have they given him Prontosil?" she asked, trying to make her question sound matter-of-fact when she well knew this drug, its infection-fighting properties discovered only a handful of years earlier, was not available to prisoners.

"And, my darling, what do you know of Prontosil? I had no idea you stayed current on available medical treatments."

"I know of it because of the children, Reinhard. Every mother who is concerned about infectious diseases of childhood followed the development of this German miracle—this wonder drug. They use it on the battlefield, I understand, and it has reduced incidents of sepsis."

"This is true, Annalise, which means we wouldn't waste it on a prisoner of war. They are not treating him. He is an English officer, remember, not a German one. They're just keeping him in the medical building until he dies."

"Reinhard, my arbor! Are you saying he will not be available to complete it?"

"Available?" Reinhard gave a laugh at her question. "Yes. It is safe to say he will be unavailable, my love, unavailable for anything at all. We will have to find you a new helper."

"But how is that fair to me," she demanded, face flushing, "when I have spent hours upon hours discussing this project with this lieutenant? Refining the design to this point? I cannot start over with anyone else, Reinhard. I will not."

He did not like her tone, her overly agitated demeanor. Her melodramatics, he was familiar with, but this was different. She displayed a genuine, frantic concern that was improper. He heard it in the pitch of her voice, saw the alarm on her face. Her interest in the Englishman seemed to extend beyond his utility as a handyman for her project. As he formulated the words to confront her with this, to accuse her of being inappropriate and regain control of the direction of this conversation, she switched tactics, making this a question not of her power but of his.

"Reinhard," she asked evenly, "Do you mean to say, as the commandant of this Stalag, you are unable to get him medication to make him well?"

The camp commandant blanched at the way she said "unable"—her over-articulation that seemed to signify an inalterable failing, a near-criminal act. Rather than risk her thinking him impotent, he assured her he could secure whatever he needed with a snap of his fingers. Anything.

"Then I trust you will do it, Reinhard, not for the *Kriegie*, of course, but because the *Kriegie* is useful to me, your wife, and therefore useful to you." She smiled, but it was forced and pinched, an effort to camouflage intense emotion. She transitioned swiftly to a new topic—yet another discussion of Clara's shortcomings—the gummy quality of the potatoes she had prepared. What could Annalise possibly do to improve the woman's skills? As she continued to talk, slipping casually from one thing to the next, her husband had a grave, uneasy sense that there was more at stake than the arbor. Well, fine, he thought. Perhaps the lieutenant will recover and complete this project—but after that, he need not return to this house.

That night, Annalise approached their lovemaking with such passionate enthusiasm that Reinhard concluded he had misjudged her intentions. She was kind, that's all, and simply wished that an unfortunate man not die prematurely when there were means to save him. That was surely her position, he believed, that and her wish to complete this new garden piece about which she was so enamored. He reached this conclusion because, in his pride, he simply could not conceive that the sexual aggressiveness and willingness his young, eager wife directed toward him could be contrived. His failure of imagination would prove costly.

· · · ·

The following day, Annalise called the driver to take her to the camp, where she slipped inside the medical building to see Gordon's condition for herself. He lay completely still, his skin hot and dry, the rash profuse. She asked the nurse if she had given him the medication the commandant had authorized.

"Not yet, ma'am. We attend to the patients on a schedule and we have..."

Annalise exploded in fury. "You have purposely ignored an order from the commandant?" she spat. "How dare you? Where is your supervisor?"

"Frau Schröder," the woman sputtered, "I am only an aide and I do as I'm directed. I meant no disrespect."

"Bring the medication now, so I may be assured this man is being treated as my husband ordered. If he dies, it will be due to your insubordination."

The woman ran to get the head nurse, terrified and confused at the Frau's sudden anger. This was a prisoner. Prisoners died every day. Why was this one getting unusual consideration? Usually, the staff was informed why a prisoner merited special treatment.

Within twenty-four hours of the first infusion, Gordon opened his eyes and gestured that he needed some water. Annalise was unsure if he realized it was she who gave it to him, she who cooled his face with a wet cloth. The next day, his fever broke, the rash receded, and the medical staff determined he had a good chance of survival. Two days after that, Annalise returned with soft bread Clara had baked for him, along with sweet fig preserves. She was so relieved to see Gordon's smile, the color beginning to return to his face, that she ignored the comments from the medical staff, who told her directly that her interference was irregular and unwelcome. Some quietly discussed how best to report her, but the fact that her husband ran the camp made it especially complicated. She would have time to repair all this later, she decided, once this crisis had truly passed. Gordon was returning to her. That's what mattered. She sat at his bedside and watched him sleep, the miracle of his recovery convincing her that he returned the feelings she had developed for him. He must, she thought. He has responded to every small gesture. This is evidence of his regard for me. And believing there was very little to tie him to his home country, believing they had formed a bond that transcended countries and roles and allegiances, she began to daydream a life in which he stayed with her—always—even if they both had to pay a high cost.

The next week, she brought fruit—a rare commodity—along with bread and three bottles of splendid French wine to the staff of the medical building, saying she owed them an apology. As she explained it, the ill English prisoner was halfway through a vital project at the commandant's home and had left the place torn apart and in pieces. She had desperately needed the prisoner to return to untangle it all and put things back together, her anger at him causing her to become overwrought at the notion of having to find another work detail to finish this important project in advance of a big event she was soon to host. She was so very sorry and begged them to forgive her childish tantrum. She found them happy to do just that. And while they were enjoying the warm bread and toasting one another with the lovely Bordeaux, Annalise managed to insert a card into a waiting stack of documents that would soon be sent through the post. They comprised the latest tally of men who had been treated in the medical building, details of which were sent every three months to the International Red Cross. The card had formerly indicated that Gordon S. Clarke had received a diagnosis of typhus, had recovered, and would be returned to the general POW population. But with Annalise's slight revisions, the card now indicated that Gordon had succumbed to his infection. That evening, the same very nursing aide whom Annalise had blasted for not quickly administering

Gordon's antibiotic shuffled through the cards, ostensibly reviewing them for error. But after a long day—many long days—her eyes spotted no mistakes.

.   .   .

Fully two months after he'd fallen ill, Gordon returned to the commandant's home. Hearing the car pull into the drive, Clara met him at the garden gate, hands clasped in front of her, smile wide. As Friedrich walked ahead toward the guest house, where he presumed Gordon would begin the day, she whispered that she and Helene considered Gordon's recovery an answer to their prayers. Gordon squeezed her hand in thanks and followed Friedrich up the stairs, eager for his first bath in more than two months. He returned to the kitchen where he handed his uniform over for washing. Clara, Helene, and Friedrich then departed for the dining room, saying Frau Schröder would be down shortly, Clara saying pointedly that she had a new bread recipe she intended to prepare for him in the coming days.

Annalise appeared silently at the kitchen threshold. Her hair fell down around her shoulders, blonde strands against a powder blue dress that matched her eyes. She had taken pains to prepare for his return.

"You're here," she said simply, the words catching in her throat.

"I am, ma'am. That I am."

"Thank God it worked," she continued.

"Worked Frau Schröder?" he asked quizzically. "I'm not sure I know what you mean."

"The medicine that cured you. Thank goodness they could secure it for you and that the treatment was successful, Lieutenant."

"Was this something out of the ordinary protocol, Frau Schröder? Did the commandant keep you apprised of what was happening?"

At this, she gave a rueful laugh, disappointed that he was unaware of how she had saved him.

"I insisted Reinhard administer you Prontosil. It is a drug produced here in Germany, grown from a fungus, that reverses infection. That is what cured you. You were near death when I intervened."

And then he remembered, realizing that it was indeed her voice he had heard berating the workers in the medical building, that it was she he had smelled as he lay near death. He owed her his life.

"My deepest gratitude, Frau Schröder," he said finally. "I am in your debt."

Later that afternoon, Annalise followed Gordon as he returned to the car for the trip back to camp. As he climbed in the back seat, he did not see the driver hand Annalise a packet of envelopes—just one or two this time. There would surely be more.

. . .

By spring, the cement was poured and the posts were planed smooth, installed with the intricate trellis above. Annalise had even ordered the vines she planned to train up and over the top. They would be shipped in from Spain, and she hoped they would do well in Germany's cooler climate. She was delighted with the result and grateful to both her husband and the lieutenant for seeing the project through. All would be ready for the party she would host in several weeks' time for the Waffen-SS officers arriving to review camp operations. They would be impressed with the outdoor elegance she had introduced; it would reflect well on her husband. With the arbor completed, Annalise asked Gordon to assist with planting some new annuals to give the garden early color. She then requested he attend to smaller projects around the house—the warped floorboards in the guest house, the water stain that had appeared in the kitchen ceiling, the re-hanging of drapery rods that had come loose from the plaster. Reinhard did not object, finding her ongoing use of the POW—the evident distance between them and the absolute command he observed her exercise over him—satisfying. She required him to bathe as one did a child and made him follow her around the house, attending to this and that like a puppy. "The feckless British," he observed to Friedrich. "Chamberlains, all of them."

Gordon worked one morning on the upper floor of the guest house, late spring sunshine streaming through the many windows, the sparrows completing their morning trills as the sun moved higher in the sky. His strength and stamina had returned, aided by the fruit and meats and breads Clara and Annalise continued to provide. His hair had begun to grow again and his nails had lost their yellow cast. As he worked, enjoying the warmth on his arms and face, Annalise appeared, waiting quietly, watching him from the door frame until he took notice of her. He was surprised that she was alone: Friedrich did not appear behind her to pace the hallway, as had become his custom.

"Just a few more minutes of sanding this window frame, ma'am, and then I'll need to paint it. After that, you'll be able to open and close it as necessary to move air through these rooms." He turned back to his work.

She approached, arms crossed, standing close behind him, observing aloud that he had not yet made use of the bath.

"Apologies, Frau Schröder. I had expected to stay out of your way today and spend my time finishing this. But certainly, I do not wish to offend you. If you'll excuse me."

"Danke, Lieutenant. We shall meet after you're finished. Be quick." Their eyes did not meet.

Gordon entered the bathroom and closed the door, heartbeat accelerating, a vague sense of anxiety settling in his gut. On the vanity had been laid a razor, cup and brush for lathering, items he had not seen in the guest house bathroom before this day—a silent request from the lady of the house. He obliged, taking care to smooth the stubble on his face, working slowly so as not to cut himself and leave drops of his blood on the towel or the tile. He stepped into the warm bathtub and did not rush, despite her admonition to hurry. He needed time to consider the contest that lay before him. Gordon soaped his body, defined musculature having returned to his chest and arms because of the physical work that filled his days and the fortifying provisions Annalise afforded him. She seemed determined to do this. For months now, they'd engaged in a delicate dance, she taking the lead, endeavoring to camouflage their growing intimacy, the boundaries they no longer observed, and probably failing. Clara and Helene, he didn't worry about. But a word to the commandant from Friedrich or an observation shared by the driver would have grave consequences. But Annalise seemed determined to press down this path.

A towel wrapped at his waist, he returned to the bedroom where, as he expected, Annalise waited. Gordon held no power in this moment and knew that whatever happened next would proceed only on her terms, not his. He could protest, finally giving a name to what had been developing between them over these weeks and months. But if he had misread all this—if it was not sexual desire but a trap she'd set, a bit of fun to alleviate the humdrum and not her plan to move into the narrative he expected—she could summon Friedrich instantly and construct another story, a plausible story with an allegation that could imperil his life. He waited, head bowed.

"Lieutenant—Gordon—Friedrich has been summoned back to the camp," she said. Her eyes, unblinking and vulnerable, met his. "Clara and Helene have gone to market for last-minute things for tonight's supper. There is no one else here." She stepped back several paces, feeling with a trembling hand for the bed. She sat.

"This is dangerous for me, Frau Schröder, being alone with you."

"I have notified my husband you are ill—a vestige of the typhus. I have told him you are indisposed and therefore not in need of an armed guard. He believes you are shut away here in our guest house, sleeping, weak with fever."

"And how long am I to be ill, Frau?"

"The entire day, Lieutenant. Until the driver returns at dusk." She heaved a deep sigh, gathering herself for what she planned to say. "Lieutenant—Gordon—would you say you and I have become friends? It feels artificial that I continue to call you lieutenant, after all the time we have spent together, all our lovely conversations. They have meant a great deal to me. Do you agree? Have we not created a kinship? Despite the difficult circumstance, I'm sure you would say that I have been kind, yes? With the intervention for your medical care, food that has nourished you and..." she waved a hand through the air "... all these make-believe projects in the house and the garden that I have devised to keep you here—away from that godforsaken camp. And now, this free time I have found for you."

Gordon stood unmoving, still clutching the towel, runnels of water falling from the hair at his neck, dampening his torso and back.

"You have been more than kind, Frau. You have made these months bearable for me. You have. You restored my health and my sanity—and the health of other POWs, if I might say so—with your generosity. I am grateful for your protection."

"Then for me—if you are grateful—I would have a different request today. One that goes beyond protection, as you call it. Would you, I mean, I would like to ask—could you consent to remove that towel for me? That is, if you wish it too."

He stood frozen for a moment, then nodded, eyes locked intensely on hers. She leaned toward him and pulled his hand so the towel fell. Her eyes fell on his clean, naked body and she reached for him. He moved over her on the bed, pulling her free from her sweater and skirt, reaching at last for the body she had used to tease him from the moment they met. He covered her neck and chest and arms with his mouth, inhaling her strong, musky scent, forgetting she was his enemy, breathing her name for the first time, reciting it again and again. With that, she was unleashed, pinning him on his back, sitting astride him, eyes fixed on his, her straight pale hair hanging like a curtain, swinging as she moved.

Afterwards, they lay intertwined, listening to the soft rustle of the leaves outside the open window, Annalise curled under his arm, nestled into his side, hand on his chest.

"It is me now, Gordon, who is the prisoner," she whispered, moving her hand down the length of his stomach. "But there is something I must ask you, now that we have become closer: who is it you write to in London if, as you say, you suffered a tragic end to your love affair?"

He stilled, holding his breath to think. Of course, they'd been reading his letters home, gathering what facts they could about him. His duties had continued here, so clearly, they had discovered nothing disqualifying. How else to explain the wide freedoms he enjoyed and Annalise's determination to assign him this latest household duty—to bed her under her husband's nose? He reached his free arm around her, cupping her cheek, kissing the top of her golden head.

"She's no one, really. A wartime marriage that will not last, so it did not seem important to share. I write only to get news of people we know, and of home. She is no more than a friend who had the misfortune of finding me after my ill-fated affair."

Annalise looked him hard in the eye. "May it be as you describe," she said. "We do not need additional complications."

"Annalise," he said. "Am I to understand you want to pursue an affair? Despite the risks? Friedrich and the household staff will surely notice. I am a dead man if we're discovered. And what would happen to you? Even if your husband wanted to protect you, the SS could execute you as a spy."

"Don't you think I've considered this over your many months here?" she asked. "This was hardly an impulsive act on my part. It is not simply that I have tired of my husband. I am fascinated by you—by your artistic gifts, your love of music, the way you attend to my point of view in any number of languages. And yes, your physical attributes. I enjoy this especially. I have tired of this life, Gordon, this all-consuming loyalty to the Reich by which my husband and all others are measured. It has begun to exhaust us all and more than that, it has grown dangerous, even to me and Reinhard. Thousand-year Reich? Germany could not even beat back the Russians. There is talk the Americans will invade and we may not prevail. I do not intend to wait for them to find me here when that happens."

He looked at her with concern. "Annalise," he began and upon hearing her name on his lips—something she had longed for and waited so many months to hear—she cut off their discussion, reaching for him again and finding him ready for her.

"I wish we could go away," she whispered, hips moving, her breath warm over his face, "that you and I could leave all this and start again."

"Yes," he agreed. "We could go away."

CHAPTER SEVENTEEN

A little truth helps the lie go down.
–Italian proverb

London, early 1944

It did not require much effort to tidy Jesse's beauty shop. With so little traffic, she found herself sweeping, then sweeping again to clear the tile floor of non-existent hair shorn from non-existent customers. She felt it important to look busy, to behave as if the salon were a viable concern. Cash from the *Abwehr* kept her bills paid, little bundles wrapped and dropped at intervals in a hedgerow outside the Tube station, made to look like a stack of newspapers. She had failed to pick up just one bundle in the past two years, believing some lucky person had stumbled upon her payment. Now she went to the Tube station at the beginning of each pickup window to make sure it didn't happen again.

The assessment of her family in Scotland notwithstanding, Jesse had not made an ill-advised marriage to an introverted Teutonic bookkeeper. In fact, she had not made a marriage at all, although she hoped to. She had met Hans while on holiday in Munich, found him magnetic and fascinating in ways Scottish men were not, and quickly fell under his influence. They had shared a glorious holiday trip through Bavaria, the birthplace of the National Socialist Party, where Hans introduced her to his bright, passionate friends who understood the world far better than she. They welcomed her into their world, sharing the burgeoning vision of Germany reborn.

In her, Hans found the ideal mix of gullibility and potential: she believed he loved her and her background could be of use once Germany asserted itself across Europe. Jesse telegrammed her parents just as Hitler was ascending to the Chancellorship and consolidating his power, saying she had found work in Germany and was staying: she was learning to cut hair. Jesse was not a true believer in the Nazi regime, but she did believe in Hans, who had convinced her she held his heart. When he outlined a plan that would involve her, as their other friends were doing, collecting intelligence to protect the Party, she promised to do whatever he asked for the good of Germany. She did not concern herself with the younger women in their circle with whom Hans met late into the night. Operatives, all of them, he assured her. These were business meetings only.

Once Britain declared war, Hans informed her she was returning to the U.K., with the cover story that her husband had died and that she had suffered because of rumors of Jewish ancestry. Initially, she felt utterly betrayed: she would sooner die than return to Scotland without him. But once she learned she would be furnished with a quaint little salon in London close to Covent Garden, she saw the possibilities. She intended to demonstrate her loyalty through her work here, believing it would one day result in a real marriage proposal. Once Germany won the war, she envisioned her triumphant return to an indebted Hans. Then their life would truly begin.

What she couldn't know was that with the success of the code-breakers over at Bletchley Park, who could decipher encoded German messages via their Enigma machine, her activities were well known to MI5, Britain's domestic intelligence agency. The little drips and drabs of information she'd penned never made it to the post office box in Iowa, USA: the Americans had made quick work dismantling that clutch of spies long before Pearl Harbor, so Jesse's letters were regularly intercepted, then reviewed by German agents who had been turned and were now assisting MI5 in order to save their necks. Jesse's lack of skill with following the code books often exhausted the translators, who were never sure if they had something consequential or useless before them. Partly out of amusement, and, some said, for the sake of the handful of women who still frequented her salon, MI5 did not arrest her immediately, but continued to leave her little packets of money outside the Tube station and surveil her in the event she turned up something important, even responding on occasion with a letter meant to look like it came from her contact in America. Her visits with Beryl had been closely observed and had Jack not stepped forward to confess he'd accidentally let strategic information slip to a British civilian, he might well have spent the rest of the war locked up under suspicion as an enemy agent.

After Jesse expressed a too-avid interest in his upcoming assignments, Jack met with his commanding officer and the combat intelligence officer at Kimbolton. The intel officer had leaned on him hard about his undisciplined talk and the lives it could cost. Operation Argument—Big Week—aimed to take out the German aircraft industry in six successive days of unrelenting fury. What the hell had he been doing talking about it? The losses of Allied men and aircraft would be bad enough without Jack giving the Germans forewarning. He attempted without success to explain the extenuating circumstances—the grief that proved disorienting to both Beryl and himself. His C.O. confined him to base until such time the damage from his disclosure was understood and contained. He was to have no contact with Beryl or the English children who frequented Kimbolton. The violation was a serious one, said his superior, not one he would expect an officer like Jack to commit. The intel officer then sent the information up the chain to American then British intelligence who examined it, then acted. When Jesse sent word to the Iowans of "something big" commencing in mid-February 1944, she had signed her own arrest warrant. It was time to shut her down.

·   ·   ·

As she leaned on her broom, Jesse's thoughts ran to the day she would see Hans again: she believed it was drawing closer—the Brits couldn't even figure out how to get across the Channel and would surely capitulate soon. Her contact with Hans over the past three years had been limited, just a line or two relayed by her Iowa "friends" urging her to continue her good work. How she had wished for a more intimate message, one that assured her he was well and still cared for her.

The bell on the door jangled and a man unfamiliar to her entered the salon.

"Afternoon, sir. Hello to you. So very sorry but we don't cut gentlemen's hair. There's a barber 'round that corner who's open until late today, so you can try there."

"Thanks awfully, but I won't be needing a haircut," said the man, his eyes locked on her in a way she found deeply uncomfortable.

"This is a salon for ladies, sir, so I'm sorry I won't be able to do the shampoo for ya either," responded Jesse, who did not appreciate the way this stranger leaned over her reception desk, seeming to scan the papers laid there. "If there won't be anything else then, sir, I'll be locking the door, so if you'll be off then..."

"Miss Jordan, it's not a hair washing I need either. A mutual friend suggested I come by and meet you. I understand you are a refugee of sorts, forced to leave Germany because of your Jewish heritage?"

Jesse's mouth opened as if she intended to speak, the patches of rosacea on her checks burning as her alarm grew. Mutual friend? She had no real friends in London, just scant customers with whom she pushed her cover story. Who could have sent this man to her? Was he her handler? She had no clear sense if he was friend or enemy. Stick to your story, she reminded herself. Play the part.

"Well, yes, no, although it's not true," she sputtered. "There were those saying that... back in Munich... and, well, after my husband died with all that going on there, I thought it best to return here and stay clear of any issues involving, you know, all of that."

"Wise decision. And how is your dead husband, Hans? In Berlin, now, right? Although, I guess more correctly I should say your friend Hans, since you never actually married, and he remains, shall we say, active with any number of women of his choosing. Isn't that so?" The man smiled, in no hurry for her reply.

Color drained from her face. "I'm not sure what you mean. My husband was a bookkeeper who passed away. I am not married now." Jesse gripped the broom, wondering in a panic if she was strong enough to draw it up quickly and press it into the man's windpipe before he seized her.

"Indeed, you're not, nor have you ever been," said the man, now approaching her and reaching for something in his pocket. "Miss Jordan, I am arresting you on suspicion of espionage..."

And at this, Jesse threw her broom in his general direction and darted towards the back door of the salon where two other men waited, MI5 agents all, to end Jesse's amateurish foray into espionage. They seized her and drew her arms to her back to place her in handcuffs.

"I don't know what you're talking about!" she shrieked. "I am a hairdresser! Nothing more! Leave me be now! Let go of me, I say."

"We shall do no such thing," said the first man. "These kind gentlemen are taking you off to Scotland Yard for a little chat. I shall place a sign in the window to say you are no longer in business—wartime hardship and all that. Ah, look. Not even a quid in the cash drawer. How in the world were you making ends meet?"

• • •

On February 20, 1944, more than one thousand bombers and nearly as many fighter planes lifted off from airfields across East Anglia to drive the Luftwaffe from the skies over Europe. Jack and Buck piloted the Gator that first day and would fly two more missions before the assault concluded. Their targets were the massive aircraft factories, assembly, and component plants spread across the Reich. While Allied losses were heavy, the fervent hope was that the pounding they inflicted for those six days would clear the skies of German aircraft, making possible an Allied invasion. While there had been no official announcement, of course, that this colossal attack was coming, the British whispered among themselves that something must be up because there were so few Americans on the streets: the country had grown altogether quiet because every airman and ground crewman, it seemed, was either preparing for a mission, getting briefed on a mission, or recovering from a mission and preparing for the next one. Where Londoners once commiserated over the ill-mannered rubes who had descended so loudly, so conspicuously, on their mannered city barely two years ago, they now fretted over these boys—their Yanks—and prayed for their safety.

At Jack's persistent request, his combat intelligence officer had finally relayed a message to Beryl at the hospital, saying Jack would be out of contact for the next number of weeks, regretting that he could not be more available to her under the circumstances. A week after she received the news from the War Office, she returned to work, finding the familiar smells and sounds and activity soothed her, cueing her to the pattern of her duties. With Jack indisposed, she had delayed plans to go to Elsworth and deliver the news of Gordon's death to Colin. Every day her son lived free of the eventual grief to come was her gift to him. Ignorance is bliss, the saying went, and in this case, she wished she, too, were ignorant.

A month later, Beryl made her way home from work, preoccupied as she always was, hardly noticing the hint of spring that made her walk far more pleasant. It occurred to her she had not seen Jesse since that afternoon she had appeared while Jack was at the flat. She counted back to estimate how many weeks it had been. Five—no, a bit more, she decided. Jesse had promised to check on Beryl once Jack returned to base, but had not done so. It had been a relief to Beryl, actually, who did not consider Jesse a close friend. Their acquaintance spanned only a few years. But the war had forced casual friendships into something much more intense, as people of all backgrounds found themselves side by side in the Tube station, clutching perfect strangers during air raids, hailing them as dearest friends the next time they met because of what they had survived together. She and Jesse had endured the destruction of Densmore's, the constant threat of attack, and the daily privation of their circumstances. And, of course, taming Beryl's hair had been Jesse's ongoing challenge. She prepared herself to stop by the shop and field the questions about Gordon that Jesse would no doubt pose.

But there, on the inside window, was a little sign indicating the salon had closed down. It was dated six weeks earlier. How had she not noticed this? Poor Jesse, having to close her doors for lack of business. As she turned to cross the street and enter her flat, she could not have noticed the man watching her from the window of Jesse's tiny sitting room just above the salon.

· · ·

Knowing Jesse as he did, Hans should have foreseen, perhaps, that her earnest but inept espionage would not only fail to elucidate British war plans for the Nazis but accomplish precisely the opposite. The thing had gone wrong fairly early: once England declared war on Germany, every piece of international mail—incoming and outgoing—underwent thorough scrutiny, so he was not surprised her communications ceased soon after the Battle of Britain began. He knew she was limited, but his handlers insisted Hans deploy her in the U.K. in the event she could unearth worthwhile tidbits. He was only too happy to comply with this order as several years of playacting romantic interest while he groomed her had worn on him. What Hans could not know was that Jesse had indeed produced actionable intelligence—for the Allies. Censors passed the story up the line of the British lieutenant regularly working in the home of a Nazi colonel, presumably with access to all the resources contained therein. Thanks to Jesse's good work, Polish paratroops serving with the RAF, who now regularly dropped behind the lines to distribute information and supplies, assist evacuees through the escape lines, and sabotage German transportation and communication, were instructed to make contact with this lieutenant. Had Jesse been working for the British, MI5 agents concluded, she might deserve a commendation for the actionable intelligence she passed along. Instead, she remained jailed, piteously pleading that this was a mistake: she was a simple Scottish hairdresser who had done nothing wrong. As time wore on and the agents shared information with her on Hans' activities in Germany, she came to understand she had indeed done something very, very wrong: it was trusting a liar like Hans who had used her, trading on her love which he did not reciprocate.

CHAPTER EIGHTEEN

The wise man does not expose himself needlessly to danger,
since there are few things for which he cares sufficiently;
but he is willing, in great crises, to give even his life—knowing that under
certain conditions it is not worthwhile to live.
–Aristotle

Occupied France

It is an odd thing, how time passes.

There are the joyous, gossamer moments that hurtle past, that cannot be grasped or gripped or held still, their beauty and bliss replayed and savored, again and again, but only in memory.

And the stunningly painful passages, when the debilitating burden of loss is so grave that time freezes, refusing to advance, the forfeiture of the beloved clouding the present, heavy and dark.

Then there is the routine of life; hectic, over-filled days that become weeks, then months—how did it get to be summer already? Where did autumn go?—prompting the sudden realization that this thing or the other was never finished, despite the best of intentions, provoking the blithely repeated question: where did the time go? This explains in a fair way why a particular wall never does get painted and why the crewelwork for the pillow cover is interminably set aside. It also accounts in part for why Lieutenant William Hughes had not yet come home. With so much to do, he never seemed to get around to it.

It wasn't that Wills intended to live four, five years in hiding, working with the Resistance, shepherding others to freedom but living apart from his own wife and son. Like many, he had expected the Allies to draw things to a quick conclusion. But they had not, and day stretched into week and then month and then ultimately, years. From his earliest days in hiding when he resolved he must live out his gratitude for all Albert's family had done for him, he had expected that he, eventually, would be among those walking to freedom after the next rescue. Or the next. Or the one after that. He had access to forged documents that could protect him and his French had improved dramatically. But he felt himself essential here, skilled and equipped for the rigorous trip across the mountains, his butcher training always put to good use to trap and prepare game to serve the travelers. He knew how to read the signs—when the German shifted their surveillance sequences to try to find escapees. The British Special Operations Executive airdropped supplies and agents with regularity and as a key operative along this portion of the escape route, and like all leaders consumed and gratified by demanding work, Wills found himself unable to relinquish command to someone else. Many of the courageous guerrilla partisans—the Maquis— had given their lives to the effort, some making only a tiny, fatal slip. Fatigue usually played a part, instincts and intuition dulled just enough that key signs were missed. One fighter met two German soldiers dressed as American fliers at Dax. He fed and resupplied them and in return, they broke his neck as he slept, the three Brits in the group waking to the struggle and fleeing into the woods. A teenage boy working the line learned the story when he recovered the Brits hiding miles off course. Each exposure meant an entire rework of the escape lines, which increased the danger and created more room for missteps. With young Frenchmen and women—children, really, as some were young teens—continuing to place themselves at risk, Wills could not see his way to abandoning the work. Nor could he risk exposing his true identity or his whereabouts without endangering those with whom he worked. But at least now, Ivy knew he lived.

While escorting the fliers presented certain challenges—the Americans often tried to direct the whole business, questioning each stop, each fork in the road, always believing they could enhance the plan—the Jewish families gave Wills the most sleepless nights. Most were French Jews who realized too late their French citizenship would not protect them. By the time they found their way to the underground network and those who would help them escape, they were badly weakened after months in hiding with limited food, no medical care. He had buried more than one during the crossing, believing that they allowed themselves to die once they recognized their children were steps from freedom and would survive. Their children were often frail, docile, and worried when they deserved to be rambunctious and curious, normal children living free and safe lives. They bore the emotional cost of leaving behind grandparents who were too old or too ill to flee, who mistakenly believed the Germans would have no interest in old people minding their own business. Many of these children, Wills hauled over his shoulder to carry across the mountains, depositing them at the monastery where they were fed and restored, the monks giving over their small stone chapel for Shabbat services, the Benedictines themselves reading from the Torah they now kept alongside their Bible. Wills had attended more than one of these services, heartened when he saw the haunted look in the children's eyes change to recognition as they heard the cantor begin the familiar melody. It was this Wills found impossible to abandon. Would these souls survive if he were not doing this work?

While he had not seen them in over a year now, he knew Albert, Ginette, and their children continued offering the aid that started with Wills' accidental escape. He'd heard snippets of conversation of more recent escapees, which assured him the family had not been compromised. Sylvi had moved off the farm and ran lines below Orleans. Wills had encountered her a handful of times and found her nearly unrecognizable from her teenaged self: black beret, styled hair, her body fit and strong, her ability to transform herself proving indispensable to the Maquis. A hat, a scarf, glasses, a man's jacket and shoes or a woman's—she could come across variously as a teenage boy, a thirty-something farmhand, or a pubescent girl. When her work took her into cities, she took on the style of an office worker, too busy with her own concerns to trouble herself with whatever the Germans were doing. Head high, tote basket in her hand, false papers sewed into the lining, she marched escapees into safe houses in plain sight of the occupiers. She had dreamt of a life more varied, more interesting than the one she led on the farm. She could not have imagined she would inhabit a world so fraught with risk, or that she would grow so brave and resilient.

Wills had spotted her some months earlier in Toulouse. He was there to ferry explosives his compatriots would use to sabotage German supply lines to the coast. He had stopped in a café and there she sat, this time, a demure French schoolgirl, her algèbre textbook posed before her. Taking a table next to her, Wills dropped his handkerchief and watched it settle at her feet. She picked it up and extended her hand to return it. Wills gripped her hand tightly and looked her in the eye.

"Merci. Merci beaucoup pour tout. Je ne suis rien sans ton aide." Thank you. Thank you for all you have done. I could not have done it without you.

She allowed herself a flicker of a smile. "Bien sûr, monsieur. Tu parles bien français."

"Merci," he responded. "Dear friends devoted many hours to helping me learn."

CHAPTER NINETEEN

If you tell a big enough lie and tell it frequently enough, it will be believed.
–Adolph Hitler

Sagan, 1944

The night of her much-anticipated party in late spring, Reinhard found Annalise especially happy, her contented movements almost feline as she glided into her glimmering gold gown, strapless and tight through her chest and hips. Her toenails painted a festive red, she pointed them, flexing her calves, as she stepped into peep-toe pumps. With Helene's help, Annalise had pulled her hair into a low and rather complicated bun, with thin braids weaving through it, a gardenia tucked at the center, and the sides rolled toward her face in the way of American film stars whose pictures she'd seen. She had neglected, apparently, to read the English captions of those photos that identified that particular hairdo a Victory Roll, as in victory over Germany.

"You are enchanting," Reinhard said, coming up behind her, wrapping a strong hand around the back of her neck and massaging languidly, inhaling the scent of the gardenia. "Perhaps we can delay our appearance by just a few minutes, provided we can slide that dress up enough for..."

She waved a hand—a dismissive gesture she relied on more and more that he was growing to despise.

"That would be nice, Reinhard, but you know I have much to do to ensure we are ready to receive our guests. So," and here she swept by him and moved toward the stairs, "permit me."

Nice? He repeated to himself. Nice? Her words sounded reasonable and polite, but the rebuff was pointed. Rude, in a tone he found unacceptable. He stared at her back, her narrow waist, the bare shoulders as she hurried down the staircase, her mind on other things. Where had her ardor gone? Was she impatient with him particularly, or was it just this ridiculous party preoccupying her? Either way, he would have her to himself later. He would insist on it, reminding her such things were his decision, not hers.

.   .   .

The garden and *Terrasse* were as visually stunning as Annalise had hoped, the lights strung over the arbor giving it a magical, ethereal look, worlds away from the prison camp just a few miles away, the death camps across the Reich, and the theatres of war soon to encroach. The flowers and shrubs had cooperated, many at the peak of bloom thanks to Gordon's careful cultivation over the past number of weeks. As the guests arrived, Clara and Helene poured drinks and offered hors d'oeuvres (that were to have included Russian caviar until circumstances prevented its acquisition), circulating through the party picking up snatches of conversation they were not meant to hear. Despite the live music, the abundant liquor, and the expertly prepared food, many of the Heer and Waffen-SS officers seemed distracted, even grim-faced. The word the women heard most often: invasion. As much as they wished they could ask a few clarifying questions, they kept moving, affecting disinterest. As Helene pretended to tidy up the bar, she strained to hear two Heer officers, both colonels, whisper concern over some of Hitler's recent decisions, one tossing out his comments between long drafts of whiskey and the other speaking quietly but emphatically out of the side of his mouth, a task especially difficult given the amount of liquor he had consumed. They spoke out of the presence of the two guests of honor, Reichsführer Himmler and Minister of Propaganda Goebbels, who both seemed enthusiastic in their enjoyment of the evening, Himmler, squinting through his thick glasses as he offered a few too many toasts to the Führer.

The Reichsführer had brought the Schröders several cases of French wine—bottles of Bordeaux, Burgundy, even some Champagne—a curated assortment from the well-appointed wine cellar of the Berchtesgaden. He selected one for Clara to uncork and pour for him immediately, Annalise silently communicating to her cook to hide the rest away. No point in wasting wine of this caliber on guests whose speech was already beginning to slur.

The guests of honor did not profess any concern about the status of the war and Goebbels, whose wife, Marta, was not present, managed more than once to sidle up to Annalise and place a hand low on her back—too low— as he inquired about her children, life in Sagan, the provenance of the beautifully lit arbor, how her parents were faring in Berlin. He was known for his sybaritic appetites and his many affairs, and while Annalise had no interest in being counted among them, she would do nothing that could harm her husband's prospects. Ensuring his superiors thought well of Reinhard was the reason she staged this party. At least, that was what she told herself. As they stood side by side listening to the string quartet, the Minister of Propaganda slid his hand slowly down the small of her back to her backside, resting his hand there before massaging her, the pressure growing progressively more intense. She neither responded nor resisted, which had the effect of encouraging him to step a hair closer, wrap his arm low on her hip, and press himself into her.

"Why, Minister," she said, turning demurely toward him, whispering over her shoulder to draw his face to hers. "It has been a very long time then, since you've been home to see your wife? I thrill over the notion that I remind you of her." She leaned in, her eyes lingering on his lips. "Thank you for this kindness. Now, please excuse me as I must see to my other guests. Heil Hitler." And giving an enigmatic smile that an overconfident man might interpret as genuine delight at his touch, she disappeared into the house. He would think the door was still open; she would keep herself out of his reach for the remainder of the night.

Traveling from one conversation circle to another, Annalise listened as if every shopworn story and oft-told joke dazzled and delighted her. She described for her guests the building of the arbor, attributing the construction to a work detail, rather than revealing a single POW had completed it. She deflected compliments about the design, the intricate woodwork, the fragrant vines that intertwined it, while still managing to take a bit of credit for it. As she sipped her Riesling, flirting with high-ranking officers, disarming their wives by complimenting their gowns and hairstyles, she thought suddenly of Gordon—his tall, taut physique, his beautifully lean face—and wished the world were different somehow and that he could be the handsome man at her side, the one with whom she slept at the end of this evening. She felt pressed between two visions of her future. One, she was inhabiting in this moment as the beautiful, educated wife of a Nazi officer, a man poised for widening power and influence once the war was won. The other—a life with an artistic, far more intriguing man who treated her as his equal and whose mere presence caused her heartbeat to quicken. She had spent many hours contemplating which future would serve her best, which would offer the greater advantage—social, personal, sexual—that she believed essential to a fully satisfying life. She had not worked out where her children fit into an alternative picture.

"How long now, Frau Schröder?"

She missed her guest's question while lost in her reverie.

"My apologies, Oberst, I was watching to ensure my staff is attending properly to the needs of the Reichsführer. And yes, now he seems satisfied—there's a drink in his hand. Again, your question?"

"How long have you lived in this splendid home?" the colonel repeated.

"We arrived in 1940, but there was truly so much to do to get the property in hand. Jews inhabited it before, you know, so there were things we needed to dispose of. Of course, we had to clean absolutely everything. I've had a constant stream of workers here to address this and that, make repairs. This is our very first outdoor party and do you know, I had wanted to host a gathering from the very first moment I arrived? But it took me four years!"

Her admirers laughed indulgently, assuring her the evening was well worth her years of preparation. Annalise gazed out over the grounds, inhaling the intoxicating scent of gardenias that mixed with cigarette smoke, ladies' perfumes, and warm male bodies perspiring in their dress uniforms.

She had grown to love this house and the cloaked life it had made possible for her. The tears she had shed four years ago upon leaving Berlin seemed to belong to another woman entirely. She lamented that circumstances would permit her to host but one magnificent party on these grounds. Just one.

Throughout the night, Reinhard played the magnanimous, expansive host, joining in several rousing verses of Horst-Wessel-Lied in the music room as the party reached its festive climax. Annalise took a turn at the piano, impressing her guests with the Schumann etudes that so enchanted Gordon, smiling at her oblivious, beaming husband. Afterwards, she nestled next to him, the adoring wife, hand on his forearm, sunny, compliant.

"Here is my Annalise," he whispered to her, reaching to wrap his arms around her, the pearl-white skin of her neck and décolletage arousing him even with others in the room. Drinks in hand, the guests watched the commandant embrace her, the two of them the very embodiment of the Aryan ideal with his self-assured strength and her pale beauty. Sensing she had taken center stage, Annalise prepared to deliver her lines. She looked into her husband's eyes and placed her manicured hands on either side of his face.

"My esteemed guests, ladies and gentlemen," she said, her eyes never leaving his. "Please join me in thanking my marvelously talented husband—and he is talented in many, many ways, I might add," prompting several whistles and knowing laughs from the crowd, "for planning this unforgettable evening for us." The group began to applaud and raise their glasses, some calling out a "Heil Hitler" for good measure, as Reinhard pulled Annalise in closer, reaching for the clip at the back of her head to release her hair, Annalise moving her head to allow it to fall, sensuously combing her fingers through her strands to pull out the braids. Amidst oohs and ahs and a few nervous giggles, several men pulled their own wives closer while others reached for whomever was handy. Annalise gave Reinhard a playful look, tongue at the corner of her partly opened mouth, a gesture that reassured him that with the party nearly over, she would now be available to him.

As the last sleepy, sodden guests took their leave, Annalise slipped up the stairs while Clara and Helene helped reunite officers with the uniform jackets they had shed over the course of the warm night. Reinhard escorted several couples who could not seem to find the way themselves, to the staff cars that lined the drive, offering his arm to women unsteady on their feet and sharing a few closing words with their husbands, end-of-the-evening blather spoken by drunken men at the height of their powers, full of promises and proclamations. It had been a fine night, they declared, an exemplary one, and they had nothing—not a single thing—to worry about because the officers here represented the vast and capable strength of the Reich that could overcome any assault on its primacy. Any at all. Enemies be damned. Heil Hitler! Reinhard affirmed their pronouncements as he tucked couples into their vehicles, snapping a salute and remarking again and again that Germany most certainly will prevail, given its resources, talent, and superior preparation. When at last he mounted the stairs— leaving the cleanup to Clara and Helene—he anticipated Annalise waiting for him, seated at her dressing table, as eager as he for an appropriate culmination to their successful evening. He hoped she still wore her gold dress so he could remove it himself, slip the black shoes from her lovely feet. Instead, he found her burrowed under the quilts on their bed, wearing her plain Batiste nightgown, feigning a sleep so deep that her husband, while frustrated, was reluctant to disturb her.

As the party guests traveled the silent streets to their homes and headquarters, the rhythmic rocking of the ride prompting their eyes to close, their heads to droop, they failed to note a surprising coincidence: many had lost a button from their jackets. Battle ribbons, too, had become detached from more than one jacket front. Insignia pins, including the double slash of lightning of the SS, had dropped from their collars.

.   .   .

Thanks to the successful assembly of bits and pieces culled from a variety of sources, the *Kriegie* radio was now fully operational, hidden in a carved-out portion of the wall of Gordon's barracks, camouflaged by a calendar hand-drawn on scraps of cardboard, affixed to the wall with chewing gum. A single nail over the radio powered it using electricity from the single light bulb that hung from the ceiling. A second nail powered the makeshift headphones. Both the nails and the wire transmitting the signal were among the lesser-known ingredients in Clara's bread recipe.

One Tuesday in June, several weeks after the Schröder's grand soiree, the POWs of Stalag-Luft III gathered to hear BBC announcer John Snagge proclaim "D-Day is here." The Allies had landed on the beaches of Normandy, Operation Overlord underway to wrest Europe from Hitler's brutal grasp. While hope swelled among the prisoners, Lieutenant Colonel Leonard cautioned that the most dangerous time could be ahead of them—when the vice tightened and the Nazis believed they had nothing to lose.

The POWs drove the guards crazy over the next few days, making off-hand remarks about all the tourists suddenly visiting France and suggesting that if perhaps the Nazis ran a missing persons ad in the newspaper, they might find out where the Luftwaffe had gotten to.

"They cannot know anything," the guards told one another. "How could they? They are bluffing." When the commandant finally briefed the staff and confirmed the Allied invasion was in fact underway, he assured them that elite SS units were blanketed across Normandy to repulse it. Perhaps so, whispered the guards. But how did the *Kriegies* know about this before we did?

When Gordon arrived for his next workday on the Schröder estate, he did not proceed directly to the guesthouse, but lingered in the yard hoping to assess how the news from France might be affecting the household. As he dead-headed the geraniums and pulled a few weeds, he overheard a violent fight between Annalise and the commandant. She was yelling, demanding to know if an evacuation was planned. Was he to remain in charge of the camp? What did he plan to do with the prisoners with the Soviets pushing from one direction and the Allies from another? Where did this leave her?

"Where are you getting this information, Annalise? What makes you think it is accurate?" His voice boomed and carried out the French doors and into the garden. "What impertinence to ask these questions, as if the high command has not prepared a strategy long ago."

"Long ago?" she screamed. "Long ago? Why? Because they know the cause is lost? Did they leave us out in Poland—yes, Poland—as fodder for the Red Army? And you cooperated with them on this?"

"I am not listening to your facile, uninformed accusations. The Führer, the Reichsführer, have the prosecution of the war well in hand and I have no use for your hysterical…"

"Hysterical?" Annalise's voice grew in rage and Gordon heard a crash—a plate? A vase? "It is not a question of how I'm taking this news, Reinhard, it's the news itself. The threat it poses. Pay attention, my dear, darling, overconfident husband. You may be content to end up in the custody of the Allies, but I am not."

Gordon heard a door slam, then saw Reinhard charge from the music room, crossing the *Terrasse*. Face red and angry, he strode past Gordon, who by this point was on his hands and knees collecting invisible weeds under the Rose of Sharon hedge, and left through the garden gate. After the staff car was safely away, Gordon headed to the kitchen to find Clara. She stood before the stove, one index finger at her lips, the other pointing to the washroom where Friedrich was occupied.

"Is it true?" she mouthed, and he nodded. Mouth wide in a silent squeal, she hugged him, then returned quickly to the stove to resume her task.

At that moment, Annalise appeared in the kitchen, face red and blotchy, strands of hair escaping from the ribbon tied at her neck. When Friedrich emerged from the lavatory, she asked him and the staff to leave the kitchen, as she had important instructions to give the lieutenant for house repairs she needed him to complete.

"We must make our plans to leave, Gordon, soon," she whispered once they were alone.

"What is it, Annalise? What has made you so upset?"

"The Allies. They have come ashore in France. How long before they are at our doorstep? We must not wait for this." She grabbed his hands in hers. "We must go."

"But how? I have no papers, no standing."

"I can get these for you. Reinhard has access to documents that will get us out. We will take a car and drive to Switzerland, where the children are. I will tell Reinhard I am going to visit them and hide you. You can drive a car, yes?"

Gordon's mind raced. "Yes, but Annalise, I doubt your husband would release a car to you and..." She moved close to him, reaching her arm around his back, pulling herself to him. He felt the moist warmth of her breath on his neck. She did not wish to hear his objections.

"The driver will accompany me," she whispered. "You will have to dispose of him." Her eyes searched his. "Can you do that?"

"Probably—yes. When? When are you planning to go? There are arrangements I will have to make to allow us as much time as possible before we are discovered. I will be missed at the camp and they'll blame your husband. I need to think how to make this work."

"Do that, then. How quickly will the Allies move across Europe? That will determine our departure. We must stay ahead of them and I will learn as much as I can of their progress from Reinhard."

Gordon knew the BBC broadcasts the POWs tuned in to each day would be much more reliable than anything Reinhard would admit to Annalise.

"A year perhaps? They have a lot of ground to cover before they get as far as Poland, Annalise."

At this, she relaxed a little. "Then we will have enough time to ensure we can do this without discovery. Perhaps I can convince Reinhard I wish to spend Christmas with the children in Geneva."

· · ·

From that moment, Annalise concentrated on two things, and two things alone.

The first was devising a detailed plan of escape, along with fallbacks for every eventuality that might confront them. She collected and hid the civilian clothes Gordon would need to make the escape, along with a uniform jacket of Reinhard's—a cast off that had grown too tight. Her unexpected visits to Reinhard's office, ostensibly to surprise him with a picnic lunch or a mid-afternoon walk in the forest, pleased him immensely.

As he set about notifying his staff that he would be off campus with his wife for an hour or so, Annalise examined the maps strewn about his office and rifled through his files for documents that could help her and Gordon cross the border into Switzerland.

Her second priority was keeping the house staff occupied so she and Gordon could pursue their affair. After years of managing Reinhard, she trusted her sexual aptitude—her creativity, her relentlessness—to cement Gordon's commitment to build a life with her away from all he had known before. She dispatched the staff—along with Friedrich—to the market in the staff car each time Gordon was at the house, all but instructing them to stay away for the bulk of the afternoon, making arcane requests for things she knew they would never find. Once the car was safely away, it became her custom to discover new ways and places to please her lover. They improvised on the staircase, in various rooms across the house, the risk of their discovery heightening her pleasure. Her favorite setting became the music room, with its the thick carpets and the sunlight that streamed through the tall windows, because afterwards, while he lay contentedly, she could move to the piano bench and play—Schumann, most often, with its emotional, minor key melodies, that for her, captured their liaison in all its complexity. She loved the smile that played on his lips as he listened, how he followed the movement of her naked body, her talented fingers, and how often the music moved him to take her a second time.

. . .

As the staff undertook one particular shopping expedition, the driver declared the Frau was up to something. He had a sense.

"Indeed, it's true," responded Helene. "I've heard them."

"As have I," said Clara. "Such a surprise. The Frau is tutoring the lieutenant in German."

Even Friedrich bought the story the women peddled. The Englishman, he said, parroting what Clara had fed him, had developed an affinity, a love even, of Germany and the German people. Clara and Helene had overheard him discussing this with the Frau. The secretiveness came about because the prisoner was rather shy. So deep was Friedrich's commitment to the notion of Aryan German superiority, that he could not conceive the Frau found a weak, captive Englishman even remotely attractive. Helene wondered aloud if the lieutenant would stay in the Reich after the Germans won the war. Not completely convinced, the driver observed that the lieutenant had spoken German fairly well when he'd arrived—why the shyness now? He and Friedrich mused about the irregularity of the circumstances as the women exited the car and began their shopping. The driver opted not to tell Friedrich about the thing that had really raised his suspicion, the reason he had brought this up in the first place, because he wished not to forfeit the benefit he'd derived from cooperating with it.

It was the height of the summer growing season and Clara was delighted to see tomatoes and carrots, along with a variety of fruits for sale. As she stood considering which potatoes to add to her basket, a man drew alongside her, selected a firm, large one and suddenly handed it to her.

"This looks like an excellent candidate for the lieutenant's soup, does it not, Clara?"

Her stomach fluttered. She held her breath as she considered how to respond. She did not recognize him and if he knew her name, he was most surely a collaborator. His dress was unremarkable, that of a farmer, which confused her. He did not look like one who benefited from Gestapo favor. He spoke impeccable Polish, highly cultured, with the accent of someone from Warsaw.

"Przepraszam?" she stalled. Excuse me?

The man continued to survey the potatoes, reaching across the bins for the best ones, extending his arm in a way that brought him close to her and ensured he could to continue to speak without drawing attention.

· · ·

At the end of August, the BBC trumpeted the liberation of Paris, reporting the German army was scrambling east, the retreat in disarray. Embedded in the broadcast were strings of greetings, oddly worded coded messages that indicated the Allies crossing France and would soon press into the Reich—

that the POWs would see freedom in a matter of months. But as summer turned to autumn, the Allied offensive in Holland stalled, troops failing to gain purchase in Germany. The Red Army, now blasting its way into Poland, would certainly arrive before the Americans and the Brits. Conditions at the camp deteriorated, each prisoner subsisting on two meals a day of a barely flavored broth, plus one small piece of bread every other day. The provisions Gordon smuggled from the manor house proved life-saving for many, doled out to the weakest man first. Still, prisoners died every day.

Wishing to get out of Sagan before the thick of winter set in and before the Red Army arrived, Gordon and Annalise agreed to a day and set their plan in motion. Their conspiracy became more and more obvious, Clara and Helene wondering what the commandant would say if he were to witness the brazen way his wife looked at the lieutenant, making jokes, touching him, signaling things had fundamentally shifted in ways that could imperil them all. Annalise no longer planned to craft a story for her husband that she wished to visit their children. Any travel was risky now, and he would most certainly forbid it. She planned to simply leave him, acknowledging to Gordon that this would take him by surprise—shock him—which, she said, was precisely why she must leave. In her carefully constructed rationale, it was he who had wronged her, bringing her so near a war zone, not at all the life promised her when she left the Conservatoire for him. Far from extending her horizons, Reinhard had limited her prospects. That he was unaware of this, verified their unsuitability, she concluded. The ill-suited marriage was the reason she must leave. It was unrecoverable, she insisted, even without Gordon's intrusion. Just as she had learned to cope with life's vicissitudes, her husband would have to find a way to confront his own.

CHAPTER TWENTY

Scatter thou the people that delight in war.
–Psalms 69:30 (KJV)

France, 1944

In military vernacular, it's called "clearing," a purposeful camouflage of the violence involved in sweeping acre upon acre of French soil of steadfast German troops. Clearing the cities and towns of France of the enemy, including pockets of collaborators who had much to lose with the Allied advance, was a brutal if fairly swift endeavor, initiated with Operation Overlord at Normandy and reinforced with Operation Dragoon, as the Allies came ashore in the South of France. Aided by tens of thousands of Resistance fighters, the Allies eventually pushed the Germans back to the Vosges, the low range of mountains between France and Germany which had only now recovered from the battles fought there during The Great War. But weeks of aerial bombing, artillery and cannon fire, and finally, house-to-house fighting in which soldiers looked one another in the eye before pulling their triggers, proved costly. To retake each street, each block, each tavern cost thousands of lives, with homes, churches—entire villages— regularly blown to pieces in the crossfire.

The escape lines would soon be rendered obsolete. Wills emerged from his long-shrouded existence and proceeded to Avignon, making himself known to a captain in charge of a group of British paratroopers moving north. As he attempted to explain his identity—his capture at Calais, his work with the Resistance—the platoon sergeant raised his machine gun and held it steady. He believed this man, who looked French but spoke perfect English, was most likely a German spy.

"Identification, please," said the captain.

"I have none, sir. My name is William Hughes. Second Lieutenant William Hughes. I have worked with the French Resistance since 1940. Codenamed Carlos. My area of operation was south of Bordeaux, through the Pyrenees."

This rang a few bells with the captain, but it was information anyone could have cobbled together as the conflict neared its pivotal moments and practical men abandoned long held loyalties in favor of keeping themselves alive. "Hands up, on your head, then. We'll take you with us and run down your serial number to see who you might be."

Had Wills opted to traverse the well-worn path to Spain—a path much safer with the Germans in retreat, he'd have been welcomed as a hero at the British Embassy—fed and cleaned up, his country and his family joyously notified that another young British soldier feared lost was in fact, safe and well. Instead, he placed his hands on his head as instructed, a prisoner of war again, of the Allies this time. They placed him on a truck bound for Paris with a German platoon that had been overrun in vicious fire at Toulouse. Seated directly across from him, a face he knew in an instant: the Unteroffizier from Calais, the very man who had trained his machine gun on the surrendered soldiers in the British garrison so long ago. Wills would never forget the terror of those moments, the soldier's finger playing over the trigger, the intensity in his gaze, his anxiety exposed in the way he ran his tongue across his lower lip again and again. That ferocity had abandoned him in the months since, his eyes tired now, vacant. He slumped on the bench, the ruts in the road bouncing him into the bodies of his fellow detainees. One took umbrage and pushed him hard, causing him to tumble from the bench and strike his head. He stayed there in a heap on the floor of the truck bed for the rest of the trip, eyes closed, blood dripping from a spot on his head, not a single one of his compatriots interested in learning the extent of his injury. Wills knelt next to him long enough to make sure he saw the chest rise and fall, the heart beating. Nearly comatose, the soldier fell into his deepest sleep in months, flinching now and again, moaning at some unseen horror. Wills wondered if the images that floated behind the soldier's eyes still included a glorious German victory.

.   .   .

They arrived in Paris at dusk, the city bustling and animated after the repression of occupation, the long, blood-red Swastika banners gone from the erstwhile Nazi headquarters at the Hotel Majestic on Avenue Kléber. Prisoners were processed here, then taken to the coast where waiting transports would take them to England. The pall had lifted from the city, replaced variously with jubilation and outrage—emotions vigorously suppressed during occupation that insisted, now on a full hearing. Loud, laughing, exuberant Parisians filled the sidewalk cafés—the restaurants finally free of the hated Germans. As the truck paused at a stoplight, passersby shouted epithets at Wills and his fellow captives, their explicit gestures needing no translation. Suddenly, a group of people coalesced into a shouting, furious mob. At the center, two women, forced to kneel before men with shears. *Les tondues*, Wills learned: women whose hair was shorn to humiliate them, to make clear they had collaborated with the occupiers. The purges had already begun. He thought about the many women with whom he had worked, those who decided early in the occupation that risking death was preferable to bending to the Nazis' evil. Some, like Sylvi, ran the escape lines in and out of southern France aided by countless observers—farmers, bakers, schoolteachers—who gathered vital intelligence on troop movements that they passed to couriers who relayed it to the Allied command. Wills knew of young women who had plied themselves in physics and chemistry, mastering the art of explosives they repeatedly used to sabotage German communication and transportation links. Many of these brave resisters had been caught and very publicly executed, their leaders appearing to take each loss matter-of-factly—but, in truth, they suffered, absorbing each life lost like a body blow. And there were some, Wills knew, who lived a double life, who seduced their way into the beds of German officers to gain crucial information that aided the Allies and the Resistance. The uninformed called them whores: to Wills, they were heroes of France.

The truck came to a stop outside the provisional headquarters of the rapidly reforming French government. Wills and the others were directed to exit and form a cue at makeshift tables arranged across a courtyard; clerks would take their names and serial numbers to compile the POW lists. An American colonel supervised the proceedings. When Wills reached the head of the line, a British corporal handed him a form. Once again, he tried to explain himself.

"Corporal, may I speak with the officer in charge?" he asked.

The corporal lifted his head, surprised. "I've heard about you blokes," he said, "looking and sounding like a Brit. Your spyin' days are up, mate."

"That's just it. I'm from Elsworth. I'm a British lieutenant, name of Hughes, William. I served with the 30th Infantry Brigade of the BEF at Calais where I was taken prisoner. I escaped outside Lille with the help of a farmer and his family and made my way to the south of France. I have worked with the French Resistance since then, getting men through Spain with the support of the Special Operations Executive."

"That's quite a story, old man. Nice the way you worked all the details in there. You did this for four years, you're saying?"

Wills scribbled his serial number and thrust it in front of the clerk. "Look it up. Please. You'll see when I was captured and when I was declared MIA."

The corporal summoned an assistant.

"Take this bloke for a debrief," he whispered to the private. "Maybe he'll cough up something that can help us find other German spies or collaborators lurking about." The private asked Wills to step out of line and follow him.

"Good luck, mate," called the corporal. "Hope you get home... to Berlin, I mean... real soon."

Wills grimaced and followed the private through the foyer of the building and into a converted ballroom. There, he found an odd array of ostensibly German soldiers claiming special circumstances, like British or American citizenship. Overseeing this was an assemblage of Allied officers and top leaders of the Resistance who were being assimilated into the FFI—the French Forces of the Interior—in improvised ways. They surely deserved the recognition and respect, Wills thought. The Maquis he had worked alongside were as valiant as any British soldier he knew and they had accomplished immeasurably much, tying up German units that would have otherwise engaged the Allies. But Wills wondered just how successfully these men who fought with a ruthless gut instinct could be engrafted into a regular army with its firm set of rules and protocols.

As he scanned the room, he saw a young man looking intently in his direction, a vaguely familiar face, leaner and more mature now, but still recognizable. Gilles, from the farm in Lille. He wore the uniform of a private in the French army. He nodded to Wills, then headed out of the ballroom, returning sometime later with the American colonel Wills had seen in the courtyard. They approached. Gilles extended his hand, then began the introductions.

"Guillaume, I am so happy to see you," he began before turning to the colonel. "There is a mistake. This man is British. My family rescued him after Calais."

The colonel's eyebrows arched skeptically. "As you can imagine, this is a fraught time, Private, not a moment to take anybody's word for much of anything. How can you be sure of this?" He turned to Wills. "Where have you been, then? Roaming about the French countryside?"

"No, sir. I chose to stay and help the Resistance. I worked near Bayonne, sometimes over to Toulouse. I took soldiers and families across the Pyrenees. My code name was..."

"Carlos." The colonel finished it for him.

"Yes. That's it," said Wills, dropping his head in relief. "I am—was—Carlos."

"You got out a right many of our fliers, Lieutenant. You did a terrific job for us. But son, that was a helluva long time to stay behind enemy lines hiding yourself like that. Had they found you, no POW conventions would have applied to you, you know. You'd a been shot. It is incomprehensible that you stayed at it... what... four years?"

"I never planned to do it for so long. But it seemed I couldn't let it go, Colonel. Gilles' family saved my life—and dozens of others. Crossing the mountains was not easy—but after a few months, I got better at it and knew that this odd set of skills I'd developed could not be replaced easily—that people would die if I left and others had to take over my routes."

"Well, I'm not sure if that's hubris or courage, Lieutenant. But I do know we need both to win this war. So, what of your family? Will they forgive you for choosing to live in the woods like this, for not making your way home earlier?"

"I'm praying so, sir. And I'm hoping you can get my status here reclassified so I can see them sooner rather than later. Right now, I'm lumped in with the German POWs. They think I'm a very clever spy for Hitler."

"Private, take this man to my office and arrange for his transfer home. You'll need to confirm his details with the British duty officer—serial number, service unit, all that. There is also likely to be an inquiry into why you didn't immediately return to service. That may take a bit of time, Lieutenant, but hold tight. We'll get you home soon enough."

And despite his peasant dress, his dirty face and hands, the long, unkept hair secured by a red bandana, Wills saluted like the soldier he was. "Thank you, sir. Most appreciative." The colonel returned the salute, then reached to clasp Wills' arm. He leaned in.

"Thank you, soldier. You saved my own son's life. Did you know that?"

Wills smiled. "Delighted to hear that, sir. Truly."

As the colonel turned to other duties, Gilles exhaled with relief, then pointed towards an exit door. He escorted Wills through a hallway, then a stairwell, to a warren of rooms and the colonel's basement office.

"And your parents?" Wills asked once they arrived in the office. "How have they fared?"

Gilles gave a tense smile, his eyes clouding, remembering. After a few long minutes, he spoke, his voice tight.

"We lost them almost two months ago. Right after Normandy."

"Lost them? How, Gilles?"

"It began with Sucre. I loved that little dog. She was so very smart, *non?* We found her dead outside the barn one morning, foam around her mouth. Then we discovered several of the cattle, lowing in pain. Poison, we think, scattered in their feed. The Gauleiter had watched our farm for years—never could get anything on us because father was so clever, always varying his practices. The collaborators knew their opportunity to expose us was closing with every kilometer the Allies advanced from the coast. They knew my father would bear witness to all they had done in service to the Gestapo these past four years. Without Sucre keeping guard, they probably had run of the house and found the trapdoor in the living room that opened to the crawl space. We kept the radio there—and there could have been documents, maps, clothing, any number of things. They were probably disappointed no one was hiding at the moment, but they'd gathered enough evidence for their purposes. My parents were taken to the churchyard and executed. Both of them hanged. I'm told they were very brave, heads high, father yelling *Vive la France* to his last breath. They gather everyone, you know, summon them to town to make them watch it, thinking it will encourage them to collaborate, not resist. But all it's done is confirm the godlessness of the *Boche.*"

"Gilles, I am so sorry. And now. After everything. How did you escape?"

"Father sent me off to the partisans after we found Sucre. He had made the calculation. We heard over the BBC when the Allies landed and he knew anything could happen before Lille was liberated. He was always right in these kinds of judgements. Right about Petain, right about Hitler. But my parents were not the only ones caught in the final sweep. Every farmer with land adjacent to ours was arrested and killed. Their children, their livestock." He paused, gathered himself. "It was vicious. And impels me to tell their story. My parents—who, you know, never sought any of this—saved one hundred and sixteen lives. How do I know this? Because mother tallied every one. After we sent you on your way, she placed a tiny notch at the base of her wooden spoon—her best stew spoon, the one she always used. You know the one. She counted from the very start because she knew there would be others after you. The last time I saw it, there were notches all the way up the handle. I can see her at the stove, stirring, stirring, the palm of her hand probably feeling each nick in the wood, reminding her of the lives she'd saved. Yours being the first. And after that, pilots, British and American, even a Pole or two working with the RAF. And the Jews—some who ran shops in the village, people we'd known for years. Our neighbors who lost everything. She was overjoyed we could do that. We all were."

"And Sylvi? Is she safe?"

"She is, Lieutenant, back at the farm now, trying to put things back together with our parents gone."

They talked a few moments about Sylvi—her determined work on behalf of the Resistance, her resolute confidence when Wills had seen in her in Toulouse. Even so, she had lost her parents. Wills offered further words of sympathy that came out muddled and fragmented as he worked to absorb what he'd learned.

"I admire my big sister," said Gilles. "She certainly got the adventurous life she had hoped for—more adventurous than she could have imagined even three years ago. She is taking stock now, resting, deciding what to do with the farm once all this is over—whether we sell it or put the work in to restore it. She is cut of the same cloth as my parents and they were so proud of her."

"Never forget their pride in you, too, Gilles. Barely eighteen and helping bring all those people to safety. And now, a soldier in the FFI."

"Yes, I think father would like this," smiled Gilles, "both of us fighting to keep France free—he in The Great War and me in this one. *Vive la France*."

"Indeed," responded Wills. "Always. And your dear parents will live on too, both in legend, and in those whose lives they saved."

•   •   •

Grief over the news of Albert and Ginette's murders stayed with Wills even as he was directed to new rooms to talk to new officials who, inch by inch, began the process of transforming him from a Maquisard into a British lieutenant once again. The sacrifice of the farmer and his wife had made it possible, Albert adhering to a moral imperative, in which, in effect, he exchanged his life for Wills' and so many others. It was only right that Wills had followed suit. He would hold to that belief no matter who challenged it. As he received a clean uniform and dog tags with a name he had not used in four years, he hoped his wife and son, who had been bereft of his companionship these past four years, would understand his reasons for taking the treacherous path he'd taken.

CHAPTER TWENTY-ONE

God giveth the shoulder according to the burden.
–German Proverb

London and Elsworth, 1944

Some days as she dressed for work, Beryl stood before the armoire and ran her hands along the sleeves of Gordon's good shirts, one after the other. She remembered what it felt like to touch the crisp cotton on his arm, the way he rolled the sleeves so carefully when he worked—two times—so he would not get ink on his cuffs. She had never removed his shirts from the cramped, shared space—a testament to the strength of her denial. In the earliest days of the war, despite the terror-bombing, she still believed her family would reunite quickly and all would be set right in Europe once the right people got to the table. Four years later, the shirts no longer smelled of him—his hair tonic, his shaving cream—but still, she often brought a shirttail to her face and inhaled, hoping.

Beryl never intended to keep the news of Gordon from Colin for so many months, but circumstances conspired to delay her visit to Elsworth to tell him. It took her weeks to reach the point where she felt emotionally prepared to walk her son through this heartbreak. She wanted Jack at her side when she told him, but Jack was not soon available, given the acceleration of the air war. He was restricted to base until late spring, by which point they agreed it would be better to wait until the end of Colin's school term. In the interim, Beryl continued to badger the War Office to locate what remained of Gordon's things. The dog tags at the very least—evidence of his dutiful service—but what about his boots or his watch or his wedding ring or the letters she had written him? She wished to hold a thing, a tangible anchor to his beautiful, truncated life and the years he had lived apart from her. It would help her and Colin move forward—was that so much to ask? The vapid clerks had been useless in this, offering little information on what they termed "the most unusual of cases."

Then suddenly, it was June and the wards of Grove Park overflowed with the wounded from Normandy, men who had charged out of landing craft into churning waters and onto the sand amidst shredding artillery fire. The losses were unfathomable, but those lucky enough to make it back to London had a good chance of survival, albeit without arms and legs they had left on the beach. And as the Nazis were pushed from the coast, their leader, safe in his lair in Berlin, ordered his supply of V-1 bombs be armed and aimed across the Channel. All hospital leaves were cancelled: every nurse, doctor, orderly, and ward clerk worked sixteen-hour shifts day after day, as more wounded fighters came in not just from France, then Belgium, then Holland, but from neighborhoods across central London as the buzz bombs cruised over quiet streets, hunting for victims. Despite this fresh horror— anonymized, unmanned missiles, a more sophisticated iteration of what England endured in the early months of the war; despite the volume of wounded soldiers and civilians that exhausted medical supplies and workers at hospitals city-wide, there grew a sense of optimism that this was the beginning of the end, that things might be turning and the Allies could prevail. Londoners lifted their heads, greeted one another again on the streets, chatted with waiters and news agents and bus drivers, allowing themselves to entertain notions of the future, of themselves remaining free, that the tyrant to their east would soon be forced to capitulate.

Beryl had not seen her son in six months when she finally found an August Saturday to take the train to Elsworth. As she watched the countryside from the train, the greens and golds faded now after summer's draining heat, she placed herself back in the days before the war, when she and Gordon had taken toddler Colin on holiday to the shore, chasing him as he pursued butterflies and gathered seashells he presented proudly to his mother; the three of them drowsing in the afternoon on the worn blanket; she and Gordon watching the face of their boy as he slept, lying on his back, arms splayed as if to say he was ready to embrace the world when it arrived for him. Now she would have to tell him a very different future awaited them both.

All this had been difficult for Jack in a different way, as he grasped the depth of Beryl's love for her husband and anticipated the grief the news would bring to Colin. He knew he could never replace Gordon, but still hoped he could interlace his future with Beryl and her son. Perhaps when the war ended—and some were saying it was a matter of a few more months—if he survived, he could stay in England and help with the drawdown, with deactivating the air bases. Then maybe muster out and stay. These ideas he kept to himself, knowing how unseemly it was to lay plans to replace a father, a husband. He found Beryl extraordinarily strong, unwavering, continuing her dutiful work at the hospital despite her own loss. He had visited her in London as often as he could through the summer, spending nights on her living room sofa, bringing chocolate bars and tea bags to her at Grove Park, leaving flowers on her doorstep, even meeting her in the middle of the night—her dinner break—to share a meal in the cafeteria. She had responded kindly to all of it, grasping his arm as they walked, kissing him hello and goodbye every time they met, too early, Jack understood, for intimacy beyond that. But he dreamt of it. The shattering things she had faced in this war had given her a depth, a grace, a wisdom he felt sure he would never find in another woman. The chaos of the war had strengthened and shaped them into better people, Jack believed, conjoining them in that way unique to survivors of catastrophe, who have only to exchange a glance to understand one another wholly, completely. Jack did not believe the folks back home would ever fully understand him now, the way Beryl did. And Colin. Jack couldn't imagine loving his own child any more deeply and wished only to do what he could, so Colin had the full and happy life Gordon would have wanted. So, he remained available to Beryl as she wished him to be, waiting, hopeful that he would be the man to fill the chasm left by Gordon's death.

Jack watched Beryl step from the train, dark hair a swirl of energy, smile constrained, eyes softening when she spotted him. He parked the jeep in front of Ivy's house and as they made the trip up the cobblestoned walk,

Beryl reached for his hand, her own damp, sweating. Margaret swung the door wide, nine and a half years-old now, pencil parked behind her ear, notebook in hand, a writer these days of plays and short stories.

"Mrs. C!" she cried, reaching for a hug, then quickly reading the look on the adults' faces. "News, then, is it? Well, I'm still happy to see you both. Glad you're here. Let me find Colin."

"Tell him we'll meet him in the garden, will you, sweet girl? We'll be out back."

They proceeded through the kitchen where Ivy waited silently, apprised of the purpose of the visit the day before.

"Shall I join you, or no?" she asked gently. "Whatever you think best."

"Take the girls and Hugo, Ivy, and if you could, please let them know while we talk with Colin outside. And thank you. Thank you for all of this. For four years of this, really. For providing Colin—and me as well—this safe place."

With tears in her eyes, Ivy turned to gather the other children. How could it have worked out that Gordon had died, with her own husband improbably alive behind the lines? She had tucked Wills' wedding ring away last winter in her bureau, speaking of its provenance to no one. Oliver Dowd said talk would endanger Wills' life and the lives of those Wills worked to save: people tended to find details of things like this so hopeful and exciting, the information had a way of getting across the Channel to the wrong people. With effort, she put it out of her head—keeping it from her son and the rest of the children, her neighbors, even the vicar. But daily, she awoke mindful of this miracle that for now she had to protect, unaware that others noticed, but could not explain, the palpable lightening of her spirit.

Jack and Beryl waited on the garden bench only a few minutes before Colin bounded out the door.

"Son," she said, standing, clenching and twisting the handkerchief in her hands. Jack stubbed out his cigarette and stood next to her.

Looking at his mother—the anguish in her eyes, the defeat in her posture—Colin knew.

"Dad?"

She gave a single nod. He asked how, absorbing the bitter details like a boxer conditioned to withstand repeated, brutal blows, his face working to hide his grief, to drive away any tears.

"I had rather wondered about this, Mum," he said quietly. "It's been so long since there's been a letter from him."

"I'd hoped you hadn't noticed, that with your busy life here, with Hugo and your friends, school... I had hoped to give you a few more months of— I don't know—peace? Happiness?"

He looked at her, surprised. "It's always there for me, Mum, always. Whether we talk about it or not. Ever since I came to Elsworth, I worried about him. I worry about you. I love Mrs. Hughes and Hugo and the people here—my God, the Dowds are practically grandparents to me. And Jack and Buck and the guys at Kimbolton. I'll love them my whole life long. But I miss you and dad every day and I feel sick and uneasy when time passes and I don't see you or hear from you. That's when my mind starts to reason things out, figure out what must be happening. And when you stopped bringing new letters from Dad... I knew. I think I've known for months."

His words brought a fresh swell of tears, Beryl grasping that instead of shielding her son from grief, she had compounded his pain, month after month, with her avoidance and obviation. Colin reached for her hand, then moved to embrace her. Fighting tears of his own, Jack wrapped his arms around them both and there they stood, resting, leaning against one another. Once they summoned the strength to let go, Colin leaned into his mother's ear to say wouldn't it have been bloody tremendous if Dad had gotten to meet their Yank.

·   ·   ·

That afternoon, Reverend Dowd paid a pastoral visit, quietly observing that Lieutenant Clarke must have been a remarkable man because look—just look—at his exceptional boy. At this, Colin and Beryl recalled Gordon in his essence, the things he loved: drawing and architecture, listening to fine music, a sassy, witty remark of the kind that drew him to Beryl in the first place. His high character, his integrity and kindness. The vicar took those little anecdotes and wove them into a narrative fabric of Colin's particular gifts, both his wit and his many kindnesses—with the twins, at school, with the American airmen—stories that distracted Beryl and Colin and everyone else from the pain of the present moment, as the vicar intended they do. The girls giggled when Reverend Dowd described them learning to ride their bicycles, how Colin and Hugo caught them when they faltered—never once letting them fall—and how the boys tricked them into thinking they were still holding them steady when they were really just running alongside. This was among the vicar's best talents, not learned in seminary necessarily, evident only to congregants in the midst of loss and turmoil. This simple, soothing, storytelling helped the grieving understand that life would go on because it could still contain incandescent moments of love and beauty. That this is precisely what life is, he affirmed, without saying the words: searing loss and extravagant blessing, both. The voices drew Marigold from the upstairs and she slowly wound her way through the long legs of the children sprawled on the floor, climbing into Patsy's lap once she found her. The room grew quiet, Marigold the only one speaking with her steady purr, the right moment, the vicar determined, to lift a prayer of thanksgiving for Gordon's life and service. It was so simple and heartfelt that Beryl extended her own prayer, thanking God for this man's influence on Colin's life, resolving that later—after all of this—she and Colin would find a parish to attend in London. They would. It would get them through this. Then Reverend Dowd asked about honoring Gordon more formally, about a memorial service over which he would be pleased to preside. Beryl said she would like to do exactly that. The timing would depend on the War Office, from which she still hoped to receive some of her late husband's personal effects.

"When the timing is right, then," said the vicar. "We stand ready."

A rap on the door broke the stillness that had settled in and, at first, they looked helplessly at one another wondering how to respond. Hugo, finally, hopped to his feet and opened the door, finding a courier from the telegraph office. He accepted the folded message and turned to his mother, who rose to her feet, hands pressed to her mouth.

"Shall I read it, Mum?" he asked, hands shaking, knowing rare is the telegram that contains happy news.

"Yes. Do." Ivy responded, eyes bright, hopeful.

Hugo scanned it, then read it again, more carefully, before erupting into tears.

"It's from Dad. He's in France. And he's headed home."

And despite his own anguish, the shock of the news he himself had just received, Colin swept Hugo up in his arms, the two of them jumping in circles, knocking into an armchair, a floor lamp, driving the cat up the stairs. The others asked to know details—how could this be? He'd been missing for four years. Ivy shared what she knew, explaining to all of them how Oliver had brought the wedding ring, how Wills had helped him get to freedom. The children were stunned.

"Well, I'm absolutely gobsmacked!" declared the vicar. "You're saying our very own butcher helped bring my grandson home?"

"He did, Reverend Dowd, he did. And you understand, Hugo, why I couldn't tell you this, right? Your father was still at grave risk. But I suppose now that Paris is liberated, he's able to find his way home."

"So, Dad was a spy, Mum, is that it? Did you hear that, Colin? Me own father, a spy for the Resistance! I'm not surprised a bit. That's Dad. More than meets the eye. And he's coming home." He turned to his best friend, who stood with his arms crossed, clutching his upper arms, eyes red-rimmed, attempting a smile.

"Oh blast, Colin. I'm so sorry, mate," said Hugo, "I am so very sorry. Unfair for me to be celebrating when…"

"Hugo," interrupted Colin. "I can be happy for you. I can. And I can be sad for me at the same time. This is the very best possible news we could have received today of all days. Half of us gets a dad back," he said, voice breaking. "I can't wait to meet him."

Talk turned to the homecoming, speculation on how soon it might be, each of them eager to share in Ivy and Hugo's joy and relief, so long in coming. As the others laid plans, Colin walked his mother into the small kitchen and asked if he could go with her, back to London, to his old life. She wished he could, she said, but she insisted he stay in Elsworth. London was not safe with the indiscriminate buzz bombs falling in all parts of the city. Surely he could understand that she could not bear to lose him, too.

Jack drove her back home that night, the two of them pondering the day's good news layered over the sadness they'd carried these many months. Beryl felt deep relief that she was no longer keeping the truth from Colin and she was elated—truly—that Ivy's husband would return to her, that their family would be restored. The day's developments produced in her a sudden resolve to lay down the burden of her own losses in favor of cherishing what she still had. Colin, specifically. And Jack. Jack, who risked death with every mission he flew and still retained his humanity—patiently, gently, lovingly attending to her needs again and again. It was not the life she expected, but she wished now to live the life before her.

They arrived at her flat, Jack escorting her to the door as he usually did. But this time, instead of the chaste kiss she usually offered, Beryl took his hand and led him through the door, into her bedroom. As she worked the buttons on his uniform shirt, he looked at her questioningly, to confirm that she wanted him, wanted this.

"It's time," she said simply.

· · ·

Over the next number of months, Colin adjusted to two piercing changes: the permanent loss of his father and the emerging closeness between his mother and Jack. He read it on Jack's face when the boys went to Kimbolton and her name came up. Colin knew his mother and Jack were spending time together in London, but he didn't investigate specifics like where Jack stayed on his three-day passes. He was unsure how he felt about all this, these two people whom he loved and had introduced to one another who now had a relationship apart from him. Should he want his mother to be lonely? That seemed small, mean. But maybe she could have waited a bit, long enough for Colin to get used to their changed circumstance before beginning whatever this was.

Over the next few months, Colin spent many after-school hours in the vicar's study, sometimes posing theological questions as he struggled to work out how his father could perish this way—why God could let it happen. Sometimes they chewed over the latest news of the war, what Oliver had to say about it and what the vicar thought. Sometimes he simply sat in the older man's presence as they both read or wrote. And just once, he brought up his mother and Jack.

"Your mother's been through a terrible shock, Colin, as have you. It's made worse by your not being together. It would soothe you both, I think, to be a family again, and have time to remember your father and what you both loved about him."

"Yes," nodded Colin wistfully. "I miss her. I miss our life before the war. And I thought once Dad was taken prisoner, he would be safe, at least, that he would make it home."

"As did we all, son. And when horrific things happen—things that can't be reversed or made right—we're left to do the next right thing, the thing that allows us to take a tiny step forward, one at a time, to heal and get going again. Your mother loves you with her whole heart, but adults need other adults to listen to them, to reassure them, to provide friendship. Surely you would not begrudge her this friendship, as unexpected as it is."

"I'll try not to," said the boy, returning to his mathematics but unable to work a single equation on the page. They sat in silence until Dorothy came along, offering shortbread biscuits, followed by Hugo, summoning Colin home as the hour had grown late. Watching through the window as the boys walked the short distance home, the vicar's wife said she wished she could have met Lieutenant Clarke, to know the man who had helped give this boy such a deep well of reflectiveness and calm, qualities that would stand him in good stead whatever the chaos around him.

· · ·

At last, the summer warmth gave way to the first chill nights of autumn. So strange, thought Beryl, the determined way the world kept spinning, the seasons marching ahead as if life had not been upended. She pushed the War Office again to solve the mystery of Gordon's things and told Jack she had the strange sense that a new records clerk to whom she'd been referred knew more than he was saying. He had paused before answering her questions, as if working out a specific response, rather than simply putting her off as the other clerks had done for months. They set the memorial service for right before the New Year. She would take a week's leave from the hospital and Colin would be on holiday from school. They would have time to properly celebrate all Gordon had given to this world and then to mourn together, finally, without the press of having to return to school and work immediately. The vicar reminded her that the sanctuary would still be dressed for Christmas, with evergreens and candles. Beryl rather liked that, deciding it would help remind those who attended the service that Gordon's life had indeed been a gift.

CHAPTER TWENTY-TWO

There is only one kind of love, but there are a thousand imitations.
–Ibid

Inside the Reich, 1944

One late November morning, a light snow falling, Gordon arrived at the house in the back of the Mercedes as he customarily did. The driver and Friedrich took their time exiting the car, their lethargy convenient for Gordon, who ignored the tussle behind him and headed toward the guesthouse, before circling back to the manor house front door which had been left unlocked for him. He climbed the stairs two at a time to the second floor and entered Annalise's room, finding her packing the last of her jewelry in a small valise. A second suitcase, far larger, waited at the door and contained clothing and documents that would be vital to their escape. Annalise had been quite busy in the few minutes since her husband had departed for the camp.

"My love," she said, looking his way, a worried smile on her face. "Help me with this, please."

He helped her close the over-packed valise and they stood face to face, she giving a long exhale to steel herself for what was next.

"Did they see you come up here?" she asked.

"They saw me head toward the guest house. They're hardly interested now, Annalise, with the overall situation deteriorating. I am not the biggest threat they face these days." He picked up the suitcase and nodded at her. "Ready for this?" he asked.

She stepped toward him, reaching up to pull his face to hers. Her kiss was urgent, searching. Gordon pulled back, impatient to get started with the task ahead. "We must go, Annalise. If I'm to neutralize Friedrich and the driver, we have little time."

She followed him down the steps, chattering nervously that she had ordered Clara and Helene to walk to the market and that both had responded with obvious chagrin, given the foul weather. The nerve! She laughed. And here she was, giving them the rest of the day to themselves! At the base of the staircase, her eyes took in the grand hall, the fine chandeliers, the deep pile carpets and she felt a pang that she could not take it all with her. She thought about how her addition of the arbor had completed this house, making it a more handsome show piece than she could have hoped. And the piano. She might never own such a beautifully crafted instrument like this again. That she did not own the piano, nor much of anything in the house, no longer occurred to her.

As she entered the sitting room, she came face to face with her household staff, Clara holding Friedrich's Lugar while he sat, handcuffed and gagged, against the wall. Stunned, Annalise dropped the valise, which sprang open on the floor.

"What is happening here? What is the meaning of this? I told you to get to the market," she said, as if that were the thing out of place.

"The driver?" Gordon asked the women.

"Your men have contained him. He is secured in the guest house," responded Helene. "Friedrich will go next."

"What is the meaning of this?" repeated Annalise, alarm growing in her eyes. "What men?"

Gordon turned to her, speaking in a voice she didn't recognize. Not that of her lover, nor that of a cowed prisoner intent to preserve his life. "Change of plans, Annalise."

"You've brought others, Gordon?" she said, crouching to gather her things back in the valise. "And did not apprise me? But we must go. The staff can make up a story about what happened here—but we must go to the car and leave now."

She fled through the house, out the French doors to the *Terrasse*, running under her precious arbor, snowflakes drifting over her lifeless garden, covering the bare limbs that she would never again see in full flower. She rattled the lock at the garden gate and flung it wide. There stood four men—villagers, apparently—one holding a gun pointed in her direction.

"Whoa, ma'am, slow down there," said the one with the gun. Not Polish. American.

"What are you doing?" she shrieked. "You are not to be here without guards. I shall call my husband this moment..."

"Ma'am, we're not interested in hurting you, but you're not calling anybody. Not at this point, anyway."

Gordon emerged through the gate carrying Annalise's suitcase, followed by Clara and Helene. Helene placed three sacks laden with bread, jam, boiled eggs, apples, and salted ham inside the car. Clara carried a scarf and a length of heavy rope. Two of the men went back in the house to retrieve Friedrich, who, far too late, had decided he wished to reverse his stated position on the nature of the Frau's relationship with the *Kriegie*.

"What is happening, Gordon? What have you done?" Annalise asked, bewildered.

What he had done, he had not done alone. Clara had secured the paper and the exact color of ink the camp forgers had needed to create the gate passes the men used to get out of the camp that morning. The guard who had waved Gordon through over many months had not questioned that this time, the commandant dispatched an entire work detail to his house. After all, here were the pristine gate passes that authorized it. Beneath their tattered combat uniforms, the men wore the tunics and breeches of peasants, created from scraps of fabric Clara had painstakingly collected. Tucked in the bags of food was a box with a needle and thread, along with a fine assortment of German army buttons, insignias, and uniform ribbons carefully collected over the preceding months.

"What is happening, Frau Schröder," Gordon said, "is that we are leaving. We're just not going where you had planned." Clara approached with the rope, one of the POWs coming alongside her.

"Do not touch me, you dirty Pole," Annalise spat. "You filthy, treasonous... how could you betray me like this?"

"Betray you, ma'am?" asked Clara quietly, daring to look her mistress directly in the eye as Helene pried the valise handle from Annalise's fingers. "You invaded my country. You stole this house and used the items you found here as if they were your own. The betrayal began with you, with Germany, and I pray God you live long enough to see the consequences yourself."

Clara and the POW bound Annalise's arms in front of her, then wrapped the scarf around her mouth to silence her. Annalise watched as Helene knelt and opened the valise, combing through the jewelry, removing several broaches and a pair of necklaces and tucking them in her apron pocket.

"I shall hold these for Mrs. Stroński, as they are hers, are they not, Frau Schröder? It is my prayer—mine and Clara's—that she and her husband will return here someday. If they do not, these will go to their children—provided they survive the war. But don't worry, I shall place your case and your jewels in the car with you. Because that is the fair thing to do, isn't it, Frau Schröder? And we Poles are fair people."

Annalise looked at Gordon, both grief and anger in her eyes as the POWs put her in the car. Gordon turned to Clara and Helene, gripping their hands, unable to speak for a moment.

"What you've done..." he began, "risking yourselves... your families. How can I thank you?"

"We could not have done anything but what we did," said Clara, tears welling in her eyes. "It is a small thing, while your troops are giving their lives to restore our homeland to freedom. Until we meet again, Lieutenant." They embraced. "Gentlemen. God go with you."

The six of them packed into the Mercedes, Gordon at the wheel, steering them out of town. He turned the car toward the southwest, towards Czechoslovakia not Switzerland, just over 660 kilometers to cover.

.   .   .

The camp commandant returned home that evening with a different driver, as the usual man had not yet returned to camp. This had happened a time or two, when Annalise needed something from the market late in the day, and sent the driver with her list, not wishing the staff to leave the tasks she had assigned them. With worsening shortages of meat and produce, stocking the kitchen took hours longer than it once did. On that particular night, Annalise did not greet him at the front door with a glass of wine, as had become their custom, and he detected no aroma of dinner being prepared. With some irritation, he called out for his wife, then strode into the kitchen where he found a note from Clara, saying she and Helene had enjoyed their work immensely and regretted that the Frau had seen fit to discharge them. Discharge? Annalise must have finally had enough of Clara's mediocre meals and taken her anger out on Helene as well. Surveying the pantry, the vegetable bins, Reinhard saw several bottles of wine, but little in the way of provisions. In fact, the kitchen looked cleaned out. So, Annalise must be at the market gathering items to prepare dinner herself. He would be relieved when she returned: the snow was falling thick and fast. In the interim, he would enjoy a bottle of Bordeaux—the last of the assortment the Reichsführer had brought the night of their party last spring. It would do quite nicely. Unable to locate the corkscrew, he thrashed about the kitchen, slamming drawers and cabinet doors, developing some sympathy then for what Annalise must have suffered daily with the dimwits on the household staff. Eventually, he pulled the cork out with his pocket knife, dropping granules into the bottle. Irritated, he poured a generous glass and at last settled into his chair, watching through the window as the snowflakes floated silently down, expecting the staff car to appear any minute. He closed his eyes and played out the argument that would soon commence, seeing the tears that would spring to Annalise's eyes when he scolded her for firing the staff so impetuously, for the inconvenience it had created now, of all times. Would she beg his forgiveness, eyes glistening, as she had so often in their early years together? She would, he decided, picturing it. It would be a loud and fractious fight, as there was no one else in the house to curb the dramatics. He would enjoy it. Reinhard would make her cry; her lip would tremble piteously. Perhaps he would move to strike her, a sudden thrust of his arm. He would not land a blow, but she would be frightened in that way that always reassured him, gratified him, restored his sense of himself. She would speak in that somewhat contrived, whispery voice she used when she apologized. And then he would hold her, soothe her, own her, all passion spent. Almost all. And perhaps then she would turn to preparing his belated dinner.

The passage of time blurred by the prodigious amount of wine he consumed, it was nine-o'clock before Reinhard telephoned the camp to see if the driver had turned up there. When he learned the man had not been seen all day, panic flared and he directed a contingent to scour the streets of Sagan immediately looking for the car and his wife, who had obviously had some sort of accident. He regretted he had never learned the last names of Clara and Helene; speaking with them might have provided insight into what happened at the house this day. By midnight, he called back to the camp and vented his anger at the inept soldiers who had failed to do as ordered: namely, find his wife. As he yelled, pacing on the carpets, he thought he heard a rhythmic pounding, a thump, thump, thump, somewhere in the night. Tree limbs, he decided, hitting the side of the house. There must be wind with this storm. He eventually passed out in the sitting room chair, awaking well before dawn and summoning a driver to take him back to the camp. As he rode off, unshaven, frantic, he was deaf to the sounds in the guest house that Friedrich and the driver furiously made.

Still bound, their night had been far more uncomfortable than the commandant's. They were hungry and thirsty, exhausted from breathing through their gags and trying to writhe free from the handcuffs and the ropes that wound around their necks to their ankles, secured around the leg of the heavy brass bed frame. Unfortunately for them, Reinhard would choose to spend the next week at the camp, directing the hapless search for his wife and becoming more disconsolate by the day. By the time someone thought to search the guest house for clues to what happened—weeks after Annalise disappeared—they found the decomposing bodies of two Nazi soldiers, the odor contained somewhat by the frigid winter air. The driver had died first, killing himself when he rocked his way clear of the heavy bed and maneuvered toward the staircase, arms and ankles still bound, his uncontrolled tumble down the steps concussing his brain into a fatal swell. Friedrich lay there another week, his shoulder and wrist bones broken from trying to wrest free from the handcuffs behind his back, the ensuing infection a painful one, ravaging the organs of his body and ultimately shutting them down.

·   ·   ·

As Annalise drew up her detailed escape plan—gathering supplies and documents, leveraging Reinhard for useful information, all the while envisioning the new life ahead of her—the men in Stalag-Luft III coordinated with a network outside the camp to devise the actual escape. A handful of Polish paratroopers had reconnoitered Sagan and the camp for months, transmitting what they learned back up the line. That knowledge would be enhanced now by the first-hand observations of the escapees who could convey more subtle details of the camp layout, the supervision practices, and the current conditions of the captives. Dysentery among the prisoners was rampant, along with a host of infections efficiently and continually delivered by the rats that numbered in the dozens in each of the barracks. If the Nazis evacuated the camp, few captives would survive a long march. In fact, Lieutenant Colonel Herbert worried it might provide the rationale for the guards to facilitate their own speedy escape by gunning down the prisoners first. Then there were the Soviets closing in, certain to arrive to liberate the camp ahead of the Americans. Might they take protective custody of the soldiers and move them elsewhere? The POWs could be a potent bargaining chip in the post-war world.

The escapees' orders had arrived in pieces, via coded messages passed to Clara at the market. Sometimes, she verbally relayed an apparently innocuous phrase to Gordon. Other times, she received a scrap of paper, which she slipped into the pocket of his freshly washed fatigues. In short, they were to get to Kalinov, a Czech village liberated from the Germans several months earlier, where the Soviets would receive them and, at some point, arrange transport to England. A series of rendezvous points were identified along the way, where the escapees could be resupplied and provided updated intelligence. One open and unresolved question: what to do with Annalise? It would depend completely on her.

Throughout the many months he had worked at the manor house, Gordon had assiduously briefed his commanding officer on his progress in co-opting Annalise. When the relationship had become sexual, Herbert had seen it as progress: Gordon gained more freedom to mine the house for useful resources and intelligence. And indeed, he'd stolen money—a few Reichsmarks at a time—from Annalise's dresser and the commandant's briefcase. He pilfered bullets from Reinhard's Lugar, along with bars and ribbons that had once adorned the commandant's uniform but had been replaced with fresher versions once they'd become worn and frayed. And cigarettes, always cigarettes. He had been the most popular prisoner in the Stalag because he always had smokes. Items too bulky to smuggle back into the camp, he hid in bushes only he tended or under the mattress in the guest house bedroom where he and Annalise had their trysts. Helene conducted routine sweeps to collect the contraband and secure it for Gordon's escape. Clara added the sharpest knives in the kitchen to the trove.

The night before the escape, Lieutenant Colonel Herbert found Gordon anxious and in need of absolution as he contemplated what lay ahead.

"You did your duty, son," the colonel reminded him. "This isn't just a case of you randomly buggering the girl."

Gordon offered a wry smile. "I slept with another woman, sir. I broke vows I took to my wife."

"And you're thinking that because you rather liked it, looked forward to it, that you ought to be punished, do you?"

Gordon flushed, head bowed. "I did like it. And I hated it. Being with her saved me—literally—because she got the medicine that made me well.

She did that for me at substantial risk to herself. The food has been critical—and not just for me—and the work on the arbor rescued my brain by giving me something to think about, a problem to solve, instead of just withering here in this place. You've seen her. So beautiful, but part of something so very wicked. Sleeping with her tortured my soul and at the same time, it healed me. I felt like a human being again when I was with her. A horrible, lying son of a bitch, but human at least. A man. So yes, I am ashamed: ashamed that I enjoyed the sex, enjoyed the release of it right in the middle of this bloody war while other guys were losing their lives. Ashamed that I feel intensely grateful to her for saving my life—the woman with whom I betrayed my wife. And tomorrow, I will betray her, too."

"You're free to regret what has happened. There is much to regret in any war, the vast array of inhumane things that happen, we obscure over time because they are simply too painful to remember. We forget them entirely, which is why the next war comes around. But shame? I daresay you have nothing to be ashamed of. Hear that. Shame comes from selfish motives, from putting your needs ahead of others. You're like any man, Lieutenant, presented with a willing, enthusiastic woman inviting you to take her to bed. Now if you'd gone along with her plans to escape, that would be betrayal. You'd be a damned traitor, even if I couldn't fault you for wanting to get out of this stinking camp. But what you did, Gordon, you did as an imprisoned man, with limited resources to draw from. You played the hand you were dealt: you weren't on the hunt to cheat on your wife. There was purpose in your drawing close to this woman, earning her trust. It was a small part of the big picture: to help us gain advantage so we can push the Huns back to Berlin. 'Our duty is to be useful, not according to our desires but according to our powers.' A Swiss philosopher said that. Amiel, I believe. You had a unique position of power in this situation. Your duty in this case was not to keep your wedding vows, but to use this other woman for a higher purpose."

"Beryl—my wife. She will suffer from what I've done. If I'm fortunate enough to survive all this and see her again, must she know this?"

"My boy, that is a problem for another day and as a good soldier, you know you must focus your mind on what's right in front of you. Do the next right thing tomorrow and then do it the day after and so on, and that's how you'll get yourself home. This worry will do you and the mission no good. Rest well tonight and trust that every bit of this will get sorted out as it needs to."

. . .

In the days after the men disappeared from the camp, the POWs played a shell game to cover their escape, a game made far easier because of the commandant's frantic, impulsive behavior that compromised the respect for him the guards had formerly held. Blankets and clothing stuffed in bunks portrayed men too ill to stand at *Appell*. When the roll was taken, several men responded at once, confusing the guards whose strict discipline had begun to unravel amidst whispers of evacuation. When Lieutenant Colonel Herbert was questioned about this man or that one who was rumored missing, he simply pointed around the corner and insisted that very man was just here—right in this very spot—so sorry you missed him. The commandant was near-paralyzed over his missing wife and the professional disaster it portended, failing to confirm in those critical early hours whether the POW she had taken such an interest in was AWOL, too. But after several weeks, once the driver and Friedrich were found dead and apparently innocent of any scheme involving Annalise, the guard captain and his assistant knew the British lieutenant and several other missing POWs must have fled in the missing staff car. When they dared lay out this case to the commandant, he found their theory insulting to him as their leader and offensive to him as a husband.

"You believe, what, that my wife has run off? Is that what you are saying? My wife has either suffered an accident, or she has been kidnapped, Captain," Reinhard bellowed, turning his truculent anger on the guards, accusing them of a dereliction of duty that resulted in Friedrich's fatal incompetence. "Every moment you spend spewing useless, baseless theories delays her safe return. Do you understand that? If you speak of this again, I will have you both court-martialed for implying that Frau Schröder left of her own accord. You are dismissed."

A year earlier, the guard captain might have made his case to the commandant with greater precision, gathering timelines and evidence to support his theory, tracking down the household help whom no one had yet located, who could certainly aid the investigation. But after years at the camp, apart from family, with diminishing rations, the artillery fire of the Red Army now plainly audible, the allegiance of the guard corps had waned: given the commandant's irrational ill temper, he could figure out the pieces of this mystery himself. *Fick dich ins Knie, mein Commandant.*

In December, as Hitler gambled on Operation Mist, his largest assault of the war with fourteen infantry divisions and five Panzer divisions, thrusting into the forbidding Ardennes in Belgium; as the Soviet army drew closer to the camp at Sagan; as American bombers pounded German targets practically without challenge, crippling Nazi supply lines, orders came for Reinhard to evacuate Stalag-Luft III. Immediately. Without alerting his superiors to his personal turmoil because of the opprobrium it would bring, he ordered his men to prepare the POWs to move out.

CHAPTER TWENTY-THREE

A man is not where he lives, but where he loves.
–Latin Proverb

Elsworth, 1944

As autumn deepened, Hugo tried to concentrate on his school lessons—he truly did—but he'd grown incapable of it and eventually, Schoolmistress Helms stopped expecting it of him. The boy could catch up next term. His father was due home before Christmas, having spent the previous weeks in the custody of the British Army. When a soldier walks away from enemy captivity and does not at least attempt to reunite himself with his command, there are questions to answer, even if that soldier spent the intervening time in a completely worthwhile endeavor.

Wills arrived at the Albany Street Barracks in London in September, but it was the first of December before he was finally granted leave to visit his family in Elsworth. It remained to be seen if he would be returned to 30th Infantry Brigade which had been reformed after Calais and was deployed at this moment in the Low Countries for what everyone hoped would be the final push in the war. He and Ivy had discussed this in the many phone calls and letters they'd exchanged over the weeks; she was prepared for whatever might happen. She believed God himself had preserved her husband's life in the years since Calais, and would continue to do so, whatever the army had in mind for him.

The day of Wills' return, Ivy let Hugo stay home from school. Even though the train was not due to arrive until late afternoon, Hugo's unbridled excitement would surely disrupt his classmates. Colin and the girls went on to school where, over lunchtime cheddar cheese sandwiches, classmates sought details of Lieutenant Hughes' homecoming.

"Just Hugo and his mum are going to the station later today," reported Margaret, "so's they can have a bit of family time, just the three of them. They've had chats since he came back—over the telephone—but today is the first time they will see one another."

"We're having dinner together tonight," Patsy continued with a measure of pride that she was part of the inner circle. "The Holy Trinity ladies are bringing beef roast and potatoes and carrots, with Mrs. Dowd bringing the biscuits. Shortbread, oatmeal AND gingersnaps!"

"But how is Hugo?" one of the older girls wanted to know, "with his dad returning after so very long?" For this answer, the gathering turned expectantly to Colin.

"He couldn't sleep last night," Colin allowed. "Bloody well talked the whole night. Every time I woke up, he was mumbling something. But he can't wait. He's had that fool smile on his face for two months now. He keeps reminding me that he always said his father would make it home."

And here's where the easy camaraderie of Elsworth natives and the evacuees they welcomed, whose worlds had been upended, transmuted into something far more potent, a bond that continued to heal and sustain them, first through bouts of homesickness and worry over their parents' welfare and later, as one after another navigated the heartache of loss. Colin was not the only one who had been told his father was dead: the fathers of nineteen students of the fifty enrolled in the Elsworth school were either dead, confined to a POW camp, or missing. Some evacuees no longer had homes in London to return to, one boy losing his mother and much-older sister in the explosion of a V-1. All of them had an uncle, a friend, a neighbor with whom they had celebrated holidays and the arrival of new babies and first days of school who were simply gone now, an irreplaceable thread in the tapestry of their young lives. But living here in this tiny, tranquil village, this particular set of young people had somehow not grown numb and withdrawn, bitter and overwhelmed. Influenced by the grown-ups around them who gently tended to their complicated needs, they instead moved closer to one another, trusting each other with these acute hurts, demonstrating sensitivities and sensibilities that usually required many more years to cultivate.

"We thought the odds had your dad as the one returning," said one of the older boys, coming around the table to place a hand on Colin's shoulder, bravely saying the thing that needed saying as the others nodded and Patsy murmured, as she had done countless times, that she was "so, so, so sorry" to her adoptive brother.

The older boy continued. "You're going to hear some bits tonight, I bet, about your own dad, Colin. About him being brave in holding Calais as long as he did. Astonishing that Lieutenant Hughes knew him. I want to hear all about it, alright? Tomorrow."

The boy's adroit conversational pivot earned a smile from Colin and prompted the others to share for surely the millionth time the highlights of what they knew about the battles in which their own fathers and brothers and uncles had fought. They traded stories all of them already knew by heart, of courage and sacrifice, their recitations stopping short of retelling the chain of events that resulted for some in permanent separation. These narratives instead remained in the realm of the heroic, bypassing bad decisions or bad luck that had proved fatal, echoes of the made-up tales they'd told on their train ride to Elsworth those many years ago, but without the bombast and hyperbole.

"Yes, it's a mad coincidence, isn't it? On my very first day here, it was Hugo himself who speculated that our dads had met. And I sort of rolled my eyes about it—I mean, what were the chances? And what do you know? They had. And it... I don't know why... but it makes me feel a bit better that Hugo's dad—a man I will soon meet—was with him a little farther in the journey after he had to leave us. It's like our families were meant to be connected, a part of one another."

His classmates nodded, collectively grateful for the providence that had brought them together to just this place to wait out the calamity that had seized Europe.

·   ·   ·

While Ivy and Hugo sat staring at the kitchen clock, willing it to advance sufficiently so they could begin their walk to the train station, Colin pedaled over to Kimbolton, something he had rarely done alone. He rode by the pastures and paths and woodlands that had provided the quiet space for his growing up. He remembered walking barefoot across this landscape with Hugo that first fall—something he had never done in London—the pain of each pebble and twig pressing into his tender feet. How Hugo had laughed. Proper boys didn't walk barefoot on the streets of London as they could in Elsworth, and it took a while for the soles of Colin's feet to toughen up. Life and its routines would change now that Hugo's dad was back. The two of them would no longer be the men of the house, as Ivy called them, but the time was nearing when Colin could return home to London, anyway. Why did the idea of that make him sad? He had wanted to rejoin his mother soon after he learned of his father's death, but now, leaving Elsworth felt like another loss. As he pumped the pedals in the chill air, the sun low in the gray sky, he felt dislocated, unsure of where he belonged, displaced from the comfortable nest that had been created for him here that had shielded him from missing the life in London he'd known as a much younger boy.

Colin approached the gatehouse to the base, giving a wave and not intending to slow, but the guard stepped in front of him and blocked his route.

"Whoa there, buddy. I need you to stop," said the private. "Let me let them know you're here." He picked up his radio.

"What it is, sir? I'm Colin Clarke. I'm usually with Hugo and they always wave us through. They know us here. Is something wrong? Is Lieutenant Philip okay?"

"He is son. He's coming right now."

Jack strode toward the guardhouse, uniform cap low on his brow, cigarette clenched tight in his teeth. He signed the visitor's log and tilted his head toward his barracks, signaling for Colin to follow. Colin walked his bicycle to the Nissen hut, his worry accelerating with each sympathetic look he earned from the airmen they passed on the way.

"What is it, Jack?" he implored. "What's happened?"

They sat on Jack's cot, side by side, Jack placing his broad hand on the boy's neck. Colin saw a series of deep red gashes across his forearm, along with several large bandages. "Colin, buddy. We lost Buck," he said, staring straight ahead.

Colin felt his throat constrict, bile moving up from his stomach. "What do you mean? He didn't make it home? Did he bail? What happened?"

"We got hit over Dresden. Artillery fire came right through the windshield and got him. Lost one of the waist gunners too when the engine came apart. He was all cut up. We couldn't save either of them. We tried but... no idea how the rest of us made it back." He stubbed out his cigarette and immediately lit another one.

Not Buck, who had taught them so much about flight and modern avionics—who explained things so clearly, so patiently. With whom they had laughed and joked during so many Saturday meals, hearing about Chicago and his family there and how he couldn't wait to return to write for the Tribune. Colin heaved a deep, guttural breath and began to cry the tears he had not been able to shed for his own father. Jack pulled him close.

"Purple heart corner?" Colin asked.

"No, it wasn't even that. It was just a vicious defense of the target and one we didn't completely expect. The Luftwaffe is limited now. They don't have the planes and pilots they had three years ago, so they've consolidated their defenses over some key strategic areas. They're not going to let this thing end easily. Never experienced anti-aircraft fire like that—just ruthless pounding. Tells me they're on the ropes. But it's still costing us. In a big way."

"How'd you get back? You got all the way home with a bad engine?"

Jack gave a sad smile. "It's what Boeing built these rigs to do. And after twenty-three missions with ole Buck Myers, there ain't much I don't know about handling a Fortress. I think Buck ran me through just about every set of variables we could face, so we'd be prepared for anything, have the best chance to get back. The Gator's shot up to hell, but she'll fly again once the engine's replaced. And the windshield. And, well, there's a lot of interior cleanup to do." He paused, lifting his eyes to Colin's. "We made it back because Buck was a stubborn cuss who made sure we were prepared, that I would always know what to do. And wanna know the worst part? I'm getting promoted over this, for making it back with the aircraft and saving seven lives. They're awarding me a Distinguished Flying Cross. All I can think about is the two buddies we lost, but the Army Air Corps sees it differently. It's really Buck, not me, who deserves the credit for gettin' us back to Kimbolton."

"Captain Jack Philip," Colin said, rubbing the heels of his hands under his eyes, trying in vain to erase the tears that continued to fall.

"Yeah. Captain Philip. Helluva way to get promoted."

"I can't believe this. Hugo and the twins—this will break their hearts. But I want to tell you... I am so glad you survived. So very thankful. For myself... and my mum."

"Well, that's mighty kind of you to say, Colin," said Jack, his voice husky. "It's a generous thing for you to say. I'm glad I made it. And I'm glad you're glad. I guess we'll have to stick together to get through the rest of this mess, huh? Deal?"

They shook on it, clasping hands then embracing before Colin turned to leave. At the door, he had a sudden thought. "Does my mother know?"

"Calling her tonight."

Colin nodded. "Who will tell his parents, Jack? You?"

"The army sends a couple of officers to the house but yes, I'll be writing them a letter about what happened."

"Could I, do you think, write them too? Just to tell them how much better Buck made everything for us here. All the things I learned from him about flying. So they know that he was our American and everything?"

"Absolutely. You'd be doing them a kindness. Maybe I can put your note in with mine."

. . .

Colin would not share the news about Buck with his Elsworth family yet. Hugo and Ivy had a right to joyfully celebrate Lieutenant Hughes' homecoming, so he resolved to put a smile on his face and bear up for the welcome tonight and the next number of days as needed. He pulled his bicycle up to the house as dusk settled in and looked at the dark house, the interior light hidden by the blackout curtains. What joy must be taking place inside right now, he thought. He entered and there, seated on the sofa, he saw an older version of Hugo. Marigold was ensconced in his lap while Margaret and Patsy perched on either side of him, explaining the plot of

Margaret's latest story. (It was a wartime adventure featuring twins who were spies.) Wills rose, his hand extended.

"My other son, is it? Colin, I'm Hugo's dad," he said, an utterly superfluous statement.

"Yes, sir." They shook hands. "Hello and welcome back, sir. Are you well, then? They've treated you alright in all of this?"

"Surprisingly so, yes. I'm in one piece. As are Hugo and my wife, thanks in large measure, I believe to you. They say you've been a champ here, helping with the two young ones."

"We're not awfully young now," said Patsy, scooping the cat to her side.

"I hope I've done my part, sir," said Colin, chuckling a bit, "keeping them in line, you know," evincing loud protestations from both girls.

"Indeed, you have. More than ought to be asked of you."

Hugo emerged from the kitchen with a tray holding whiskey for his father and mother and Coca-Colas for the rest of them. "Colin! We're having a toast to Dad," he said. "Tried to talk mom into letting us have a spot of whiskey to celebrate but, well, she said no."

Ivy followed, bearing a basket of salted crackers and a wedge of cheese. Already, Colin saw, there was a different aspect to her face, to Hugo's. The worry that had knotted their foreheads, dulled the light in their eyes, had been chased away by Wills' return. In its place, Colin saw hope and relief, bliss wrought by the miracle that stood before them. Even on this day, when he had learned of Buck's fate, it seemed possible, just slightly possible, for there to be happy moments once more in the world. It was not the unbounded, limitless joy that he had once believed, as a little boy, life to be— one adventure after another, more exciting than the last, the sky's the limit—but it was enough. There could still be bursts of pleasure.

A knock at the door heralded the vicar and Dorothy Dowd, delivering the promised biscuits for after dinner. At the sight of Elsworth's butcher, Reverend Dowd laid a hand on each shoulder, his booming voice lifting in a prayer of thanksgiving, the rest of them freezing in place as he did so, Margaret with one eye opened, peeking to take in the scene. The vicar's voice grew weak and whispery and the tears dropped down his face and off his mutton chops as he thanked God and William himself for his role in seeing the vicar's grandson to safety. As he finished, he drew his handkerchief from his pocket and offered apologies.

"Took me by surprise, that one," he said, as Patsy sidled up and took his hand.

"Quite alright, Reverend," she assured him. "You're entitled to be a bit weepy these days, just like the rest of us. Jesus wept, you know. It's in the Bible."

"Yes, I'm rather aware, Patsy. But I do so appreciate the reminder," said the vicar, bowing officiously, allowing her to reach up and give his wet beard a pat.

The Dowds declined to stay for dinner, but did raise a toast to Wills before they departed. Over their meal, the succulent roast surprising Wills utterly in its competent preparation, he recounted what he could about his work in France, general truths that would not give too much away about particular methods as there were still plenty of people behind the lines in Poland, Czechoslovakia, and elsewhere whom partisans were still passing through the network. He shared details of his own accidental escape, of his time with Albert and his family, of Sylvi's bravery and finding Gilles in Paris. He left out, on this night of nights, how Albert and Ginette had met their end. The children were enthralled, Hugo saying again and again "just WAIT 'til the mates hear this" while Ivy sat chin in hand, gazing at her long-lost husband. She was proud of him, certainly, but she was still weighing the cost of his protracted absence, his choosing to stay in the most dangerous kind of work. How had he not grown desperate to get to them—his own family? It was almost unbelievable to her, this man with whom she shared a child and a simple, unremarkable life, becoming a spy, his clandestine activities spanning years.

Colin cleared his throat. "I've another question," he said. "You knew my dad at Calais."

The room grew very quiet. "I did, in fact, yes, Colin. We had no idea that you'd come to Elsworth, of course, but I remember your father as a very brave sort. The battle at Calais was buggered up from the start." Patsy's eyes grew wide at his profanity, and she leaned into Margaret's shoulder, stifling a giggle as Ivy swatted her husband's arm. "Yes, sorry. My apologies. Anyway, our forces were no match for the Germans, but your dad, Colin, even as things were getting worse and worse, he remained steady and calm. He stayed on the front lines protecting the garrison when, I'm a bit ashamed to say, some members of the French army and even some Brits managed to sneak away and head inland. No telling what happened to them because we surely didn't have any escape routes in play then. But your dad, when he could have hung back behind all the privates, stayed up with them. He never quit until the Nazis charged our location."

"What about after you were captured?"

"I was with him about a month after that, as we were marched into northern France and then Germany. We learned pretty quickly that the enemy was brutal, unsparing. But the men looked up to your father, him being a bit older and having a reassuring way about him."

"That does sound like dad," agreed Colin. "Something trustworthy about him, I'd say."

"Sounds like you, Colin," said Ivy. "I'd say you're much the same way."

"I know, I know. Apple doesn't fall far from the tree and all that." Colin waggled a finger at Ivy. "We all see what you're doing here." He smiled.

· · ·

That night, Ivy laughed as she entered her bedroom, seeing that the girls had relocated their palettes to the boys' room to afford her and her husband some privacy. The moment the door was closed, Wills swept her up into his arms, his chin resting on her head, taking in her scent, so warm, familiar. Feeling just the slightest bit of resistance, he pulled back and she stood primly before him. Was she feeling shy after all this time? Reluctant to give herself to him?

"What is it?" he asked. "Ivy?"

"I'm sorry, Wills. I'm sorry. I don't mean to act this way. I told myself not to. But before... before we go on, I need to understand. Because," and here the tears came unbidden, "I could never abandon you for so long and leave you to wonder and worry as I've had to do. I am proud of you, my husband, so proud. But knowing I was less important than the excitement you found in France..."

"Ivy. Oh, Ivy. It was never that. Never the thrill of it. I didn't do it because I felt a lesser commitment to you and Hugo. I did it because the only way you and our son will be free is if we beat these bastards. If we do not prevail, our way of life is over and to not fight in the best way I could would be consigning our boy to a life run by tyrants. I wanted to come home to you, take a respite from the war, but I was so grateful to have my life, grateful to the strangers who sacrificed everything for me, that I had to stay and do what I could. Albert and Ginette? The couple who saved me? What I didn't tell the children is that the Nazis executed them, caught them with evidence they'd been passing people through the lines."

Ivy's hands covered to her mouth. She leaned her head heavily into his chest. "God bless them," she whispered.

Wills' voice grew quiet. "Every man I got out of France was one who could return to battle—fliers, mostly, far more skilled in warfare than I was at my capture. These are the men who will win the war. And the families, Ivy, the hunted, forsaken families who came to us because they had no other hope. It's because of what we have here, because of our precious family and the safe and happy life we've known—I had to give others a chance to have that too. The Nazis have no regard for anyone but themselves. It was my duty—to my country, yes, but also to you and Hugo—to stay in France and fight. Not because I didn't love you well enough, but because I had to do everything in my power to make the world safe for you. Because I love you that much."

She pulled back from his embrace to look him in the eye. And because of her practical nature, cultivated and sustained by the people of Elsworth, and the steadfast optimism that had attracted him to her in the first place and had carried her through the worst moments of this war, she pronounced her questions answered. She would not spend another minute wondering. Because if she had learned anything, it was that time was limited; the future was not promised. Best to make the most of the present.

With a gleam in her eye, she requested that her husband unbutton her dress and remove her underclothes and shoes, as well as his own, and climb into bed with her because it was well-nigh past time they become reacquainted. Her manner—flirty, bossy, direct—would have shocked the children. Always one to fulfill his duty as he saw it, Wills obliged, picking her up in his arms and laying her gently on the faded eiderdown quilt.

CHAPTER TWENTY-FOUR

Soldiers are citizens of death's grey land,
drawing no dividend from time's tomorrows.
♀–Siegfried Sassoon

Inside the Reich, 1944

The twin Swastika flags on the Mercedes' hood grew stiff in the blowing snow, the small rectangles of fabric, the angry slash of black, potential guarantors of safe passage. The escapees took a circuitous route out of Sagan, formulated during Gordon's many rides to the manor house, aided by maps Clara furnished, information Annalise gathered in her strategic visits to Reinhard's office, and intelligence provided by paratroopers infiltrating Poland. Gordon wore their one good German officer's cap and the uniform coat the commandant had no idea he'd donated. The others positioned themselves under blankets and would pretend to doze at the checkpoints ahead. The fallback plan would be to shoot their way through with the two handguns they possessed—hardly a failsafe and an option they hoped not to exercise. Each was equipped with a forged *Ausweis* that identified them as Heer soldiers, ostensibly members of an engineering battalion headed to the southernmost boundary of the Reich to reconnoiter and recommend the men and resources needed to hold it. It was a flimsy cover that would work only if they lucked up on border guards who lacked imagination or were easily bullied by higher-ranking officers in a luxury sedan.

Fifteen kilometers from town stood the first checkpoint. Well in advance, Gordon pulled the car behind a ramshackle barn so the mission team could make some adjustments, placing Annalise in the car's boot, along with the smallest British escapee, Sergeant Melvin McGruder. His job was to keep her from screaming or banging a foot on the inside of the boot to draw attention. The sergeant rather liked this assignment, wrapping his arms and legs around a gorgeous, writhing female, climbing on top of her as necessary to keep her quiet. He took readily to the task.

Each man had been selected for this mission based on his skills and background. Graham Fletcher was the BEF private Gordon had served with since Calais, the man who first alerted Lieutenant Colonel Herbert that Gordon had fallen seriously ill with typhus. After four years in the camp, he spoke a serviceable German, and his light-blonde hair and blue eyes could potentially delay the detection of his nationality. The two Americans—a sergeant and a captain—were airmen shot down soon after DeGaulle made his triumphant return to Paris. Captain Floyd Harris was a pilot and wing commander who knew the terrain of the European Theater of Operations better than most. He had completed twenty missions in his B-17, bombing runs on the ordnance depot at Magdeburg, the synthetic oil refinery at Regensburg, the marshaling yards in the Ruhr among them. An aeronautical engineer by training, his navigational instincts had been sharpened in hours of detailed pre- and post-mission briefings. Sergeant Al Balducci, Junior was a waist gunner from Philadelphia who was on his twenty-fifth and final mission when his plane was shot down. Al joked he had the record for the shortest length of evasion from the enemy: a line of Nazi soldiers, rifles raised, had calmly tracked the descent of his parachute as it deposited him into the center of their column. They had cut off his chute, picked him up, and marched him several miles to headquarters, the German platoon sergeant happy to accept Al's offer of a Camel cigarette. Sergeant Balducci was far more fortunate than the plane's tail gunner: after parachuting into a wheat field, he was pitchforked to death by a group of infuriated German farmers. A storied sharpshooter, Al carried one of the Lugars.

Gordon approached the checkpoint, the six forged IDs tucked in the visor, gun on his hip. The men pulled their blankets to their chins, eyes scanning for signs of danger, hands gripping the door handles in case they had to move quickly. But as Gordon slowed the staff car and moved to roll down his window, the Nazi guard simply saluted and waved them through.

In the cold snow, he was not eager to leave the relative warmth of his guard house to review the travel documents of what appeared to be high-ranking Nazi officers. Gordon gave a quick nod and drove on.

"Bob's your uncle," exclaimed Graham.

"Holy Mother of God," exhaled Al. "Are you kidding me? That's it? They're idiots, these guys. I don't think they give a shit anymore."

Floyd laughed. "That's just the first one, Al. We got a few more to get through before we're out of this mess."

"Well, Captain, sir, I'm praying they're all like that one."

"You do that, Al. Keep praying. And when you're not using that rosary, hand it over to me, why don't you?"

"Ain't you a Baptist, Captain?" Al chided him.

"Yeah, well, let's say I'm covering my bases."

.   .   .

Retrieved from the boot, Floyd removed the scarf around her mouth and offered Annalise some bread and a bit of cheese. She had no appetite for either. Along with the food Clara packed, Annalise spotted two bottles of Burgundy, part of the assortment delivered to her by the Reichsführer at her party last spring. There was the corkscrew from the *Terrasse* bar, even. She seethed. How lovely that her loyal house staff had secreted the prized bottles away for this purpose. How long had these men, Annalise wondered, and Clara and Helene, been planning this with Gordon? From the center of the back seat, she spat a stream of angry questions and accusations at Gordon, demanding to know where they were going. What would happen to her? Who was making him do this? Gordon, responding in English in deference to the others, told her she need not worry: if she cooperated, she would survive, healthy and well. He did not respond to her pleadings about whether he had ever really cared for her and the rhetorical follow up: how could he do this to her after they'd been lovers? Eyebrows raised and eyes wide, Floyd shot Al a look. Graham shifted uncomfortably in the front seat. Melvin suggested, politely, that it was time for Annalise to shut up and enjoy the scenery.

Eventually, the car grew quiet, Annalise closing her eyes in fatigue and resignation, the men hyper vigilant, transfixed by the incongruous beauty of the gently falling snow and the open terrain. After several hours, they neared Bunzlau, their first pickup point. They found the dairy farm as described, just south of town, and the small weathered shack on the grounds. Inside, a rusted trough held pants and jackets and caps that, from a distance, could pass for Wehrmacht-issued uniforms once the men added the buttons and insignias from their stash. They left their Allied fatigues in exchange, relieved to shed the emblems that could give them away. Their castoffs would be reworked to camouflage whomever passed this way next—a Jewish family, perhaps, or a Polish partisan helping others escape. Tucked beneath the trough were two containers of petrol that would allow them to continue driving through the next several days, as well as detailed directions to a safe house. This, they each committed to memory before shredding the paper. As Gordon pulled the car back onto the roadway, a lone farmer stood at the edge of his field, shovel in hand, scraping it aimlessly on the snowy ground. From the near-imperceptible nod he gave as they passed, the men concluded that farming was only part of how this gentleman spent his time.

Above Görlitz, as Gordon drove up over a small rise, a dense mass of men and vehicles—hundreds and hundreds of POWs—came into view. So. The camps were being evacuated. The group was headed directly toward them, towards the northwest. Gordon slipped the car quickly behind a line of evergreens to allow Melvin to move Annalise into the boot. The others settled into their seats, more confident now in their makeshift Nazi uniforms. Graham took the wheel and Gordon moved to the back seat as the most "senior" Nazi among the contingent. They pulled back onto the road, then parked, as if they were purposely on scene to review the evacuation. It was a ragtag contingent—cadaverous prisoners so obviously malnourished with little protection from the cold. Their guards, wrapped in their greatcoats, fur-lined hats, and scarves, walked beside the long columns, with more senior officers traveling in trucks and on motor scooters. When they spotted the staff car, many snapped a salute, palms raised in esteem of their Führer.

"Nothing like hiding in plain sight," Al observed wryly.

"Act the part, gentlemen," advised Floyd, "so they have no reason to take a second look."

These were broken men trudging past, many shoeless and scuffling, disoriented by the cold and lack of food. Americans, British, Canadians, Australians—many walking arm in arm, the stronger ones pulling the sicker men along. Their uniforms were horribly soiled; those who left the column to piss or defecate were swiftly shot so the POWs had learned to shit as they walked, those with dysentery producing a ceaseless, churning stream down their legs, brown liquid drawing lines in the snow behind them.

"I suppose our mates are evacuating our camp as well," said Graham, easing the vehicle down the road as the last cluster of prisoners passed. "This is utterly shambolic. Where in the world are they headed? How will they survive this march?"

"I'm not sure they're supposed to," said Floyd.

. . .

The next checkpoint loomed at Görlitz. They were certain to be carefully questioned here, driving against the surge of POWs headed the other way. Gordon offered Annalise an option: she could climb back into the boot with her eager chaperone, or don a uniform jacket and cap, stay in the car, and pretend to sleep, a Lugar pressed into her ribs. Her eyes filled with tears, rebuking Gordon for speaking so harshly with her. She would stay in the car, she said. She would do as told. Gordon was greatly relieved: this close to the border with Czechoslovakia, the boot would most surely be searched.

Their props in place, each man signaling his readiness, Graham pulled the car toward the checkpoint and lowered his window.

"Was ist Ihr Geschäft?" What is your business? the guard asked.

His throat dry, tongue thick, Gordon called gruffly from the back seat that he was the lead of this engineering task group, the battalion to follow shortly. Graham handed over the stack of *Ausweis,* keeping his gaze attentively forward.

The guard shivered, stamped his feet to fight off the cold, and flipped through the stack of papers. He paused at one, then peered in the car and counted. He observed aloud that it was a fine night for travel.

Gordon barked an irritated response, letting the guard know they were not there to make idle conversation. The guard got the message, returning the documents quickly and offering an earnest Heil Hitler. Graham responded with the same and rolled up the window. The guard lifted the gate arm and waved the car through. But as it passed, he seemed to remember a key part of his job, one he was loathe to neglect even in this weather.

"Der Kofferraum," he yelled, pointing, walking after the car. The boot. The trunk.

"Bollocks," breathed Graham.

"Drive. Drive. Drive. Drive. Slowly. Don't stop." Gordon chanted quietly from the back seat, head turned to disguise his anxiety, to ensure the guard could not catch his eye. Graham continued on, accelerating slightly, just an obtuse, overworked driver of a self-important Nazi officer, simply trying to do his job at this difficult juncture in the war. The guard continued to try to get Graham's attention, beginning a trot alongside the vehicle, waving his right hand in hopes of catching his peripheral vision. But then he stopped and watched the car pull away, giving a small shrug and returning to tend the small fire burning outside his drafty guard shack. Fine, then. This could be someone else's concern. He radioed ahead to the next checkpoint at Legnica to say a staff car with an odd assortment of officers was en route.

The men drove through the night, trading off behind the wheel, two of them keeping eyes on Annalise at all times in case she got any ideas. Their progress was slow over the rutted roads, but visibility improved when the snow tapered off into tiny flakes before stopping altogether. Melvin took charge of the food, subdividing it over the four days they expected to need it. If they added to their provisions, so much the better. But that wasn't a given. Melvin's curation ensured they would not, despite their longstanding hunger, consume everything in the first twenty-four hours.

"That cook really knows how to boil an egg and bake a potato," said Al, directing the comment to Annalise, who didn't respond. The men, Gordon excepted, groaned in pleasure at the aroma, the texture of the freshly prepared food compared to the thin cabbage soup they'd subsisted on the past months. The boiled eggs became gourmet delicacies thanks to Clara, who had thoughtfully sent several envelopes—Swastikas engraved on the flaps—full of salt, pepper, and dried dill.

"God's honest truth—this meal ranks right up there with my mama's ravioli. When this whole thing is over, I'm thinking we could open up a little restaurant, right in south Philly, and I can cook there right alongside her. I'll tell her to put me in charge of the egg boiling." The men laughed, Floyd promising he would make reservations to eat there as soon as it opened. Gordon said little, thinking of the meat, the fruit, the breads he'd consumed during his days at the manor house, the wine he and Annalise savored together after their trysts. Perhaps he could have brought more back to hungry men at the camp. Perhaps he should have.

They headed east now, their progress hampered by the accumulated snow that would not be cleared from the roadways until spring or until the T-34 tanks of the Red Army thundered over them—whichever came first. German troops were engaged in furious battles with Slovakian partisans miles to their south, hopefully too absorbed with that to spot a lone German staff car trundling down the road in the dark.

As they neared Legnica, they fell into their roles, buttoning their uniform coats, tossing egg shells and apple cores out the window, pushing the box of buttons under the seat and sheaves of forged documents into slits they'd cut into the roof liner of the car. Graham drove and Gordon, once again, acted the part of highest-ranked officer in the group. They were traveling at dawn, they would say, to catch up with a contingent from whom they'd been separated. They were trying to make up time.

In the dim light, the high turret of the Piast Castle and the soaring steeple of the Legnica Cathedral appeared on the horizon. Legnica is known for its medieval architecture, Floyd noted, adding he did not recommend they stick around for any tours while they were in town.

They spotted the checkpoint, ran down their security checklist one more time, then settled in as Graham drove to the gate. The young guard seemed to be expecting them, prompting Gordon's first frisson of concern.

The guard requested they step out of the car as soon as it drew to a halt, his machine gun hanging loosely from his right hand. Gordon barked a furious retort, but the guard held firm: he would summon his superior if they did not comply. Behind the young German was the small guard house—apparently empty—and behind that, an outbuilding that could house sleeping quarters and perhaps the guard's supervisor. Or might not. One thing was sure: the moment they stepped out of the car, the mission was compromised. Even if they managed to explain Annalise's presence, their cobbled-together uniforms, upon close inspection, would give them away, along with their worn army-issue boots and the fact that only three of them spoke German.

"What do ya say, Captain?" Al whispered, his lips barely moving.

"We're too close to town to shoot him out in the open. You have your implements, gentlemen. Al and I stay outside. The three of you, go in." Floyd responded. "Mrs. Schröder, take off the uniform jacket. You have your wish: you're married to Gordon here. Our German colonel. Go."

Annalise did as she was told, wriggling out of the jacket and pushing it under the front seat of the car with her foot.

They moved out of the car suddenly, surprising the guard who had expected this to take longer, to give him time to summon back-up. He waved the gun to move them away from the vehicle, all the while appraising their odd uniforms, their irregular haircuts, the stubble on their faces. And Annalise. He spoke first to her, asking why she was on a military mission so close to live fire.

"I never wish to be away from the commandant," she said, linking her arm through Gordon's and pressing into his side. "His work is my work. I am greatly honored to accompany him."

He turned next to Al, taking in his olive complexion, his dark eyes and hair.

"Dieser Mann ist Deutsch?" asked the guard, turning to Gordon. You expect me to believe this man is German?

Al shrugged, then laughed, sensing the thread. "Ich bin Italienerin," he offered. I'm Italian. Gordon added that after Italy went over to the Allies, this brave fighter stayed on with the Reich. The guard nodded slowly, skeptically.

He backed up to the car, the weapon still trained on the escapees. He opened the driver's side door and looked in. Nothing. He moved to the passenger side, seeing nothing on the seat. But there, on the floor, what were those? Pebbles? Small, round rocks, along with some bright snatches of color. He peered in more closely and saw the assortment of Wehrmacht buttons, the double lightening slashes of the SS insignia, Nazi uniform ribbons. Annalise's kick to hide the uniform jacket had dislodged and overturned the button box. The Görlitz guard was right. It fit now—these odd uniforms, this irregular group. They were imposters. He would alert the colonel.

But the guard's eyes lingered a second too long trying to sort out the apparent contraband. Al slipped soundlessly behind him, pulling from his boot the kitchen knife Clara had provided. He drew it quickly across the guard's throat as Graham and Gordon moved toward the outbuilding. Melvin wrestled Annalise back into the car, worried she would scream for help but the violence, the blood pouring from the man's neck onto the once-pristine snow, the way his eyes had registered the attack, the gurgling in his throat, stunned her into silence. She covered her face with her hands as Melvin moved to cover the man's body with snow.

Gordon eased open the door to the outbuilding—a small, spare barracks—to find a couple asleep. A Nazi colonel, his jacket hung on a hook at the door, and a young woman—a teenager, probably—lay entwined, skin to skin, in a twin bed. The girl stirred at the squeak of the door hinge and at first seemed not to recognize that strangers had entered the room.

"Du bist früh dran." You're early, she mumbled, her sleepy mind thinking her next customer had arrived, that she must rouse the colonel and send him on his way. But when she saw there were two men, both completely unfamiliar to her, she bolted upright and screamed.

The colonel awoke and stumbled from the bed, scrambling for the radio that sat on a small table on the back wall.

"The weapon, you idiot!" the girl screamed, as she rolled over to the colonel's side of the bed to retrieve a handgun tucked under the mattress.

She swung around to shoot, but Gordon leapt, butcher knife in his hand, and slashed her, cutting viciously into her neck until her hand released the weapon. Her head dropped grotesquely onto her shoulder, her small body crumpling into the bed. She made no further sound. Graham seized the gun and shot the colonel, then shot out the radio for good measure.

Their clothes spattered with blood, they grabbed the colonel's uniform jacket from the hook and returned to the car to find the others waiting, the engine revving. Graham asked if someone else could drive for a bit, so Al climbed behind the wheel.

"How many?" asked Floyd.

"Two," responded Gordon. "A colonel and... a young girl."

"Killed?" Floyd pressed. "Are you sure?"

"Quite."

"Had to do it, Lieutenant," Al reasoned. "We couldn't have them radioing up ahead that we're coming. That's what happened here. After Görlitz. They were waiting for us."

"Quite," Gordon repeated, astonished at the brutal new proficiency he had just demonstrated. A girl. A young girl. He saw again the white skin of her neck, the bloom of blood that quickly soaked her braids, her small, bare breasts.

"So, hear me, sir: you did the right thing. You had to. No question."

Floyd continued. "He's right, Gordon. Shake it off. We've got miles to go before we sleep."

The task now was to put some distance between themselves and the checkpoint. There was no telling how long it might be before the dead were discovered. After two hours' time, Al pulled the car off the road and into a copse of trees. They would stay hidden for the remainder of the day and resume the journey after sunset. Their next objective was the safe house in Kraków, some 300 kilometers away, where they would stay overnight. They would reach Kalinov, Czechoslovakia two days later. That was the plan, anyway.

CHAPTER TWENTY-FIVE

People never lie so much as after a hunt, during a war or before an election.
–Otto von Bismarck

London 1944

While the Allied commanders—Eisenhower, McArthur, Montgomery, Bradley, Zhukov—headlined the newsreels as their armies made their inexorable march to the Rhine, the agents of the British Special Operations Executive continued their own quiet and deadly work in the shadows, supporting the underground fighters at war with the Germans. The SOE had been formed from the consolidation of several spy offices and agencies, its official inception coming just months after the collapse at Calais, Winston Churchill charging its leader to go and set Europe ablaze. The Ministry of Ungentlemanly Warfare, as it was known to insiders, handled the most unsavory aspects of spy craft—assassinating the Nazi governor of the Protectorate of Bohemia and Moravia is one example—while furnishing life-giving support that fueled the work of the Maquis and the partisans across the occupied continent. Its protean moral framework made for a fraught and complicated relationship with the commanders of the British military.

It was an SOE agent who had handed the plump potato to Clara at the market in Sagan, his section that ran the team that supported and tracked the progress of the Stalag-Luft III escapees as they headed south, arranging to resupply them with food and petrol. Members of his team furnished the seemingly nonsensical messages relayed over the BBC that instructed embedded agents and partisans on the lines to prepare for visitors. And it was members of his team that safely ferried Clara and Helene and six members of their families away from Sagan, to ensure the camp commandant's staff could not pay them a visit and wring from them the truth about what had happened that final morning in Sagan.

On the morning Gordon and the men had departed the manor house, the women set about their normal duties. If someone from the Gestapo or the camp came, it would appear only that the driver had chauffeured Mrs. Schröder, along with the POW and his guard, on some sort of errand. It would not be their duty to know anything beyond that. Only the stripped kitchen offered a clue that something was amiss: the women had sent the contents of the larder and pantry with the escapees, a few mostly rotten potatoes and onions, some curdled cream the only items remaining. Late in the day, after composing the farewell note that lamented their firing, they locked the premises as they typically did and began their usual route home through the snow, stolen gold coins and pieces of Mrs. Stroński's jewelry sewn into their skirts, bottles of liquor they had lifted from the commandant's bar clanking in their burlap satchels. They had thoughtfully left several bottles of wine for the commandant, knowing he was likely to need it upon his return home that evening. After midnight, in the blowing snow, they began their escape from Sagan in earnest, a slow and arduous trip through the dense woods in the back of a farm wagon. They headed north in hopes of avoiding the Soviet army that often did not differentiate between Germans and their Polish subordinates. With Clara were her daughter and the daughter's eight-year-old twins, along with Clara's great uncle whom the Nazis had deemed too old to send to the Russian front. Accompanying Helene were her husband and their teenage son. The group traveled only at night, hiding out for weeks at a time in a series of villages and farmhouses, before arriving at the ruined port city of Danzig. There, hidden in the hold of a fishing boat, they set sail for Karlskrona, part of the Swedish archipelago, the tense passage made worse by roiling waters that made all but the youngest seasick. They floated up to a small jetty at dawn on a crisp but sunny day, shocked at the enthusiastic welcome they received from the Special Operations Executive section that, as it turned out, was well-equipped in ostensibly neutral Sweden. The next day, the eight of them found their way to morning Mass at the one tiny Catholic church on Karlskrona, all of them overwhelmed with joy that they could worship free from the black tarnish of Nazi regulation that had contaminated their church in Sagan. As Clara knelt at the altar, receiving the bread and wine, her tears flowed unimpeded, wetting the hands of the young priest as he brought the cup to her mouth. "För att vi skola vara fria, har Kristus frigjort oss," he whispered. Christ has made us free. Clara knew not a word of Swedish, but she understood him exactly.

It was this same SOE that had directed the War Office clerk to play dumb each time Mrs. Gordon Clarke called to ask if there was any updated news on the details of her husband's death and the disposition of his things. After MI5 had moved on Jesse, they undertook surveillance of Beryl and the American with whom she spent considerable time, an agent often parked in Jesse's former sitting room to observe comings and goings, mostly to put to rest any concerns that Beryl had cooperated with Jesse's inept undercover work. It took a number of months, but eventually the various entities—the branches of the intelligence service, the SOE, and the War Office, prompted by an earnest army records clerk who sought once and for all to get answers about Lieutenant Clarke—compared their sets of facts and realized the POW the International Red Cross declared dead of disease at Stalag-Luft III was the same officer Jesse Jordan said found work within the home of a Nazi colonel and was, in fact, the same bloke the SOE was supplying as he rattled through the Polish hinterlands in a stolen Nazi staff car with a group of escapees. Military practice and protocol required officers to immediately contact the soldier's wife to correct this grievous mistake and essentially declare the lieutenant no longer dead. But the SOE forbid it. The man remained in danger, went the argument, until he was back on British soil. Were he to die in the course of their escape, they could hopefully secure something of his and return it to the widow and she would be none the wiser that he had lived months past his alleged fatal case of typhus. But certainly, at this juncture, there was no reason to apprise her of anything because the chance of these men escaping the Reich were slim to nil. It was resolved among them all that they would keep their cruel secret for now. The records clerk would make known in the office that any inquiries regarding Clarke should come to him. Hopefully, they could mislead and obviate until such time the man was actually free and they could tell the truth.

Andrew Wilkins, the London-based agent who continued to surveil Beryl, observed that there was another reason not to inform Mrs. Clarke of her husband's status. "It does not appear that she misses her husband too awfully much," he told those gathered to discuss the case at the Baker Street offices. He offered dates and times—and they were numerous—wherein the American pilot stayed overnight at her flat and accompanied her on visits to her son. In Wilkins' judgement, she appeared quite dedicated to the flier. "She's having a fine time, my good men, so there is no reason to apprise her of what we know until absolutely necessary. Then it is she who will find herself in a tough spot, I suppose."

But soon after the lieutenant and his colleagues began their run for the Czech border, Wilkins learned that the memorial service had been scheduled for the end of December. He knew the strait-laced military types would draw the line at allowing the funeral to proceed given the facts they knew. At some point, they would have to take Mrs. Clarke into their confidence, even if the outcome of the escape was unclear. But they allowed Wilkins to play out the string, all of them agreeing that the next several days would determine the story Mrs. Clarke would ultimately hear.

CHAPTER TWENTY-SIX

No power can the impenitent absolve.
—Dante's *Inferno*

Inside the Reich, 1944

They pressed on, Gordon taking a turn behind the wheel while Annalise squirmed uncomfortably between Al and Melvin in the back seat of the car. They had removed the flags and license plate because surely, by now, a bulletin had gone out to find those responsible for the murders at the Legnica checkpoint. Seventy miles outside Kraków, the air hung smoky and dense, particles of ash dirtying the car windows and darkening the snow. The men could smell it, even with their windows closed. A munitions factory, they speculated, close to the railroad supply lines. But what of this acrid chemical odor?

"This whole area is about to be overrun by the Reds," said Floyd. "The Germans would have moved any armament production west by now. That's not what this is." He knew the tendrils of soot and fog that soiled the air represented a different aspect entirely of fascist Germany's attempt to remake the face of Europe.

Annalise gave a derisive laugh. "What you smell is evidence of diligent, young Germans still on the job. That is smoke from a work camp, where they employ undesirables—Jews, the gypsies, the communists, the deviants. When they work earnestly, they live. When they do not, they are killed and cremated."

"It is not exactly that," said Floyd, voice even, his gaze unblinking and directly on her, "as I'm quite sure you're aware. We bombed the tracks more than once to keep the trains from bringing in more people, but when we did, they just rerouted the trains to other camps. This is one of the places people from across Europe are taken to be exterminated. Entire Jewish families— doctors and business owners and academics—by the thousands. There were reports of camps like this all over Poland, Upper Silesia, Germany—even France, although I expect those have been liberated by now. And, Mrs. Schröder, you've got it partly right: the Nazis work people to death. But others—young mothers with children, old people—are brought in by train and taken straight to their deaths. Next time you see your commandant husband, you can ask him about it."

Annalise's pale face colored. "You are mistaken, Captain. You have taken disparate facts and thrown them together, but they are not correct. These people—most of questionable background, many of them criminals, in fact—are brought here to work for the Reich. It's a labor camp and unfortunately, some workers die. Disease develops and spreads and it cannot be helped. It is no fault of the camp. My husband and I have discussed the uglier rumors, and he was adamant about this. Your BBC has stretched the facts so grotesquely to inspire more passion in the Allied ranks, to make your soldiers fight more viciously. Like you did at Legnica."

"Oh, ma'am, you don't have to worry about us needing a reason to fight harder," responded Al, lighting a cigarette and exhaling broadly before he spoke again. "Our guys are doing that already. And I ain't apologizing for what I did. After your team took over Austria and Poland and France—and what else? Holland, Belgium. Tried to take over Africa. That was enough to rev us up pretty good. But killing people for nothing? Just because they're Jews? That pretty much guarantees that we ain't gonna stop 'til we get to Berlin."

"As I said, Sergeant, this is not true. It is a fabrication."

"And the Strońskis?" Gordon asked. "What happened to them, do you think?"

"Who?" Annalise asked, agitated, annoyed.

"The family who owned the house you lived in, in Sagan. The house where I built your arbor, where we tended that unbelievably lovely garden.

The owners of that house were forced from it, Annalise, because they were Jews."

"What would you know of them? They were never forced from that home," she said, mocking his tone. "They moved away. Reinhard told me this. They did not wish to live so near the camp that was being built there, so they moved away."

"So that's your line, is it Annalise? The one you'll tell the Allied authorities when they win this war. I recall your saying many months ago that you did not wish to be found in the home of a Polish Jew if the Germans didn't triumph. Remember that flash of insight? I do. And as Clara tells it, the Strońskis didn't up and move: they were forcibly removed and quickly. They left their silver, the heirloom jewelry you're so fond of, and their antiques—the Steinway you loved to play. Who moves without taking their things with them? They left everything because they were not permitted to take anything. They were taken to a death camp, Annalise, while you were pouring tea from their tea service."

"Clara knows nothing. I know nothing of this," she said. "In war, things happen over which we have no control. I did not want to move from Berlin, but I did my part. I made the best of it. Others have had to do likewise. It's nobody's fault. I bear no blame for decisions our leaders make for reasons I am not privy to."

"He was a doctor. He was beloved. Not just because he saw children through serious illnesses, but because he was kind. Generous. He convinced the SS that Clara and Helene hated him and his wife to spare them from suspicion—guilt by association. He hid radio components for them—now, that's something I honestly believe you don't know—and that's how we learned the Allies landed in France. Thanks to him."

"Oh, that's fiction, Gordon," Annalise said, waving a hand dismissively to signal she did not wish to hear more.

"It's true, ma'am," offered Graham. "We built a bloody fine radio and rigged it up in our barracks at your husband's camp. The Polish guards weren't as loyal to your side as you imagined. Blitzkrieg tends to create hard feelings. But we most certainly enjoyed our BBC broadcasts which kept us apprised of the landing, then the liberation of Paris and so on. Quite lovely, that little radio."

Annalise stared at the back of Gordon's head. "I was the one who told you the enemy had landed in France, Gordon. It was me. I remember the day and I remembered how surprised you were."

"Well, sir, is appears Jimmy Stewart isn't the only actor we've got on our side," said Melvin, "because I remember the moment the BBC announced the landings. You were standing right there with us, tossing back the *Kriegie* hooch, as I recall."

Annalise dropped her head in her hands, wounded by the men's laughter and the realization that Gordon's decision not to flee with her was no last-minute change of heart. His betrayal began months ago when he had feigned surprise at her news of the Allied invasion, soothed her anxiety, and promised they would flee together. She rewound their many conversations over the past two years, replaying encounters between them she thought proved their intense mutual pull. The loose way he stood, hand on his hip, eyes lingering on her, solicitous of her opinions, eager to know her background, sympathetic with the difficulties of her life apart from her children. She had savored how he had responded to her from his very first day at the house, marveling as time went on that even in war, wondrous things can happen. Had it been mutual? Had he reached for her first, ever? No, she realized. Not a single time. He had followed her lead, done as she had asked, and then used her for his own purposes. Despite the risks she had taken for him and the life-saving gifts she had offered him again and again, she had not secured his love. She had forfeited a useful life with Reinhard and her children for nothing.

"There will be an accounting of all this, of what the Germans did in this war," predicted Floyd. "There will be a price to pay."

Indeed, thought Annalise. But I shall not pay it.

. . .

They arrived finally in Kraków, the Carpathians looming in the distance, the icy Vistula River churning nearer to the road. They were expected at a location in Old Town, where they could rest for the night and receive final instructions for the last leg of the journey. Gordon turned the car onto the Royal Road, the ancient coronation route used by Polish kings. Back when there was a Poland, he thought. God willing, there would be again.

They found the address and Graham climbed out of the car, clasped his hands behind his back and drew himself up straight as SS officers tended to do, although a close inspection would have given him away with his worn boots, the flecks of blood on his uniform jacket. He proceeded to the door and knocked using the prescribed rhythm, so the occupants would know who was there. But when a young girl opened the door, her eyes filled with terror. She believed him an actual SS officer, calling late in the evening, with a carload of officers right behind him. Still, she breathed the password, hand tight on the doorknob in case she needed to slam it shut.

"Drozd," she said, eyes worried. Thrush.

"Wróbel," he responded. Sparrow. She smiled and swung the door wide.

The others fairly leapt from the car, Melvin on one side of Annalise, Gordon on the other, gripping her upper arms to propel her forward and through the door. They entered a modestly appointed house, a fire blazing in the hearth, the smell of something delicious on the stove. Just a simple family home where this young girl lived with her parents.

"Welcome. Glad you made it," said a man, the girl's father, apparently. "Any problems?"

"None, really," responded Floyd. "An incident at a checkpoint, but we're past it, I think. I'm Captain Harris," he began.

"No, please, none of that. Details of this sort can prove deadly. Call me Piotr. I'm glad you got here safely. We're going to need you all to change out of those uniforms," he said, eyeing the blood, most profuse on the cuffs of Gordon's jacket. "Aside from the... soil, that was fairly good sewing on somebody's part. Then we'll get some warm food in you."

"We have a change of clothes out in the car," said Gordon just as a young man came through the front door bearing a wicker basket.

"Got 'em," he said, "and the rest of the food, too. There's also a small valise and a big suitcase. I'll put them under your bed."

"The car?" Piotr asked.

"Taking it to the motor pool at Rynek Główny 28," the young man smiled. "German headquarters, where it will be one of many parked there for repairs. If they are scouring the countryside for this particular vehicle, that is the one place they will not expect it to be."

The escapees exchanged a relieved look, Al saying if he never saw that car again, it would be too soon.

Their host escorted them to a small lavatory where, one by one, they rinsed in the frigid water at the sink, then changed into their peasant tunics and breeches. After, they joined Annalise in the kitchen, where she warmed her hands around a steaming bowl of vegetable soup prepared by Piotr's wife. As the others sat down to eat, Gordon and Floyd approached their host for a private word.

"All's well, as far as you know?" Gordon asked.

Piotr nodded. "The woman?"

"She's been fine. Angry, but she's cooperated. We ran into a little trouble at the last checkpoint. I think she's still recovering from that."

"Well, she'll have more to sort through tomorrow, won't she?" observed Piotr. "But we have it well in hand."

. . .

After their meal, Annalise asked if she might bathe and change into fresher clothes. After a nod from Piotr, the man's wife took her off, allowing her to pull some items from her suitcase—a clean sweater and skirt, lace undergarments, and surprisingly, a satin nightgown. The suitcase would remain under Piotr's bed. Melvin observed her from the doorframe, one of the handguns tucked in his waistband. After a look into the windowless bathroom, he allowed her to proceed.

The rest of the group remained at the table, smoking the few cigarettes they had left, sipping the tea they had brought with them, and enjoying the quiet of the home, the sheer luxury of sufficient space to move and lean, to cross and stretch their legs, to stand and pace. Piotr reported that Polish partisans were certain German workers were now evacuating the headquarters building they'd held in Kraków since 1939. Just a handful at a time, but offices that once buzzed with activity were now dark, piles of papers sent to the incinerator. The chaos, he said, was most convenient. It was easier to bluff and delay and obfuscate than just a few months ago. The name of the game now, he said, was to buy time enough to survive.

"Any German male who can walk is being sent to the front," said Piotr, "so they are pulling staff out every day and rounding up grandfathers, ten-year-olds to deploy. They are evacuating POWs and consolidating them at camps in Germany, probably thinking fewer guards will be required to supervise them." He smiled. "Yet another sign the Reich is nearing collapse. Pray God their overwhelm will distract them as you continue to your destination."

The men shared what they had seen in the journey from Sagan, the deadly evacuation of the ill and malnourished POWs. Piotr nodded solemnly and summoned the young man who'd handled the car drop into the kitchen. He asked the escapees to repeat all they'd reported.

"Make sure command learns this, yes? We must ensure the allied bombers do not mistake their compatriots for retreating German soldiers. There will be dozens of camps evacuating. Get the word to them now." The young man slipped out, his orders clear.

Gordon's eyes were drawn to the faded wallpaper on the kitchen walls, a pattern of tiny yellow flowers encircled by busy scrollwork in a faded blue. Weathered and worn, it seemed to contain irregularities one would only notice by doing this—sitting hours over tea and conversation, staring off, unconsciously gazing at the design while one's mind sorted it out. Gordon rose and walked over to the portion of the wall where the phone hung to have a closer look.

"Yes, young man. You've found it," said Piotr. "Our story of the war."

On very close inspection, Gordon saw numbers, some in ink, some in pencil, drawn in the style of the blue curlicues of the wallpaper, hundreds of them, grouped in random clusters, close to the baseboard and up to the ceiling, balanced across the wall to retain symmetry in the design.

"Would you believe the Gestapo has searched our home many times and has yet to do what you have just now done? Their urgency and immature impatience work against them because they believe physical power is all that is needed to overcome their adversaries. Hitler believes this too. But had they done what you have, sir, they would have closed down our part of the operation many years ago."

On the wall, in a tiny script, engrafted into the broader pattern of the design and camouflaged by kitchen grease and gravy spatters and water spots and pipe smoke, were phone numbers, latitudes and longitudes, dates—vital intelligence that helped the family in this home safely shepherd endangered persons through the lines to safety.

"What do you know?" said Floyd.

"Bloody brilliant," agreed Graham.

"The information about your arrival is written there," said Piotr, puffing contentedly on his pipe, "but I shan't tell you where because the less each of us knows, the better. My dear wife has already told me that when this is over, she would like me to put up fresh wallpaper. But I've come to love this particular pattern. So, perhaps, I might... resist." They laughed at his use of the word.

This was not the only wonder of this old, unassuming house. Small, hollowed out spaces had been constructed high in the walls, adjacent the dormer windows, and in the alcove below the stairs for stashing people, weapons, and forged documents. The men's mock uniforms would be hidden in these cavities until they could be safely removed. Four of the men would lodge in a back room, but Piotr insisted Annalise stay in the space beneath the steps, a false panel wall covered by a faded tapestry, and that one of the men stay with her. After a hot, healing bath, Gordon stepped into the carved-out niche where Annalise waited, her hair smoothed, her body clean, the satin nightgown incongruous in the tight space. Inside were blankets and pillows, a chamber pot. They sat quietly in their first moments alone since they'd left the manor house, a flickering candle their only light. He did not relish the conversation sure to come.

"How long were you planning this, Lieutenant?" she began. It was back to lieutenant now, was it?

"I have wanted to escape since the day I was captured, Annalise," he said wearily. "So, let's say May 25, 1940. I've wanted to escape since then. It has nothing to do with you. I want my life back."

"We were planning a life—or so you led me to believe. A life that would have given you so much more, would have made you infinitely happier than your banal life in England with your common little wife. Beryl, is it?"

His stomach turned. He had never spoken her name to Annalise and it stung him to hear her say it. "How did you learn her name?"

She paused, pursing her lips, enjoying the power she wielded in this moment, the pain she could inflict on him. "I have my methods, Gordon, and by now, I would imagine that Beryl has probably found another man because many, many months ago she learned that typhus killed you. Prepare yourself, dearest: you may not have a wife to return to at all."

Gordon interrupted. "She knows I survived. I have written her letters since. She knows I recovered."

"She does not, Gordon, because the Red Cross reported you deceased. Just a tiny clerical error, but it happens. See? I was clearing the way months ago for your new life with me, so the British army didn't come looking for you. Why is it, do you suppose, that she hasn't written you in, what is it, half a year?"

He moved to speak, considering whether the scenario Annalise painted could possibly be true. It had been months, he now realized, since he had received a letter. His practice of reading and re-reading her letters had masked this. He'd been so consumed with keeping up appearances with Annalise, covering his tracks at the manor house, planning the escape, gathering the resources required, even as he dreamed of life again with his wife and son, that he had not realized Beryl had not written since springtime. "I assumed it was the slow mail, with the Germans in retreat. Many of us have not received letters in months."

She gave a convulsive laugh. "It could be that, but there were men in the camp whose mail continued to arrive, yes? And you chose not to notice this. But Beryl received no mail from you, so she did not respond—on account of your death." She said the word slowly, overly articulated. "And perhaps by now, her interest lies elsewhere—another man closer at hand. But I have enjoyed your odd little letters to her, your mentions of me and the work on the arbor. I saw no passion in what you wrote her, Gordon, not really. She cannot hold your heart in the way I do. She cannot."

"What do you mean? Why has she not received my letters?"

"Because they are in my drawer, at the manor house."

The horror written on Gordon's face pleased Annalise, restored a bit of order to her shaken universe. "You stole them?" he asked.

"Absolutely not. The driver brought them to me and I reviewed them. As I explained to him, I was obliged to censor anything you might disclose about your work on my property. He followed my directive discreetly, and I rewarded him for it. And then, I kept them because, as you explained to me, this was just a wartime marriage—no children—expendable. Better to cut it off sooner rather than later."

So, Beryl believed him dead for what, ten months, almost a year now? He hung his head in his hands. "You had no right."

She erupted, swinging the back of her hand at his face. He caught and held it, repressing his desire to squeeze the life out of her for what she'd done. "I had no right? I, who saved you from that deplorable camp, who broke every rule for you! I risked everything—EVERYTHING—for you!"

Her voice cracked, imperiousness giving way to self-pity, the dissimulation second nature, a tactical shift because this man was not responding the way men reliably did to her. She could not read him. Since her earliest years, her acuity at detecting the emotional milieu then applying her subtle, skilled dramatics had helped her overcome obstacles to getting what she desired, win her most crucial battles. With her father, her abjectly despairing sobs, an entreating look, had secured her separation from the Conservatoire—despite her mother's objections. Reinhard did her bidding when she assured him of his power, his importance, leading him to trust their cooperative symbiosis. But it was not cooperative: he rarely held sway. This had happened when she made the case for the children to attend school in Geneva. His objections evaporated as she described (eyes moist, hand outstretched) her desire to be absolutely available to him—however he needed her—as he became camp commandant in Sagan. It was the same when she wanted to construct the arbor and expand the garden, insisted that the piano tuner be brought in from Berlin to restring the Steinway, that Gordon be treated for his typhus, that they host the glorious party. But how to win Gordon in this moment? He no longer needed her to safeguard his life. Surely their relationship—the potent chemistry that brought them together, then compelled them to share a bed (or a Persian carpet or a table or a staircase) again and again—surely that was real. So strong was her belief in herself that she could not entertain the notion he could abandon that.

"I love you, Gordon. Still. After all you've put me through. The lies. This betrayal. I realize your desire to be a free man again was paramount and forced you to do what you did—to bring others into our escape. To kill as you did in Legnica. I still want to go with you—wherever that is. I will cooperate. Do you understand? I still trust you after all this. I will wait while you properly conclude your marriage. I have to end my own. I believe we can still share all we had hoped—lives enriched by art and music, with beauty and the passion we have discovered together. We cannot forsake what we have shared."

They were face to face now, Annalise pressing her forehead to his, moving her head around to kiss him, her chapped lips grazing his cheek, his mouth. He was still, eyes closed, his lips receiving her familiar, careful caresses, her gentle, teasing movements inviting him to respond. He marveled at her protean practicality, trying any number of approaches with him until she hit on the one that would work. She had caused immeasurable pain to his wife in multiple ways and yet still believed they had a basis for a life together. He could take her another time and perhaps gain release from the bloody images that played nonstop in his head, the horror of the past few days. Gordon wrapped an arm around her and pulled her to the blanket, closing his eyes as she sighed and settled into him, telling her he was too weary to discuss it further tonight. She took as a hopeful sign that he didn't reject out of hand the picture she painted of the life they could share, that he hadn't removed himself from her when he learned what she'd done with his letters. They could discuss it tomorrow, or the next day. Gordon blew out the candle, knowing he no longer needed to stay alert to watch her; she wished only to lie with him, to press her body into his. Just before he slipped into unconsciousness, her hand went to his chest, then lingered on his stomach, caressing. But as she attempted to reach lower, he moved her hand away, whispering that the house was too small. They needed to be quiet. At this she rejoiced, thinking he had not rejected her, but was only protecting her privacy, her honor.

. . .

When she awoke, she was alone. She gave a few knocks on the wall and Piotr's daughter came to slide back the panel and help her climb out. The house was quiet, the curtains drawn against the sunlight.

"Where is the lieutenant?" she asked. The girl just shook her head and pointed to her father, seated in the kitchen.

"Good morning," said Piotr. "Your quarters must have suited you. It's nearly noon. Did you rest well?"

"Where is the lieutenant—the British lieutenant?" she asked.

"The tea is steaming and I even have an egg for you, if you like, and a bit of bread..."

"Where is he?" she repeated.

"Nearly to Kalinov by now, I would expect," he said, placing the tea cup just so before her.

"What? What do you mean? I am supposed to be with them. They have left? All of them?"

He sat and smiled at her. "They have, Frau, and I do not think you are supposed to be with them. They are escapees from the German Reich. You, on the other hand, are a citizen of the German Reich."

She did not appreciate his playing with her like this, the direct way he spoke to her, his amusement at her plight. Infuriated, she slammed her hand on the old wooden table, formulating a threat. "Find me a way to catch up to them. I demand it. Or I shall let the German High Command know all about you and what you're doing here. All of you, including your little girl, will be executed if you don't do as I say."

Piotr sighed, chin in his hand, leaning on the table, impressed by her fortitude. He was armed, after all, and she knew it.

"To visit Headquarters, you will need papers. Do you have those?"

"Yes. Perhaps. Somewhere. It doesn't matter: I will tell them who I am," she said.

"Because you cannot do anything here without your *Ausweis*. You know that, don't you? They do not take anyone's word for anything."

"Do not concern yourself about that, old man. That is hardly your problem. But you'll soon have a host of things to worry about."

"Will I now?" he asked. Piotr took a small sip of tea, then patted the pocket of his vest. "Ah, yes. Now I remember. I have your papers here. The men left them. Is this what you are needing?"

She seized the documents from his hand and unfolded them. There was her photograph, her age, her address at the manor house in Sagan. But what was this? These papers listed Stroński as her surname and indicated she was Polish. A Polish Jew.

"What in God's name is this?" she screamed, prompting Piotr's wife to rush into the kitchen and beseech her husband to contain this woman, tie her up if needed, but at the very least, to keep her quiet.

"Silence yourself and I will explain," he said, waiting until she stilled.

"As I see it, you have several options. You may take these papers to the German High Command here in Kraków, where I suspect you will be taken into custody and placed on a train bound for the camps. Auschwitz is but a brief ride from here. Be my guest. Bon voyage."

She gave a hysterical little laugh. "That is preposterous. Who would believe I'm a Jew? Me?"

"You must not know, Frau, that the leaders of this regime stopped thinking, stopped being reasonable, a long time ago. They will not even notice your fair skin or fair hair. The Führer is dark-haired, after all, so the determinant of such things is your identification papers, not your appearance. Your papers say you're Jewish, so you are and there is but one outcome when that is the case. You will not be able to talk your way out of it."

Annalise trembled in anger. "What are my other choices?"

"You may stay here for the next day or so—until the men you traveled with have made it to freedom." He pulled the keys to the staff car from his pocket. "Then we will retrieve the car from the carpark at German headquarters and you may take yourself home—or wherever you'd like to go, avoiding the Allies, of course, who seem to be advancing from every direction. The POW camps are being evacuated and Sagan will soon be occupied by the Russians, so you would be unwise to drive there. Or," Piotr took a slow, conspicuous sip of his tea, "we can pass you through our network if you wish to continue south. If that is your preference, I can equip you with a different set of papers. Which will it be?"

Annalise's eyes flashed. "And what's to stop me from waiting a few days, then taking the other papers, the real *Ausweis*, and informing the High Command all about you?"

"Oh, you are welcome to try that, if you wish. But you'll find the market for informants is just not what it once was, what with the Germans trying to get their own asses out of town before the Soviets arrive. They still care about exterminating the Jews, mind you, but investigating claims that could help destroy the partisan network? It's just too late for that. They don't give a damn about that anymore. When you're running for your life, you lose interest in such things. More tea?"

CHAPTER TWENTY-SEVEN

Be still, my soul: The Lord is on thy side;
With patience bear thy cross of grief or pain.
Leave to thy God to order and provide;
In ev'ry change he faithful will remain.
Be still, my soul: Thy best, thy heav'nly Friend
Thru thorny ways leads to a joyful end.
                    –Katharina von Schlegel

London and Elsworth, 1944

On Friday, December twenty-ninth, Beryl rose early to greet a day she had
anticipated with both dread and an odd kind of hope. In the same, sad way
she felt a rush of relief after telling Colin, finally, of Gordon's death, she
expected the ritual of the memorial service to close a door that she'd been
unable to shut, to allow her to lay down at least a portion of this burden even
though she believed elements of grief would persist all her life. Neither her
parents nor Gordon's would attend today and for that, she was both relieved
and resigned. His father was aged and infirm, his grief masquerading as anger
that he assuaged with copious amounts of brandy. "Why hold a memorial
service in the name of a Creator," he had furiously asked his daughter-in-
law, "when God has betrayed me so completely?" Her own mother became
tremulous over the notion of traveling to a service in Elsworth, proposing
instead they hold a small memorial on the grounds of the family estate. She
did not consider what her presence in Elsworth, among the people who
loved Colin best, might mean for her grandson. Where wartime deprivation
had made so many more resilient or generous, such was not the case with

Beryl's mother. But it was all to the good, Beryl decided, as her relationship with Jack was not something she was ready to reveal to her in-laws or her parents, and he would be at her side throughout this emotionally fraught day.

She stepped reluctantly from her bath, wrapped herself in her robe, and returned to her bedroom where Jack lay asleep, having arrived the previous night to escort her back to Elsworth for the service. Days earlier, they'd shared a humble Christmas at Ivy's, meeting Wills for the first time and finding him Ivy's perfect, if somewhat surprising, complement. Ivy quietly confessed to Beryl that he was not exactly the same man she had known, the near-flawless French he now spoke a testament to how his world had widened while hers had remained focused as it always had on child-rearing and housekeeping and more recently, volunteering in support of the war effort. She harbored a twinge of fear that Wills would find this life too provincial and unsatisfying, that he might not be able to wean himself from the adrenaline that had propelled him through his purposeful work with the French Resistance. The enthusiastic delight with which he served their Christmas dinner—goose and Yorkshire pudding and roasted potatoes with crispy, caramelized edges—persuaded Beryl that Ivy was utterly wrong. Here was a man entirely absorbed in the present moment, his eyes scanning from his wife to his son and back again, his head occasionally giving a small shake as if he were taking in the wonder, the gift of his return home all over again. "There will be adjustments, certainly," Beryl told Ivy, "but his devotion to you and Hugo is beautifully obvious to all of us. He adores you. This life here? Seems to me it's exactly where he wants to be. And you? You're enough. Exactly as you are." Ivy reached for Beryl's hand and squeezed, reassured.

Over their meal, Wills reprised stories about the few months he shared with Gordon, brief anecdotes that pointed to his stable courage, stories Colin continued to request. Jack sat through their telling with a stiff smile on his face and frequent slugs of bourbon, wrestling with an atavistic jealousy that shamed him—the irrational envy of a dead man into whose family Jack was now wholly assimilated. He wondered how long it might take for Colin's apparent hunger for remembrances of his father to ease, for all of them to shed the pervasive regret and melancholy and live into a new future together.

His internal struggle mostly hidden, Jack had become a balm to Beryl since their mutual surrender to one another in late summer. Their relationship had elicited some chatter in Elsworth, along with a brief period of consternation for Colin, but in truth, their romance had revived her. Jack was careful and loving with Colin, still patient in answering his endless questions about Florida and flying and the war, saying funny things in his fresh way that was so different from the British men Beryl knew—including Gordon. He visited London as often as he could get a pass, eventually leaving some T-shirts and boxers in the armoire for when he stayed over. His visits gave her an excuse to dress for dinner and fuss over herself a bit, something she had not done in four years. Afterwards, he made love to her with great tenderness if she felt blue, with athletic exuberance when she wished for that.

But the loss of Buck had hit him hard and temporarily robbed him of the persistently sunny outlook they all counted on him to manifest. He often awoke in a panic, heart hammering, reliving the hours in the blood-spattered cockpit, nursing his wounded aircraft west, his buddy caved in next to him, a sodden heap. Beryl worried a depression could endanger him in flight and knew she must bear hope to him. She found their physical relationship did much to soothe him, salve to his psychic wounds. Lying in her embrace, safe in their sacred refuge, he had pondered more than once why it was Buck who died. She had no answer but assured him she was unbelievably grateful that he was here, that they had found one another, taking this tiniest step to mitigate their losses. Sometimes, afterwards, as he dozed and they lay together satiated and content, her mind would wander, trying to remember the particular way Gordon had made love to her, the sensation of him astride her or nestled into her back. As time passed, the touch of her husband's mouth on hers, the feel of his hand on her skin, became harder and harder to recollect. It's true. Time heals, she told herself. It just heals by helping you forget the things you love so you don't miss them quite as much. It was not, she decided, a fair exchange.

Colin had made the hard shift, accepting without censure the unmistakable closeness of his mother and the American he'd introduced her to. He had far preferred when he was their intermediary, the liaison between them, both of them going through him to learn about the other. He had echoed the vicar's words to Hugo—that his mum deserved a measure of happiness and that of all the men who could have found their way into his mother's heart, Jack was a pretty good choice.

Beryl opened the drapes and Jack stirred, pushing the covers aside despite the coolness of the room, his flat belly moving in and out with his breath, the blonde hair on his chest and muscled legs catching the faint rays of the winter sun.

"Morning," he said finally. "You're up early."

"Big day," she responded, returning to the bed to sit near him. "Do I have to do this?"

"You do not," he responded sleepily, reaching for her. "But I think you'll feel better on the other side of it."

"I half-wish I could just crawl back into bed and forget the whole thing."

"Well, ma'am, don't let me stop you. There's a little space for you right here. If that's what you'd rather do, I am happy to provide whatever support you need." She leaned in to kiss him and he reached to pull the covers back over her. After a prolonged and deep kiss, she pulled away and rose to her feet.

"I'm a complete shit, I am. Making jokes and thinking about such things on the day of my own husband's funeral. I'm a shit."

Jack sat up, fully awake now, pulling the sheets to his waist. They had had versions of this conversation before. "We've had a long time to get used to this, Beryl. You've lived with this for a very, very long time. It'd be different if you'd gotten this news two days ago. But if Gordon was half as kind and reasonable as you say, he'd be happy you're living your life, that you've found some pleasure again. I doubt he would want you to be lonely. Or celibate. Can't imagine that. But I know what you're saying. Today is not a day for us. I need to get showered and dressed and think about what we've got on our plate. Sorry. You just get to me, you know? You're beautiful and when you're half-dressed, you're pretty hard to resist. And one more thing:

you're about as unshitty a person as I've ever met. And I promise you, that is an actual word. Or is it nonshitty? Maybe it's deshitty. Let me think here."

In spite of herself, she laughed, reassured as his humor reemerged after his sorrow of recent weeks. He had written a long, detail-filled, loving letter to Buck's parents, attesting that Buck was among the most respected men on the base, describing how his high standards, his keen preparation, had safeguarded lives. Colin had followed through with his promise to write a letter of his own, which prompted Hugo, Margaret, and Patsy to do likewise, Margaret supervising the final edits to ensure they did not all tell the same anecdotes but as many different ones as possible so Buck's parents would know how much they'd loved him. Patsy also drew a picture of Buck with the Gator, Marigold smiling at their feet, a bright golden sun over their heads. Each day, the children hoped to receive a reply, but so far, nothing.

They drove to Holy Trinity in a U.S. military staff car, requisitioned for this most solemn occasion. A contingent from the British army would be at the church to serve as an honor guard but they would do little more than stand at the front of the chancel as the service began, then retreat to a pew together: there was no casket upon which to drape the Union Jack, not even an urn to bear down the center aisle. Beryl and Jack met the members of Ivy's household in the small parlor of the church, where the vicar said a brief prayer. Ivy stood calmly next to a uniformed Wills, having met the near-impossible challenge of outfitting four children for the service in clothes and shoes that were appropriate and actually fit. The girls wore matching navy dresses and held hands, standing as still and quiet as Beryl had ever seen them. Hugo had his arm crooked around Colin's neck, both of them in ties and vests, sharing some last-minute wisdom meant to support and encourage.

The group made its way to the sanctuary and found the entire village had turned out, along with scores of American airmen, members of the Home Guard proudly attired in their uniforms, and the military representatives. Friends from London had made the trip, including several of Gordon's colleagues from his firm. And the children. All the children from the school crowded into the pews directly behind the family. Wilbert was there, Colin's red-headed train mate from evacuation day 1939, now a newly minted army private awaiting his orders. He'd received special dispensation to attend the service and was seated in the midst of the family that had taken him in and seen to his safety five years ago. They all prayed his training would extend a measure longer to keep him out of the fight.

The small chancel was bright with Christmas color, pewter vases filled with pine branches and red berried-holly, snipped from the trees in the courtyard. Fresh flowers were near impossible to come by, but that had not stopped the members of the Holy Trinity Flower Guild. They had leaned on the owner of a private greenhouse in the next village to furnish dozens of white phalaenopsis. The orchids were a favorite of Gordon's, they had learned, the Lieutenant blessed with a green thumb himself.

The prelude concluded, followed by the Reverend Dowd's invocation and then the opening hymn. "Be still my soul, the Lord is on thy side," they sang, Beryl not entirely believing that to be true. But the melancholy chords, the almost hesitant way the organist played them, did what the vicar hoped they would—encouraging those gathered to remember they must always, always continue on, despite uncertainty, despite the unknowns of life. Trust and take the next step.

As the organ swelled at the final verse, there was one late arrival, a man who stood at the back of the sanctuary. He entered just ahead of the courier from the telegraph office, a young man who hastened down the side aisle—perhaps the only person in Elsworth who had reported to work that Friday. Vexed, the vicar beckoned him to climb the chancel and explain himself. He whispered something in the vicar's ear, at which point the Reverend stilled, closed his eyes, then slowly reopened them as he asked the courier for a fuller explanation. He handed the vicar a telegram, which Reverend Dowd unfolded and read. At this point, he dismissed the courier and made his way to the organist, cueing her to continue playing even though the congregants had sung the hymn's last words. The vicar then waved those gathered to sit and walked to the front pew to beckon Beryl and Colin to follow him, the expression on his face unreadable. Jack moved to follow Beryl, but the vicar asked him to remain in the pew: they would return shortly.

CHAPTER TWENTY-EIGHT

And blood in torrents pour
In vain–always in vain,
For war breeds war again.
–John Davidson "War Song," 7, 1899

South of Kraków, 1944

The men departed the safe house at three in the morning, Gordon slipping from the hidden alcove, pausing for a last look at Annalise as she slept, her face placid, untroubled. She had been a formidable enemy—he had to give her that—ruthless and willing to leverage every tool at her disposal. Chief among them, her pale, ethereal beauty which had commanded his attention from the start, physical gifts not reflective of inner goodness. Her allure and her ability to appear devoted had inclined her husband over many years to believe her lies and overlook wild, laughable inconsistencies, even as he shaped a life of comfort and plenty for her with no real responsibilities, no inherent purpose. What must he be thinking with her gone over a week now? No doubt he'd concluded she'd been kidnapped—blameless and at risk in the hands of the escapees. But one does not pack one's jewelry and finest lingerie when kidnapped. Not usually.

As he gathered his things, Gordon considered the lengths to which they had each gone for mutually exclusive objectives: he, acceding to their affair in hopes of finding his way to freedom and she, carrying out a series of ruses, including intercepting his letters to cut him off from his former life, to keep him at her side. Had she gotten her way, had they somehow ended up together, he was certain she would have soon tired of him and used her machinations with someone else. She had wanted Gordon, had fed him, and delivered him medicine not because of who Gordon was, but because she had relished the audacious, dramatic pursuit right under her husband's nose. Genuine love and regard for the welfare of another requires a generosity she had not yet learned to cultivate. Gordon pitied her children.

The men left the safe house one at a time on foot, their multiple layers of clothes causing each to look like an especially well-fed peasant, their pockets laden with food and supplies because a satchel would draw too much attention. They crept out of Old Town, rendezvousing at the Vistula below the city, which they would cross and re-cross as they made their way south. The city maintained a curfew so the five men moved carefully around corners, staying in the shadows praying they would not encounter city policemen or worse, a drunken Nazi soldier headed to quarters after a long night, someone likely to shoot first and ask questions later. Soon, they were in the safety of the countryside, traversing rocky outcroppings as they climbed into the Silesian foothills, moving quickly to stay warm. It was fifty kilometers to their next objective, Wadowice, a distance they could have easily made in twelve hours, but because of the need to skirt villages and populated areas, it would take far longer. Most of the travel would have to take place at night. Floyd used the hand drawn map that he had refined over the past months to keep them headed in the proper direction, as well as the compass he'd trusted since his very first bombing run, a tiny device embedded in a button that had once been attached to his flight jacket.

Dawn arrived late in southern Poland on the cusp of winter and by the time a weak sun ascended, they'd been traveling a good six hours, their feet stiff and cold, their legs heavy. They constructed a little hideaway in the woods, pulling long pine branches over fallen logs and there they rested through the day, ears tuned to any unusual sound that might lead to their discovery. They slept in shifts, ate small portions of their apples and cheese, reviewed contingency plans, then resumed their trek as darkness fell. Al and Gordon remained in charge of their two weapons.

They reached Wadowice at midnight, renamed Wadowitz by the German occupiers who had effectively cleansed it not only of Jews, but priests, academics, and artists—all lost in mass executions and deportations.

Still, Polish partisans—the Home Army—operated within the city and throughout the Beskid mountains to the south with support from the British Special Operations Executive. The men eased their way into the forest at the spot where the Skawa River tributary spilled into the Vistula and waited in the frigid air for further instructions. For three full days, they dispersed, hid, and regrouped again and again, concern escalating that something was amiss, the odds falling that they could hide successfully much longer. On the fourth day, a young woman approached, walking her German Shepherd on the path that followed the river. She paced up and back, up and back, the same stretch of path until the dog broke from his leash and exposed Melvin's position in a culvert behind a stack of downed trees. The Nazis favored Shepherds, Melvin knew. She was looking for escapees or contraband—something. He was done for. She ran toward the spot where the dog stood whining and pawing. Without acknowledging the man crouched at her feet, the woman reached down to pick up the dog's leash, chiding him for misbehaving as she dropped a small square of paper on the ground. Then she turned and made her way back up the path in the direction she'd come. The paper contained a license plate number, an intersection, an address, and a time: eight p.m., roughly twelve hours from now. On the back was a hand-drawn map; at the bottom was the anchor emblem that signified the Home Army along with the phrase "zniszcz po przeczytaniu." Destroy after reading. Melvin rounded up the others, and they committed the information to memory before setting the paper aflame.

After another long day of waiting, the men followed the river into town and found the described intersection, an unlocked car parked there, keys tucked into the visor. They piled in, Graham at the wheel, glad to be out of the elements and seated somewhere besides the cold ground. Well before curfew, they pulled into the address, a warehouse complex where Graham slipped the vehicle into a garage bay. An unknown person closed the garage door behind them seconds later. A group of men emerged from the shadows, opening the car doors and guiding the men down hall after hall of abandoned rooms until they'd traveled deep into the complex, arriving at what was once an office, where, blessedly, an old radiator still operated, piles of worn blankets lay on the floor, and a teakettle gurgled on a hot plate.

"Come in, come in," said a man, drawing them through the doorway. A second man removed a pack from his back and placed it on the broad desk. He removed bread, dried meats, cash, and a weapon. He waved to offer his guests the food.

"All's well with you?" the first man asked.

"It is," responded Floyd, "although the last four days at the riverbank have been a bit... brisk."

"Please, there is instant coffee and many blankets to warm you up. I am Jarek, and I welcome you on behalf of Polish patriots. While I wish the hardest part of your journey was behind you, I fear it may not be. We apologize for your extended stay near the river. Three divisions of German troops have moved through Wadowice in the past two days. They are abandoning their positions in Czechoslovakia to join their misguided brethren in Belgium."

"How many remain here?" Gordon asked.

"Less than a battalion perhaps, maybe a thousand men. Very manageable, but you understand that we needed to allow that to settle out before we made contact with you. The complication from losing these three days, however, is that word has circulated about your escape. We have intercepted communications about the kidnapping you are responsible for. But where is the woman?"

"We left her at the safe house," said Gordon.

"Ah. Excellent. One less complication. But it is imperative we get you in the hands of the Red Army as fast as we can. After you enjoy a few hours of refreshment here, we will drive you into the highlands to Babia Góra, which lies just this side of the frontier. A long day's walk awaits you after that."

"Who's looking for us? Do you know?" Floyd asked.

"We've learned some details from POWs who escaped when your camp was evacuated and made their way down the lines," said Jarek. "Plus, the SOE has infiltrated that corner of Poland most thoroughly. The camp commandant, they say, was frantic over his missing wife but tried to hide it from his superiors, maybe hoping the evacuation of the camp would provide cover. A contingent of SS came to oversee the withdrawal and the junior officers—aspiring SS no doubt and bootlickers, most certainly—dropped broad hints about the missing prisoners and the missing wife. The commandant was relieved of his command, taken into custody. He's probably jailed in Berlin. Senior camp guards were dispatched to find you."

"What of the driver and the guard we left bound at the house?" Gordon asked.

"The house was not checked for well over a week, Lieutenant, and by that time, they were dead. Most fortunate that they were not able to offer information that could have headed off your escape at its inception. You should have shot them both in the head before you departed. That kind of sentimentality can catch up with you."

"What about the cook and the housekeeper?" Gordon wanted to know. "They were most helpful to us. Are they safe?"

"I'm impressed, soldier, with your concern for them. Safely away, we believe. We can't be absolutely certain, but they are out of Sagan and we've had no reports of anything going awry. Now, there is a washroom around the corner and I would encourage you to get a bite to eat. Then we'll talk about tomorrow."

The men relished removing their many layers of wet, dirt-caked clothes, all of them rinsing their filthy socks and laying them to dry over the radiator. They took turns washing up, lathering their red, chapped faces with a bar of harsh soap and shaving with the single razor that had been left for them. Returning to the office, they waited for Jarek to continue.

"It is nearly eleven. You have four or five more hours to rest before we load up to take you to Babia Góra. We have a newspaper truck that does not draw suspicion when it's on the streets in the early morning. The occupiers do not molest us because they believe we are distributing their propaganda and we are. If they looked more closely, they would find our leaflets in the folds of the paper that tell the truth of what is happening in the war. From Babia Góra, it is a brief trek over the border and from there, it is seventy kilometers to Kalinov, Czechoslovakia. The terrain is forested and rocky but affords safety. You must follow a path that stays south of the ridge—the highest in the Carpathians, by the way—so that you don't accidentally wander back into Poland. Questions?"

.   .   .

Fortified by sleep and cups of hot coffee, the men's conversation was hopeful and energetic as they traveled south. One of Jarek's young aides was at the wheel, offering all he knew about the terrain they would soon face and the odds they would encounter German patrols this high up in the mountains. He hoped not, but with the Nazis withdrawing, there could be stragglers who would like nothing better than to pick off an Allied soldier. As the men leapt from the truck bed, eager for this final leg of a mission six months in the making, the young Pole made the sign of the cross over each of them, thanking them, and wishing them powodzenia—good luck—in the hours ahead.

It was mid-morning and after a good look at Floyd's map, updated with Jarek's notations, the group began their long walk. As they walked, silently, purposefully, Gordon finally allowed himself to consider the possibility he might soon see his family, that the nightmare of his long captivity could end. He wondered suddenly where Annalise was, whether she had left Kraków, only to discover the camp closed and her husband jailed. What were her options? Perhaps she would she try to get to Switzerland and her children because backtracking to Berlin held its own dangers.

Within an hour, they had crossed into Czechoslovakia, an event they had expected to involve more high-stakes drama. They paused for a brief moment, shook hands, and clapped one another on the back before proceeding on their way. After several more hours, they emerged from the most thickly forested portion of the mountain crest and heard the rumble of trucks. They hoped these belonged to the Soviet army. They did not. The men melted into the forest and waited, ears straining for any sound that might signal a soldier's approach. Melvin stood behind a tree, his eyes trained on the direction from which the vehicle sounds had come, wondering how they had managed to progress this close to a road without realizing it. He peeked out, waited, and seeing nothing, stepped into the open, believing he and his colleagues were alone. The machine gun fire shattered the pastoral quiet of the woods and Melvin fell, blood erupting from the many holes in his chest, his torso.

Al sprang from the ditch in which he'd hidden, coming at the shooter from behind. He raised the Lugar and fired, Gordon racing with him to provide cover, scanning for a second shooter. The German sentry took the bullet in his back and he fell forward onto his knees. As he dropped, he waved his weapon, his finger still pressed on the trigger, releasing another storm of bullets, one that ricocheted off a tree to strike Graham in his femoral artery, another hitting Gordon first in his shoulder, then piercing his side. As the landscape went black, Gordon heard a loud howl, not realizing that it was his own voice, crying in pain as the bullet shredded the tissue and muscle of his chest and worked its way just above his heart.

CHAPTER TWENTY-NINE

No one can serve two masters.
–Jesus of Nazareth
Matthew 6:24

Kraków, 1944

Annalise took so long to take stock, to decide her next steps, that after a few days, Piotr flirted with the idea of calling the Gestapo himself to come get her out from underfoot. She seemed to think of him and his family as her new house staff and took to demanding food and beverage when she wished them instead of waiting for it to be offered, turning up her nose at dishes she disliked and suggesting ways they could be improved. Sitting in the mornings with her tea, she chose to ignore the peril she faced, for the first time in her life having no man to oversee her passage from one place of relative safety to the next. Her options were narrowing. The staff car had been discovered and impounded and while it had not yet been linked back to the escapes from Stalag-Luft III, officious Nazi investigators would eventually discover its provenance. If Annalise revealed herself to the High Command as a kidnapping victim who needed the Germans to transfer her back to Berlin, they would quickly put the critical puzzle pieces together—that the escapees had traveled through Kraków and could be nearby.

"They will interrogate you," said Piotr. "They may look for evidence you played a part in assisting the escape."

"There is no evidence to uncover," she responded. "I will persuade them I did not cooperate and they will believe me and arrange my passage home.

It is mostly the truth. I certainly did not plan to make a trip here. They will reach out to Reinhard and he will vouch for me."

Piotr smiled. The commandant would not be in a position to vouch for anyone for some time, perhaps ever. "The way back will be difficult, you know. The Germans are in full retreat west, jamming the roads with troops and trucks and armored vehicles. Your husband's camp has been evacuated and the Home Army is asserting its control over more territory every day. You may be a liability, rather than the high priority for repatriation you think you should be."

He could see it irritated her that he refused to display the deference she was accustomed to.

"Only months ago," she spat, "I hosted the best minds of the Reich at a party that was talked about for months, and now I'm consigned to debating a vile little man I could get before a firing squad if I wished."

"Indeed, Frau, I'm sure if you'd had a hint you would be mistreated this way, apart from the commandant's rank and authority, you might have thought twice before leaving him. Nevertheless, we've one more thing to discuss: the valise. What about that?" Piotr had kept the small suitcase locked away from her since she arrived, a safeguard for her cooperation.

"What about it? I expect you to return it to me. I will tell the authorities the prisoners allowed me to pack before they carried me off."

"But its contents—pieces of exquisite jewelry, many, many, in fact. The fine French lingerie, and that very thick pile of Reichmarks. How will you explain that?"

She closed her eyes, gathering herself before she spoke. "I do not appreciate you pawing through my things."

"Frau Schröder, the Gestapo will not simply paw through your things. They will seize them. And before they steal them, they will assert that they have evidence of your mutually cooperative relationship with escaped Allied prisoners who allowed you to retain valuables instead of stealing them from you—the lingerie perhaps not, but the other things certainly. I do not think that even you, with your considerable interpersonal skills, could settle those questions satisfactorily. Remember, the Gestapo does not require a complete set of facts; a hint of wrongdoing is enough for them to exact retribution."

They sat in silence, Annalise sipping her cold tea.

"You could abandon the valise here, my dear. Showing up at the High Command without your possessions—with only your tattered *Ausweis*, no change of clothes—will make the story more believable and ensure..."

"What? Leave my family heirlooms with you? And the money? That is what you're after, is it, to appropriate my things?"

"Frau, if you wish to leave here with the items in your valise, be my guest. Good luck to you. Should you point the Gestapo my way, remember that I have the second *Ausweis*, the Jewish version, that I do not believe you wish disclosed. I am respected in this town. It's how I have managed to survive this long without getting caught: they believe me loyal. So, in my view, you have but one choice to ensure your freedom and the retention of these items that seem so very important to you: avoid the authorities and allow the network to pass you through the lines. You may be questioned at the Swiss border, but you won't be shot on the spot. The Swiss are accustomed to all kinds of wild stories. Alternatively, you can stay here and we'll sip tea together like this for the remainder of the war. It should not be all that long, and at that point, I shall turn you in to the Allies."

"When I return to Germany," Annalise said imperiously, rising to her feet to make her point, "and tell my husband of this blackmail, it will be you who is in danger. He will dispatch agents to your door and close down your little operation here."

Piotr raised a hand to his head, as if an important piece of information had just come to mind, something that could not wait.

"A moment, Frau, because I realize there is one more thing I neglected to tell you. A thousand apologies. Forgive me if I implied that your husband had moved with the camp, that he was still in command of a relocated operation. He is not. He is in Berlin, in jail, charged with high treason because his wife ran off with her lover, a British solider, a bit of news he tried to hide from his superiors. So, alas, he cannot do you terribly much good now. Perhaps not ever." Piotr rose and stood eye to eye with Annalise, who had no quick retort, no sharp dismissal this time. "So, do what you like, Frau.

But whatever it is, it's time you removed yourself from this home because as well-mannered houseguests go, you have much to learn."

·   ·   ·

The next morning, her jewelry and soon-to-be worthless Reichmarks sewn into the multiple layers of clothes she wore, Annalise walked out of the row house behind a partisan who would take her the first few miles on her journey to freedom. Her blonde hair was hidden underneath a leather cap, her face streaked with tears in fear of what lay ahead, her stomach roiled with nausea. Piotr handed over both sets of identification papers to her as she left, not knowing which might afford her safer passage at this moment in the war.

CHAPTER THIRTY

Truth is a divine word. Duty is a divine law.
–Douglas Clyde Macintosh

Elsworth, 1944

Beryl's mind raced as she and Colin followed Reverend Dowd back to the parlor—was she needed at the hospital? Had there been a fresh attack in London?

The man who had arrived late to the service intercepted the vicar as the little group made its way toward the parlor. The two exchanged a whispered conversation, the vicar nodding, the man falling in with Colin and Beryl.

"Vicar, what is it?" She implored as they arrived in the tiny meeting room.

"Colin, Beryl." He took their hands. "There is news. This is Andrew Wilkins, an agent with British intelligence. I have just this moment read a telegram with news of your husband."

Mother and son stared dumbly at the old man. "His things, do you mean? His ashes?" asked Beryl. "What further news?"

"Only that he is alive, in France. Alive and well."

"That cannot be," Beryl said firmly, hands reaching for the bookcase to steady herself. "Who is claiming this?"

Wilkins responded. "The War Office, the information confirmed by agents in my section. Lieutenant Clarke is in the company of a British unit in southern France. He escaped through Czechoslovakia with assistance from a variety of special operatives. He was shot and wounded, Mrs. Clarke, but we are confident he will fully recover."

The news stunned mother and son. Beryl swayed, then reached for Colin for ballast. He gripped her wrists and guided her to the settee, their eyes locking, tears gathering. With his mother safely seated, Colin bent at the waist, hands on his knees, searching for equilibrium.

"Where was he shot?" he asked, breathless, bewildered.

"Well, if you're asking geographically, he was shot outside Kalinov, Czechoslovakia, as he attempted to escape with four other soldiers. If you're asking where he was hit, his shoulder took the initial fire, but the bullet traveled into his torso. He's had several surgeries, but appears now to be on the mend. No lasting damage."

"But how did this happen?" Beryl asked finally. "Why was I told he'd died of typhus?"

Wilkins let out a long sigh. "That is a complicated story. It took some work for us to unravel, put some pieces together, but we had reliable intelligence on the lieutenant so by mid-summer..."

"Midsummer?" said Beryl sharply. "You knew last summer that he was alive? Why was I not apprised? Why, in God's name, would you leave me and our son to grieve over this when it wasn't true?"

"To be perfectly frank, Mrs. Clarke, it was because of some activities he was involved in, in Poland, that we did not think he would survive. Would you have preferred we tell you he survived the infection, only to tell you now that he had been caught and killed attempting an escape six months later? Does it make that much difference?"

"Yes," she said to no one in particular. "It makes a tremendous difference. Had I known Gordon was alive—even if it had only been for the past six months—well, it would have made more difference to me than you can possibly know."

But the intelligence officer did know. Their delay in informing her was unfortunate, certainly, as the woman had only taken up with the American after she believed she'd been widowed. But his office and the agencies with whom he coordinated did not make decisions to defend the United Kingdom predicated on such things.

After a few minutes of silence, the vicar gently inquired what Beryl would like to do now. "Your friends are still gathered in the sanctuary and we must offer an explanation of what's happened. They will perhaps want to speak with you so you can stay here and be less available for that or we can return to the service and I'll explain and send them on their way as best I can. I can't say there's a Church of England protocol for an occasion such as this."

They would return to the sanctuary, they decided, to share this unbelievable news with the people whose love had sustained them these many months. After that, they would reconvene with the intelligence officer to learn details of Gordon's return. The Clarkes clasped hands tightly and followed the vicar back thru the narrow hallways to the sanctuary, Wilkins following at a distance. Beryl's head was bowed as she took her seat next to Jack. After failing to catch her eye, Jack reached his arm protectively around her, gave her a squeeze, then rested it on the top of the pew.

The vicar whispered a few more directives to the organist, then mounted the pulpit, dabbing at his forehead with his handkerchief. The music ended, and he spoke.

"Dear friends," he began, "the family would like to express their deepest thanks to each of you for your steadfast friendship and support. But we have just learned that Lieutenant Gordon Clarke, the one whom we gather to mourn today, has no need of our grief. He has been found alive, in blessed good health, having escaped to France. He is with the British army and most certainly eager to return to his dear family." The murmurs built as the assemblage expressed astonishment at the news. Reverend Dowd charged right into a prayer because, despite there being no Anglican liturgy to cover this very specific set of circumstances, he well knew prayer was always the proper response to miracles.

"Blimy!" Hugo exclaimed as he leapt from the pew and threw his arms around Colin. Both boys sobbed, as Hugo repeated over and over, "Colin... your dad! Your bloody dad!"

The twins began a little jig, prompting Ivy to pull the closest one to her back into the pew, reminding them laughingly, "We're still in church!"

Seeing the odd paleness of her skin, Wills rose and sat next to Beryl to ask if she needed water—anything—whispering phrases that were incomprehensible to her along the lines of "How did... when did... what do you...?" She could not respond because by this time, she had turned to Jack, her eyes sorrowful, anticipating the pain ahead. He nodded, trying valiantly to smile, mouthing that this was great news. Wonderful news. The best news. Good for Colin—again and again.

Encouraged by the vicar to allow the family a time of privacy to absorb this joyful albeit shocking news, the attendees shuffled past Beryl's pew as they departed, several giving Colin a pat, offering Beryl a wave or blowing a kiss, many of them signaling to Ivy that they would be over soon to hear all the details. As the church emptied, Beryl asked Ivy if she could take the children to allow her a moment with Jack. When they had left, Beryl reached for Jack's hand, so comfortingly familiar to her now, a hand that had dried her tears too many times to count.

"Holy moly," he said. "Didn't see this coming."

"Nor did I," Beryl responded. "Obviously."

"It's good news. Tremendous news. I'll bet he has quite a story." Jack said, his enthusiasm false and forced. And then he waited, knowing that whatever she said next would tell him everything he needed to know. Whether she was torn—in love with them both, maybe. Or the best possibility, for him anyway, that she'd grown to love him too much to let him go—that their bond, forged by the fires of this war, was too powerful to relinquish. From his earliest days at Kimbolton, her little boy had given him purpose, a flesh and blood reason to keep climbing up into his bomber every few days and flying into hell. This makeshift family had become his strength, had imbued him with resolute courage to face the day. Beryl had done this with her determined selflessness in the worst of all situations. He found her noble—that's what it was—and as the word came to him, he knew what she would say and what she would do.

"I love you, Jack." He nodded, knowing what would come next. "But I loved him first and I owe him. I owe him and Colin after all they've been through. We took vows. I'm his wife. Whatever I've meant to you, I am still his wife."

"Right. I know. Of course," Jack responded, suddenly on his feet, working his cap in his hands, trying to keep his voice steady, unemotional. "I'll need to head back to the base, so..."

"Stop it," she said. "Sit. Now." He did. "Please don't make this worse. You're sturdier than that. Given everything we've been through, you'd better be. It's not like we can just trade the two of you out, you know, one for the other. Colin still needs you and he will suffer if you up and disappear. Gordon's return doesn't change our love for you."

Our love for you. Already so familial, friendly when Jack wished it to remain intimate, passionate.

"What would you have me do, Beryl? Help plan his welcome home bash? Am I supposed to flip a switch? Is that what you've managed to do in the last, oh, fifteen minutes? Because it doesn't seem to be working that way for me. I have loved you with everything I have. Everything. I stupidly thought that there would be one honest and true thing to come out of this war—and that would be us. Us and Colin, becoming a family. Maybe we'd add another kid. I actually wondered if we would someday. We couldn't forget the things we've seen and the losses... but we would get past it because through that pain, we found each other. That's how I've made sense of this, Beryl."

"And you, you have literally dragged me out of the depths, helped me limp through this, and brought some normalcy to my life. But a future? You're young and handsome and an American soldier, Jack, and I'm older and somebody's mother and I just imagined you wouldn't need to settle for..."

"You're saying I could do better? That I was doing you a favor? If it was just that, there are lots of women in London I could have climbed into bed with. Listen, Beryl, I tried like hell not to fall in love with you. That day we found out about Gordon? Which wasn't even the truth, but anyway, that day? I planned to apologize for kissing you—planned to keep my distance. But when you let me in your life, that was it. I finally got a clue about what makes life worth living—that when you truly love someone, you'll do whatever it takes to make them happy—to show that love. Doing that—for you, for Colin—has made me happier than I ever thought I could be. Even here, now." He paused, lifting her hand to his mouth to kiss it. "And now your husband is returning. I thought this war couldn't get any harder."

She wept, leaning her head on his shoulder, knowing that the mending of her own heart meant breaking his. He held her trembling frame, hating himself for contributing to her sadness on what ought to have been a day of abject joy. "Your love restored me," she whispered. "You held me upright when I thought I would crumple. You've been my anchor—Colin's anchor. He and I are in right mind now because of the love and reassurance you lent when the worry threatened to sink us. You won that war on our behalf. We'd have been lost without our Yank." Jack stroked her hair, bowing his head in sorrow.

Having turned out the lights and secured the back door, the vicar strode to the front pew.

"How may I help you both?" he asked, looking from Beryl to Jack, his face kind, serious.

Beryl straightened, accepting the vicar's handkerchief to dry her tears. "You know about us, do you not, Reverend?" she began.

"I do. I know you both to be fine people who have demonstrated utmost courage in difficult circumstances."

"No," Beryl interrupted him, shifting uncomfortably in the pew. "I mean us. Jack and me... together."

"That is precisely what I am referring to. You are a pair of human beings, imperfect as we all are, who have looked to one another for love and comfort to help you through the cruelties of this war. God does not fault you for the love you have shown one another, nor do I. I would say it has sustained you both."

"But now, I fear..."

"Tosh. Do not fear, dear Beryl, or as the angels tend to say, whenever something huge and earth-shattering is about to happen in the Bible: 'fear not.' Hear that: fear not. You two did your best, for each other, for Colin, for the Allies, I'd say. And now, with your husband returning, things will need to change. That will be enormously difficult for both of you because of the love and regard you have developed for one another. But what you must not do is make it worse with recriminations. No one set out to deceive or hurt anyone here. Be as kind to one another as you've ever been—let grace do its work. There can be healing from even this. Not immediately, but with time. And in the interim, think of the boy, who he needs you both to be. Summon your courage one more time for him."

"But I love her, vicar, and the idea of losing her..." Jack's voice choked with grief.

"If that is true, Captain, then seek her best. Be grateful for all you've learned in loving her, but seek the right thing for her life. Can you do that? Keeping your own wants out of it for a bit?"

Jack's face contorted in pain. He wrestled with simultaneously wanting her to himself again, but not wanting to make the coming days harder for her. Eventually, he spoke.

"I can try, vicar. I can certainly try."

"That's all I ask. That and your promise to trust that God has not forsaken you, that there will be joy once again in your life. Every bit of pain and disappointment in our lives, Jack, is seed. Seed that makes us who God intends us to be and from that seed, joy will grow again. Now..." he looked at them both. "The man from the intelligence service went with the Hughes and is waiting for you at their house. He has more to tell you about Gordon and when he might come home. Under the circumstances, I think it best that I accompany the two of you to over to Boxworth Road to ease any awkwardness. Shall we?"

. . .

When they came through the door, Wilkins was seated at the Hughes' dining table, eating a bite of lunch. Wills had made a fragrant onion soup with a veal stock the way Ginette had taught him and set out some cheeses and baguettes—very French—for the party that replaced the planned post-funeral luncheon. Wilkins was enjoying it immensely.

Colin rushed to the door, his eyes full of worry. "We wondered where you'd gotten to," he said.

"Colin, my good man," said the vicar, "I believe it's time for you to stop bothering with all that worry that tends to follow you around."

At this, Hugo let out a little snicker.

The vicar sat, drawing Colin close, speaking softly, reasonably. "Think about it for a moment: we all believed the very worst thing that could happen had happened. And did you and your mother fall to pieces? On the contrary. Despite your sadness, you grew more resourceful and more resilient and pressed your way through with the help of Ivy and her family and Jack, of course, and Buck, whom we all miss, and all your friends at school. And now, miracle of miracles, your father is returning. He returns to a family that has seen the worst and survived it. A family that is now grown, actually, interconnected with all these lovely people here. So, it would seem to me, there is very little you ought to worry about, very little you aren't completely capable of handling—even if your mother and your friend Jack take their sweet time crossing the street."

Colin looked from his mother to Jack and back again. It was not their delayed arrival, of course, that troubled him. It was who they would be, with each other, with him, now that his father would soon reenter their lives. How was this to work? But looking into the faces of both these people whom he loved and trusted so completely, he saw no anger, no confusion. They seemed spent, but calm, settled. And both looked on him with love in their eyes.

Jack spoke. "The vicar's got a point, Colin. Your dad's comin' home. Maybe today we can enjoy the good stuff—just happiness—for a change. Forget about the war and the tough stuff. At least for today."

A smile grew on Colin's face and his shoulders, which he had not recognized were raised and tight with tension, relaxed in relief. "I can't believe you're going to meet him. My dad. I can't believe this is real, you know? This is the kind of thing Hugo and I used to dream about—this very thing with our dads and you and... well... Buck too."

"That would have been even better, wouldn't it? If Buck were here."

.   .   .

After they'd all had a bite of lunch, they gathered in Ivy's sitting room as Wilkins recounted the events that would culminate in Gordon's return to them. He painted broad outlines of the escape from Sagan—leaving out the relationship with the commandant's wife, saying simply that the escapees had stolen a car and fled. Hugo provided color commentary, imagining they had crashed through the gate of the prison camp in a hail of bullets, Lieutenant Clarke at the wheel. Wilkins neither corrected nor affirmed Hugo's imaginings, believing the Lieutenant himself could provide all the details he wished once he was home. The group, said Wilkins, ran into a sentry in the mountains at the Czech border; two soldiers—both British— were killed and Gordon was critically wounded in his right shoulder. Instead of abandoning him there in the snow, two Americans, Captain Floyd Harris and Sergeant Al Balducci, carried him across the frontier to safety. They eventually flagged down a Red Army tank outside Kalinov, which transported Gordon to a field hospital where, after a week's time, he stabilized. A surgeon scrubbed his wounds to obviate infection and the shoulder began to heal, but the bullet remained lodged in his torso. So, he and the others travelled on a series of puddle-jumpers from Zagreb to Bologna to Lyon, skirting Austria and southern portions of the now-failing Reich. Once in France, Lieutenant Clarke had undergone more surgery to remove the bullet and in only the past few days, had turned a corner, begun to eat solid food, and communicate with his nurses and doctors.

"For this reason," concluded the intelligence agent, "we thought it best to wait as long as we did to bring you news of his survival."

Beryl understood the rationale, the need to cloak Gordon's mission as it progressed. But she resented the way the cold calculus of it all played out against real life, magnifying Jack's hurt, complicating her situation.

"And when's he coming?" asked Hugo. "When can he travel?"

"In a few weeks' time, I would say," said Wilkins. "You'll be having a grand start to the new year, to 1945. Let's hope it's a sign of good things to come for all of us."

"Man," said Jack, turning to Beryl. "What a lucky, lucky guy," and all those present—except perhaps the twins and Marigold—knew that Jack referred to more than Gordon's fortuitous escape. Standing beside him, Ivy placed a hand on his back and rubbed, her palm circling in quiet recognition of the crushing loss Jack worked so hard to conceal.

CHAPTER THIRTY-ONE

Any fool can tell the truth,
but it requires a man of some sense to know how to lie well.
–Samuel Butler

London, January 1945

After Andrew Wilkins' revelations on the day that did not, in fact, turn out to be the day of Gordon's memorial service, Beryl was left to wrestle with a series of unanswered questions. Why had her husband been seized with the notion to steal a vehicle and run for the border at this point in the war? Did he fear the Nazis would liquidate his prison camp? There was grave talk across Britain about just that possibility, something Gordon must have anticipated. And what of the time he spent in a private home outside the camp? Did the War Office or the intelligence service know if this had made him a target, placed him at greater risk? And mixed up in all of it: his survival of the typhus. Why had he not written her in nearly a year—not a single letter—after she received the false news from the War Office?

Once back in London, Beryl made her way to Baker Street to seek out Wilkins to ask questions she did not want to investigate in front of her son. After a string of secretaries and clerks made a series of awkward excuses why she could not wait for him in their offices, why she could not set up an appointment, the man himself finally telephoned her and agreed, reluctantly, to a conversation. He suggested they meet at the Cross Keys Pub near Covent Garden, wishing to keep her away from the office, away from those who might inadvertently reveal the peculiar specifics of Lieutenant Clarke's activity in Poland.

They sat at the small, polished table amidst patrons energized by news of the Allies' success in Germany and the anticipation that their loved ones might soon return home. After offering a bit of an update on what he knew about when the war in Europe might actually end, Wilkins launched into a sanitized account of Gordon's wartime exploits. Beryl leaned back in the banquette, listening, arms folded, cigarette between her fingers. Lieutenant Clarke, said Wilkins, gained unusual access to the camp commandant's home when it was learned he was a skilled architect and builder. He completed a large project in the garden over a number of months and was then assigned to general maintenance of the house—a rather large manor house with an extensive garden along with a separate guest house. When he fell ill, the commandant and his wife secured an anti-infection medicine for him and the treatment proved successful. Some months after that, he and his group of escapees used the resources the lieutenant had gathered over many months at the house—weapons, cash, maps—to execute an escape. A treacherous journey to the relative safety of Czechoslovakia followed "and now," he concluded, "the Lieutenant is headed home in the very near future." He lifted his beer in salute.

Beryl sat quietly in the din of the pub, considering the still-spare details Wilkins provided.

"They treated him with this new medicine?" she finally asked. "A POW? Is that common?"

Wilkins looked at her steadily, eyes unblinking. "It is not."

"So, explain it."

"It appears the commandant and his wife found your husband extremely valuable to the running of the household and developed a sense of obligation, or perhaps appreciation, towards him, given his fluent German and the other talents he brought."

"The commandant and his wife," Beryl repeated. "The commandant of a prison camp concerned himself with one British prisoner to this extent. How lovely of this officer, as Nazis are not entirely known for this type of compassionate behavior. I'm most indebted. I shall have to send a note to express my profound thanks." She returned Wilkins' stare. "What are you not saying, Mr. Wilkins?"

Wilkins took another sip of beer, then another small step toward the truth, deeply hoping he'd be able to avoid spilling details that would injure this woman.

"Well, the old wife truly believed she could not manage the house without your husband, so she apparently pressed for the medication."

"How is it the Red Cross recorded him dead, then?"

"We're not entirely sure," he lied, "but it seems the woman was utterly worried about the poor quality of her help given her hosting responsibilities as the wife of the commandant, that she wrongly believed she could keep your husband in her employ—well, not employ, actually, because he was not paid of course—but anyway, she thought if the British army believed him dead, she would gain some latitude with him. She believed the Germans would win the war, and perhaps, that she could retain him on her household staff."

"Retain, you say." Beryl took a deep pull from her cigarette, considering what would cause this woman to believe herself entitled to retain an enemy combatant once the war had ended. Perhaps she believed the combatant would choose to stay. "As you've spoken, Mr. Wilkins, I've conjured an image in my mind of these people—from what the newsreels show us of our German enemies, from the propaganda posters we see now all over London. I picture the commandant officious, self-important, all brass buttons and bluster, and with the wife, I see a sturdy German matron with her hair in a bun in her dirndl skirt and wool tunic. Wide and solid. Am I correct in this, would you say?"

"Half-right," he said.

"Which half?"

"You have described the commandant well."

·   ·   ·

Beryl pressed him further, learning the woman was much younger than the commandant, a pianist of some talent who had studied in Paris. It was not a hard leap to conclude she had grown dependent, overly attached to Gordon, a man closer in age, ultimately saving his life by supplying the typhus treatment. But another detail truly unsettled Beryl: the notion that Gordon had sufficient access over many months to the commandant's private quarters to pilfer items to use in the escape. Had he not been under guard? Had he been alone in the house with the wife, month upon month, and was that what inclined him to stop writing to Beryl a year ago? Even before that, his letters had been odd and empty, impersonal messages without a tender thought or a sign he yearned for her or for Colin and the life they had shared. It had contributed to her despair, the all-consuming loneliness for which Jack became the antidote, first as a friend and then as her lover.

She recalled how Gordon had chafed in his earliest years of fatherhood. Perhaps he had found some independence as a prisoner—as ridiculous as that sounded—but maybe some relief from the constraints of marriage and the obligations to family. She closed her eyes and considered how war left no one untouched: even the lives of those lucky enough to survive were utterly reshaped. At this moment, she wished only for peace, peace of mind, peace in the world, but she worried Gordon's return would bring further upheaval.

"I appreciate your meeting me," she said, standing and extending her hand to Wilkins. "I only wish I'd been apprised of all this in a more... timely manner."

"War is a messy enterprise, Mrs. Clarke. Unfortunately, you were not the only consideration."

"Apparently not," she said. "Apparently not."

CHAPTER THIRTY-TWO

What we love we shall grow to resemble.
–Saint Bernard of Clairvaux

London, January 1945

On the eve of each bombing mission, Jack tucked into bed early for a few hours of restless sleep. He had adhered to this schedule from the very start, routine mutating into superstition, reinforced every time he returned to base, alive if not well. Sometime after midnight, two or three in the morning, a member of the Gator ground crew who'd been fussing over the plane all night to ensure it was equipped and ready, would enter his hut to rouse him: "Mission today, Captain!" the man would whisper, giving Jack's shoulder a shake and moving a cup of hot coffee in front of his face. The coffee quelled the biliousness in Jack's stomach, allowing the adrenaline to course that would drive the day.

On evenings that did not precede a mission, Jack developed a new habit: throwing back multiple shots of bourbon at the officers' club. The raucous group of airmen around him on these evenings shared a unifying goal: to anesthetize their pain in such a way they could make it to the end of this unholy war and get home. Each had lost too many friends to count in sudden, gruesome ways and found that the alcohol was the one sure tool that helped mitigate and blur the images that shadowed them. Most wondered why Jack, who had completed his twenty-five missions, continued to stay when he could rotate home, perhaps lead a training command in the States. Jack previously said he was staying because the war was nearing its decisive point and he wanted to see things through to the end. But given the change in his personal circumstances, he considered whether it was time he asked that his stateside orders to be put through.

After hearing the intelligence officer's recounting of Gordon's heroic escape, Jack returned to base feeling like he'd been socked in the gut. He and Beryl agreed it would be unwise for him to join the celebrants at the homecoming party for Gordon, Jack finding it painful to relinquish the place he had known, comfortably embedded into the lives of these families in Elsworth, Colin's surrogate father, one of the Yanks sent to save them. The idea of staying after the war for mop-up and to decommission the bases across England seemed ludicrous now and would only magnify his sense of loss. Better to return home to a life and a setting that would not constantly remind him of Beryl and her son. To rum and Cokes in the shadow of a Florida palm, beneath bright, cloudless skies with sun-splashed waves rolling in the distance, to sunburned skin and bare feet he could finally—finally—warm in the hot, white sand.

He had sent hints in letters home to his parents about "special people" he'd met in Britain, hints he hoped had gone undetected so he would not have to explain anything once he got home. What he wanted now was a clean exit: for Gordon to not learn of the affair, for Colin to go on loving all of them, being proud of them. At least, that's what he wanted in his best moments. With every shot of bourbon he ordered around the table at the officers' club, he became incrementally less committed to his promise to the vicar to recede and allow Beryl the room to resume her life with Gordon, protecting Colin from further hurt. A better course might be to drive into London and pound on the door of her flat and plead with her to be with him after all they'd been through together. Fortunately for him, army rules forbade requisition of a jeep or staff car when a soldier was plastered. He had spoken to Beryl by telephone several times, assuring her he would comply with Colin's keen wish to introduce him to Gordon when he returned. Colin seemed content to believe that the bond between his mother and Jack had shifted back to a safe and uncomplicated place, and they cooperated with this idea.

In a telephone call weeks before Gordon returned, Jack asked if he could come to London to see Beryl alone, just one more time. She agreed, suggesting they meet in public—not her flat—because even now, she worried their closeness, the attachment she still felt, might overwhelm their best intentions. He suggested the café at the Dorchester, the very place where they had failed to convene a year earlier on that day when Beryl had received the false news. Beryl was finally working the day shift at Grove Park so they could share a proper dinner. As she freshened up at her flat, she took the same care she formerly did to look her best for him, the way she had done in the months before, when she thought she was free to love him. But she paused often as she powdered her face and worked to tame her curls, dabbing at the tears that spilled down her cheeks, tears that acknowledged that this would be their last evening together.

He stood as she entered the dining room, brushing a kiss on her cheek, his eyes clouded in a way only she could detect. They ordered wine—French vineyards once again shipping to Britain—and made small talk for a bit, afraid to open themselves, to speak aloud the cost they felt in losing each other, caught together in the bittersweet intersection of the tragedy of the war and the hope they'd found in spite of it. He shared that Colin had apprised him of plans to bring Gordon to the base just as soon as he could, assuring her he could handle it because of how it would thrill Colin. She shared what she knew of Gordon's convalescence now in Bristol, that he was healing well and would most likely be able to resume his architectural career. She paused, fiddling with her wineglass, repositioning the salt cellar and the pepper grinder, before looking up at Jack.

"There's another thing," she said.

"Okay. Let's hear it," he offered, half-thinking it had to do with him.

"It's something odd. Perhaps I don't have the right to bring this to you..."

"Anything, Beryl. If I can help, I want to."

"You know how he—Gordon—worked outside the prison camp. For quite a while. Years."

Jack nodded.

"There are things that feel odd to me, the lengths the people went to for him—the couple he worked for."

"Well, those Nazis probably appreciated having such a fun-loving guy around," Jack joked. She frowned. "I'm sorry. Please. Continue."

"It seems it was the wife who protected him, got him the medicine that cured the typhus."

"Well, good job, grandma. Typhus epidemics have killed plenty of POWs. So, what's odd?"

"She was the one who misinformed the authorities that he had died. And she's not a grandmother. She's rather young and a pianist, apparently, and probably beautiful. According to Wilkins, the man from the intelligence service? She had this plan for Gordon to stay with her—with the household—after the war."

Jack crossed his arms and looked off, considering. "How in the world would she think that could happen? Even if Germany wins this whole thing—which it can't now—but even if it did, Gordon wouldn't choose to stay there. He'd come home."

"One would think so. But Gordon stopped writing to me after the news came from the War Office. So, I'm wondering if maybe he cooperated with her. Or, if... maybe... there was something between them."

As much as Jack wanted to seize on this idea—foster and embellish and sky-write the notion that Gordon was a turncoat who had fallen under the spell of a Nazi socialite, who should be banished from Beryl's life, from his son's—he could not do it. He reached across the table for her hand, wishing such a narrative were true because then he could resurrect his dreams of a future with her, make extravagant promises to protect her from a man who had betrayed her. Instead, he carefully chose the words he would need to settle her heart once more.

"I've never been one, mind you, but Beryl, being a prisoner of war is about as bad as it gets. Desperate straits. And he was held as long as anybody in the war—no guarantee he'd come out of it. You hope the bad guys follow the rules, but when things get dicey, when they run out of food, out of room, they play fast and loose. Gordon's goal was to survive. Working at that house, he probably got better food, stayed a little warmer. He got medicine that cured him of typhus. He said anything and maybe did anything he had to do to make it. I mean, we did what we thought we needed to do to get through this, right? You and I?" she nodded, her eyes pensive and sad. "And we weren't under armed guard. Beryl, if I had to guess, I'd say he didn't cooperate to please her, but to fool her. Her and her Nazi officer husband. Fool them so's he could get the hell out of there and get back to you. Which is what he did when he got the chance. He escaped. As all good soldiers are taught to do. He did his job."

Beryl nodded. "He did. He did."

"And why did he escape?" He paused, leaning close to her over the table, fortifying himself to speak, his expression resigned. "He escaped because he knows he belongs with you and with Colin. Because he loves you. Still. Because he knows, as I have come to know, that there is absolutely no one like you, and not just your beautiful green eyes and your wild hair, but your heart. Your honesty. Your damn integrity, that Colin has inherited and that I have learned from. So as much as I'd like to agree with you and tell you to come away with me because he's a son of a bitch because of whatever he's done..." he shrugged, "I can't say that. Your husband, I'm thinking, did the best he could."

The ensuing silence encouraged the waiter to rush in to refresh their wine glasses, let them know the entrees were coming. Beryl failed to acknowledge his fluttering about, her expression infused with gratitude that her life and Jack's had intertwined, even with the profound sorrow of their disentangling.

"You are good medicine," she said. "Despite that funny accent of yours, you tend to choose exactly the right words."

He smiled and gave a seated bow, his bent arm across his middle. "Then I have a few more for you, that I want you to remember if nothing else, so you'll know what you've been to me: in the worst moments of my worst days, when I was scared as hell and thought it might just be easier to bail out of the Gator and take my chances because I wasn't real sure I could keep going, I would picture Colin's face. When Buck was killed and I had one engine and half an airplane, it was that trusting, hopeful face I saw, a boy who expected me and our guys to be braver than we knew we could ever be, expected us to do our jobs and end this thing. That's how I kept doing it.

First for him and later for you. So, thank you for seeing me home, Beryl. I owe you my life."

They rode back to her flat in silence, their last private moments, without Colin, without the Hughes, without Gordon. In the days ahead, time alone together would only add salt to their wounds, so they would avoid it. Jack walked her to her door as he'd done the first time he drove her back to London and extended his hand, prompting her to laugh and lean fully into his chest, her arms around his waist. He asked if he could kiss her—"one for the road" he said—and she answered by pulling his face to hers, moving her mouth slowly, languidly over his as if she wanted to commit each part of his lips, his tongue to memory. He pulled away first, took a step back, and touched a hand to the brim of his uniform cap.

"Captain." She responded with a salute of her own, eyes glistening. "It's been lovely."

"It has, Mrs. Clarke, ma'am," he said, a catch in his throat. "Sorry to see it end."

"As am I," Beryl responded, "as am I."

CHAPTER THIRTY-THREE

The soldier above all others prays for peace, for it is the soldier who must suffer the deepest wounds and scars of war.
–General Douglas MacArthur

London, February 1945

She paced the length of the platform, taking shallow drafts of the cold air, too nervous even to smoke, heart hammering in her chest. Colin had stayed in Elsworth, graciously understanding that his mother wished to see Gordon alone first because it had been so very long and she wished to orient him as best she could to all that had happened to them these past five years. In their former life, Gordon had only to observe the set of Beryl's jaw, the stillness in her eyes, to detect something unsaid between them. She hoped this ability of his might have dulled because there was so much she wished not to say today, fearing even an unsettling hint would mar his homecoming. He and Colin both, deserved more than that. Would Gordon sense her continued attachment to Jack, that apart from their physical intimacy, she felt indebted to him for how he had unburdened her, cheered her time and again? Would she give herself away when she spoke, when Jack's name crept into the conversation one too many times? That would wound Gordon after all he'd suffered, the risks he'd taken to escape. Could he be made to appreciate the set of circumstances that had forged the bond she and Jack had shared—one that Colin continued to experience with him? Her thoughts twirled and spun as she waited and watched the many trains arrive and depart. Her mind would not quiet.

Her husband had departed in 1939 from this very platform and the next train in would return him home. Gordon Clarke was among the fortunate few. Across Europe, she knew, countless others had boarded trains that took them one direction only, never to return to family, to safety, to the lives they had lived simply and happily before Hitler developed his unspeakable plans. She thought of the innocent millions he packed into cattle cars, the first step of his scheme of extirpation of those he considered racially inferior. Then followed the soldiers who willingly climbed aboard trains in free countries across the world, the first stage of the years-long journey each would take to join forces to undermine Hitler's scheme. What ironic justice it would be, Beryl thought, if the Allies could catch Hitler on a train somewhere and bomb it all to hell. She recalled how his hubristic love affair with trains had caused him to do outrageous and impractical things—dragging out the railcar used when Germany signed terms of surrender in the first world war to host the signing of the Armistice at Compiègne after France fell. He'd had a luxury railcar constructed, with silk drapes, gold filigreed fixtures, and soft leather couches—laden with drink and gourmet food and beautiful young serving girls. She'd seen photos. He'd planned to use this train to speed VIPs to Russia once he'd conquered it. Both of those railcars were in the hands of his enemies now, as Hitler, hopefully, would be in the very near future. The incursion of the Germans into the Ardennes had been repulsed; they had retreated now to defend the Siegfried Line. With the Luftwaffe shattered, could the Reich be in its death throes at last?

German rockets continued to fall over London, but Gordon's wartime service would soon end: his medical discharge would be completed over the next few weeks. Wills, too, would soon relinquish the uniform after an upcoming ceremony, during which he would be awarded the French Commemorative War Medal as well as the Croix de Guerre for his service with the Resistance. Beryl and Colin—and of course, Gordon—would attend the ceremony with the Hughes in London. It was all Hugo could talk about. Margaret and Patsy were lobbying to come, the odds slim they would be permitted to leave the safety of Elsworth until the fighting was truly over.

The whistle sounded, and Beryl saw the train at a distance.

. . .

After he was deemed well enough to travel, Gordon had been flown from Lyon to the large airfield at Bristol. He continued his convalescence there and underwent a lengthy debrief on the movement of POWs he'd observed and his sense of German troop morale. After three weeks, he boarded the train to London, the penultimate leg of the long journey from Sagan. They would go to Elsworth after this. He and Beryl had not spoken, their communications relayed by a team of combat intelligence officers who had arranged his transport home. There had been an emotional farewell with Floyd and Al at Lyon, Gordon attempting but feeling he'd failed to fully express his gratitude for their superhuman effort after the sentry had shot him, lugging him nearly twenty kilometers inside Czechoslovakia before they'd been able to flag down help. By this point, the three were so covered in Gordon's blood that when the Soviet tank driver had spotted them, he thought them a trio of Polish partisans whose courage exceeded their skills. The driver delivered them to a field hospital, Floyd recovering from his exhaustion enough to forcefully insist that American and British officers be contacted after the Soviets doubted their story of escape. "You cannot be Allied soldiers," insisted the Polkovnik, who oversaw the medical unit. "Your clothes are Polish-made—your only weapons a pair of German Lugars! We have no reason to believe you are whom you say." But after a number of days, agents arrived to confirm their tale. Then they waited to see if Gordon would survive.

As he lay on the hospital cot, willing himself to hang on, to resist slipping into death to end his acute physical pain, Al sat at Gordon's side, smoking one acrid Soviet cigarette after another, berating him, saying Gordon couldn't give up now. Not after getting this far. They'd already lost Graham and Melvin, and that was enough. "Listen, Lieutenant," he whispered conspiratorially, "it'll make a lot better story for the folks back home if you survive this, okay? Might even mean a medal for me and the Captain, bringing you out, when you were mostly dead. Holy Mother of God, your skin was whiter than the snow—just as cold, too. And now, look at you here, pink-cheeked, cozy under a couple of blankets, and these Red Army nurses

takin' care of ya. Hoo-boy, a bunch a lookers, I gotta say. But not the kind
you think. I'm saying they're even scarier-looking than the nuns at St.
Bridget's back in Philly—"

His eyes still closed, Gordon gave just the slightest shake of his head, the
corners of his mouth turning up. So, Al continued.

"And when you get well, you're coming to the restaurant I'm gonna
open at home, in Philadelphia, right there in Little Italy, and I'm gonna
serve, well, boiled eggs of course, as I said a couple weeks back in Poland, but
also, stuffed ziti with basil and oregano and three kinds of cheeses and
cannelloni that'll be packed with the freshest whipped cream and eggs and
sugar and..."

The last few ingredients proved too much for Gordon, who was
suddenly upright, gesturing urgently for a bin, a bowl, a bucket, something
into which he could heave the contents of his stomach. Up came blood and
bile, dark, profuse, foul-smelling, spilling onto his hands, his clothes, his
bedding. As he wretched and convulsed, Gordon surrendered to what his
body wished to do, to rid itself of infection, to expel hidden toxins—shame,
guilt, the hurt that consumed him—that he believed he'd inflicted on Beryl,
on Colin, and even Annalise. The events of Legnica that continued to haunt
him. His failure to get Melvin and Graham to freedom. His stomach roiled.
His head pounded. For a few minutes, he lay still. Then he turned toward
Al, and gave him a look.

"Few too many things on that menu, old man."

"And there he is," said Al, already removing the soiled blankets, waving
a nurse over to come check the patient. "Welcome back, Lieutenant. We
weren't real sure we'd hear from you again. We've missed you." A damp
cloth in his hand, Al reached to wipe the drying blood from around
Gordon's mouth, his cheeks, and up under his chin.

· · ·

After hopscotching all over southern Europe together, they parted. Gordon
boarded a flight that carried him across the Channel to Bristol, while Floyd
and Al proceeded to Paris to report in to an American unit for a trip back to

the States. They would reconvene next, they agreed, at Al's restaurant once it was opened in Philadelphia.

The pain in Gordon's shoulder persisted; he still wore a sling to incline those around him to give him a wide berth. His internal injuries had healed with less pain, he decided, because no one was constantly knocking into them. His hand seemed unaffected and he hoped his ability to draw hadn't been compromised. With each phase of his journey home, his world grew discernibly safer, more familiar. Having cast off Mussolini, the Italians had been genial and welcoming. The French in Lyon treated him like he was the single reason their country was now free. When he arrived in Bristol, finally back on British soil, he wept—copiously, profusely—a steward on the plane patting his bowed head saying he was hardly the first Tommie to do that.

And now, London. Battle-scarred but still standing, the home he'd naïvely left five years before, never imagining all he'd lose, the pieces of himself he would leave on the battlefield. The violence he'd so easily summoned, his ability to lie, be so deeply duplicitous, left scars in his psyche: he knew himself capable of things that, before the war, he would have been sure his sense of honor would never permit. Circumstances had demanded that he push open the door to that darkness and step through it, do what needed to be done. He wondered if he would be able to seal off that door now that he was home, banish the fearsome images that came to him at night and the pervasive sense of dread that stayed with him in the day. He prayed he could.

The train slowed and Gordon rose to his feet, pulling his duffel from the rack, an older man behind him leaning in to help heave it over his good shoulder. "Welcome home, soldier," he said, patting Gordon on the back. "So glad you made it home." Riders seated nearby added their applause. Gordon nodded gratefully, offering his thanks in a voice thick with emotion.

. . .

Beryl stood in the middle of the platform, head swiveling left and right, wishing she'd had time for a haircut, that she'd bought a prettier dress, noticing for the first time the frayed cuffs of her coat. Despite having taken extra time and care in dressing, she felt a bit shopworn, comparing herself to the picture she'd conjured of the German wife with her household staff and her extravagant house. Beryl had anticipated this very moment for five years and now, suddenly, felt completely ill-prepared.

But there he was, stepping from the carriage, striding towards her, a head taller than most in the crowd. His blonde hair was darker, now, his body thinner. His eyes looked tired but, she could tell, happy to see her. He reached for her with his left arm—his good one—and buried his face in her neck, inhaling the rosewater scent she'd placed there, her soft curls draping his face, camouflaging his gathering tears.

"Beryl, am I truly here? Am I to believe it?" He leaned hard into her, his posture one of release, surrender.

"Gordon," she breathed again and again, one hand traveling the length of his long, familiar back, the other arm crooked around his waist, gingerly avoiding his wounded arm. After they stood a few minutes, getting ahold of their breath, acclimating to the idea of each other, she took his face in her hands and turned it to look into his eyes. He dropped his head to avert her gaze, eyes downcast.

"What is it, Gordon? Can't you look at me?" she asked, alarmed. Would he have news for her this quickly that his experiences had changed him, that he couldn't play along with something he no longer felt? "Please, Gordon. Have I turned into an old crone?"

He shook his head and steeled himself to face her. "It's that... it's that..." His tears fell freely. "I have dreamt of you, Beryl, longed for you from the very start—every day. Every single day. For so many years. And now that I see your face, you are more lovely, more perfect than I even remember."

She closed her eyes in relief. She wrapped both arms around him, observing how he felt to her, his torso longer, slimmer than the one she had lately known. She looked up at him.

"We are neither of us perfect, my love," she said quietly, steadily, "after all we've had to do to muddle through all this." Her first small confession. "But we are still us. We're here. We've made it this far"—she reached gingerly for his wounded shoulder—"mostly in one piece. We've done a far bit better than many. We have you back. We have our family. Still."

"Indeed, we do," he said, Beryl's calm steadiness an aspect of her he'd missed. He drew close and kissed her, both of them surprised to find they fit together in much the same way they formerly did.

. . .

They rested for a bit at their flat, the cat circling and circling suspiciously before leaping onto Gordon's lap and pawing at his chest, demanding an explanation. Gordon told him there was too much to get into just yet, Beryl knowing he was really saying that to her. They were careful and polite with each other, providing scattershot facts on a random timeline of the past five years—Colin's progress in school and his continued fascination with aviation, the friends he'd made at school and at Kimbolton. Gordon was incredulous over the loss of the Densmores, shaking his head that Beryl might have been lost too had the bomb landed a few meters closer at a different time of day. They steered clear of discussing the very things each most wanted to know: whether their demonstrated ability to manage without the other would have lasting consequences, whether each truly believed they could knit their hearts and lives back together.

That afternoon, they boarded the train for Elsworth, where Colin, the Hughes, and various others assembled to give Gordon a proper welcome. Just like the day in September 1939 when Colin and Margaret and Patsy and so many others first arrived in the country, Elsworth families assembled at the station, waiting to welcome the train from London, Reverend and Mrs. Dowd included, only this time there was no bullhorn to assist in the sorting of refugees, no list-makers to track where those newly arrived would live. Beryl briefed Gordon on whom he was about to meet, quizzing him on their names as they pulled into the station in hopes he would not feel completely at sea.

Gordon helped Beryl down from the train with his left arm, then searched the platform for the boy he'd left so many years ago. Instead, he spotted a tall, rangy, young man with dark, curly hair over smiling, familiar green eyes. Colin ran towards them like the little boy he'd once been.

"Dad!" Colin cried, the voice deep and mature and startling to his father. "You're in one piece! Nearly!" He slipped his arms tenderly around Gordon's middle, working around the sling, the two of them nearly identical in height.

"Son," said Gordon, leaning into Colin, their foreheads meeting, their eyes moist. "My boy."

"How's about it, Dad? You made it. We made it. I'd say, except for that sling there, you don't seem all that different. Some gray hairs, maybe, and some crinkles around those eyes."

"Ah yes," said Gordon, drawing himself back with a laugh. "That's all that's changed with me, to be certain. And you? Clearly, they've been feeding you out here in the country. You've grown taller than I am."

"They've done far more than feed me, Dad. They've been everything these past five years. Come meet them."

Margaret charged to the front, pulling Patsy along, both executing a practiced curtsy.

"I'm Margaret and this is my sister Patsy and we're ten now and essentially Colin's sisters. And Hugo's, of course. I am a writer also and I have written a story about your heroic service to the British Empire, for which we are most grateful. In my story, aided by twin girls from Manchester who are actually spies who steal secret plans to..."

"Lovely, Margaret. Very good. That's enough for now. Gordon, I'm Ivy, the one who's kept Colin. I believe you've met my husband, William."

Somehow, in all that had happened in the past few weeks, this astonishing bit of information had not been communicated to Lieutenant Clarke.

"Hughes?" he asked, extending his good hand, realization dawning, "from Calais?"

"That's right, Lieutenant—Gordon, if I may," said Wills.

"But we thought you were killed in France," Gordon looked worriedly in Ivy's direction, "in the hayloft."

"Fortunately, that was a different chap." Wills winked. "I hid under the hay and it saved me. Got help from the family there and, well, like you, I was very, very lucky."

"And then he went on to save others," volunteered Hugo, who stepped up and thrust out his hand. "I'm Hugo. Your son's me very best mate in all the world, and this is my father and, of course, my mother and we are all just so bloody glad you're home."

.   .   .

The common room at Holy Trinity hosted the welcome home dinner, attended by all manner of Elsworth residents. Jack's absence was lamented aloud by some attendees, either obtuse members of the parish who had not grasped the extra-marital connection between Colin's mother and Jack, or the gossips who had hoped to see some fireworks. The vicar presided, beaming as he welcomed them, saying a rousing grace, lifting a series of toasts, wherein he called Gordon one of Elsworth's own. Gordon found it all a bit disconcerting, how much these strangers knew about him, recalling the contained, private life he and Beryl had lived before the war. Mrs. Dowd told him Colin had spent many afternoons at the vicarage, where she saw up close his mature and composed way of handling difficult circumstances. Gordon had much to be proud of, she said. Gordon could see the good these people had done for his son and Beryl, too, as she moved through the room after the meal, happily accepting hugs and pats, the twins trailing her like ladies-in-waiting. He spotted Colin and Hugo through the window, horsing around on the lawn with boys from the school, their shirts untucked, ties askew, their faces pure joy. Gordon gave an involuntary shudder, thinking suddenly of Annalise and her conviction that he would willingly trade all this for her. He did not want to think of how very close he came to missing this moment, to dying first in the camp and later, in Czechoslovakia.

It had been two months since he walked away from Annalise, but he still thought of her every day. Not because he missed her, but because he found it hard to shake the idea that he was no longer subjugated to her, didn't have to lie to protect himself anymore. He wished he knew where she was, having dreamt more than once that she turned up in London, having devised a way to marry him without his knowing. She haunted him, he knew, because of the secrets she carried.

At the close of the evening, Colin argued hard to accompany them back to London but Beryl stood firm: the Germans were still dispatching their buzz bombs over the Channel—one had taken out a Woolworth's in November at great cost to human life—so until peace was declared, Colin would stay with the Hughes. Beryl and Gordon planned to return the following weekend, at which point Colin wished to take his father over to meet the Americans at Kimbolton.

.   .   .

Gordon dozed as they rode the train back to Kings Cross, worn out from the travel and the emotions of the day, while Beryl sat keyed up and nervous. Now that they'd visited with Colin and enthusiastically celebrated Gordon's return, they would take a few more days to rest, then perhaps consider, after all this war had brought into their lives, what their future held. He had seemed genuinely happy to see her at the station and his words had buoyed her. But the wistful look in his eye. The distance. She worried he was missing someone. Or worse, that he sensed a change in her because of the pull she still felt from Jack.

CHAPTER THIRTY-FOUR

The pleasures of love are always in proportion to our fears.
–Stendhal

London and Elsworth, 1945

Gordon did not wait until the weekend, when Beryl was off work and could accompany him, to return to Elsworth. He rattled around the flat alone for a day and a half and found it unsettling after so many years in the noisy company of men. He left Beryl a note to say he was taking the train to see Colin for a quick visit while she worked her shift at the hospital. He had slept so soundly the past several nights, tumbling into their cocoon of a bed earlier than he intended, then falling asleep before he could rouse himself to reach for his wife to begin, in earnest, their reconnecting. They had yet to have a conversation about anything substantial, their shared goal for the moment to be deferential and solicitous with one another.

Wills met him at the Elsworth station and served him a bite of lunch—a corned beef sandwich that Gordon swore was the single best sandwich he'd eaten in five, no, ten—years. They spoke in depth, finally, of the bullet that killed Graham when he was steps from freedom, the randomness of the projectile finding the artery as it did and draining him of life in seconds. Gordon described how Melvin had essentially given his life for them, drawing the machine gun fire that allowed the others to cut down the sentry. Wills described in greater detail his unexpected escape early in the war, how it compelled him to stay and fight in the shadows.

"I can see why Hugo is so proud of you," said Gordon. "I'm not sure I could have done what you did."

"Oh, you could have. You would have," responded Wills. "We have, each of us, done as the war demanded, haven't we? For Ivy, it was taking in the children and loving them like her own, doing what their mums and dads were not in a position to do. For your wife, it was the hospital, working seven days a week sometimes, taking care of one hideously injured person after another, then spending a rare day off here in Elsworth to reassure your boy that all was well. Jack and the blokes at Kimbolton pounded the Germans with bombs, hoping to convince them to give up. And you, Gordon, did all the conventional soldierly types of things, didn't you?" Wills smiled. "Getting captured, getting shot, almost dying several times. All those things in the soldier handbook. Among other things."

"Yes, just that. Among other things, yes."

"How's it going? Being back, I mean."

Gordon wondered how much to say. "I'm getting used to it, I suppose. I woke up today with a start, afraid I'd missed roll call. Walking around in public still feels odd. I have not yet adjusted to the notion that I'm not under guard or in danger of getting shot. I'm sure you felt the same. I have to remind myself when I eat that there will be more when I wish to eat again. I had it better than many, but I've spent five years rationing every morsel of food, stretching it as far as it would go, thinking about it constantly. Difficult to let go of that fear. One thing's for sure: I shall never eat cabbage again."

"For me, it's moving around in the daylight again and remembering that everyone here is exactly whom they say they are—presumably." They laughed at this. "I doubt our dear little Elsworth is home to a single Nazi spy, but I've got a wariness of people. I'd not used my real name in so very long and my wife has accused me of affecting a French accent, so I've developed a mild identity crisis, it seems. And then there is the remembering that I try not to do, but it comes to me anyway, all the things that went wrong, the people we lost. Why them and not me, you know? That's in my head a lot of the time—what we could have done to save them if we'd known a bit more detail, arrived a few minutes earlier or later. I still wish I could have another crack at it, a re-play with a better ending. But we get no do-overs, do we?"

"If only," responded Gordon.

"And with Beryl? Are things alright?"

"We're adjusting. Still a bit in shock, I'd say. A lot has happened."

"Indeed. You've both been through it. But the worst is over."

"We shall see," Gordon smiled, enigmatically, prompting a sympathetic look from his host.

That afternoon, the two men walked to the schoolhouse and when classes let out, Hugo and Colin skipped into the cold sunshine, smiling at this unprecedented event: their two fathers, waiting for them, together. Colin linked his arm through his dad's for the walk to Kimbolton, Gordon declining the offer of Hugo's bicycle as he was not confident he could stay upright one-handed. Hugo and Wills headed back to Boxworth Road, Hugo reluctant but understanding this was an introduction Colin wished to make by himself.

Father and son waved at the private at the gate and entered the base, the American soldier working to contain a grin, saluting Gordon, thanking him for his service, and welcoming him back home.

"Friend of yours, Colin?" Gordon asked.

"'Tis," said his son. "One of many."

They made their way towards Jack's Nissen hut, the airmen they passed greeting Colin, extending a hand to Gordon or patting him on the back by way of welcome. "You're a bit of a celebrity," Colin whispered. "With the escape and all."

"And how would they learn of that, I wonder?" Gordon mused.

"Hugo. Absolutely. And perhaps I said a thing or two."

They found Jack pacing outside his hut, ostensibly to ward off the chill, jacket collar, as always, pulled high on his neck, but it was really nerves that had him moving. He stopped once he spotted his visitors, seeing contentment, calm in Colin's visage. This boy no longer had to manage the loss of a father, the loneliness of his mother, the undoing of his family. The pervasive shadows of worry that the war had imposed had been pushed out to sea, joy evident in his face.

"Dad, this is Jack. When we were little, we used to call him our Yank. But that seems a bit babyish now. Jack," Colin raised his two fists exultantly, "this is my dad!"

The men locked eyes. Gordon appraised him, surprised at his youth, his lack of pretense, how overwhelmingly American he was.

"Captain," Gordon paused. "I ... Colin's told me so much about you. Well, bloody hell, I can't seem to come up with the proper words at the moment to thank you."

"Lieutenant—Gordon," responded Jack, offering a left-handed handshake, the tension dissipating. "We've been awfully worried about you for a mighty long time."

"Your work is a bit of a high-stakes gamble too, I'd say. Colin says you've lost many, many friends."

"I have. We all have."

"Indeed. We have," said Gordon. "Speaking with Wills just now, I'm seeing more clearly how different the war's been for all of us. You, here and in the skies. Wills, all over France, in all manner of circumstance. And there I was, locked up inside the Reich, not doing much good to anybody."

"You did your duty, soldier. Escape is no small thing and from what I hear, you provided some pretty damn good intel."

"We were able to get word of the POW evacuations up the line, so you and your mates didn't mistake them for retreating troops and bomb them. So yes, I'm pleased to have contributed that."

They snagged a jeep and rode out to the hardstand for an up-close look at the Gator, pockmarked and patched up, still murderously airworthy. Speaking from a design perspective, from his years of experience and training, Gordon proclaimed the artwork on the plane's nose outstanding, particularly the roundness of the protuberant Hitlerian rump. Colin said he always knew his dad would appreciate the plane's florid feature. Then he launched into a lecture on the specs of Fortresses in general, as well as the specific missions this plane had survived. Gordon declined the offer to climb up into the belly of the plane, promising he'd be back to do it once his arm healed.

"It carries ten men, Dad, and can fly about 280 miles an hour at the most, but cruises around 180. There are thirteen guns on board—M2 Browning machine guns. For the milk runs—over to France and back, for example—they carry eight thousand pounds of bombs. Four tons! But on the longer missions, Fortresses carry forty five hundred pounds."

Gordon watched his boy rattling off what he knew, so earnest and animated, wanting Gordon to understand every detail and to love that detail as much as he did. Gordon watched Jack, too, looking on proudly, never interrupting, allowing Colin to come up with a statistic even when it took a few tries.

After, they stopped at the O-Club, Jack ordering a Coke for Colin and a pair of whiskeys for the men. As they lifted their glasses, Colin drifted off to chat with some of the other airmen, pointing back at his father from across the room, his wide smile one of pleasure and pride.

It gave Gordon the moment to say what he came to say.

"You have been a father to my son over these years," he began, "and I know that assuaged his pain, helped steady him. It was generous of you, Jack, and I'm grateful. You surely didn't have to take that on in addition to your brutal duties."

"It was a two-way street, Gordon. He gave me a reason to go on when it was hard, when it got to be too much. I got a taste of being a parent, I guess, when you do what you have to do because you promised to do it. In my case, I promised Colin I'd get back safely and somehow, despite some very close calls and some horrible losses, I did."

"You seem quite attached to him. And he to you." Gordon took a slug of the whiskey. "And Beryl? Did she give you a reason to go on as well?"

"Beryl?" Jack repeated stupidly, as if he were unfamiliar with the name.

"Yes. My wife, Beryl. Somehow, I get the sense that she contributed to your positive state of mind as well, to your commitment to get back here safely, in one piece." He said this quietly, without emotion, simply stating facts as if they posed no threat to his intimate life with his wife.

"Of course. Yes. She's Colin's mother, and we've certainly become friends over the past three years." As Jack lit a cigarette, his hands would not steady.

"Friends. Yes. Whatever the nature of your relationship, Jack, I am home now." He took another drink. "And I have no intention of leaving again. Do not misunderstand me: I am deeply grateful to you and what you've meant to my son and yes, even the... the bedrock you've apparently been for Beryl. I recognize my return is unexpected and things are now somewhat... crowded. But I want Beryl and Colin and me to recover our life as a family. The three of us. When this damnable war ends, I want him back with us, in London." Gordon leaned in, his eyes moist, his voice strained by emotion. "This war cannot cost me my family, too."

"It won't," Jack said, the pain caused by his affair with Beryl no longer a nebulous, abstract thing but embodied in the man before him, arm in a sling, five years of his life lost, worried now he would lose his future too.

"We're not involved, Gordon. I've stepped back. We agreed to it, although to be perfectly honest, I didn't want to."

Gordon's eyes narrowed.

"But it didn't matter," Jack continued, "because once that telegram came, once she knew, she was clear with me about what she intended to do: restore your marriage. But one other thing you need to know: our involvement came after—months after—she got the news from the War Office. She did not knowingly betray you. That's not who she is, as I'm sure you already know." Jack gave a wry smile.

Gordon ruminated, considering the timeline Jack described. It fit more securely with what he knew of Beryl's character. Why had he assumed something more deceitful? He dropped his head, relieved.

They watched Colin circulate through the club, chatting happily, getting a refill of Coke, glancing back now and again at his father and his friend, who both smiled in response.

"You know how when people are dying—when they die young—they tell the spouse who will survive them 'I want you to remarry. I want you to be happy.'" Jack nodded, not sure he was prepared for Gordon to continue. "Rubbish, probably, but they say it anyway. Had I not returned, Jack, I believe you would have given her a happy life, would have been an able father to Colin, despite the fact that you're a Yank and a bit on the young side. And I say that because I see my son has not just endured this harrowing time, but has grown into a perceptive, hopeful young man despite it. That is partially your influence, I know. And Beryl—she is steady and generous when she could be debilitated and frazzled with nothing much to give after five long years of this. I believe this is due in part to her fortitude and determination, but also because you loved her well, helped her trust there was still some good in the world, helped her hang on to, even sharpen all the best qualities we both, apparently, love in her." Gordon lifted his glass in salute. "For that, Captain, I offer my ambivalent appreciation."

Jack lifted his own glass in response, his smile rueful but relieved. "Glad I could help, Lieutenant. And I'm glad you made it home, really I am, for her—and for your son there. But you gotta know this hurts. It hurts like hell."

"War is hell, remember? I believe one of your Confederate generals said as much."

"Yeah, well, I blame Hitler. One hundred percent."

.   .   .

Gordon returned to the flat late that night, finding Beryl sitting in the armchair in the living room, one hand around a wine glass, the other at her mouth, gnawing her fingernails. She came home from work that evening surprised to find his note, then feeling like she'd been socked in the gut when she saw what he'd left in their bedroom. Folded neatly in the center of the bed were two pairs of U.S. Army issue boxer shorts along with two U.S. Army issue T-shirts, Jack's name stamped helpfully at the neck. He had gone through her things, she thought at first, furious at the invasion. But then she realized he was only just looking for space in the armoire—their armoire—to put his few things away. He hadn't gone looking. That wasn't the kind of thing Gordon did.

He nodded at her as he came through the door, removing his coat, unwrapping the scarf from his neck. She watched him apprehensively, trying to read his expression, glean from his posture how this would go.

"I saw Colin. He sends his love. Had a good visit over at the air base. Quite fascinating." He paused, sat, and turned to her. "Did you have a mind to replace me then?" he asked finally, a conclusion, not an accusation.

"If you're talking about Jack, and I assume you are, he has been an overwhelmingly positive support for Colin. A wonderful influence in your absence, most especially so when we thought you were lost."

"Yes. Quite. I agree. But I mean with you. It appears his involvement extended beyond teaching Colin aeronautics and expressing a fatherly interest."

Beryl sat quietly, knowing whatever she said it would sound weak and selfish. "I haven't been running around on you, if that's what you're accusing me of. We didn't become close until after I heard from the War Office. I was told I was widowed."

Gordon nodded. "I'm aware. And I thank you for that, Beryl, truly. But now you know you're not widowed. I've returned. And I don't believe all this is so easily undone, is it?"

"Not easily, no."

"Do you love him?"

She stilled, the struggle hidden inside her as she considered whether it was best to deny it wholesale, or risk hurting him by acknowledging that yes, she would always love Jack, would cherish forever how he had brought calm in the maelstrom, obviated her disorienting loneliness. But how to say that her love for Jack was a separate thing from her love for her husband and her deep desire to live within the love of the family they'd once been? Could they even be that family again?

"Gordon, I must understand something first. I'm sure over time, you will tell me all that happened in the years we've been separated. I know it has been excruciating from what you've said already and what the War Office and the intelligence agent have told me. But this woman—the German woman in whose home you worked, the one who made sure the typhus didn't kill you. I know only bits and pieces, but her role in all this unsettles me. Who is she? It seems she means something to you apart from the war."

"Who is she?" Gordon repeated with a sad smile. "Annalise was my master, Beryl. She was my savior and my tormentor, reminding me that a sane world still existed outside of the prison camp and giving me the most limited glimpse of it. I was very, very lucky to be able to work there, where I ate meals with bread and fruit and meat that was not infested by maggots, smuggling bits of it back to POWs who really needed it. Prison camp is inhumane, Beryl, no matter the conventions that were meant to safeguard us. There's never enough to eat. It's filthy. The rats have the run of the place even in the daytime. Men I knew died of skin infections, scratching at lice and bugs in their sleep, tearing their flesh to the point it couldn't heal. Others killed themselves because of the futility of it all—day after day, the stench and hunger and disease. They lost hope. They ran for the fences, all of a sudden, knowing they'd draw machine gun fire that would end their agony. So, getting out of there for a few hours, working at the manor house, constructing the arbor, tending to the beautiful garden was a life-saving respite. It was a gift."

"And did your benefactress expect you to show appreciation to her for granting this gift?"

"She did."

Beryl gazed steadily at her husband. "How did you do that?"

"She sought my company."

"You spent time with her alone?"

"At her request, yes. She would arrange it, send the household staff and my guard off somewhere."

"And then?" Beryl did not want to hear what he would say next.

"And then I would do as she asked."

Beryl nodded, drawing her legs up into the chair, crossing her arms, afraid of his answer to her next question.

"And did you think of staying with her? After?"

Gordon looked at her incredulously. "What? Stay? Hell, no. Stay? Never. There was no relationship. I wanted only to get back to you."

"But, Gordon. You stopped writing. Why is that? Did you consider starting over with her—a new life in Europe once the war was over?" He tried to interrupt, but she pressed on. "Because your letters before that were... were empty. They never spoke of anything that mattered—of anything we'd shared or said that you wished to be back with us—that you were the least bit concerned for me or for Colin. Letters from a stranger, they were. It was like you'd forgotten me—lost interest in the life we'd shared."

He shook his head. "I should have told you first off, Beryl, as soon as I stepped off that train. I did write to you. Faithfully. Frequently. I never stopped. But she stole my letters, Beryl. Annalise had her driver intercept them at the camp and bring them to her. I didn't know at the time—please believe me. She only told me later, after we escaped. Said I should stay with her because she had made sure you had long since given up on me and moved on."

Her skin prickled, his words like sharp cuts, as she finally grasped the whole of Annalise's scheme, a stratagem that had somewhat succeeded. Beryl had indeed moved on, turning to Jack, engrafting him deeply into her life. All while this woman had kept Gordon at her side.

He continued. "The letters you did receive—in the early days, I nearly lost hope. I knew only that I wanted you to be safe and hoped you were staying in the shelter out back to stay clear of the bombs. The censors read everything, and I didn't want them to know about my despair—how much I missed you. They used that against us and so much of surviving the camp was holding on to a realistic hope, looking past the filth and misery right in front of you but telling yourself a normal world still exists, run by rational, sensible people, despite the lies the Germans told us. I didn't want them to rob me of that and use my love for you against me. Once I went to work at the manor house, I knew my letters would be scrutinized more carefully to make sure I wasn't passing along anything useful. And they were. It's how Annalise learned we were married. She confronted me about it and I lied to her that I'd been through a rough time and married you out of convenience. And from then on, I stayed neutral, worried to mention Colin because I didn't want her to know he was our child."

"You're not a good liar, Gordon. You've never been."

"Sadly, I've become quite skilled. It's something I'm hoping to unlearn."

"But when you escaped, why did she come with you? Wilkins omitted that detail when we talked, conveniently. What is there to think except that she thought you and she had a future?"

Gordon shook his head. "She had no choice. She had prepared for what she thought would be our escape. Ours alone. She was furious when she realized what it was—when she saw the other men and that her house staff were in on the plan. She had to come with us because we could not leave her there alive. And in spite of everything, I couldn't kill her."

The hair rose on Beryl's arms, the back of her neck, at hearing her husband say he had contemplated killing this woman. "Where is she now?"

"I'm not entirely sure. We left her at a safe house in Kraków. Maybe she's back with her husband by now. Or she may have reached Switzerland, where her children were in school. The partisans would have helped her with that, not realizing who she was."

"So, she saved your life, did all she did, believing you loved her?"

"She saved my life, Beryl, so I would feel indebted to her. It's how she operated. And I played along. I led her to believe I appreciated her and loved her. Do you understand that? I played along. I took what I could from her to survive." His face contorted in pain, hand on his head, fingers raking across his scalp as he organized his thoughts. "But I never intended to stay with her. Ever. From the start, I used her. I used her for everything I could get from her that would sustain me long enough to get out of her control. And as I did it, I had to go a bit numb. I had to block out how desperately I missed you and Colin to make it through. Despondency leads to death in that kind of place and I decided very early on to allow myself to picture your face only one time each day. I would picture you wholly, fully. Count your freckles and your curls, see Colin's round cheeks. I lay in the dark and pictured you, just before sleep, when I prayed for your safety."

He paused, not wishing to hurt Beryl further, but needing her to know, to work his way free from the veil of deceit that shackled him. "When she asked me into her bed, I had no choice. I felt enslaved to her. But I used those moments, as conflicted as I felt inside, to remind myself real life existed outside the hell I was living. That I was still fully a man and what I did with her was a pale imitation of the joy I would experience again, someday, with you. The constant lying, presenting a completely different self, wore me out, Beryl. It's like a dead weight I've hauled around for years that I can't shed.

But it served a purpose, and that's what I kept in front of me. It helped me make it back to you."

They sat in the quiet, Beryl eventually uncrossing her arms, leaning back heavily into the chair, the gravity of what she'd learned settling into her bones.

"Jack is a fine man," Gordon said suddenly. "A hero to Colin and a good man. I see that. I told him today that I intend to stay with you—that I will fight for you—for our family. But now..." he looked about, shaking his head, "I realize I've done this whole thing out of order. I hope you want me to stay. But if what I've done is too great a betrayal, I understand. If you love Jack, well then perhaps we'll work out how to help Colin understand and then..."

She rose and approached him, reaching a hand to cover his mouth, to quiet him, to soothe the frenetic dialog that had clearly echoed in his head in the hours since he'd found the items in the drawer and visited Elsworth.

"I think it's best that we be honest—that we tell the truth to each other despite how brutal it feels—as hearing all this about Annalise has been for me." She took a deep breath. "You asked if I love Jack. I do. I believe I always will, completely apart from these circumstances, because he is good. He loves our son. Even with handling his own duties in this war, he brought hope to us. Sunshine in the darkest moments."

Gordon nodded, bracing for what she would say next.

"You've been gone so very long, Gordon, and I've grown so accustomed to him, the comfort he's provided in these debilitating times. But I want to grow strong enough to let go of that comfort. I am willing—if you are—to let go of how I've cobbled my life together, to know you, to know us, again. To learn to love the man you have become through all that's happened—whoever that may be. You said when you arrived home that I looked perfect to you and while it was lovely of you to say, it is so far from the truth. I have proven, haven't I, that I am earthbound and needy. I will have to learn now not to need Jack anymore. But life is risk, isn't it? Nothing is promised—not peace, not comfort, not protection from things that wrench your heart. But still. I am hopeful. Because here you are, having risked everything, to be with me once again."

He pulled her arm to bring her to him. She moved onto his lap, burrowing her head in his neck, both of them melting into one another, releasing the tension their muscles and sinews and hearts had carried since the first days they were apart. He lifted her head to kiss her, the act a symbol of their recommitment, an erasure of the things they'd felt compelled to do that no longer had any place in their lives. They stayed nested in this way for hours, making their way, finally, in the half-light, back to their room, their future less clouded, the path in view.

EPILOGUE

We must learn to regard people less in light of what they do or omit to do,
and more in the light of what they suffer.
–Dietrich Bonhoeffer, German pastor and theologian executed at
Flossenbürg concentration camp

Paris, 1954

After the program concluded, the Clarkes lingered in the concert hall. They hoped to speak with the first pianist, inquire if she might be related to the Stroński family of Sagan. If she were in fact a relative, Gordon had much to tell her—how their selflessness had preserved the lives of Clara and Helene, and later brought real hope and help to the POWs of Stalag-Luft III through the radio components Dr. Stroński had left. It was discomfiting to consider these dependencies—that if Clara and Helene had not continued to work at the manor house, quietly aiding Gordon and the Allied effort, then Gordon most surely would not have escaped when he did and may not have survived the war. When the Stalag was evacuated in late 1944, all of eastern Europe was snowed in and frozen, the winter harsher than any in decades. Thousands of POWs died in the long and futile march west, including, Gordon learned later, Lieutenant Colonel Herbert. His strong internal compass had steadied his men since Calais. But his body had its limits and could not tolerate, together, the frigid cold, the lack of food and water, and a case of dysentery. Witnesses on the march said the colonel developed a fever and grew disoriented, wandering into a stand of trees and drawing the fire of Nazi soldiers, happy to liquidate the prisoners for any perceived infraction, even an officer of his rank.

When Gordon recalled the war years, images flitted before his eyes like a movie, where the plot is predetermined and characters lack agency, propelled forward instead by the work of an unseen hand. It's how he felt when the war ended, after living so many years directed by others who held power over him, and it produced a persistent depression that he shared with war survivors across the world. Becoming himself again—truly himself—was a years-long process. He reasserted his autonomy first in small things, like sorting out the flat once Colin moved home and asking Beryl to suspend her work at the hospital—just for a while—so they could recover the rhythm of a shared life. In this way, he felt steadied to face larger decisions, which included signing on with a new architecture firm rather than returning to the familiarity of his previous one. Six months after his military discharge, he returned to work, shoulder achy but functional, applying new vigor to projects to help rebuild his unbowed city. His depression grew less gnawing, and he found himself once again able to swim in the deep well of creativity, getting tossed in its currents, absorbed completely in the process in ways that nourished and healed him. He and Beryl steadily rebuilt their marriage, having learned over the years to extend extravagant grace to one another as their hearts and psyches healed from losses both real and perceived. The nightmares still visited him, persistent, devastating, the most frequent one in which he traveled alone over a peaceful, snow-covered tableau, always hungry and striving, encountering villagers eager to help, before turning suddenly to find the young girl from Legnica standing before him, head resting unnaturally on her shoulder, mouth shaped in a surprised "O," blood from her body staining the snow.

Jack redeployed to the States in time to celebrate V-E Day with the throngs in New York City in May 1945, writing later that strangers had plied him with one free beer after another, leaving him to sleep it off in the bar of his hotel, never having found his way to the actual room. It made for a memorable night. His departure from Kimbolton had been sudden, just six weeks after Gordon's return. By the end of May, Elsworth was a ghost town, Hugo and Colin despondent that the Americans—just as quickly as they'd arrived—were gone, Kimbolton left with a skeleton crew to oversee its deactivation, tall weeds sprouting unabated that summer on forlorn runways that would never again hum with the same brave purpose. Jack promised to write frequently and was as good as his word, sending letters to the boys that included photographs of the places he'd stopped as he'd piloted his plane home. After a few days of R&R in the Azores, he'd turned the Gator westward over the now-placid Atlantic Ocean, refueling at St. Johns, Newfoundland before alighting on American soil at Andrews Field outside Washington D. C. Months later, Jack left the military and moved to California to work for Boeing, a Christmas card the following year indicating he'd met someone special. Beryl told Gordon she deserved credit for ensuring Jack's standards were high and they laughed genuinely and fully, secure in one another again, Gordon not feeling the piercing jealousy he once had and Beryl, finally free of the wistful longing that once unsettled her.

They saw Jack one last time in 1950, at the vicar's funeral at Holy Trinity. The old man had died in his sleep, a gentle death, many in Elsworth said, for a shepherd who had been so very gentle with his sheep. Colin sent a telegram with the news to Jack, who leaned on his aviation industry connections to get an immediate seat on a flight to London. He brought his wife, along with photos of their baby girl, who had stayed back with her grandparents. At the reception after the service, Jack sought out Mrs. Dowd to say he could not have missed the opportunity to honor the vicar, whose counsel had proved invaluable to him as a younger man. "He promised God hadn't forgotten me—as bleak as things were—that I would know joy again. I didn't believe him at the time, but he was exactly right." When Jack introduced his tall, blonde wife to Beryl and Gordon, her serene face betrayed no special concern, no flicker of recognition. But when she met Colin, she swooned: "Colin!" she cried. "And Hugo! Jack talks of you still! I don't believe there's a single thing I don't already know about you."

There might be, Beryl mused silently. Just a thing or two.

At the close of the reception, Jack leaned in for a hug to say goodbye, his familiar scent, the solidity of his body, flooding Beryl with memories.

"All's well here?" he asked, eyebrows raised. "Didn't ruin anything, did I?"

Beryl smiled and shook her head. "Ruin? No. Save? Most assuredly."

Hugo and Colin retained their deep and abiding friendship, attending university together before getting hired at the French aviation company Avions Marcel Dassault, Colin in airplane design and Hugo more specifically involved in avionics. The Hughes still lived in Elsworth which was no longer the sleepy village it had been in 1939. They visited their son as often as they could, Wills saying frequent trips would keep his French sans défaut. After the war, Wills had expanded his butcher shop, adding a restaurant that featured country French fare. It proved an outrageous success, bringing diners from all over England, eager for haute cuisine along with inside stories of the Maquis that Wills could sometimes be persuaded to share. For several summers, the waitstaff included Margaret and Patsy, whose bond with the Hughes did not wane but grew ever more secure and permanent over time. Ivy would forever be their second mother, a bond their own mother respected because of the confident, cheerful people the twins had become, even with the losses that had surrounded them in the hardest years of the war. For months after they moved back home to Manchester, their parents brought them and their younger brother to Elsworth on Sundays to attend services at Holy Trinity, the entire group squishing into the pew directly behind Mrs. Dowd, Ivy pretending to fuss over the girls' belts or a loose strand of hair as she did when they were little, just to draw a smile. Afterwards, they shared a meal at the Hughes' and communed with Marigold, who raced to the front door and planted herself expectantly at their feet the moment they arrived. The poor thing spent much of the rest of the week mewling disconsolately, wandering throughout the house in hopes of discovering where the girls might be hiding.

The Hughes had not joined the Clarkes for this particular trip to Paris. It was only Gordon, Beryl, Colin, and his wife, Lisette, watching as the students made their way from the stage, moving into little family clusters for hugs and congratulations, moments bittersweet because of the family members not present whom the war had stolen. Colin allowed that he wished he'd studied music when he was younger, acknowledging the lack of opportunity. "We were just trying to make it through, step at a time, weren't we, Mum?"

"Indeed. We did the best we could under the circumstances." Beryl smiled. "Your musical development was the last thing on my mind in those days. But I'd say thanks to Ivy, and those Yanks, and perhaps a little influence of my own, you turned out alright." She turned to her husband and saw his eyes fixed on a group gathered in front of the stage. He looked stunned, the color drained from his face.

Annalise stood in the aisle talking to the Stroński girl. The years had been kind to her, the face still smooth, youthful, her long hair secured by a scarf at her neck. Her body moved in the same lithe and sensual way it always had, despite the ill-fitting jacket and skirt she wore, made of coarse fabric, not the silks and satins she once favored. As she spoke with the young pianist, she fussed with a strand of hair that had escaped the younger woman's chignon. A young man stood next to them along with a much younger girl, her light brown hair in braids.

"Go," said Beryl. "Speak to them. We'll stay here and join you when you wish us to. But see what news they have of Dr. Stroński and his wife."

He approached, unsure of what he would say, his mind working to piece together the relationships of these four people. Annalise saw him and attempted a quick exit back up the stairs to the stage. Surprising, he thought. She was many things when he knew her, but never a coward.

"Annalise, if you would, please," called Gordon.

"Maman!" called the youngest girl, running to Annalise and pulling her by the hand back toward Gordon. "Cet homme vous appelle!" This man is calling to you.

Annalise stood before him, resigned.

"Gordon. Bonjour. How surprising to see you. Children, this is Mr. Clarke. We were acquainted during the war."

"Hello, sir," said the pianist, extending an elegant hand. "I am Ilsa"

"Ilsa, it was beautiful, truly. You are quite gifted. Congratulations."

"Thank you, Mr. Clarke. You're very kind. This is my brother, Luka. And my sister, Mila."

He shook Luka's hand, then looked into Mila's blue eyes, a different hue from her siblings, a color and shape much like his own.

"And how old might you be, Mila?" Gordon asked.

"Almost ten. I was born on May 8, 1945. Mummy says all of Europe celebrated the day I was born because the war was over and the Jews were finally free." She looked up to her mother for affirmation, but Annalise was still, quiet.

"Indeed, we did, Mila," said Gordon. "It was an unforgettable day after some very, very difficult years. How wonderful that you got to begin your life after all that was behind us."

"But we did lose our father," she said solemnly, guilelessly. "He died at Auschwitz."

Before Gordon could speak, Annalise cut in.

"Ilsa, why don't you gather your things? I'll meet you all at the front entrance. I'll just be a few more minutes."

When the children had moved out of their hearing, Gordon turned in white-hot anger towards their mother. His fury nearly overwhelmed him, given that now, there was no guard pacing the Persian carpets nearby to subdue him, no threat from the Gestapo to bring him into line.

"Is she mine? Mila? Did you ever think to let me know I had a daughter?"

Annalise crossed her arms, lifted her chin, eyes glittering, all of it so familiar that a chill ran through him. But when she finally spoke, her words were not combative. "It crossed my mind, yes, but how was I to find you?" she asked wearily. "It was all I could do to survive. It took me months to make my way through the network. By the time I got to Switzerland, they had practically thrown the older children into the street, as their school fees had not been paid for the term. I sold my jewelry to satisfy the debt when they threatened me with jail. We found shelter in a camp for displaced persons. Mila was born there—in a tent, with the help of a midwife. I had no money, no means to search for you. I was not even sure you'd survived the escape."

"And Reinhard?"

"Executed," she said with an involuntary shrug. "The Gestapo took issue with his handling of your escape—my alleged kidnapping. They believed him complicit in the conspiracy given his history of criticism of the Reich, charging that he facilitated his wife's escape because he'd lost faith in the

Führer. He met his end in front of a firing squad in Berlin, just as Patton crossed the Rhine."

"Not at Auschwitz, as you've led your children to believe?"

"What does it matter, Gordon? Either way, he lost his life at the hands of Nazi madmen. He did not deserve what happened to him, but I was in no position to stop it."

"But you've led these children to believe they are Jewish, Annalise? Surely the older two know that isn't true."

She raised a hand to plead that he speak more quietly. "What Ilsa and Luka know," she said, barely above a whisper, "is the invective that would be aimed at them were it discovered what their father actually did in the war—something they, as young children, had no control over. They remember he didn't send them to Nazi schools, but allowed them to be educated in Switzerland. They remember he was not SS but Heer and didn't earn a field command because he was outspoken about decisions he disagreed with. So, there was enough to construct a plausible narrative that he had been sympathetic to Jews and it had cost his him his life. All of Europe is inventing stories, embellishing and obscuring the past. No one alive today admits to ever supporting Hitler. Nine years after the war and not a single Nazi left in Germany, so they would have us believe. I'm not alone in wanting to forget what happened. The forgers in the Stalag were quite talented, Gordon. The *Ausweis* you provided that gave me the name Stroński turned out to be most useful. I could begin anew as a Polish Jew, someone due a measure of compassion and support. Ilsa's charges here are paid for by American philanthropists eager for European Jewry to replenish its ranks of musicians and artists."

"How can you live a lie like this, Annalise? Borrowing a religion your people tried to destroy to save your skin."

"Borrowing?" She considered the word. "It may have begun that way, but I would not describe it in those terms now, Gordon. When I had nothing, when we slept in a freezing cold lean-to with precious little food to eat except what the Allies brought us and later, the Jewish groups that organized to help us, I came to see their goodness—that there was something genuine in their beliefs, in their way of life, the things they valued.

They helped us get out of the camp and find an apartment here in Paris, and later a job for me teaching piano and scholarships so the children could continue their education. Why this kindness, I thought, with no expectation I could ever repay? What kind of people do this?" She paused, tears gathering in the corners of her eyes. "The most horrible moment of my life—worse than learning you did not love me, worse than waking to find you'd abandoned me in Kraków—was when I accepted that I had participated in the murder of millions of people just like these who were sacrificing now to help my family. Hitler was a stupid little man. A feckless, fanatical idiot whose policies, I believed, would run their course. No, more accurately, I gave no thought to his policies, where they might lead. I went along with them because there were great benefits to Reinhard, to me—the lovely home in Sagan, for one thing, the luxuries and privacy I enjoyed there. I closed my eyes to the catastrophe of Hitler until I, too, was caught in the ruin."

Gordon's anger slipped into incredulousness as he studied her serious demeanor, her posture that lacked even a hint of the flirtatious manipulation that had once been her stock and trade. "I would imagine," she continued, "that having known me as you did, you doubt my perspective could change so completely. The journey from Poland was impossibly difficult, but for some reason, it did not embitter me; it opened my eyes to what I'd done, what Reinhard and all of them had done. I remember what you and the men said as we drove near the compound at Auschwitz. I tried so desperately to not see the truth. But months in a camp with thousands of other displaced persons who told horrific stories of persecution—who lost loved ones and friends and neighbors—caused me to finally consider how, exactly, I had arrived at this place, this moment in my life. My parents and sister were killed by Allied bombs as they tried to escape Berlin. So, at the close of the war, I had nothing. I concluded, eventually, that I could remain angry and dedicated to the belief that I had been wronged—by you, by Reinhard, by all of Germany, really, or I could accept that I had been party to it all in staying silent, and could begin to make some small reparation. I have chosen the latter."

As he appraised her, she gave a quick nod to emphasize she meant what she said. "I give a portion of my earnings to aid others who have struggled to find their footing after leaving their homelands. The children and I have worked with others at La Victoire synagogue to restore it after the damage the Nazis did to it. We prepare meals for elderly members of the congregation. Small things, I know, but good things for the children—for me—to do."

"Who knows the truth," Gordon asked, "besides the older children?"

"I know it, Gordon. I carry it with me every day. I have confessed at the cathedral, but the priests will not disclose it. There was a professor at the Conservatoire who seemed to remember me from my student days, but he has retired now, moved to the coast. I have told no one at the synagogue my whole story, although I'm sure there are those who suspect things. But I am not the only one with an uncertain background, eager to right wrongs. The rabbis do not judge me or ask questions. They are simply glad to have the help. I knew this day would come, but I had hoped Mila would be a little older, a bit more settled in her life. I did not imagine it would be you who exposed me, but there is justice in that, certainly. I had thought the housekeepers from Sagan would turn up one day and point the finger at me. I have dreamt of just that thing. I treated them dreadfully, I know. I was a child, petulant and selfish, something I have endeavored to prevent in my children. Over time, I've learned it will not be a German who turns me in because they are just as busy as I am trying not to draw attention. But here you are and if you wish to reveal this to the faculty at the Conservatoire, I cannot fault you. If I've a further price to pay, I shall pay it. I shall begin again."

From a distance, Beryl watched the long conversation, the intensity and emotion of it, and recognized at once who this woman must be. Observing her husband, the forceful way he spoke to her and the way the woman leaned in to speak to him confirmed the deep familiarity between them, a closeness that had crossed boundaries Gordon normally observed with other women. The hall had emptied now, just the five of them left, so Beryl beckoned her son and Lisette to follow her to where Gordon stood.

"Gordon?" she asked questioningly as she approached, her discomfort evident.

"Yes, love, sorry. So sorry. We got... involved. I apologize. This is my wife, Beryl."

Annalise extended one hand while the other went to her chest, something Gordon had seen her do when she wished to get her way with Reinhard, a gesture utterly contrived. But this time, Gordon believed it signaled a humility, a measure of regret, perhaps even an apology.

"Beryl," she said. "Of course."

"And my son, Colin, and his wife, Lisette."

Annalise's eye's narrowed for a beat, calculating. "Your son? How glorious. I recall you'd always hoped to have a family."

"And this is Annalise," said Gordon before adding, slowly, "Annalise Stroński. I knew her in Poland. In the war."

Beryl shot Gordon a confused look and he responded with a slight shake of his head, a quick closing of his eyes.

"A pleasure," Beryl said woodenly, the unease she remembered from the late days of the war returning suddenly, threateningly.

"It is I who has the pleasure," responded Annalise, "to finally see your family reunited. To meet the woman Gordon held at the center of his heart." She looked Beryl hard in the eye. "And he always did. Always. I knew that. I treated him poorly for it. I'm aware of this. I apologize. To all of you."

Her words were startling, words none of them had ever imagined they'd hear.

"Of course," Beryl responded quickly, automatically, as if the apology were attached to something minor and insignificant, a careless faux pas. "But I must... I want to thank you for curing my husband of the typhus. For saving his life. We would obviously not be here now had you not done that."

Annalise closed her eyes and gave her head the smallest shake, as if she didn't deserve to hear Beryl's gratitude. "So, there is at least one time that my selfishness did some good," she said finally, "perhaps only one. Now, Gordon, the administrator of the school is often in his office after concerts so I can take you there, or give you his telephone number—whatever you prefer." Annalise offered a contrite smile, seemingly prepared for whatever lay ahead of her. Beryl stood anchored by Colin, her arm linked through his. Gordon spoke.

"That's not necessary. I have nothing to say to him. Your children are waiting, Annalise, so you best be off. We bid you goodnight. Please tell Ilsa once again her performance was exquisite."

Annalise gave a disbelieving shake of her head, tears welling in her eyes. The group exchanged parting well-wishes, perfunctory but kind. As Gordon turned to go, Annalise reached for his hand and held it, saying simply, "Mila?"

"I leave that up to you. But I don't believe introducing all this now would serve her. She seems well-adjusted, a confident, bright little girl."

"She is. And loved deeply by her siblings."

"Then raise her well, Annalise. I trust you to do that on my behalf. Goodbye, Annalise. I wish you well."

"Goodbye, Lieutenant." They smiled at this, in spite of the memories it evoked, her first time addressing him with his wartime rank with a tone of respect and deference. "Know that I am grateful. For everything."

•   •   •

The moment they reached the street, Colin demanded to know who the woman was, why his mother was so anxious and his father had been so deadly serious with her.

They walked along the narrow sidewalk adjacent Rue La Boétie, heading toward the avenue des Champs-Élysées, Gordon taking a moment before formulating a mostly true response: "She worked with the Germans in Poland in the war, Colin. In some ways, she was very helpful to me. She made sure I was treated for typhus and that saved my life. But she took part in some awful things, as I'm sure you can imagine. I learned tonight the extent that she and her children have suffered, and that seems to have effected a genuine remorse in her. She has a sense of obligation to the world because of the people who helped her get back on her feet. Hers is a rather astonishing evolution, I must say. She even offered an apology to me—something I could never have imagined when last I saw her."

"Wouldn't the vicar have relished hearing this?" Colin mused. "He believed no one was beyond redemption. I can hear him reciting the verses from Saint Paul, how suffering produces perseverance; perseverance, character; and character, hope. In my hardest of moments, when I was growing up in Elsworth, he made sure we understood that hope was never lost, always reminding us to allow grace the time to do its work."

"It's done a mighty work with her," said Gordon.

Beryl nodded. "With all of us, I'd say."

ACKNOWLEDGEMENTS

To every friend who, year after year, graciously read my Christmas letter and said, "You should write a book" — well, okay. I did. Thanks for the push. And to the friends who refrained from eye-rolling when said I was doing it, my love and heartfelt thanks. I'm grateful beyond measure to earliest readers Karen Jordan and Linda Galle for the time they spent with my story and for their spirited debate about where the heart of a certain character truly lay. To intrepid readers Lenore Norsworthy and Julia Rogers: thank you for staying up well past your bedtimes to follow these characters home. Much love to book critic, par excellence, Joanna Pope, who asked to read WAR BONDS, then became a promoter, passing around a Xeroxed manuscript to others. To the Night Angels Book Group: thank you for bringing years of books to my bedside table—*A Gentleman in Moscow, All the Light We Cannot See* are two—that inspired me to begin a story of my own. Much love to Betty Obenshain and Deanie Quillian for their legal expertise and unfailing interest, constant support, and steady friendship. And to the dramamamas who were unfailingly supportive and always eager for an update.

Thank you, Black Rose Writing, for inviting me into this resourceful, smart, and warm writing family.

To my children who cheered me, my dogs who reminded me when it was time to stop writing and tend to other things, and to Gray, my poet-musician, writer-theologian, basketball playing World War Two aircraft-identifier, who brought the most perfect set of support skills to this project, and whose steadiness, kindness, and unflagging belief has anchored me my whole life long. I love you.

ABOUT THE AUTHOR

Pamela Norsworthy applies the same tenacity she used as a writer with CNN Headline News to ensure every detail in her historical novels is accurate and illuminating. After a career in television and corporate communications, Pamela turned to fiction writing to share her love of history and politics and explore how decisions made by a powerful few can prove cataclysmic for everyday people caught in the crossfire. A graduate of the University of Virginia (2019 NCAA Men's Basketball Champions), Pamela lives with her husband and two very spoiled dogs in Atlanta, Georgia, all four of them loyal Atlanta Braves baseball fans.

NOTE FROM PAMELA NORSWORTHY

Thank you for reading! Please visit pamelanorsworthywrites.com to find book club questions, blogs that fill in some of the historical context, and a sign-up for my newsletter.

Word-of-mouth is crucial to an author's success. If you enjoyed *War Bonds,* please leave an online review. Even a sentence or two makes all the difference.

With appreciation,
Pamela Norsworthy

We hope you enjoyed reading this title from:

BLACK ❀ ROSE
writing™

www.blackrosewriting.com

Subscribe to our mailing list – *The Rosevine* – and receive **FREE** books, daily deals, and stay current with news about upcoming releases and our hottest authors.
Scan the QR code below to sign up.

Already a subscriber? Please accept a sincere thank you for being a fan of Black Rose Writing authors.

View other Black Rose Writing titles at
www.blackrosewriting.com/books and use promo code
PRINT to receive a **20% discount** when purchasing.

Made in United States
North Haven, CT
03 July 2024

54289234R20189